THE NEXT CASEBOOK OF
DOCTOR SABABA

Lawrence
WINKLER

BOOK TWO OF THE DOCTOR SABABA SERIES

Note for Librarians: A cataloguing record for this book is available from Library and Archives Canada at www.collectionscanada.ca/amicus/index-e.html

Cover Image by prometeus (CanStockPhoto ID: csp25473021)

Cover Design by Jenny Engwer, First Choice Books

ISBN – 978-1-988429-56-4

Printed in Canada ♻ on recycled paper

 FIRST CHOICE BOOKS

firstchoicebooks.ca
Victoria, BC

10 9 8 7 6 5 4 3 2 1

PRAYER OF MAIMONIDES

Inspire in me a love for my art and for thy creatures. ◆◆ Let no thirst for profit or seeking for renown or admiration take away from my calling. ◆◆ Keep within me strength of body and of soul, ever ready with cheerfulness to help and succor rich and poor, good and bad, enemy as well as friend. In the sufferer let me see only the human being. —MOSES BEN MAIMON 1135-1204

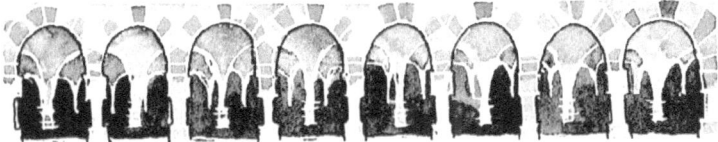

To my patients

The Next Casebook of Doctor Sababa

Prologue

The Next Casebook of Doctor Sababa

Autumn—The Book of Earth.......................... 3

13. The Case of the Universal Veil................... 5

14. The Case of the Orange Faller................... 43

15. The Case of the Tumescent Tattoos........... 77

16. The Case of the Congo Stain..................... 115

17. The Case from the Crack of Doom............ 155

18. The Case of the Sensitive Smurf............... 203

Epilogue... 241

Characters.. 243

The Further Analects of Doctor Sababa........ 247

Songs and Poems................................. 249

Acknowledgements

Fortune has smiled once more and allowed me to write this sequel to the first two seasons of the *Doctor Sababa* series.

This book is also of me, and my thirty years in practice as an Internal Medicine consultant on Vancouver Island. But, again, it is not me, although it may have been who I wanted to become.

I continue to live in eternal debt to the people who made me what I am, in the quest to become as good as I can be. For those I have forgotten to pay proper homage to, minds I have been inspired by or borrowed from, I would ask your forgiveness.

This time, I also want to thank: all the inspirational physicians and musicians and poets in my life, including Dr. Doug Farrago, Hunter S. Thompson, and Jo Walton; Jenny Engwer for putting it all together; and my patient and loving wife, Robyn, through whose tender loving care I remain alive and happy.

Disclaimer

Prologue

For those of you who have not yet read the first two collections of stories in *The Casebook of Doctor Sababa*, stop reading this one now. There is no shortcut to anyplace worth going. All legends have an origin, and that is where you must start. Go back and begin at Sababa's creation. Learn about the characters and dramatic circumstances that propelled the Good Doctor into his place in the mythical firmament.

For returning disciples, it's good to have you back. I understand your desire for more special time with the portly professor. Inside these pages live six more original stories of survival, suspense, and satire from the Sage of the Salish Sea. He will amuse you with his wit and wisdom, and the spontaneous combustion and thrust they generate, often mixed in unequal proportions, as he dances with the devil in the pale moonlight.

Go ahead. Turn on your radio. That's BC Bud, 101.3 FM. He has already announced your homecoming.

Sharpen your pencils. Put on your thinking caps. Like the stocky savant, you will have six minutes to see each patient. Don't be alarmed. Think of it as an intellectual challenge. With lives in the balance.

Welcome to the autumn of his Casebook. Welcome to Sababaland.

Autumn—The Book of Earth

Autumn came in like closing time. *Everybody out of the pool.*
The third season was Sababa's favorite time of year. A study in brown, it coaxed him into contemplation. Its sweet breath chilled the sleepy land, fading in like a softly sung hymn.

The Sage of the Salish Sea saw Harbour City's mountain etched in sharp relief against the vault of heaven, its flesh drenched in pastel watercolours, arboreal hues in their final flight to the soil. Overlapping clouds scuttled across the sky, broken only by occasional sallow shafts of sunlight. Fine morning mists coalesced into waves of rain before retreating into particles.

The lake was quiet, save for the occasional scratchy *shaaa-aak* calls of gathering Steller's jays, the tympanic *gronk* of ravens, and the *ahonk-hink* V-shaped shouting of geese in southern migration. Sababa could sense the silent steps of passing ghosts, but no human voice would ever dare break the solemnity.

Winds rose high out over the Pacific, sweeping east over Vancouver Island, down the Georgia Strait, and up the coastal ranges, animating the pools in between. Arctic air currents, in the first bite of shaggy late autumn decrepitude stained with fiery colours, whirled and swirled in frost-crisp'd frenzied spirals. Refrains of de Falla's ritual fire dance pirouetted around tree trunks. Millions of crisp crimson and copper and caramel corpses, veined with the yellow and orange that ran the brittle length of them, quivered and rolled out into gypsy carpets. They were the royal flush in a final game of poker, the grand slam of the last domino. Breezes blended these fall colours with their smells. Sababa walked unbraced and sucked up the humours of the dank morning—faint odours of wood smoke and decay. It tasted like he was kissing the whole world all at once—overflowing streams and cedar bark and muddy paths and rotting leaves and exuberant fungi. His tread made a leafy crunchwalk beneath his feet. Walking on the earth and listening to the stones and trees and space and wild animals and the pulse of all life in the great silence, filled his heart with wisdom and exultation.

His forays took the higher trails of his mountain, where the damp earth and atmosphere were cooler. Here, every breath was deeper; each crisp gulp of cold air made him want to holler, to hear his voice echo amidst the trees. He felt alive, immersed in the fermentation.

Somewhere on the high ridges, the professor sat on a log chair half-obscured by moss and lichen and sorted the mushrooms he had collected on the climb—chanterelles and matsutake and great big cauliflower mushrooms, and more. He had never needed his compass before his dog died. Shiva always found the way home. But now, he had to be more careful, especially because he refused to carry a phone. *If it was an emergency, it should be an Emergency. If it wasn't, there was no good reason to disturb his tranquility.*

Sababa arrived home to Jane's warming soups and roast dinners served with ancient Barolo, followed with big slices of Shady Mile pumpkin pie topped with dessertspoonfuls of dulce de leche. They snuggled into their evenings under a duvet of cozy comfort and joy. Sababa knew the precise word from his anesthesia days in Denmark. *Hyggelig*. The harvest moon leaned over his hedges like a ruddy-faced farmer.

Late in the season, he picked his last tomatoes and the first Marina di Choggia squash and parsnips from the garden, and crisp juicy ripe apples and pears from the orchard. On another morning, yellow jackets orbited his head while his secateurs cut through solid stems of ripe pinot noir and chardonnay grape bunches in the vineyard.

In this most melancholic black bile of seasons, ephemeral lessons rose off Musashi's *The Book of Earth*, refining his strategy within the precision timing skills he had mastered in previous lessons. Sababa learned to perceive those things which cannot be seen—the smallest things and the biggest things, the shallowest things and the deepest things, as if it were a straight road mapped out on the ground. He learned how to distinguish between gain and loss in worldly matters, to do nothing that was of no use, when to attack and when not to attack, and how not to overuse his weapons in the never-ending battles to protect his patients.

The Earth book made the professor more thoughtful and analytical, turning each third season into the gateway to renewal. But with every year, shuddering under the autumn stars, his head sank lower.

13. The Case of the Universal Veil

'I won't be trapped no more,
So raise your window baby,
I can ease out soft and slow…
Ain't but one way out baby,
And Lord I just can't go out the door…'
Allman Brothers, *One Way Out*

"Hello?" The young man appeared to be speaking to no one in particular. Two wireless earbuds protruded from his head, as white as the porous ceiling panels through which his gaze escaped the nursing station on the fifth floor of Harbour City Regional Hospital. "I'm paging Doctor Sababa?" He said.

"Congratulations." Said the disembodied voice. "Now what?"

"It's Dr. Praj Bharmal, Sir." There was a stutter. "I'm your new medical resident."

"OK."

"The Team Leader here says you're on call today." Praj said. "She called me to the medical ward to see a referral."

"OK."

"He's standing on the ledge outside his room."

"That will make the physical examination more challenging." Sababa said.

"I've tried to talk to him."

"And?"

"He said it made him want to jump sooner."

"On my way." *Click.* A few minutes later the stairwell door opened for a stocky tanned middle-aged man. Below a bouncing medusa of black curls, a Littman Master Cardiology black and brass stethoscope draped over his shoulders. He carried a well-used Colombian leather briefcase, the inside of which held secrets of survival.

"What you got?" He asked.

"I'm sorry?" The young resident spluttered.

"For what?"

"I'm sorry?'

"You just said that." Sababa countered. "Look, Mowgli, this is what we do and how we do it. I ask you about the patient. You tell me. Then we fix the patient's problems. Now how hard is that?"

"Mowgli was a Kipling character." Praj protested. "A naked feral child raised by an old bear who taught him the laws of the jungle."

"My point exactly." Sababa said. "Now let's try this again. What you got?"

5

"Tim Leery." Praj began. "23-year-old VIU student admitted early this morning with abdominal pain, vomiting and diarrhea, headache, and visual hallucinations. He had a seizure in the ER, and another one on the ward. In between, he was awake but couldn't talk. Probable Todd's paralysis."

"Named after Robert Bentley Todd, the inventor of the hot toddy."

"What's that?" Praj asked.

"Brandy, cinnamon, sugar, and water." Sababa said. "Don't they teach you anything in medical school these days."

"I'm sorry?"

"Except self-deprecation." Sababa said. "Go on."

"Yes, please go on." Sababa turned to the source of the encouragement, shivering at his powers of recognition.

"We'd like to resolve the little problem of our new base jumper client." Said the pant-suited woman with the Valentino Garavani silk scarf. "Before he slips the surly bonds of Earth, puts out his hands and touches the face of God." She clutched her hundred-dollar clipboard like she was walking through a dark alley.

"Praj, I should introduce you to the new Floor 5 head nurse, Samara Morgan." Sababa said.

"Professor Morgan." Samara's pupils constricted. "VIHA has designated me as an influential educator. "I'm the Team Leader and Care Coordinator."

"We've met." Praj related the rest of Tim Leery's history.

"Amazing how low you go to get high." Sababa perused the chart.

"I resent that." Samara tightened her scarf.

"I wasn't talking about you." Sababa said. "I was referring to your cosmonaut client."

"What do you mean?" Samara asked.

"Leery has no history of mental illness, no suicidal ideation, and was admitted with abdominal symptoms, hallucinations and two seizures. His pupils were dilated and his heart rate was elevated on admission."

"And?" Samara pursued.

"It's a toxidrome."

"What's that?" She asked.

"He's taken a hallucinogen." Sababa punched a few keys on the nursing station computer, selecting a tune from his music library on a secret drive hidden deep inside the hospital computer network. Allman Brothers filled the hallway.

> 'You're my blue sky, you're my sunny day
> Lord, you know it makes me high
> When you turn your love my way.'
> Allman Brothers, *Blue Sky*

"Which hallucinogen?" Praj asked.

6

"It's a pleasant autumn morning." Sababa raised an eyebrow. "Life on a ledge in the season of mists and mellow fruitfulness. You tell me."

"Dunno." Praj didn't know.

"Psilocybin. The psychoactive indole compound in the 200 species of magic mushrooms." Sababa said. "Illegal under international law since 1971. It's a prodrug, rapidly dephosphorylated to psilocin which then acts as a high-affinity partial agonist on 5-HT2B and 5-HT2C serotonin receptors in the brain. It was isolated by the Sandoz Swiss chemist Albert Hofmann in 1959, and has mind-altering effects similar to those of LSD, mescaline, and DMT."

"What's its purpose?" Praj asked.

"Rather a teleological question, is it not?" Sababa asked.

"What's that?"

"Relating to or involving the explanation of phenomena in terms of the purpose they serve rather than of the cause by which they arise." Sababa said. "Nobody knows the answer to your backwards question, but psilocybin may have evolved as a defense mechanism, deterring fungi-eating pests by altering the insect's mind."

"Like it alters our minds?" Praj asked.

"And has for centuries." Sababa said. "Eleven thousand-year-old Mesolithic rock paintings at Tassili n'Ajjer in the southeast Algerian Sahara depict horned dancers holding giant mushrooms. Similar 6,000-year-old murals were discovered near the Spanish town of Villar del Humo. In pre-contact Mesoamerica, Guatemalan Mayans used psychoactive 'mushroom stones' in ritual ceremonies. The Aztecs who ate theses mushrooms when emperor Moctezuma II ascended to their throne in 1502, knew them as 'teonanacatl' in Nahuatl. *Flesh of the gods*. In medieval Europe, Hungarians used *bolond gomba* 'crazy mushrooms' to prepare love potions, and English botanist John Parkinson wrote about 'foolish mushrooms' in his 1640 herbal *Theatricum Botanicum*. Psychedelic fungi grow in the gardens at Buckingham Palace. I remember reading author Carlos Castaneda's separate reality books about the spiritual effects of psilocybin mushrooms, revered as powerful spiritual sacraments that provide access to sacred worlds. They're called entheogens, 'the god within', spirituality-enhancing agents.

American psychonaut Terrence McKenna put forward a 'Stoned Ape' theory, in which he proposed that psilocybin helped humans develop better visual acuity and become better hunters. It facilitates openness and ego dissolution, and acts as an aphrodisiac to accelerate reproduction."

"You sound like you have personal experience." Samara raised an eyebrow.

"A little." Sababa reminisced about a far-away long-ago beach in the Philippines.

'One morning I left early, for breakfast at Mila's. She was my queen of paradise, with a strong but warm constitution. I sat at a table overlooking the ocean. The sun was out for a morning stroll.

"You hungry, Sababa?" She asked.

"Very hungry, Mila." I said.

"You like omelet?" She asked.

"Sure." I said.

"You like mushroom omelet?" She asked.

"Sure." I said.

"You like special mushroom omelet?" She persisted.

"Fine, Mila." I said. "Fine." And Mila brought me my omelet. It was good. But I hadn't counted on it getting better until it did. The first thing I observed was a silver shimmer that came in with the waves onto the shore. Then it lagged behind a bit and flowed as jewels in the surf. When it went three dimensional and animated, I became suspicious. The sky flashed purple and pink, and the ocean green, and my buddha Frank materialized in the middle, in a new skin of brilliant bronze.

"How you like your omelet?" asked Mila.

"Fine Mila." I said. "Fine."'

LW, *The Final Cartwheel*

"Well, call the kitchen and tell them to put it in the food." Samara said. "He's freed up a bed."

"There is something else." Sababa mused.

"What else?"

"Not sure." Sababa said. "But it's unusual for this situation to occur in someone without comorbidities or the ingestion of another substance."

"What's the treatment?" She asked.

"Only supportive." He said. "If I can get to him and through to him in time." Sababa made for the open window." Outside was a young man standing transfixed, his arms extended out to his side.

"Tim?" Sababa called. "Are you OK?"

"Don't come tomorrow... don't come alone... come together right now... over me."

"We're all here for you." Sababa held out his hand. "What did you take besides the mushrooms?"

"To fathom hell or soar angelic, take a pinch of psychedelic." The hospital grounds under him shimmered, full of matchbox cars and miniature people. "Isaac Newton discovered gravity in 1687. Before that, people could fly."

Tim looked up at the sky and the tilted horizon. The wind whipped his face. His toes shuffled to the edge. The mushroom he had eaten was like falling in love; he couldn't know if it was the real thing until it was too late. In the rarest tranquility of that day, he grew the most wonderful feathers. Blue danced into gray. The race to the concrete took four seconds. It was like nothing he had ever experienced before. It was like committing suicide.

8

The air under him fled from his lungs and the vacuum it left sucked back his eyes in their sockets. *If you live it up, you won't live it down.*

The only sounds Tim made was the worst they ever heard, a loud smacking thud of breaking ribs and tearing organs, reverberating loud enough to shatter the silence, and rupture his soul.

The meaning of life is that it stops. Sababa stared at his empty hand.

The day before Tim Leery launched himself into oblivion, one of his instructors at VIU ascended toward heaven with far less gravity. A professor in the biology department, Dr. Stoney Ridge was the recipient of several awards for his contributions to the science of mycology. Stoney loved his work. In the autumn, many of his professional development days consisted of foraging for new species of fungi.

The second motive for this activity related to his cross-appointment in the culinary arts faculty. Stoney was also an accomplished chef, and always returned from his forest forays with buckets of wild edibles—chanterelles and hedgehogs and blewits and lobster and cauliflower mushrooms and a dozen other species—put to good use in the university teaching galleys and his well-appointed home kitchen.

This accounted for the third reason he spent time exploring the alpine mountain paths above the lake. Stoney also had an appetite for young VIU coeds, susceptible to his wily strategies. One at a time, he took them on a mushroom hunt, followed by an invitation back to his College Heights condo for dinner. With encouragement, an evening feast would become an overnight fiesta. Every morel has a story.

Stoney's coed choice of the day was an attractive brunette named Holly Hill. She and Professor Ridge hiked up the mountain until they came onto a narrow plateau under a canopy of mature second-growth Douglas Fir. Draped with moss and mist, the forest enveloped them in a soft tranquility. Migrating geese cried across the lake below them.

"Early this spring, I found an indicator species here." Stoney said.

"What's that?" Holly asked.

"It's a plant that parasitizes the mycelia of a specific fungus, stealing the nutrients it needs." He said. "Its presence under a host tree indicates where that mushroom will appear in the fall."

"You have a name?" Holly asked.

"*Allotropa virgate*." He said. "Also known as 'candy cane.'"

"No, I meant the mushroom we're looking for."

"Oh." Stoney said. "Today we're hunting for the most exotic edible on Vancouver Island, *Tricholoma magnivelare*. It once fetched a thousand dollars a kilogram in Japan, where they call it *matsutake*.

Over on this side of the Pacific, we also refer to them as pine mushrooms, because they prefer to grow under conifers. Here's one in the moss beside us." Stoney reached down and began to rock a white mushroom cap back and forth until it released its grip on the mountain."

"Like pulling a tooth." Stoney said. "It's the roots that make the fruits."

"It's beautiful." Holly put the gills to her nose. "Smells like a cross between cinnamon red hots and dirty socks."

"Wait until you taste them at my place." He said. "I make a mean Matsutake Gohan, with sake and soy sauce and mirin and dashi and mitsuba."

"What's that?" Holly asked.

"Wild pine mushroom rice. Flor two." He watched her blush. Together they searched the grove for more after Stoney told her what to look for."

"You're scouting for smooth, dry, rounded, white caps connected to thick brown and white two-toned stems. Underneath the cap are notched gills shielded by a partial, cotton-like universal veil."

"Universal veil?"

"A temporary membrane that envelops the immature fruiting body." He said. "There are other lookalike poisonous mushrooms, so we have to be careful. Show me what you pick, and we should be fine."

Holly and the professor separated to explore the plateau more efficiently. Stoney plugged his iPod into his earbuds and switched to an FM station.

Good Afternoon Harbour City... This is CNDN Coast Salish radio, 101.3 FM on your Home and Native Band. I'm your host, BC Bud...

Stoney foraged with his head down. His daypack filled with the fruits of his labour.

September 22 was the first day of Autumn—the season of the west, maturity, buffalo, sage, water, emotional health, the colour blue, black people, and dusk...

He inspected Holly's contributions before adding them to his pack.

Tomorrow is Canadian Thanksgiving. It's a strange celebration of no thanks and no giving. Instead, on the Res, we're planning on hosting a Potlatch dinner. Bring a plate and everything else you own...

Intimacy lengthened with the afternoon shadows. When Holly showed him the last specimen, Stoney was looking into her eyes. He dropped it into the daypack. They held hands down the mountain.

Those who have one foot in the canoe, and one foot on the shore, are going to fall into the water.

'Feed them shit and keep them in the dark.'
Mushroom Management

The day after Stoney Ridge and Holly Hill had their matsutake mating meld, and a few minutes after Tim Leery met his maker, Sababa left his new resident to attend his mandatory monthly Department of Medicine meeting. He found most of his colleagues trying to grab a quick java in the main lobby at Code Brew, bunched up like a climbing group at Hillary step near the Everest summit.
Marquis Shu Ying had ordered his piccolo latte, Ernie 'The Big Easy' Hacker his flat white, Dasco Boet his straight black, Ed Hyde his anemic decaf, and Sid Shalimar his cappuccino.
"And you want a quadruple expresso, right?" Asked the barista.
"Espresso doppio doppio." Sababa confirmed.
All the men walked together down a side hallway, on their journey to the Forbidden Zone. Inside the Administration Board Room, the big bear patriarch of the department, Peter Zaias, Chief Defender of the Faith, seer of the Sacred Scrolls, waited for them to find their favorite fabric Mayline chairs. Their landings agitated powerful earthy union odours of dust and must and rotting corpses from the particulate debris of past deliberations, lurking under the table in the claret pile carpet. For here was the morgue of ambition.
The final department member strolled into the midst of his peers after they had all taken their seats. Dr. Wayward Woods, still missing an internal clock, arrived clutching his Tim Hortons Double Double, like a monk late for a monastery mass.
The scorn of previous hospital administrators, their picture frames lining the fuzzy light green-yellow padded walls in full black and white mediocrity, scowled down at the reluctant assembly.
The white stippled acoustic tile ceiling, constructed to absorb the screams of the defeated, bored out with pot lights and grooved in a railway yard

of track lighting, was controlled by a far wall bank of knobs and switches to focus photons and heat.

A long teak conference table, halfway between a boat and a racetrack, polished with oil and buffed with a soft towel, filled the centre, racing the waist-high wooden wall sideboard cabinet next to it down the length of the room. The only two items on the table were an open box of tissues, and a multifunction business-class conference digital phone console. Dr. Zaias picked up a handset and dialed zero.

"Lana, can you announce the beginning of the Department of Medicine meeting?" The hospital switchboard operator's Big Voice broadcast the assembly overhead.

At the far end of the room, a wall-mounted HDTV screen hung next to a melamine whiteboard on an easel with a rainbow tray of desiccated felt markers. Whoever had written this message on the whiteboard would have had to have picked the lock to the Board Room.

Instructions for Strategic Filibustering at your Next Hospital Committee Meeting

1. Ask for more data—This always works. Use phrases like 'level of confidence is low' or 'statistically insignificant' to scare the members into searching for more data. This data is never available.

2. Ask for whatever data you have to be 'analyzed' in a more effective manner—use phrases like 'confounding variables' or 'background noise' to make the members skeptical.

3. Ask for more members to be added to the group—everyone knows that more is better, but since everyone hates committees, you'll never get anyone to join.

4. Ask to have a consultant brought in—somehow this fools even the best of them. You have to first debate if a consultant is needed, and debate what type of consultant to get. Even if you get an answer on this, you still have to find a way to pay the consultant. There is never money in the budget to pay a consultant.

5. Ask to have the group broken down into smaller task forces, steering committees, or action groups—by the time you define what the goal of the 'micro committee' is, you will head right into the realization that no one will volunteer to be on it.

6. Ask to bring the issue to the largest group of the hospital (general staff meeting, etc.)—by the law of averages, some crotchety bastard will hate the issue enough to force it back into the smaller committee again where you filibuster it all over again.

7. Try bringing up a point and then slowly, but deliberately go tangential—by the time the committee realizes you are on another topic, you've made sure that new topic is controversial. That will piss off the 'hothead' in your group enough to have him speak his mind about the new topic and you are now off to the races. Sit back and enjoy.

8. Ask to have a consensus on the issue and they try to have the committee define *consensus* and see if they can have a consensus on that definition.

9. Ask the 'slow speaker' in your group to give the in-depth opinion and where he does, ask him more questions so he can elaborate on what he just said.
10. Ask if the issue at hand is that important when so many other issues are critical (they never are)—try to table this issue and promise to bring it up in the next meeting and then reapply any one of the top nine techniques.

Dr. Zaias called the council to order and requested approval of the previous meeting's minutes. A cacophony of grunts echoed around the table. They dealt with the more mundane aspects of their otherwise exciting existences, leaving a paper trail of 'ayes' and 'nays' and tabled motions until the next time. Halfway through the proceedings they were always joined by the man in the thousand-dollar suit, held together with impeccable cuffs and collars, silk ties and linen handkerchiefs, and silver cuff links in his Cardin shirt. In his manicured fingers he held a matched pen or pencil of platinum, poised to doodle on monogrammed paper holding the timeless, the ageless, reports. Malcolm Canmore was the Chief Hospital Administrator of Harbour City Regional, the CHA, the CEO, the COO, the COG, the CAD, the CON, the CUR, the grand omnipotent stomper of supermen. In a universe that used chaos as fuel, Malcolm represented order. Every day, he cleaned his navel with a cotton bud soaked in witch hazel.

Sababa muttered under his breath. He and Malcolm were natural foes, and the Good Doctor preferred it that way. And Malcolm disliked men like Sababa because, whereas men made the rules for Malcolm, Sababa knew that only Mother Nature made the rules for him, and Sababa was scornful of the ones made for and by Malcolm.

Malcolm had a special agenda item he wanted to add at the last minute, the way he always did.

"As you know, gentlemen, the Vancouver Island Health Authority, like its predecessor the Central Vancouver Island Health Authority, is no more." He said.

"What are you calling this double oxymoron now?" Sababa asked.

"You have the social skills of an eight-year-old with a Kalashnikov, Sababa." Malcolm said. "To answer your question, I have invited the latest managementship of the health region to speak to us this morning. It is my great pleasure to introduce an old friend and colleague, our new chief executive, Foster Inclusion." A tanned muscular older man with a full crop of wavy white hair above a wide grin full of perfect white teeth strode into the Boardroom, followed by six of his management minions. They were from the Underworld.

"Thank you for that glowing introduction, Malcolm." Foster began. "Our health region authority has been renamed to better reflect the values of our organization. Henceforth, we shall be known as Island Health."

"Down the way where the nights are gay and the sun shines daily on the mountain top." Sababa sang. Malcolm glared.

"This is Doctor Sababa, Foster." He said. "For every action, he has an equal and opposite criticism."

"Ah. Yes." Said Der Weisse Engel. "We have so many remarkable stories collected about you in Victoria."

"Nie mój cyrk, nie moje małpy."

"I beg your pardon." Foster's grin began to sag.

"It's Polish." Sababa said. "Not my circus, not my monkey."

"There are two innovations we will be requiring of our medical specialists from now on." Foster forced his smile into high beam. "The first is your participation in an annual performance review." The smell of cordite wafted from across the table.

"Who will be performing this review?" Asked Dasco Boet.

"We have created a committee of stakeholders." Foster explained.

"The kind with sharpened points?" Sababa asked.

"Not at all, Doctor Sababa." Foster said. "We intend to keep it as informal as possible. For example, I might ask you what you have done to improve the morale of your co-workers?"

"Neglected to give them the beatings they so richly deserved." Sababa said.

"And we would shorten that to 'team player.'"

"What's the second demand?" Asked Ed Hyde.

"As of now, we require you to be actively involved with our bed utilization efforts." Foster said. "The admitting department and ward Team Leaders will call you twice a day to enable discharge of your inpatients."

"You do know that the Health Authority has more managers than beds." Dasco said.

"Your point?" Malcolm asked.

"Here's a revolutionary idea." Sababa said. "You can take it to your next executive calypso meeting if you like. Get the managers down on all-fours, throw blankets over them, and presto, change-o!" Foster Inclusion's grin hit the floor.

"People management is not your strength, is it Doctor Sababa?"

"I am a mere mushroom on whom the dew of heaven drops now and then." He said. "If your job is to tell me how to do my job, you should at least know how to do my job."

Sababa's pager went off in his pocket. He called the number. It was Praj, on the bridge of the Death Star. He was excited.

Dr. Zaias thanked everyone and adjourned the meeting before any bloodshed could occur.

14

'Death is the veil which those who live call life; They sleep, and it is lifted.'
Percy Bysshe Shelley

On his way to the ICU, Sababa left the Board Room with Marquis Shu Ying. Shu was in one of his Chinese metaphysics moods.

"A deeper understanding of yin-yang duality will lead you to the oneness of the Tao." He said. Sababa's eyes rolled behind his upper eyelids.

"And here I was counting on these little footprints painted on the floor."

"The Five Elements live in the ICU as well." Shu smiled. "This patient you're going to see there—according to the theory, her element is earth, her emotional activity overthinking, her environmental factor dampness, her generation grief, her subjugation kidney, her five senses taste, her taste sweet, her yang organ stomach."

"You're always confusing me with this stuff, Shu." His colleague continued.

"Her time of the day is 7 a.m. to 11 a.m., her colour is yellow, her yin organ is her spleen, her five tissues muscle, her direction is middle, and her sound..."

"Is?"

"Singing." Shu veered off towards the Electrodiagnostic lab.

But nobody was singing on the bridge of the Death Star. The world stopped at the windows. Betty Boop was in full-blown nicotine withdrawal. Two of the critical care nurses, Mary and Angie, pointed to the curtain of cubicle four, behind which he could hear Praj trying to pacify Charmeine's impatience. He pulled back the barrier. Shu had been correct. Her colour was yellow. Sababa could smell the poison.

"Amuse me." He said.,

"Theresa Terrace." Praj began. "22-year-old hospitality management instructor at the university who Buddy Benway operated on last night for acute appendicitis." He handed Sababa the chart.

"Because?"

"Because she presented with fever and abdominal pain and nausea and vomiting, she was tender in both lower quadrants on exam, her white count was high with a left shift, her abdominal ultrasound showed free fluid and a few dilated bowel loops and enlarged lymph nodes in her right lower abdomen, and her Alvarado score for the diagnosis of acute appendicitis was 7 out of 10."

"But Buddy didn't find an inflamed appendix, did he?" Sababa asked.

"He told me it looked normal." Praj said. "He told me to call you."

"A chance to cut is a chance to cure." Sababa noted. "But it's only a chance. How did she end up here?"

"She had a seizure that responded to glucose injection." Praj said. "The anesthetist noticed oozing from her IV sites and wounds. He ordered a stat coagulation profile."

"And?"

"It came back seven times more prolonged than it should have been."

"Did anyone notice she was yellow?" Sababa asked. "And comatose."

"I did." Charmeine chimed in. "She also made her first appearance in Emergency five days ago, with nausea and vomiting. Trace Pangloss sent her home."

"What else?" Sababa asked.

"Her kidney function is zilch." Praj handed him Theresa's most recent lab numbers.

"So, what you got?" Sababa asked.

"I'm sorry."

"As you always are." Sababa said. "But I need to hear a synthesis of Theresa's history and exam and labwork and clinical course into some kind of coherent narrative so that we might have a chance of saving her life."

"Of course." Praj said. "Previously well young woman with a long prodrome of GI symptoms followed by liver and kidney failure."

"And what categories of disease can you name that can cause these two organs to fail?" Sababa asked.

"Infection, collagen-vascular disease, and toxic-metabolic." Praj offered.

"What kinds of toxins?"

"All kinds." Praj said.

"What's the season?" Sababa asked.

"The season?"

"It's autumn."

"So?"

"So, what toxins can cause furtive multisystem failure in the fall?" Sababa gazed into dead eyes.

"How about a bicyclic polypeptide with a tryptophan residue substitution at position two of the indole ring cross-linked by a 2-prime-bound sulfur group." He said. "α-amanitin- induced intracellular RNA polymerase II synthesis inhibition."

"From what?" Praj asked.

"Mushrooms." Charmeine said.

"What kind of mushrooms?" Both Praj and the nurse had the same expression.

"Ce plat de champignons a changé la destinée de l'Europe." Sababa said. *This dish of mushrooms changed the destiny of Europe.* "Voltaire wrote that in his *Mémoires*. This fungus arrived from the old world on the roots of chestnuts after killing off numerous notables in accidental poisonings or assassination plots—The Buddha Siddharta Gautama in 479 BC, Roman Emperor Claudius in 54 AD, Pope Clement VII, the Russian

16

tsaritsa Natalia Naryshkina, the Holy Roman Emperor Charles VI, whose death in 1740 led to the War of the Austrian Succession, and the composer Johann Schobert in Paris, along with his wife, one of his children, maidservant, and four acquaintances after insisting that these mushrooms were edible."

Sababa looked at his house staff. Still nothing.

"Amanita phalloides." He said. "Otherwise known as the 'Death Cap.' Half a mushroom contains enough heat-resistant toxin to kill an adult human. Young specimens first emerge from the ground resembling a white egg covered by a universal veil. Puffball hunters are encouraged to always cut fruiting bodies in half, to reveal the outline of any developing amanitas still encased within their structure."

"Theresa's mother is in the waiting room, Sab." Betty Boop interrupted the tutorial.

"Let's go talk to her, Mowgli." He motioned to Praj. "Charmeine, change her IV to D10 at 100 ml/hour, give her 5 mg of Vitamin K, begin an N-acetylcysteine protocol, and an infusion of silibinin, 20 mg/kg over 24 hours. Betty, get me Dr. Ziggy Stardust in Vancouver when we get back." The ward clerk raised her handset high.

The small vestibule that masqueraded as a waiting room was furnished with several retro vintage chairs, a coffee table on which sat a vase of withering gladiolas, and a wire rack of support group pamphlets. It could have been a cave if there had been more light. Theresa's mother confirmed that she had cooked up some mushrooms the young woman had picked five days previously.

"I don't like wild mushrooms." She said, when Sababa asked her if she had eaten any. "Will Theresa be OK?"

"I've put in a call to a friend of mine in Vancouver." Sababa said. "Theresa will need all the help we can give her." He and Praj excused themselves and reentered the unit through the hiss of the frosted automatic door under the overhead sign. *Tranquility Base.*

"Ziggy Stardust on line 2 for you, Sab." Betty Boop held up her handset.

"How come you only call me when you're after something." Ziggy asked. "What do you want this time?"

"I need a liver, Zig." Sababa said. "And a kidney."

"What you need is to be less of a shit magnet." Dr. Stardust was the best liver guy in the big city. "Another fearless forager dancing with the death caps?"

"Something like that." Sababa told him Theresa's story. "We're in stage four, far too late for gastric decontamination."

"Send her over by chopper." Ziggy said. "You know the odds."

"Call in the Big Bird, Betty." He hung up his handset and watched Betty Boop pick hers up again. Twenty minutes later, Tranquility Base was rocked by a racket of rotors. *Dubdubdubdub whumpawhumpa whupwhup wuppawuppa whopwhop batabata tocotoco flacflac chakkchackk chakachak akk-chk thiththith sssssssss...*

Five minutes after that, two blue air ambulance jumpsuits rolled a shortbox stretcher into the unit. It was piled high with advanced life support instruments and equipment—oral and nasal airways, bag-valve masks, portable suction, combitubes, King laryngeal tubes, laryngeal mask airways, endotracheal tubes and laryngoscopes with blades and handles, stylets and lubricant, Magill forceps, bougies, tourniquets, cleaning agents, IV catheters, fluid bags, and tubing, meds for rapid sequence intubation, and an automated external defibrillator. Sababa brought them back up to speed.

"Will she make it?" Asked one of the flyboys.

"Fifty-fifty." He studied the reaction on their faces.

"The world is a beautiful place if you don't mind some people dying all the time." Sababa said. "How thin the veil that lies between the pain of hell and paradise. For there is no life on the other side."

'And my head is aching and my hands are cold
And I'm looking for the silver lining, silver lining in the clouds
And I'm searching for and
I'm searching for the philosophers stone.'
Van Morrison, *Philosopher's Stone*

"Praj on Line 1, Sab." Betty had returned from her break dragging a tobacco smoke tornado.

"Digame." Sababa answered. *Tell me.*

"Dr. Capitaine wants us to see a VIU philosophy professor just back from Holland."

"Coming now." *Click.*

Two white wireless earbuds rotated towards the source of the footsteps. A big man topped with thick dancing curly hair bounced through the automatic sliding frosted glass doors, into a carnival of Care Card numbers, wristbands, and pain.

"What you got?" He asked.

"Truffle brothers." Came from Sababa's port side. He turned to the source.

"Myles." Sababa smiled. "How are you?"

"Living the dream." Myles said.

"Dreams are the touchstones of our character." Sababa replied.

"Who are the Truffle brothers?" Praj asked.

"Two Turkish boys, Ali and Murat Kucuksen." Sababa said. "They own a quaint Dutch farm in the bucolic pastures of Hazerswoude-Dorp, 30 kilometers south of Amsterdam, nestled in verdant fields of ruminating Holsteins, lazy windmills, and pert tulips."

"And?"

"It's the world's largest psilocybin-containing-truffle factory."

"I thought magic mushrooms were illegal everywhere except Brazil, Jamaica, Samoa, and the Czech Republic." Myles offered.

"Holland only passed a law against the possession and sale of psychedelic mushrooms in 2008, after Gaelle Caroff, a pretty French tourist, jumped off a Dutch bridge, and a 29-year-old schizophrenic Frenchman living in Amsterdam ritualistically dismembered his dog in a van beside the Herengracht to 'free its spirit.' Using a technique he claimed to be of Moroccan origin, he slit his dog's throat, tore open its chest cavity, and spread its entrails all over his naked body. Both had taken shrooms. But there was a loophole in the Netherlands ban of 186 species of magic mushrooms."

"Magic truffles." Myles said.

"They forgot to include sclerotia in the 2008 law."

"What's a sclerotia?" Praj was engaged.

"Sclerotium." Sababa corrected. "Scerlotia is plural. To be more exact, sclerotia are not truffles nor bulbs, caudices, corms, rhizomes, tubers, or other hypogeal swellings. A truffle is a reproductive structure that attracts animals who disperse its spores after digestion. A sclerotium is a vegetative structure unique to fungi. It has no direct reproductive purpose."

"What's it for then?" Praj asked.

"Two teleological questions in less than three hours, and it's only your first day on the job." Sababa said. "It's a survival mechanism. If a given environment cannot support the growth of a mushroom, the mycelium—a cottony subterranean net made of totipotent cells similar to animal stem cells—may produce a sclerotium. The mycelium's cellular threads bifurcate and fuse, forming an interwoven clod that can last indefinitely and give rise to a mushroom should environmental conditions improve. Few biological structures rival the sclerotium's adamantine resilience; in certain species, sclerotia can survive desiccated to the point of combustibility, subjected to freezing temperatures, mired in acidic soils, and deprived of nutrients. Some varieties quiesce for decades before sudden and vigorous myceliogenesis, emerging phoenixlike from the ashes of burned forests, which is why they survived the slash-and-burn agriculture all along the Mesoamerican biological corridor. The Olmec unwittingly selected psilocybin-containing sclerotia to endure their firestorms.

In the kingdom of fungi, sclerotia assume many forms. The Gogodala people of Papua New Guinea's Western Province live in an alluvial swamp completely devoid of the stones required to make hard tools. They seek out the mushroom *Pleurotus tuber-regium* and carve its giant sclerotia into club heads carried on hunting expeditions and into battle. The dark purple tendrils that emerge from florets of ryegrass parasitized by ergot, the culprit for the medieval scourge of St. Anthony's Fire, are also sclerotia, and it was their study that resulted in the discovery of LSD by that very same Albert Hofmann who found the chemical formula for psilocybin. There is also a parasitic *Fibulorhizoctonia* species that forms sclerotia capable of mimicking the size and shape of common termite eggs so exactly that the termites nurture the sclerotia as their brood, salivating on them to maintain their moisture. Sababa pulled his little Black Book, his repository of divine revelation, from inside his Colombian leather briefcase.

"And the psychedelic stuff?" Praj asked.

"Interesting story of their discovery by another physician, Dr. Steven Hayden Pollock of San Antonio, Texas." Sababa said. "On September 3, 1977, he and fellow mycologist Gary Lincoff skipped out of an afternoon session of the Second International Mycological Congress in Tampa, Florida to go foraging. Young, hirsute, and wearing a Day-Glo T-shirt, Pollock drove around in a hand-painted Winnebago Chieftain. He had converted the interior into a rolling fungus laboratory, outfitted with an autoclave, Petri dishes, desiccators, and everything else necessary to culture and preserve mushrooms on the road.

Pollock had heard of a bluing *Panaeolus* rumored to exist on the outskirts of Tampa. The two men found a single specimen of a new species of *Strophariaceae* growing in a wild sandy meadow. An excited Pollock called it the rock of ages, the cosmic camote, the superfantastic megagalactic camotillo, the philosopher's stone. Lincoff named it *Psilocybe tampanensis*.

Pollock worked 7 days a week, cloned the specimen, produced a pure culture, and isolated a strain of *P. tampanensis* that produced sclerotia of breathtaking enormousness, the size of ostrich eggs, and so alien that a trained mycologist with a scanning electron microscope would fail to identify its taxon. Looked like muesli, tasted like walnuts.

Recognizing its market potential, the mad mycologist founded a company called Hidden Creek in 1979 to sell philosopher stone kits by mail. Advertising in the monthly magazine *High Times* made Dr. Steven Pollock the largest magic mushroom vendor in the world within a year. He became the god Prometheus, bringing humans the gift of fire.

But in the Greek myth, Zeus was outraged. In the end, Steven Pollock had cloned a blood spore.

On the evening of January 31, 1981, the last 'patient' in his San Antonio clinic put a bullet in his forehead. Pollock was 33 years old. The DEA burned everything in his laboratory."

"So, where do philosopher stones come from now?" Praj asked.

"From a spore library in the Netherlands." Sababa said. "Turns out that another mycologist named Steven Peele had sent them a sample in the early cloning days of cultivation."

"And?"

"Enter the Truffle brothers." He said. "The implementation of the 2008 Dutch psychedelic mushroom ban had forced the two Turkish entrepreneurs to destroy their remaining stock. What had once been a minor novelty item to all but the most rarefied fungal connoisseurs now became the foundation of their business.

When Gary Lincoff traveled to Amsterdam that year he was astonished to find that the species he had discovered with Pollock—one he was certain had long since gone extinct—was advertised and sold all over the city. The species had not only survived; it had overtaken the market in the form of vials labeled 'Pollack', filled with injectable spores and arrayed in refrigerated display cases. Tourists were leaving smart shops with what had once been the rarest mushroom in the world.

On their Dutch farm, Ali and Murat Kucuksen created the superlab of Pollock's dreams. Inside the sclerotium-packaging facility, they built fifteen temperature-controlled growth chambers, each capable of accommodating 600 ten-pound bags of ryegrass media, a walk-in autoclave the size of a bank vault, and a double-air-locked clean room where technicians outfitted in surgical scrubs maintain tanks of liquid mycelial cultures. The Truffle brothers produce 20,000 tons per year, a quantity large enough to require a forklift to shuttle the product as it's processed. Every smart shop in Amsterdam boasts images of their mascot, a blue truffle hog named Mr. Truffles. The sclerotium, a structure that existed to carry the fungus through inhospitable environments, had done its job remarkably. Who's the patient?"

"Elias Ashmole." Myles said. "32-year-old philosophy professor at VIU. Just back from Amsterdam, where he bought some philosopher stones for his cluster headaches."

"Hmmmm... serotonin analogue." Sababa said. "It might work. And?"

"Got a headache on the ferry to the island early this morning." Myles said. "He brewed a tea onboard with about 30 grams of truffles, twice the recommended dose for a strong trip. The ambulance crew brought him in an hour ago. Vitals stable, seems happy enough. Says he's God. I told him you were. He wants to meet you."

"We're a little busy today, Myles." Sababa said. "Praj and I have already seen one hallucinating Elvis leave the building this morning. Watch him for another 6 hours. By then he should have recovered enough to send home. We'll come back if we have to."

"OK." Myles asked. Sababa's pager hummed in his pocket. He called Lana and wrote down two names on a piece of paper, which he passed to Praj.

"Go see these two referrals back on Elvis' floor." He said. "Call me when you're done. Try not to let them slip the surly bonds of Earth before I have a chance to see them." Praj looked at the two names. *Duke Point...* *Rollrim Brown.* And was gone.

"You see many psychedelic mushroom patients?" Myles asked.

"A few." Sababa said. "Most psilocybin day-trippers are supervised and safe enough. It's the muscarine and isoxazole derivative-producing mushrooms that come to our attention more often. Like the Fly agaric Santa Claus poisonings."

"Santa Claus?" Myles asked.

"*Amanita muscaria.*" He said. "Main hallucinogens are chemicals known as muscimol and ibotenic acid. Most people don't know that Father Christmas is a mushroom trip."

"How so?" Myles asked.

"In the 17th Century, the indigenous Sami people of Lapland waited in their houses on the Winter Solstice for special visitors. Siberian shamans would arrive from their Arctic abodes on reindeer-drawn sleds with a special gift. Often the snow was so heavy it blocked the doors of some family dwellings, so the shamans would enter and exit through an opening in the roof, dressed in red suits with white spots."

"Why red and white?"

"The gift was red and white." Sababa said. "Like Christmas candy canes are now. The shamans brought *Amanita muscaria,* a hallucinogenic red-and-white toadstool they considered holy. Collected and dried in the autumn, they gave them as gifts of introspection that would solve the family's problems in healing rituals and, as conduits between the spirit and human world, provide advice. Upon arrival, the healers were regaled with food."

"Santa Claus is a psychedelic-eating mushroom shaman from the Arctic." Myles said. "Who knew?"

"It fits." Sababa said. "It's why we place our own Christmas gifts under the same kinds of coniferous trees that *Amanita muscaria* grows at the base of. It's why Santa's reindeer fly. Any yellow snow urine of humans these shamanic spirit animals consume still contains hallucinogenic psilocybin, and reindeer are known for their fantastic fungal fondness. They brought healing and problem solving to the tribes."

"As do you." Myles said.

"Pretty much all the drugs I prescribe are more dangerous." Sababa said. "Every culture dabbles in alternative universes. Even Smurfs are little blue people who live in magic mushrooms. Think about it."

"You ever had a full-blown hallucination?" Myles asked.

"Once, during my training." Sababa said. "I was into my fourth day on call in the ICU without any sleep. Rounds were about to begin. I ducked into the washroom to throw some cold water on my face. When I turned on the tap, a little man came out and said 'Hi'. Slept right through my day off."

'So give them blood, blood, gallons of the stuff
Give them all that they can drink and it will never be enough
So give them blood, blood, blood
Grab a glass because there's going to be a flood.'
My Chemical Romance, Blood

Dr. Praj Bharmal was beginning to interview the second patient when his preceptor emerged from the stairwell. Samara Morgan glowered.

"Who's on first?" Sababa asked. Praj handed him the referral request from Dr. Nicholas Rivera. *Stay on white sheets. Asthma getting worse.*

"Tell me the story." Sababa said.

"Duke Point." Praj began. "37-year-old laborer at a local compost facility with a six-month history of cough, shortness of breath, fatigue, and weight loss. But no wheezing, and his symptoms don't appear to be reversible over time."

"So."

"It doesn't sound like asthma." Praj said. "Claims he was never a smoker."

"Exam?"

"He's on oxygen by nasal cannula. His respiratory rate is up and I can hear dry crackles in his lower lungs when he inhales. His oxygen saturation is 89%, almost normal."

"Never trust to general impressions, Mowgli, but concentrate upon details." Sababa said. "It's off by one percentage point."

"It's within range." Praj argued. "It's normal."

"If his DNA was off by one percentage point, he'd be a wombat."

You know how people say, 'you can't live without love?'" Sababa asked. "Oxygen is even more important. What do you call a guy who finished at the bottom of his class in med school?"

"Dunno." Praj admitted.

"Doctor." Sababa said. "Let's go see him."

At the patient's bedside, Praj made introductions.

"What do you do?" Duke asked the first question.

"I'm an internist." Sababa said. "I solve problems you don't know you have in ways you can't understand. To save time, let's assume I am never wrong." He held up the fingertips of the hand he had shaken. They were little blue footballs.

"Well lookee here." He said. "What's this, my young protégé?"

"Clubbing." Praj hung his head for having missed it. "Hippocratic fingers. And peripheral cyanosis."

"And what kinds of respiratory conditions cause clubbing and peripheral cyanosis?" Sababa asked.

"Lung cancer and mesothelioma, interstitial lung diseases like idiopathic pulmonary fibrosis, complicated tuberculosis, suppurative lung diseases like lung abscess, empyema, bronchiectasis, cystic fibrosis, arteriovenous fistula or malformation, sarcoidosis, congenital cyanotic heart disease, subacute bacterial endocarditis, atrial myxoma, and hepatopulmonary syndrome." Praj offered.

"And Pierre Marie-Bamberger syndrome and Touraine-Solente-Golé syndrome." Sababa added. "Have you seen his chest x-ray?"

"Not yet." Praj admitted.

"It's not the fault of the post that the blind man didn't see it."

"I'm sorry."

"You should be." Sababa said. "Let's go." He turned to the patient.

"We'll be back in a minute, Mr. Point."

Outside his room, Sababa filled a flat screen with x-ray images of Duke's chest.

"What do you see, Praj?"

"Fibrotic and emphysematous changes with loss of lung volume particularly in the upper lobes." He said.

"Permit me to introduce you to Sababa's Three Rules of Medical Analysis."

"Which are?" Praj asked.

"(1) What you got you got, (2) What you don't got, you don't got, and (3) Context is everything." Sababa said.

"So?"

"So, what you got?"

"Young male with clubbing, peripheral cyanosis, and some kind of bad lung disease." Praj said.

"What you don't got?" Sababa asked.

"A reason for his bad lung disease."

"Permit me to introduce you to Sababa's Existential Slap." Sababa said.

"What's the question?"

"And?"

"What's the cause of Duke's bad lung disease." Praj said.

"Let's go ask him."

At the bedside again, Sababa's first question was for his apprentice.

"What's Sababa's third rule of medical analysis, Praj?"

"Context is everything?" Sababa turned to the patient.

"What kind of compost do you work with, Duke?" Sababa asked.

"Mushroom." He said.

"Attend to mushrooms and all other things will answer up."

"So, what's wrong with me?" Duke asked.

"You have something called Mushroom Compost Worker's Lung." Sababa said. "It's a form of what we refer to as either chronic hypersensitivity pneumonitis or extrinsic allergic alveolitis."

"But they've been telling me it was asthma."

"They've been wrong." Sababa said. "Asthma, especially occupational asthma is a Type I form of hypersensitivity. Your exaggerated immune response to mushroom antigens is Type III or Type IV, and unlike asthma, targets your lung airspaces rather than your bronchi."

"I didn't get any of that." Duke said. "Can you fix it?"

"With your help." Sababa said. "First, you need to find another job in a different industry. Second, Dr. Bharmal here will arrange for some investigations."

"I will?" Asked Praj.

"If you want to continue to play doctor, you will." Sababa said. "Precipitating IgG antibodies to *Thermophilic actinomycetes* using the Ouchterlony double immunodiffusion method, arterial blood gas, full pulmonary function studies, high-resolution CT scan of his chest, and a transbronchial biopsy. Put in a referral to our resident pulmonologist, Dr. Ed Hyde."

"Why do I need a lung biopsy?" Duke asked.

"To distinguish what you've got from a group of diseases called idiopathic interstitial pneumonias." Sababa said. "And some other stuff. Once we have a tissue diagnosis, we'll give you a course of corticosteroids to jump-start your recovery. Dr. Bharmal will come back later to further detail your discharge on home oxygen."

"I sure won't miss that smell." Duke said. Sababa shook his hand before he and Praj left the room.

"Who's the other referral?" He asked.

"Next room down." Praj said. "Rollrim Brown is a 49-year-old lifeguard admitted last night by Dr. Tarmac for severe anemia. Just back from a holiday in Romania. Healthy until two days ago when he developed vomiting, diarrhea, and abdominal pain. That's as far as I got before you arrived." Praj opened the patient's chart.

"His hemoglobin and haptoglobin are low, retic count and indirect bilirubin and free hemoglobin and d-dimer are elevated, and there are smashtocytes in his peripheral smear. Poor kidney function and he has hemoglobin in his urine. Looks like idiopathic immune hemolytic anemia."

"It may not be idiopathic." Sababa said.

"Why not?"

"Because there may be a reason."

"Last set of vital signs showed falling blood pressure and urine output, and elevated heart and respiratory rate." Praj closed the chart.

"We need to see him now." Sababa said. Inside Rollrim's room, he asked Praj to describe his observations.

"Pallor, jaundiced sclera…"

"Sick or not sick?" Sababa asked.

"Sick." Said Praj and Rollrim at the same time.

"What were you doing in Romania, Mr. Brown?" Sababa asked.

"Visiting relatives." He said. "I go every year. Our original name was Cafeniu in Romanian."

"It was the saddest country I travelled through on my world tour, years ago, during Ceausescu's rule." Sababa said.

"Ceausescu was mad, and he made half of Romania mad." Rollrim agreed. "Still, kiss French, wear Italian, drive German, drink Russian, be Romanian."

"What did you do in the last few days you were there?"

"Nothing much." He said. "Visited the monasteries, hiked the mountains, picked some mushrooms, played some music, ate well."

"Which mushrooms did you pick?" Sababa asked.

"Same ones we pick every year." He said. "We call them 'bureti porcesti.'"

"*Paxillus involutus*." Sababa said. "You've had a reaction."

"But I eat them every year." Rollrim protested.

"Yes, you do." Sababa said. "But this is not a toxic reaction to a poison. This is a hypersensitivity response to a mushroom antigen that your immune system confuses with a protein in the cell wall of your red blood cells. Discovered after the death of the German mycologist Dr. Julius Schäffer, but it wasn't until the mid-1980s that a Swiss physician named René Flammer identified the mushroom molecule responsible. It doesn't happen with recurrent ingestion, and then one day it does."

"Sare din lac în puţ." *Out of the frying pan into the fire.* Rollrim said. "My immune cells are attacking my blood?"

"Your B cells are producing an IgG antibody which forms an immune complex with the mushroom antigen which adheres itself to the surface of your red cells and activates the complement cascade. We call it opsonization."

"Not good?"

"Paxillus immunohemolytic syndrome." Sababa said. "Bad blood from mud and blood. The smashed red cells cause fat emboli and clotting factors to coagulate in your bloodstream, clogging up the vessels to your kidneys and lungs and heart and adrenal glands and liver and spleen. Not good."

"Toate cele frumoase, poartă şi ponoase." Rollrim said. *All that is fair must fade.*

"Totu lucru la vrema sa." Sababa replied. *Man proposes, God disposes.*

"What can you do for it?" He asked.

"You're going to the ICU, my friend." Sababa said. "Until I can transfer you out as soon as I can, to a tertiary care hospital for dialysis and plasmapheresis."

"Plasmapheresis?"

"It's a form of blood exchange." Sababa said.

"In much knowledge, there is also much grief." Rollrim said. Our ways are not your ways, and there shall be to you many strange things."

"Marie of Romania?"

"You know us." Rollrim gazed far into the distance. "From what you have told me of your experiences already, you know something of what strange things there may be."

"Bram Stoker's *Dracula*." Sababa said. *We are in Transylvania, and Transylvania is not England.* "Another form of blood exchange. Praj, give Rollrim here a gram of solumedrol while you're working the rest of this into shape."

"A gram?" Praj asked.

"Go big or go home." Sababa said. "You have a set of wheels?"

"I have a car."

"Meet me at my office at one."

"Office?"

"For our afternoon clinic experience." Sababa said. "By three methods we may learn wisdom: First, by reflection, which is noblest; Second, by imitation, which is easiest; and third by experience, which is the bitterest."

"Who said that?" Praj asked.

"Me." Sababa said. "And Confucius."

> Caterpillar: …and the other side will make you grow shorter.
> Alice: The other side of what?
> Caterpillar: The mushroom, of course!
> Lewis Carrol, *Alice in Wonderland*

Doctor Sababa's clinic was halfway across Harbour City, an eight-minute drive from the hospital. Praj did it in ten. Sababa would do it in five, right behind him.

The young resident pulled into the parking lot next to a beautiful old white two-storey heritage building. A small brass plaque graced the main floor entrance. *Harbour City Research Institute.* Praj was aware that Sababa was a principal investigator in several Phase III clinical trials, including some from the Harvard TIMI and Canadian Vigour research groups.

"Come with me." Sababa had removed a small object from his Colombian leather briefcase and indicated for Praj to follow him around the back of an ancient plum tree, still laden with hundreds of egg-shaped purple fruit. He could smell the fermentation from the ones on the ground that had tried to escape. The wasps were having a fiesta.

"Italian prune plum." Sababa pulled open a shiny steel curved blade from a groove in his rosewood mushroom knife. "Also Italian." The professor pointed to an immense bracket fungus above their heads and sliced off the bright yellow outer edge in a single motion.

"Sulfur shelf." He handed half the ribbon to Praj. "Chicken of the woods. For your dinner."

"I don't know how to thank you." Praj didn't know how to thank him.

Together, they climbed the stairs to another doorway, inlaid with stained glass, and marked by another sign. *Manzanita Medical.* Sababa had told him that other clinics were named for native trees, but his office was denominated after a local shrub that lived on the ridges behind the city because he loved its flowers.

Praj accompanied Doctor Sababa through the open door and into a sunlit foyer. A redheaded middle-aged woman with cat-eyed frame glasses sat typing behind a counter and a big screen PowerMac G4, under a photo of a bowl of multicoloured cereal with a diagonal red line through it. *No fruit loops.*

"Hi, Mercy." A bag of chanterelles he pushed over the counter drew a smile.

"It's toadstool week, Boss." She said.

"Mercy often inflicts death." Sababa mused. He pulled the first chart off the pile Mercy had assembled for the afternoon clinic and handed it to his trainee.

"Batter up." He said.

"Perry Lepistopsis?" Praj called into the full waiting room. A middle-aged man with a red nose and hands got up from the leather chair in the corner and followed him into the resident's examining room.

"Smokey Crescent?" Sababa picked up the second chart and motioned the young man who rose from his chair to follow him into his office.

"How can I help?" Asked the stocky savant.

"I'm whipped." Smokey said.

"Whipped?"

"See for yourself." Smokey pulled off his T-shirt to reveal purple raised welts all over his torso. "And it's not the first time. Whipped." Sababa took a magnifying lens from his Columbian leather briefcase to better examine Smokey's skin.

"Hmmmm." He said. "Flagellate dermatitis. Only two things cause this pattern of rash."

"What?" Smokey asked.

"A cancer drug called bleomycin, a sulfur-containing polypeptide derived from *Streptomyces verticillus.*" He said. "But that usually leaves hyperpigmentation after the inflammation settles, and you don't have any."

"No cancer treatment either." Smokey added. "What's the other cause?"

"Shiitake Dermatitis Syndrome." Sababa said. "First described in 1977 by Nakamura, it's a toxic reaction to eating shiitake mushrooms, usually undercooked, but there are cases reported after consumption of fully cooked *Lentinula edodes*. Affects less than two percent of the population. Have you eaten them recently, say in the last ten days?"

"I eat them all the time. Smokey said. "I grow them in alder logs to sell to restaurants. It's what I do."

"You need to stop the eating part." Sababa said.

"What causes it?" Smokey asked.

"Shiitakes contain a starch-like polysaccharide called lentinan which triggers blood vessels to dilate and leak inflammatory compounds beneath the skin surface. The rash begins as linear micropapules and then blisters and forms welts a day or two after ingestion because of Koebnerization from scratching. It's an itchy rash."

"It's horrible." Smokey said. "What's the treatment?"

"I've just told you." Sababa said. "If you don't eat another shiitake, the rash will be gone forever in less than three weeks." Praj poked his head in through Sababa's doorway.

"OK." Smokey put his shirt back on. "Thanks, Doc."

"Pleasure." Sababa said. "I'll write a letter to your GP, Dr. Bloom." When Smokey had gone, Praj settled into the other chair across from the professor's desk.

"What you got?" Sababa asked.

"Perry Lepistopsis." Praj began. "42-year-old cheese and foie gras and specialty food importer back from a buying trip to France. Presents with a two-week problem of painful red hands and feet and nose. That's all."

"That's all?" Sababa was skeptical. "No other history or exam or lab findings you found to help make an accurate diagnosis."

"Nope."

"You have a name?" Sababa asked.

"Primary erythromelalgia." Praj offered.

"How do you know it's primary?"

"Because there is no other obvious reason for it." Praj said.

"What's the difference between primary and secondary?" Sababa asked.

"One has no obvious cause, and the other does."

"This is what you should have said." Sababa leaned back in his chair. "Primary erythromelalgia is an autosomal dominant disorder caused by mutation of the voltage-gated sodium channel α-subunit in the SCN9A gene, leading to hyperexcitability of the C-fiber nociceptors responsible for pain perception, along with hypoexcitability of the sympathetic nerves that control cutaneous microvascular tone. This causes so much blood flow through open vessels that the patient's hands and feet, and nose and ears and face, turn bright red and hot to the touch. Episodes can be triggered by heat, pressure, mild activity, exertion, insomnia, stress, and sugar or alcohol or caffeine, spicy food or even melon consumption. Attacks can last from an hour to several months, infrequently to multiple times a day, and mostly at night. The burning pain is similar to that of chronic regional pain, phantom limb or thalamic pain syndromes, so excruciating that, as recently as 1903, a surgeon named H. Batty Shaw resorted to amputation of the affected limbs. Let's go see him." Praj opened the resident room door to a floridly flushed procurer of comestible delicacies.

"Mr. Lepistopsis?" Sababa began. "I'm Doctor Sababa. Dr. Bharmal here has told me most of your story."

"Ah, yes." Perry said. "The Sage of the Salish Sea."

"Compliments are like mushrooms—the most beautiful are the most poisonous." Sababa inspected the man's hands. "I get credit all the time for things I never said."

"What did you mean by 'most' of my story?" Perry asked.

"Where were you in France?"

"I travel all over France."

"Where were you two weeks ago?" Sababa asked.

"The French Alps. Savoie." He said. "I rented a chalet in the Maurienne valley."

"I know it well." Sababa continued his exam. "And what did you do in the Maurienne valley?"

"Some horseback riding and hiking." He said. "Prepared some wonderful meals with local ingredients. It's my passion, you know."

"So I've heard." Sababa said. "Did you gather any local mushrooms for your culinary indulgences."

"One day I picked some funnel caps." Perry said. "Delicious."

"You didn't pick funnel caps."

"I didn't?"

"Funnel caps are *Clitocybe gibba* or *Paralepista flaccida*." Sababa said. "What you picked was the paralysis funnel, *Clitocybe amoenolens*."

"And so?"

"There are two kinds of mushrooms known to cause secondary erythromelalgia, which is the condition you have." Sababa said. "*Clitocybe acromelalga*, from Japan and South Korea, and *Clitocybe amoenolens*, first described from Morocco in 1975 by the French mycologist Malençon."

"But I wasn't in Morocco."

"Like other Moroccans, it also lives in France."

"What does it do?"

"It contains acromelic acids, compounds that mimic the neurotransmitter glutamate." He said. "The resulting syndrome of mushroom-induced erythromelalgia can last from 8 days to 5 months, although one patient had symptoms for three years."

"The pain is so bad, I'd kill myself first." Perry said.

"We can help you with that." Sababa said. "Avoid things that trigger the pain. Try elevating the most affected limbs or placing them inside a thin, heat transparent, water-impermeable, plastic food storage bag submerged in cool but never cold water. Sababa wrote a script for a stepped regimen of serial mexiletine, followed by duloxetine and pregabalin. He told Perry he would prescribe him a long-acting narcotic if lesser analgesics failed to control his symptoms.

"Tell Mercy to make an appointment for you to see me in three weeks." Sababa didn't shake his hand.

"You like foie gras, Doc?" Perry asked. Sababa raised his eyebrows.

"I'll bring some next time." He said as he left. Sababa turned his attention to Praj.

"Sorry." He said.

"You need to quit saying that." Sababa said. "Save it for a time you'll need it. There are, in truth, no specialties in medicine, since to know fully many of the most important diseases a man must be familiar with their manifestations in many organs."

"William Osler?" Praj asked.

"The same. When I was a resident, patients were never 'clients living with their disease.' He said. "We either cured them, or they died from it. The time you spend here will be the best and worst of your life. You will be pushed. I will test you in ways that you will often consider unfair, demeaning and illegal, and you'll be right. True warriors are fierce because their training is fierce. This is your starting line, your arena. How well you play is up to you."

"I want to know as much as you know." Praj said.

"Any man who wants to master the essence of my strategy must research diligently, training morning and evening." Sababa said. "Thus can he polish his skill, become free from self, and realise extraordinary ability. He will come to possess miraculous power."

"Who said that?" Praj asked.

"Miyamoto Musashi."

"Who's he?"

"Look him up. We're on call tonight, Praj." He said. "You go first. Carry these with you wherever you go." Sababa handed Praj his pager and a heavy monkey wrench from beside the desk.

"What's this for?"

"To build muscle." He said. "And so you don't fall asleep."

'In every walk with nature, one receives far more than he seeks.'
John Muir

When Sababa had the pleasure and responsibility of hosting a medical resident, the duty of making sure no mistakes were made was offset to some degree by fleeting opportunities for the enjoyment of more personal time and space. The professor might get more sleep, and sometimes even make it home for dinner on his nights on call. It was on this night, as he was enjoying one of Jane's delicious chanterelle soups and cauliflower mushroom lasagnas, that the ringing of his landline interrupted an interval of gastronomic contentment.

"We have a patient." It was Praj.

"On my way." Sababa grabbed his camo poncho and fired up his dimpled and dented white Honda. The wind had blown the rain away and blown the sky away and all the leaves away, and the trees stood naked in the dark. For a brief moment, Sababa felt that he had known autumn for too long.

Wide emergency room glass doors slid open and shut in symphonic saccades. The stocky savant timed his entry behind an ambulance crew, to find Drs. Gung Ho and Praj Bharmal conferring at the nursing station. A monkey wrench lay on the counter beside them.

"What you got?" He asked.

"Tippler Spain." Gung said. "53-year-old commercial printer brought in sick tonight. He presented in rapid atrial fibrillation with palpitations, nausea, hypersalivation, vomiting, headache, agitation, malaise, a heavy tingling in his arms and legs, and warmth and facial reddening and flushing."

"And?"

"It began ten minutes after he drank a beer." Praj added.

"Like you after your Singapore Sling at Raffles, Gung." Sababa said.

"I remember it all too well." Gung admitted.

"What do you mean?" Praj asked.

"Up to fifty percent of Asians have a genetic mutation of ALDH2, the gene encoding the liver enzyme, aldehyde dehydrogenase, leading to an accumulation of acetaldehyde and the so-called 'Asian flush syndrome.' Acetaldehyde is the intermediate metabolite of ethanol responsible for most symptoms of a hangover; its effect on autonomic β receptors causes the vasomotor symptoms."

"But Tippler's not Asian." Praj protested.

"No, he's not." Sababa agreed. "But there are other compounds that inhibit aldehyde dehydrogenase. One is the chemical disulfiram. We know it as the drug Antabuse and use it in the treatment of alcoholism as a form of operant conditioning, to make the consumption of alcohol an unpleasant experience."

32

"But Tippler's not an alcoholic." Gung added. "And he's not taking Antabuse."

"Is it possible to have a poison that's not a poison unless there is another poison around?" Sababa asked. He looked into the confused faces of his two colleagues. "It looks like Tippler Spain is back in normal heart rhythm. Let's go see him." Gung and Praj pulled back the curtain of one of the cubicles and introduced the professor.

"This is Doctor Sababa." Gung said.

"What does he do?" Asked the pink printer.

"He controls the universe by describing it." He said.

"Have you eaten anything unusual in the last five days?" Sababa asked.

"Not that I remember." Tippler said. "No, wait a minute… Two days ago, I brought home some big inky cap clumps that had pushed their way up through the tennis courts up at the lake. I love inky caps. My wife makes a mean mushroom soup."

"That would be the right adjective." Sababa said.

"What do you mean?" He asked.

"The Linneas scientific name for your Inky cap is *Coprinopsis atramentaria*, from the Latin word 'atramentum.' *Ink.* The liquid that the mushroom releases as its gills decompose into a black goo was once used as ink. You might know that as a printer."

"I do." Tippler said. "But what makes you think it was the soup that made me sick two days after I ate it?"

"Inky caps contain a cyclopropylglutamine mycotoxin called coprine. It's a non-proteinogenic amino acid, like the hypoglycin of Jamaican ackee fruit. One of coprine's active hydrolyzed metabolites, 1-aminocyclopropanol or one of its cyclopropanone or cyclopropyliminium intermediates, blocks the action of acetaldehyde dehydrogenase, which breaks down acetaldehyde in the body. Without aldehyde dehydrogenase, acetaldehyde accumulates with disastrous results."

"Mother nature is a bitch." Tippler said. "And inky caps can have this effect after one beer, two days after I ate them?"

"I consider them mushrooms of a deadly poisonous disposition." Sababa said. "Can't eat them."

"So, it's a natural version of the 'Antabuse effect?'" Praj asked.

"First described in 1916 as 'Coprinus syndrome' when it hurt three amateur mycologists after a drinking session." Sababa said. "There are several other alcohol-induced mushroom syndromes, but this one is my favorite."

"What's the treatment?" Tippler asked.

"Three 'R's." Sababa said. "Reassurance, rehydration, and replacement of electrolytes from the vomiting. Looks like Drs. Gung and Bharmal have already done the last two. You're free to go, as am I." Sababa handed Praj his monkey wrench as he was leaving.

"Don't forget your little friend." He said. "Be alert. The world needs more lerts."

'There are old mushroom pickers and bold mushroom pickers, but no old bold mushroom pickers.'

Anon

Sababa's first stop next morning was the consultant's desk in the Harbour City Regional Emergency Department. The rain had increased. Umbrellas sprouted like mushrooms amongst the graves. Cliffy Carlton had called the professor early that morning to hand off two referrals that should have gone to the intake consultant internist on the new day's roster.

"Ed Hyde is on call today." Sababa was only half awake.

"I know." Cliffy said.

"So why don't you call him?"

"I like you better." Sababa found it difficult to argue with Cliffy Carlton when he was only half awake.

Praj and Cliffy waited for him behind the frosted sliding glass doors.

"What you got?" Sababa asked.

"A twofer." Cliffy volunteered.

"Twofer?" Sababa asked.

"Yeah." Cliffy said. "I have two people who know each other and, who between them, have no kidneys."

"What do you mean?"

"I've got a page into the nephrologist on call in Victoria."

"So, why call me?" Sababa asked.

You tell him, Praj." Cliffy left them to see other patients.

"He said that you are the only one who can ID the fungal culprit."

"Tell me stories." Sababa said.

"Dr. Stoney Ridge is a 36-year-old VIU biology professor." Praj began. "Holly Hill is a 21-year-old student. Both came in within three hours of each other after midnight. Both complained of gastrointestinal cramping, thirst, malaise, sweating, weakness, and feverishness and chills. Both were anxious and mildly disoriented. Both were in profound kidney failure."

"Because?"

"Not sure." Praj said. "But they were both picking mushrooms above the lake on the mountain two days ago. Ridge used them to make dinner for two that evening and the rest, as they say, is history."

"A meal without mushrooms is like a day without rain." Sababa said.

"That's the strange part."

"What's the strange part?" Sababa asked.

"Stoney Ridge is the recipient of numerous awards for his contributions to the science of mycology, particularly for the discovery of new species of fungi." Praj said. "You would think he knew what he was doing."

"You would think so." Sababa agreed. "But you would be wrong. The prevailing wisdom is that on the subject of wild mushrooms, it is easy to tell who is an expert and who is not—the expert is the one who is still alive. However, in my experience, I bury the experts more often because, in their confidant familiarity, they think they can skip the usual steps in proper identification. They take more risks. And it sounds as if Stoney here might have been distracted."

"Distracted?"

"Falling in love is like eating mushrooms." Sababa said. "You never know if it's the real thing until it's too late."

"You think he was inadvertently poisoned by the mushrooms he picked?" Praj asked.

"They picked." Sababa said. "And yes. You are aware of Prachett's guide to mushrooms?"

"I don't think so."

"One: All fungi are edible." Sababa noted. "Two: Some fungi are not edible more than once. Let's go see them. Where are they?"

"They're both in the acute room." Praj said. The two physicians walked across the hallway. When they reached the door, Sababa switched off the lights and switched on an ultraviolet lamp. Two bodies glowed fluorescent bluish-green on their gurneys in the middle of the room. It was bright enough to read by. Praj let out a low whistle.

"Whoa." He said. "What's that?'

"Orellanine." Sababa said. "We first thought it was the orellanine."

"Orellanine?"

"Causes late kidney failure in 3-6 days."

"It's not late." Praj said.

"Allenic norleucine." Sababa said. "We thought it was the 2-amino-4,5-hexadienoic acid."

"Allenic norleucine?"

"Causes early kidney failure in 4 to 11 hours."

"It is early." Praj said.

"But then we discovered that it's not the allenic norleucine." Sababa said.

"So, what is it then?" Praj asked.

"We don't know." Sababa said. "If they were decaying wood instead of poisoned mammals, we would call it foxfire, or fairy fire or chimpanzee fire. The glow is from an oxidative enzyme called luciferase, which emits light as it reacts with a luciferin. This bioluminescence was first documented by Aristotle in 383 BC, and later by Pliny the Elder, who observed it in olive groves at night. Its source was discovered in 1823, from the glow emitted from wooden support beams in mines. Foxfire was used to illuminate the needles on the barometer and the compass of the *Turtle*, an early submarine."

"What's it for?" Praj asked.

"Third teleology in 24 hours." Sababa said. "The light may attract insects to help spread spores, or act as a warning to hungry animals, or both."

He turned the lights back on. The two men went over to see the patients.

"What did you think you were picking?" Sababa asked.

"Matsutake." Stoney said. "Pine mushrooms. *Tricholoma magnivelare*. I've been doing this for years without any problems."

"I wasn't sure about the last one I picked, Stoney." Holly admitted.

"What do you mean?" Stoney asked.

"Well, it looked different from the others and didn't smell the same and you didn't examine it as much before you put it in with the others and…"

"Why didn't you say something at the time?" The biology professor was upset. "It must have been a matsutake."

"It wasn't a matsutake." Sababa said. "It was an *Amanita smithiana*."

"Are you serious?"

"Deadly serious." Sababa said. "Happens every autumn."

"Oh, shit." Stoney said.

"What does that mean?" Holly asked.

"You both have kidney failure." Sababa said. "There's an ambulance on its way to take you to Victoria for hemodialysis. Don't worry. Everybody goes home."

Outside the acute room, Praj asked Sababa again about their chances for survival."

"Most get by with dialysis until their kidneys recover." He said. "A few more require transplants."

"And the others?" Praj asked.

"Get downloaded to Dropbox." He said.

"You mean uploaded."

"Depends on if they were naughty or nice." Sababa said.

> 'Out mushroom hunting--
> dangerously close to caught in
> late autumn showers.'
> Basho

Jane had asked Praj over for dinner at the Good Doctor's homestead on the lake in a weekend when he and her husband were not on call. Sababa arranged to meet him a few hours before that, on the lake at the base of the mountain. The professor's old clothes emanated a collection of subtle odors produced and gathered during his many foraging forays.

"Where are we going?" Praj asked.

"To the fungus among us." Sababa said. "The clearest way into the universe is through a forest wilderness, wandering where the wifi is weak." Together in silence, they climbed towards the ridges above the lake until they arrived at a broken fence. The sign on the ground beside the trail issued a threat. *Warning. Do Not Enter. Department of Defense Firing Range.*

"We're going up there?" Praj asked.

"In the woods, we return to reason and faith like a contrite prodigal from the husks of artificial life. Back to that subtle something, that quality of air, that emanation from old trees, that renew the spirit." Sababa said. "Relax. It's Sunday. They'll only shoot you on a weekday. Better a mushroom than a bullet. Why die with the taste of blood in your mouth when it could be butter and garlic?" They breached the barbed barrier and continued their ascent. Under an old-growth canopy on a high plateau, Sababa found what he was seeking.

"Are you sure about these ones?" Praj asked. "We've had quite a week."

"Of the more than 16,000 known fungi species found worldwide, only about 100 of them are poisonous to humans." Sababa said. "The majority of mushroom poisonings are not fatal, mostly small children on the lawn in their 'grazing' stage.' The majority of fatal poisonings are from the *Amanita phalloides* Death Cap, mistaken for common paddy mushrooms in Asia." Praj stared at the different toadstools around them. "Are any of these poisonous?" He asked.

"You bet." Sababa said. "There are several types of mycotoxins, 14 distinct types of mushroom poisoning on the planet, with about 10 distinctive reaction patterns here in North America. So far. An estimated 800 new mushroom species are registered every year.

In 1978, a fellow named Lampe grouped toxic mushrooms according to six main syndromes. The most frequent are gastrointestinal irritants, more frequently affecting toddlers eating *Chlorophyllum molybdites* 'greengill' lawn mushrooms. The *Amanita phalloides* group is next, containing cyclic polypeptides responsible for the most serious and often fatal intoxications from liver and kidney failure, as you saw with Theresa Terrace. There's a variety which induces muscarine-related symptoms of salivation and increased gastrointestinal motility treatable with atropine.

37

And you've already seen examples of the hallucinogenics and alcohol sensitivity subsets."

"That's only five." Praj said. Sababa pointed to a contorted silver mushroom which looked like it was poured into its alien shape.

"Elfin saddle." He said. *Gyromitra esculenta*. Some northern Europeans parboil and eat them, but not for nothing are they known as the 'fugu of Finnish cuisine.' Elfin saddles and false morels contain a molecule called gyromitrin which is hydrolyzed in the body to monomethylhydrazine (MMH), a colorless, volatile, toxic carcinogen, which blocks the important neurotransmitter GABA and is used by NASA as rocket fuel. Its boiling point is so low that, in Europe, it has sometimes only been the cooks who have died.

The problem with Lampe's 1978 classification system is that it is incomplete. Doesn't account for some other toxicities we now know about—the kidney killers in *Amanita Smithiana* in our last two patients; severe muscle breakdown from *Tricholoma equestre* 'man-on-horseback,' thought edible and good until recently, or from *Russula subnigricans* in Japan and Taiwan; convulsive encephalopathies from the polyporic acid in *Hapalopilus rutilans* here, some other nasty compound from *Pleurocybella porrigens* in Japan, and otherwise edible angel's wings in people with pre-existing kidney disease; and rashes from even handling *Suillus americanus* and similar species. There's also the possibility of ingesting herbicides and pesticides from mushrooms picked in non-natural landscapes, contamination with heavy metals or radiation, and just good old food poisoning from mushrooms 'over the hill.'"

"But aren't there some rules that can indicate which mushrooms are safe to eat?" Praj asked.

"Nope." Sababa said. "There is no folklore that will save you. Not all poisonous species have a pointed cap or are brightly-coloured or blacken silver or turn rice red when boiled, or taste bad, or are safe if cooked or dried or pickled or whatever. Insects and other animals don't necessarily avoid toxic mushrooms. The adage that all pored mushrooms are safe to eat never met Lurid or Devil Boletes."

"But these are good?"

"These are the food of the gods." Sababa cut several kinds of fungi from the undergrowth with his Italian blade and cleaned them with the wild boar bristle brush before placing them inside his pack. He looked up to a soldier, emerging from a thicket.

"You know you're not allowed to be up here." He said. "Trespassing is a Federal offense."

"I'm not trespassing." Sababa protested. "I'm foraging for food. And you're scaring it away."

"Didn't I catch you picking mushrooms up here last year?" Asked the soldier.

"That was my brother, Mycroft." Sababa said.

"I swear he looked exactly like you do."

"We're conjoined monozygotic isomeric doppelgangers."

"You must be twins." Said the soldier.

"Inseparable." Sababa crossed his eyes.

"Well, don't be long." The soldier headed down another side trail. "You make me look bad."

"We are not here." Sababa pressed his hands together and bowed. And then it rained.

Later that evening, after Jane had served a wonderful meal enhanced with the fruits of their forest foraging, Sababa and Praj retired to the portly professor's study for a vintage port, a Montecristo No. 2 Cuban cigar, and a review of the day's events.

"You place tremendous importance on this mushroom thing, Doctor Sababa."

"Perhaps." Sababa said. "But consider the evidence for their significance: (1) Life on land would collapse without the activities of mushrooms, (2) We owe our existence to mushrooms, and (3) There is no God. The logic is irrefutable.

First, Nature alone is antique, and the oldest art a mushroom. Fungi have flourished on this planet for more than 2 billion years. Some ancient forms grew 30 feet tall before trees existed. Today a 400-acre mushroom mycelium in Oregon is the largest organism on the planet.

Their activities are indispensable for the operation of the biosphere. Through their interdependent relationships with plants and animals, mushrooms are essential for forest and grassland ecology, climate control and atmospheric chemistry, water purification, and the maintenance of biodiversity. And yet, the thousands of species of mushroom-forming fungi are the most poorly understood kingdom of life.

The cedars and Douglas fir under your feet today speak to each other and share resources, using a mycorrhizal internet. Some plants used this system to support their offspring, while others hijack it to sabotage their rivals. Just like us.

Mushrooms are natural engineering masterpieces. The overnight appearance of a fruiting body occurs from the pneumatic inflation of millions of cells, extending the stem, pushing earth and even asphalt aside, and unfolding the cap. Exposed gills can shed 30,000 spores per second, delivering billions of life-generating particles into the air every day. Mushrooms work with insects, fed by and feeding leaf-cutter ants in the New World and termites in the Old. They produce strange apparitions of phallic eruptions with loathsome aromas, gigantic puffballs, and tiny 'bird's nests' with spore-filled eggs splashed out by raindrops.

Second, we have used mushrooms as food, medicine, poisons, and spiritual and religious rituals across the world for seven thousand years. Because humans evolved in ecosystems dependent upon mushrooms there would be no us without them. This is not a reciprocal relationship. Without us, there would still be them. Compared to the rest of life on Earth, humans are a recent and pernicious afterthought. This was a great neighborhood until the monkeys got out of control.

Finally, mushrooms persuasively demonstrate that gods are mere figments of our imagination. After ingestion, when psilocybin is converted into psilocin, after docking with serotonin receptors, it contorts neocortical function, conjuring up deities from out of thin air. Experiments with this single chemical reproduce spiritual feelings of kinship with something greater than oneself, other mystical experiences, and insights into the meaning of life. Our belief in God is a toadstool dream.

So then, life on earth depends on mushrooms, humans wouldn't have evolved without them, and they afford formidable support for the nonexistence of God. Our reality is that we are manufactured from stardust, rescued from disorder, and destined to diffusion. And although mushrooms are everywhere and will outlive us by an eternity, what a wonderful and rare fortune to be alive at this moment. You must be the mushroom you wish to see in the world."

'Every mushroom knows its time.'
Russian proverb

Advice is like mushrooms. The wrong kind can prove fatal. Buddy Benway's advice for Theresa Terrace to have her appendix out did nothing for her appendix and even less for Theresa. She died on life support in Vancouver before Ziggy Stardust could find her a new liver and kidney. He sent Sababa a copy of her discharge summary. *That's why they call it a Death Cap.*

The pathologist who performed Tim Leery's autopsy, Dr. Juan Leyblanca, signed off the causes of his demise as 'Multiple trauma secondary to a psilocybin-induced psychosis,' although gravity likely also played a magical role. His advice to idiot-proof the windows in the wards on Harbour City Regional's upper floors never rose above the administrative proven idiots on the first one.

A year after Elias Ashmole recovered from his philosopher's stones bad trip, his department at VIU tenured him for his work on altered states.

Duke Point has trouble remembering if his breathing is much better since beginning work at the Tilray marijuana facility next door.

Despite dialysis and plasmapheresis in Vancouver, Rollrim Brown died from his Romanian mushroom reaction. It took Perry Lepistopsis several months to return to normal from the erythromelalgia that caused him so much pain. He now funnels big glass jars of foie gras in Doctor Sababa's direction whenever he returns from his French buying trips.

Smokey Crescent switched his alder log fungi growing operation over from shiitake to oyster mushrooms. Tippler Spain gave up eating inky caps to drink beer.

Dr. Ridge and Holly Hill survived their collective kidney failure with several sessions of hemodialysis. Since Holly put the word out about what happened, Stoney can't persuade any other VIU coeds to go with him into the forest.

It didn't take long for Sababa to run afoul of the new 'utilization' bed police, shunning the magnetic goals that drew together the destinies of the masters of control.

"You act like you don't care." Said one unfortunate bureaucrat.

"It's not an act." Sababa said.

14. The Case of the Orange Faller

'I wanted to be... a lumberjack! Leaping from tree to tree,
as they float down the mighty rivers of British Columbia.'
Monty Python, *Lumberjack Song*

"Daylight in the swamp!" The bossman shouted into the cougar den. "All hands and the cook and the whiskey jacks." Sleeping timber beast savages roused themselves from their bunkhouse berths, just as the foreman's phone went off in his pocket. It was Red Snapper, the manager of the Cutthroat Tavern down in Honeymoon Bay.

"Got two of yours in the snake room." He said. "Didn't make it back to your camp last night and I've got other problems of my own."

"Tell them not to bother, except to collect their kit." Bossman said. "They can count the ties." From the days when the only way to leave was to walk down the railroad.

Honeymoon Bay was a secluded village of 600 souls nestled along the southern shoreline of Lake Cowichan and surrounded by stunning mountains, an hour south of Harbour City.

In the springtime, Honeymoon Bay was a wildflower reserve of pink fawn lilies and violets and bleeding hearts. The summers were hot and the winters were short. In the lazy hazy Indian autumn days, you could picnic under the old big leaf maples of Stoltz Pool along the Cowichan River, play a nine-hole round at the village March Meadows Golf and Country Club, or head into the deep pristine wilderness of the Carmanah Walbran old-growth forest, home to the world's largest spruce trees.

But the autumn for Bossman was no different from the other seasons in the Cowichan Valley. He had work to do. The McDonald Murphy company began logging outside of Honeymoon Bay in 1929. Western Forest Industries Limited took it over in 1947, the same year that Bossman first signed on as a logger.

He kicked the protruding feet of the last man in the amen corner cot, the place in the bunkhouse his men used for storytelling.

"What the hell's wrong with you, Alder?" He howled. "You never had blanket fever before. Maybe you need to board with Aunt Polly for a while or see an iodine." An iodine was the doctor that looked after the men in a logging camp. Polly was slang for a chamber pot but boarding with Aunt Polly referred to drawing insurance for sickness or an accident. Alder knew there was only one medical plan for a logger. *Don't fall.* Bossman was getting used to dealing with the meth heads and alcoholics he was forced to hire these days. He preferred men like Alder Way, but they were an increasingly rare breed.

The faller rubbed his eyes and his head as he swung his legs over the edge of his wooden enclosure.

"Dunno, Boss." He said. "I'm tired all the time now, I itch, my head and eyes and throat and guts and bones and muscles are sore, everything smells bad, I feel like I want to puke, this diarrhea is driving me nuts, I have these fainting attacks and I'm dizzy, and I can't afford to be." Bossman looked down at him. Alder's hands were gnarled like the bark he roared through with his chainsaw and his face was as brown as the timber.

"Well, hurry along to breakfast, Alder." The foreman said. "I'm down two men today." He shouted out the window at the camp cook.

"Box up the dough, Fung Lee." He said. "Alder here is gonna need some morning glory. Rustle him up some stove lid flapjacks and forty-five-ninety sausages." The fallers had another name for Fung's tough pancakes. *Sweat pads.*

In what passed for a dining hall in the bush camp, Alder took his place along the breakfast bench. Fung tuned the radio to a Harbour City station.

The Salish swing their paddles past the ancient taboos… to the rhythm of the drums in their crested canoes… Good Morning, Indian country… This is BC Bud… bringing you CNDN Coast Salish radio, 101.3 FM on your Home and Native Band…

Alder Way loved this life—free as a ptarmigan, deep in the bush, no time clocks to punch, no papers to push. He was his own man, tucked into a Cascadian forest.

Non-white babies now outnumber white babies in Canada… for the second time… White men claim they are descended from monkeys and I believe them… The doctor told me I don't have any white cells.

History was a tapestry and the land a loom of swaying spar trees and notched trunks transformed into silver snags surrounded by brilliant pink fire weeds in the gullies. Petroglyphs spoke in pictures beneath the vines.

Hold on to what you believe, even if it's a tree that stands by itself…

Hundreds of logging camps once floated close to the head of inlets. They were manned by bull buckers and rigging slingers and cat skinners and boom men and whistle punks working fuel and grease and generators into rusting red donkeys and hoisting winches and creaking cables. Overtime overcutting by undervalued underlings had turned the forest into a farm.

Hold on to what you must do, even if it's a long way from here…

Alder had been unable to finish a fraction of his lumberjack breakfast before his guts ached and he had to hurry to the long drop. He emerged in time to grab his helmet and gear and chainsaw, and board the bus that would take the fallers to the cut site. It was less than a minute after the yellow Bluebird disgorged its passengers and their equipment that the whine of chainsaws filled up the mountainside. The big Doug Firs and Cedars groaned and moaned in agony. *But the axe forgets what the tree remembers.*

Alder climbed his cleats up the side of a fir as big as a skyscraper. He transected the top and began to thunder through its uppermost limbs as he rappelled his way down the massive furrowed trunk. He had done it a thousand times before.

But today would be different. As he went to readjust his waist belt, a tsunami of nausea and dizziness overwhelmed his head and limbs. His chainsaw fell as silent as a man who had sinned. Alder Way went sky west and crooked. The undergrowth far below rushed up to meet him, breaking his fall, and breaking the faller. The call of the wild, it makes the pulse pound, but a falling dream in the woods, it don't make a sound.

Hold on to your life, even if it's easier to let go…

> 'Discover me
> Discovering you
> One mile to every inch of
> Your skin like porcelain…'
> John Mayer, *Your Body Is A Wonderland*

The day before Alder Way fell out of his tree, Dr. Praj Bharmal paged his mentor from the Harbour City Regional emergency room. His call display lit up a response from the bridge of the Death Star.

"What you got?"

"Dr. Capitaine wants us to see a patient with joint pains." Praj said.

"In the ER?" Sababa asked. "Why not refer her to the office?"

"He thinks there's something more serious going on that's moving faster."

"See you in five." Sababa said. He found Praj speaking with Myles Capitaine at the consultant's desk.

"How are you Myles?" He asked.

"Living the dream."

"Deep into that darkness peering, long I stood there." Sababa said. "Wondering, fearing, doubting, dreaming dreams no mortal ever dared to dream before. Who's the victim?"

"Adelle Davis." Myles began. 55-year-old personal trainer who presents with a 3-month history of fatigue, a ten-pound weight loss, and progressive disabling pain and swelling involving several joints."

"Which joints?"

"Knees, shoulders, wrists and small hand joints. Her hand function is so impaired that she can no longer feed herself." Sababa turned to Praj.

"Exam?"

"Pale. Weak and wasted." Praj said. "She has soft tissue swelling of her hands, with reduced wrist movement, but no synovitis. Tinel's and Phalen's tests are positive consistent with carpal tunnel syndrome. Cool effusions are present in both knees. I've tapped one and sent it for the usual. The rest of her examination was normal."

"Lab?" Sababa asked.

"She has a normochromic anemia with a lowish white cell count and a raised sedimentation rate. Her calcium is in the sky, her liver function is deranged, and she has significant kidney disease with a lot of protein in her urine. Serum bicarb is low and her chloride is high. Her family doc did some tests as an outpatient and found that her rheumatoid factor, ANA, ENA, and ANCA were all negative."

"Imaging?" Praj threw up a film on the adjacent view box.

"Hand radiographs show demineralization and wrist joint space narrowing with juxta-articular erosions." Sababa raised an eyebrow.

"So, gentlemen, what's happening to Adelle Davis?"

"She has an erosive seronegative polyarthritis." Praj said.

"From what?" Sababa asked.

"Well, that's the question then, isn't it?' Myles asked.

"I know the question." Sababa said. "What's the answer?" He looked into two sets of lost eyes.

"CRAB." He said.

"Crab?" Myles and Praj asked in unison.

"CRAB." He said. "Calcium (elevated), Renal failure, Anemia, and Bone lesions."

"Meaning what?" Praj asked.

"Put that together with her Fanconi Syndrome and it's a slam-dunk." Sababa said.

"Fanconi Syndrome?"

"Her type II renal tubular acidosis from light chains."

"Light chains?"

"Are you processing any of this or are you just going to repeat everything I say as a question?" Sababa called over to the ER ward clerk. "Cheri Sundae, please see if you can raise the pathologist on call for me."

"On it, Sab." She said. Cheri raised her handpiece in the air, less than a minute later.

"Dr. Leyblanca on line 2." The Argentinian voice on the other end of the line was irascible.

"¿What do ju want, Cabrón?" Asked the pathologist.

"Juan, the ER sent you down a sample of synovial fluid about an hour ago." Sababa said. "Patient named Adelle Davis."

"Ju theenk thees ees Taco Bell?" Juan asked. "Ju hab to wait in line like eberybudee else."

"Pull it." Sababa said. "We'll be right there." *Click.*

Sababa and Praj dropped down a stairwell into the basement, where all brilliant troglodyte pathologists lived. Down a long hallway, they found Juan Leyblanca sitting on the other side of a teaching microscope, making Latin noises of appreciation punctuated in profane Spanish.

"Hijo de puta!" Escaped his lips as they entered. "¿Hey Cabrón, what hab ju got up there?"

"What do you mean, Juan." Sababa asked.

"Look." He pointed to the teaching eyepiece. Praj and Sababa looked.

"Atypical cells." Praj offered.

"Plasmablasts and multinucleate cells with products of chondrolysees." The pathologist said. "Thees ees from maleegnant infiltration of her carteelage."

"Erosive arthritis, carpal tunnel syndrome and invasive tumoural arthritis." Sababa said. "All three pathogenic features associated with arthritis in multiple myeloma."

"Seguro." Juan said. *Sure.*

"Let's go see her, Praj." Sababa said. "Thanks, Juan."

"I call ju." His eyes hadn't left his microscope.

Back in the ER, Praj introduced the portly professor to Adelle Davis.

"Is he a subspecialist, Praj?" She asked.

"He's a superspecialist."

"We're in the same line of work, Eleazar." She said. "I'm a personal trainer. I make my clients better as well."

"Perhaps our challenges are more extreme." Sababa said. "And our methods are different."

"But we both get the same results." She said.

"Only sometimes."

"Are you a people person, Eleazar?" Adelle asked.

"I used to be." Sababa said. "People ruined that for me."

"I know why."

"People hate people who have theories about people." He said. "Like Jean-Paul Sartre."

"What?"

"Hell is other people."

"What's your zodiac sign, Eleazar?" She asked. Praj felt Sababa's core temperature rise.

"Glowworm."

"But that doesn't even exist."

"None of them exist." Sababa explained the nature of her illness.

"I'm positive by nature." She said. "You'd be surprised what diet and exercise and determination can do."

"I would indeed." Sababa said.

"I've been on Google." Adelle handed him a list. "I know what's wrong. Here's a list of natural remedies I've chosen."

"What do you think you've got?"

"Myalgic encephalomyelitis."

"There are known knowns. These are things we know that we know. There are known unknowns. That is to say, there are things that we know we don't know." He said. "But there are also unknown unknowns. There are things we don't know we don't know."

"Donald Rumsfeld?"

"Socrates said it first."

"And you think you know something I don't, Eleazar?' Adelle asked.

"I know I do." Sababa said. "Problems interest me, conversations don't."

"Because conversations go both ways?" She asked.

"Because I don't engage in mental combat with the unarmed." Sababa told Adelle that he was going to admit her for some more tests and treatment and that Praj would explain the details.

"But I don't have time for this." She said. "My clients depend on me."

"I'm sure they'll understand." Sababa observed Dr. Trace Pangloss moving towards him.

"Have a look at this guy for me, won't you, Sab?"

"What you got?"

"Bert Sézary." Trace began. "52-year-old provincial park ranger down at Gordon Bay on Lake Cowichan. Saw our local skin guy, Dr. Commodus Sitsofsky, five months ago for psoriasis of his palms and soles. Prescribed a course of medium-potency topical corticosteroids without relief."

"Ah, yes. dermatology, the well-dressed specialty. If it's wet, dry it. If it's dry, wet it. If all else fails, use steroids. And then?"

"Since then, Bert has developed itchy red-violet nodules on his face and scalp and neck and upper limbs and trunk. Most have coalesced into reddish-brown plaques and ulcerated masses. Commodus saw him again last week and prescribed a course of high-potency topical corticosteroids."

"Dr. Skin Laser has no skin in the game." Sababa said. "Why is Bert here this morning?"

"Says he can't stand the itch anymore." Trace said.

"Anything else on his physical exam?' Sababa asked.

"His face looks like a lion." Trace said.

"Lab?"

"High white cell count, with a few more eosinophils and basophils than I would have expected." Trace offered. "Elevated sedimentation rate."

"Let's go see him." Sababa and Trace entered cubicle 5 to find an uncomfortable-looking lion with a disseminated rash as angry as his face. Trace made introductions.

"Bert, this is Doctor Sababa." He said. "A lot of people hate him because he's smart."

"I don't care about that." Bert said. "As long as he can make me better." Sababa held up the ranger's fingertips.

"What do you see, Trace?"

"Nothing."

"Exactly." Sababa said. "And what would you expect to see if Bert had psoriasis?" An African sun dawned on Trace's face.

"Pitting or dystrophy of his fingernails."

"And what do we call these?' Sababa indicated the enlarged lymph nodes he was feeling in Bert's scalp and neck and underarms and groin.

"Oh, shit." Trace said.

"What?" Bert asked.

"We'll be back in a minute, my lone ranger friend." Sababa took Trace over to the consultant's computer and pulled up an image of Bert's peripheral smear. Praj joined the two men at the monitor. Sababa pointed to some white blood cells with notched nuclei.

"What are these, gentlemen?" His two companions shook their heads.

"Separate nuclear lobes divided by a sharp cleft and connected by chromatin bridges." Sababa said. "Buttock cells." He raised his head to catch the attention of the ER ward clerk."

"Cheri Sundae, please raise Drs. Ted Billroth and Commodus Sitsofsky, in that order."

"You got it, Sab." Cheri punched her buttons through to Lana, the paging operator. Sababa then caught the attention of one of the emergency nurses.

"Michaela, can you set up a 4 mm punch biopsy tray for us please?" She headed towards the procedure room while the three doctors went back behind the curtain of cubicle 5.

"Bert, you appear to have a condition we call mycosis fungoides." Sababa said.

"What does it mean?" The ranger asked.

"It means 'mushroom-like fungal disease,' but it's not." Sababa said. "From what the French dermatologist who first described it in 1806, Jean-Louis-Marc Alibert, thought it looked like. It used to be known as

Alibert-Bazin syndrome, but we're all finished with that chapter. It's the commonest variant of primary cutaneous T cell lymphoma."

"But Dr. Sitsofsky said I had psoriasis." Bert protested.

"You have pseudopsoriasis." Sababa said. "It's just pretending to be psoriasis."

"Look who's Dr. Teleology now." Praj said. Sababa smiled.

"Can you make it disappear?" Bert asked.

"First, we have to prove what it is." Sababa said. "Dr. Bharmal here will do a skin biopsy, order you a total body CT scan, and prescribe some naloxone lotion for the itch. We'll ask one of the surgeons to take out a lymph node from your neck for analysis. There are lots of treatments available and we often use them in combination—everything from sunlight to various systemic therapies. We'll talk about the most appropriate way to go in your office follow-up visit. Here's Mercy's number."

"Mercy?"

"She's my medical office assistant." Sababa said.

"Will you let Dr. Sitsofsky know?"

"You bet." Sababa said. "Praj, when you're finished here, we have hospital ward consults this morning" He handed him two names on a piece of paper. *Denis Parsons... Chilly Marrow...*

"Dr. Billroth on line 1, Sab." Cheri called.

"Hi Ted." Sababa said. "I need a cervical lymph node biopsy." He gave details of the patient and his concern to the ENT surgeon.

"And one for you, Sab." Ted said. "I took out another lymph node three days ago from a guy admitted by Cliffy Carlton. I have no idea what the pathology report means, an alphabet soup of some kind. Patient's name is Morrie Bund, on Floor 5." Sababa agreed to see the patient.

"Dr. Sitsofsky on line 2, Sab." Cheri held up her handset.

"Hey, Commodus." Sababa began.

"What?" The skin swami answered.

"What's the most dangerous place in the hospital at 3 p.m.?"

"I'm too busy for this crap, Sababa." He said. "I give up. What?"

"The space between a dermatologist and his Ferrari."

'Starry, starry night
Portraits hung in empty halls
Frameless heads on nameless walls
With eyes that watch the world and can't forget.'
Don McLean, *Vincent (Starry, Starry Night)*

The large blur came off the elevator like a tornado through a trailer park. A Colombian leather briefcase barrel rolled over the nursing station and landed next to the pant-suited woman with a fancy scarf and clipboard. There may have been an element of surprise.

"Doctor Sababa!" Samara Morgan struggled to catch her breath. "You scared me."

"Fear resides in all things." He said. "And at the heart of fear is the unexpected."

"What do you want?" Pantsuit's pupils constricted. Her scarf was Valentino Garavani silk. She clutched her hundred-dollar clipboard like she was walking through a dark alley.

"I need to see this patient." He handed her a name. "We need not talk."

"Mr. Bund isn't a patient." Samara said. "He's a client. You can look up his room on the chart rack." Samara stormed off down the stairwell to see the Grand Galactic Governess of Nightingales.

Sababa found the man's record and began to scan it for clues. Cliff's notes were as basic as his namesake:

'42-year-old logging truck driver from Cowichan who presented with fatigue and a fever of 4 days duration, and a solitary lymph node swelling on the right side of his neck. Examination showed intrabdominal fluid, an enlarged liver, and a massive spleen.'

Sababa looked at the lab results. All three peripheral blood cell lines were down, with anemia and decreased white blood cells and platelets. Morrie also had circulating immune complexes, cold agglutinins, positive rheumatoid factor and Epstein-Barr virus, and anti-smooth muscle antibodies. He turned the page to the lymph node biopsy report, signed off by Juan Leyblanca.

'Findings: a polymorphous infiltrate of oligoclonal T-cells expressing CD10, CXCL13 and PD1 demonstrated at the boundary between the mantle zone and hyperplastic germinal center light zones with Reed-Sternberg-like cells, prominent arborization and proliferation of endothelial venules, and a marked increase in CD21+ follicular dendritic cells.
Diagnosis: AITL.'

Sababa found Morrie's room down the fifth-floor hallway.

"Who are you?" Challenged the logging truck driver. "I've been cooped up in this cage for three days. What the hell is going on?"

"I'm Doctor Sababa, Morrie." The professor shook Bund's big hand. "I do many things, but today I'm Dr. Billroth's clinical translator."

"Meaning what exactly?" He asked.

"You have something called angioimmunoblastic T-cell lymphoma." Sababa said. "It usually presents with enlarged lymph nodes all over the place, but you only had one."

"I've always been lucky like that."

"Not sure that's the right descriptor." Sababa said. "You know how you can get crosstalk on your CB radio?"

"Yeah."

"Well, this is a kind of crosstalk between the bad lymphoma cells and the immunologic microenvironment."

"I didn't get any of that." Morrie said. "What's the cause?"

"Don't know, like many of these conditions, but human herpes viruses HHV6 and HHV8 might play some role." Sababa said. "Could also explain why it responds to antiviral therapy with valacyclovir."

"So, it's easy to get rid of?"

"Sorry, no." Sababa said. "It's an aggressive disease, even with high-dose chemotherapy and allogeneic stem cell transplantation."

"What's that?"

"We need to replace your bone marrow with stem cells from someone else." Sababa said.

"What if you're wrong?"

"It has happened." Sababa said. "But not this time."

"I don't think I've got this thing."

"Nobody cares what you think, Morrie." Sababa said. "This is not a democracy. We only care about helping you."

"Would you be telling me the same shit if we were friends?"

"I'm an internist." Sababa said. "I don't have friends." His pager went off in his pocket. It was Praj, on the third floor surgical ward. Sababa told Morrie he would get his wheels rolling and return to tell him more the next day. It was sealed with a second handshake.

Sababa arrived on Floor 3 to find Praj engaged in conversation with Sariel, the head nurse on the general surgical ward.

"Who's Denis Parsons, Sariel?" He asked.

"Patient of Dr. Falstaff, Sab." She said. "Admitted four days ago with a small bowel obstruction."

"From?"

"You tell him, Praj." She said. "It wasn't any of the usual causes." Sababa looked at Praj.

"44-year-old IT guru." Praj began. "Presented with a month-long history of frequent abdominal pain, fullness, and distension, accompanied by fever and vomiting over the last week before admission. This, and a rapid pulse, was what Dr. Ho found in the ER. He did an ultrasound which showed dilated small gut loops with fluid collections in the peritoneal cavity. A contrast-enhanced CT scan revealed diffuse mucosal thickening of small bowel loops and the stomach wall. Dr. Falstaff performed an emergency laparotomy and biopsy."

"So, what kinds of malignant tumors can cause this presentation, Praj?" Sababa asked.

"Adenocarcinoma, sarcoma, lymphoma, and carcinoid."

"And peritoneal mesothelioma. And which kind did Mr. Parsons have?"

"Lymphoma."

"And what kind of lymphoma?"

"Non-Hodgkins."

"And what kind of…" Praj beat him to it.

"Burkitt's." He watched one of Sababa's eyebrows head northward. "Confirmed on immunohistochemistry."

"Starry, starry night." Sababa said, after the microscopic appearance of the tumour, which looks like Van Gogh's painting of the same name. "Malignancy of germinal center B lymphocytes and named after the surgeon who first described the disease in 1958 while working in equatorial Africa."

"Starry, starry night." Praj agreed.

"So why didn't John Falstaff get our in-house equatorial African oncologist Henry Chibueze, to see the patient?"

"He did." Praj said. "Dr. Chibueze put in the referral to us."

"Because?"

"Well, you know how there are three kinds of Burkitt's lymphoma?" Praj turned Socrates over in his grave.

"The endemic kind affecting the facial bones of young African children, associated with Epstein-Barr virus and contaminant malarial infection." Sababa said. "The nonendemic sporadic American variant involving the abdominal viscera."

"And?" Praj was enjoying the role reversal.

"The immunodeficiency-associated form." Sababa said. "Bingo. Chibueze wouldn't have consulted us for either of the first two variants."

"Bingo." Praj showed Sababa the results of the other tests. "Let's go see him." Sababa followed his resident down the hallway.

"Mr. Parsons?" Sababa began. "I'm Doctor Sababa."

"Dr. Bharmal said you were coming." Denis said. "It can't be a good thing to have so many physicians."

"Usually not." Sababa agreed.

"And this time?"

"Also not." Sababa said. "The tumour that was blocking your bowel is a rare animal, caused by dysregulation of the c-myc gene in one of three chromosomal translocations."

"Why did I get it?" Denis asked. Sababa showed him the results of his HIV investigations. *Like the strangers that you've met… The ragged men in ragged clothes.*

"I have AIDS?"

"Something like that." Sababa said. "Dr. Chibueze has arranged for you to receive dose-adjusted EPOCH with rituximab chemotherapy. You'll also need several spinal taps so we can give you intrathecal methotrexate."

"It's in my brain?"

"Sometimes it goes there." Sababa said.

"And you're going to treat my HIV infection?"

"Exactly that."

"What are my chances?" Denis asked.

"Fifty-fifty." Sababa said. "We're not making cars here, we don't give guarantees, but we'll be leaning hard on the first fifty." He and Praj excused themselves to see the third ward patient on the first floor. They found Dr. Tictac Tarmac perusing the patient's chart at the nursing station.

"What you got, Tictac?" Sababa asked.

"Chilly Marrow." He said. "63-year-old golf pro at the March Meadows Course in Honeymoon Bay down Cowichan way. You remember Bernadine Soulier, patient in her mid-40's who claimed she felt like Tiger Woods' first wife?"

"The golf widow who Pretty Boy Troy cut into without looking at her coagulation profile?" Sababa asked. "She went to Victoria to have her 'Mommy Makeover.'"

"He's the cause of all that." Tictac said.

"Why is he here?" Sababa asked.

"Presented with a four-month history of progressive fatigue and shortness of breath, abdominal fullness, bone pain, gout, easy bruising, and weight loss on a background of a 24-pack year smoking history discontinued 20 years ago." Dr. Tarmac replied. "Pale and short of breath on arrival. Chest exam showed no breath sounds and dullness on percussion in the middle and lower zones of his left lung. I could feel his spleen seven centimetres below where it should have been."

"Lab?" Praj asked.

"His hemoglobin and platelet counts were low and white blood cell count was high with abnormal myelocytes, metamyelocytes, band forms, and eosinophils." Tictac continued. "Peripheral blood smear showed a leucoerythroblastic picture with teardrop cells, anisocytosis, polychromasia, and nucleated red blood cells. His serum lactate dehydrogenase was in the sky."

"Imaging?" Praj was getting the hang of it.

"Chest radiograph showed a left-sided pleural effusion extending up to mid-zone." Tictac said. "Our respirologist, Dr. Hyde, tapped it and got a litre of bloody fluid. Also did a pleural biopsy."

"Ed has already seen him?" Sababa asked. "What are we doing here?"

"Chilly didn't like him much." Tictac said. "He remembered your involvement in his wife's case. I tried to warn him, but…"

"The interruptions are the journey." Sababa said. "What did the pleural fluid analysis and biopsy show?"

"Atypical cells in the first." Tictac said. "Dense infiltrate of lymphocytes, immature granulocytes, neutrophils, histiocytes, eosinophils and occasional megakaryocytes in the second."

"I don't like where this is going." Sababa said. "Tell me he had a bone marrow."

"Aspirate got a dry tap."

"Jeezuz." Sababa let out a low whistle. Tictac read the rest of the report. "Trephine biopsy showed medullary fibrosis, dysplastic megakaryocyte hyperplasia and osteosclerosis. Silver staining of his bone marrow showed moderate to severe collagen fibrosis. He has scar tissue where his bone marrow should be." *Thy bones are marrowless, thy blood is cold.*

"And I assume no one has told him."

"Nope." Tictac said. "We thought we'd wait for you."

"How thoughtful." Sababa said. "Let's go see him." Tictac led the way to Chilly's room and introduced the professor.

"I've been waiting to see you, Doctor Sababa." Chilly said. "I've heard nothing but good things."

"It's much easier to do good than to be good." Sababa said.

"I hope you can do me some good." Chilly stared out the window. "I used to coach two of your colleagues, Ernie Hacker and Buddy Benway. What's happening to me?"

"You have a rare blood disorder." Sababa began.

"What's wrong with it?"

"You're not making any." Sababa said. "It's a condition we call primary myelofibrosis but it has a dozen other names. Your bone marrow is turning into scar tissue, and the only blood you're making is in your spleen and the lining of your left lung."

"Is there treatment?"

"There is." Sababa said. "We have a biological called ruxolitinib which inhibits the JAK 2 protein mutation which prevents you from making blood cells. It will improve your symptoms and your chance of survival."

"And when it doesn't?" Chilly asked. "I guess I'm used to putting my balls into a hole in the ground."

"You've hooked quite a chip shot into the rough, Chilly. But we do have other options and you have Bernadine for support." Sababa said. "Whatever happens will be par for the course."

'We can't return we can only look behind
From where we came
And go round and round and round
In the circle game.'
                    Joni Mitchell, *Circle Game*

"How did you like the chicken of the woods, Praj?" Sababa asked.
"Tasty." Praj said. Sababa cut another rim for him from the plum tree
bracket fungus in the Manzanita Medical parking lot before they climbed
the steps to his office.
"It's pink and purple people eater week, Boss." She hadn't looked up
from her typing.
"Sweet Mercy is nobility's true badge." Sababa handed Praj the first
chart off the top of a tall pile. "Looks like we'll be running today."
"Mr. Snapper?" Praj called into the assembled multitude. A middle-aged
couple rose from their chairs. The woman had to help the man follow
the young doctor down the hallway into the resident's room.
"Dmitri Romanowsky?" Sababa called. Another middle-aged man got
up from the leather chair in the corner of the waiting room and followed
the professor into his sanctum sanctorum. Time stood idle as Sababa
read Cliffy Carlton's referral. *57-year-old cider maker with persistent right-sided
community-acquired pneumonia. Drained his effusion yesterday but it looks like he
needs a real doctor.*
Sababa pressed his intercom button.
"Yes, Boss."
"Mercy, I need the lab results from a pleural tap that Dr. Carlton
performed yesterday. Please and thank you."
"On it." *Squelch.*
"How can I help you, Dmitri?" Sababa began. Dmitri pushed a large
bottle of cider across the consultant's desk. Its migration continued over
the other side and into the interior of a Colombian leather briefcase.
"I have mild asthma for twenty years but now I have pneumonia for two
months." Dmitri said. "Three different doctors give me three different
pills. I still have a fever and cough and I am tired. I soak my sheets with
sweat at night and I lose ten pounds of weight. So short of breath now is
hard for me to work."
"Why didn't Dr. Carlton admit you to hospital?" Sababa asked.
"He tried." Dmitri said. "I told him I have to make cider." Sababa had
Dmitri change into a gown so he could examine him.
"You have a fever, Dmitri." He said. "And I can hear signs of pneumonia
in your right lung." Mercy dropped in the results of Dmitri's lab tests.
"Hmmmm." He said. "Your white blood cell count is elevated with an
excess of pink cells we call eosinophils. They also appear to be the
predominant cell type in your sputum exam and pleural transudate. As
Miley Cyrus would tell you, pink isn't just a colour, it's an attitude. You
also have a high erythrocyte sedimentation rate, iron deficiency anemia,

and increased platelets." Sababa pulled up Dmitri's imaging on his laptop.

"Chest x-ray showed peripheral pulmonary infiltrates mainly in your right lung with a pleural effusion on the same side, and CT scan demonstrated peripheral pulmonary opacities. It's a photographic negative of what we see in pulmonary edema. There is no evidence of allergic reaction, connective tissue disease, infection, drug reaction, or other secondary causes of eosinophilia, although I should refer you for a bronchoscopic biopsy and lavage."

"No more tests." Dmitri said.

"What?"

"No more tests!" The cider maker was resolute. "I been poked and prodded for two months and now I want it fixed. You think you know what this is?"

"I do." Sababa said. "But I like to be certain."

"No more tests." Dmitri gritted his teeth. "You're supposed to be the hotshot. What do think it is?"

"There is no absolute consensus on the diagnostic criteria…"

"What is it?"

"Chronic eosinophilic pneumonia." Sababa said.

"Well, fix it then." Sababa wrote a prescription for prednisone and told Dmitri about the possible side effects.

"If this doesn't work like a hot damn, if I don't like anything about how you're doing, I will drag you into Harbour City Regional Hospital by your toes." Sababa handed him another set of requisitions. "Capisce?" Dmitri nodded. Praj hovered in the doorway

"Get these tests done in a week." Sababa said. "Tell Mercy I'll see you in two. I'll write to Dr. Carlton and tell him about our deal. You OK?"

"Tickled pink, Doc." Dmitri smiled. "See you in a month."

"What have you got down there, Mowgli?" Sababa asked.

"Red Snapper." Praj said. "48-year-old manager of the Cutthroat Tavern down in Honeymoon Bay. Referred by Dr. Poldy Bloom for a ten-month history of worsening shortness of breath and low-grade fever, and four days of headache and light sensitivity. His wife brought him here today. She says his behavior has been abnormal and aggressive in the last 24 hours."

"What has Poldy been doing the last ten months?" Sababa asked.

"Not enough." Praj said. "I'm concerned about his exam. You need to see him."

"Let's go then." Sababa said. "Fill me in on the rest of it."

"The investigations Dr. Bloom has done have revealed high white blood cell count, mostly eosinophils. More than fifty percent."

"Pink is the colour making the boldest statement today." Sababa looked through the barkeep's results as they walked the hallway. "What else?"

"Sedimentation rate and C-reactive protein are high." Praj said. "He has ECG changes, restrictive lung disease on pulmonary function testing, and prominent airspace markings everywhere on his chest x-ray." Sababa opened the door to the resident's room to find a worried countenance standing over a drowsy middle-aged man lying on the examining table.

"I'm Doctor Sababa, Mrs. Snapper." He said. "We'll try to make this right."

"Please." Was all she had.

The professor put his hand behind her husband's neck and lifted. Mr. Snapper's upper torso came along for the ride. Sababa did as brief a neurological exam as he dared, before hitting the intercom button.

"Yes, Boss?"

"Mercy, get me an ambulance, bells and whistles." He said. "And whichever one of the ER docs who can to talk to us."

"On it." She said.

"What is it, Doctor?" Mrs. Snapper asked.

"Red has some inflammation of the lining of his brain." Sababa said. "We need to find out from what." The sound of a siren filled the distance.

"Dr. Capitaine on line 1, Boss."

"Thanks, Mercy." Sababa picked up the handset. "Myles, I'm sending you a patient. I need a favour."

"What kind?" Myles asked.

"Red Snapper is a 48-year-old patient of Poldy Bloom's." Sababa said. "Presents with big-league eosinophilia and meningeal signs. Decreased Glasgow Coma Scale of 10 out of 15, hypertonia and hyperreflexia."

"What does he need?"

"Quite a bit." Sababa said. "My usual assault and battery, lumbar puncture, bone marrow with cytogenetics, serum tryptase, B12, immunoglobulins and IgE, FIP1L1/PDGFRA analysis by RT-PCR, ANCA, HIV and parasitic serologies, T-cell and B-cell receptor rearrangement studies, lymphocyte immunophenotyping, ECG, EEG, chest x-ray, CT and echo, for starters."

"Is that all?"

"Give him a gram of solumedrol." Sababa looked over at his wife. "I'll be the most responsible physician. We'll see him tonight." Mrs. Snapper forced a smile.

"A gram." Myles seemed uncertain. "What do you think is going on?"

"Some kind of hypereosinophilic syndrome." Sababa said. "We'll find out soon enough."

Once the ambulance attendants had removed Mr. and Mrs. Snapper to Harbour City Regional, Sababa handed Praj another chart from the shrinking pile.

"Perry Romberg?" The resident called into the congregation. A young man rose from his chair, hiding his face with a magazine. He followed Praj down to the resident's room.

"Joan Mitchell." Sababa called. A young woman accompanied the professor to his office. A stream of autumn sunlight poured in through the windows behind his desk and onto the chart he opened. He read the referral letter from her family physician, Dr. James Ruben Andrews.

22-year-old folk singer with a 6-month history of intermittent low white blood cell count associated with fever, mouth ulcers, sore throat, abdominal pain and diarrhea, and lymph node enlargement. Have no idea why.

"How can I help, Joan?" Sababa began.

"I get these infections every month." She said. "Last for a week at a time. Sometimes they're severe."

"What kinds of infections have you had?" Sababa asked.

"All kinds." Joan said. "I've had strep throat, sinus and ear infections, bronchitis and pneumonia, and perianal cellulitis and a bladder infection. In between, I feel quite normal. All Dr. Andrews does is send me for blood tests. I'm at the end of my tether." Sababa pulled a sheet of graph paper from his desk and began plotting points at specific intervals.

"What are you doing?" Joan asked.

"Measuring your tether." After a few minutes, he held up his chart. It looked like a sine wave on an oscilloscope.

"What does that show?"

"The relationship of your white blood cell counts over time."

"Meaning what exactly?" She sat forward in her chair.

"Here are the regular intervals during which your infections occurred." Sababa pointed to the depressions in the undulating curve. "They've all happened in periods when your neutrophils were way below normal and you have these large granular lymphocytes on your peripheral smear. You've likely felt fine at the peaks of the sinusoidal oscillations when your white count was normal."

"Why that looks like you've hit on something." Joan traced the curve with a finger. "But what?"

"If I'm right, you appear to have a condition called adult cyclic neutropenia." Sababa said. "It's a one in a million condition in which the ELANE gene on chromosome 19 responsible for encoding the enzyme neutrophil elastase, a serine proteinase that destroys bacteria, is either an autosomal dominant or spontaneous mutation. This causes cyclical accelerated apoptosis of neutrophil precursors leading to the periodic oscillation of bone marrow neutrophil production. When you go low, you get infected."

"Can you do something about it?" She asked.

"We'll need a bone marrow for some special studies, and we can detect ELANE mutations on genetic testing with a 100% accuracy." Sababa said. "This will confirm the diagnosis with certainty."

"No, I mean can you treat it?" Joan asked.

"Mais bien sûr." Sababa said. "We'll treat you with infusions of G-CSF granulocyte colony-stimulating factor and antibiotics, at the top of the roller coaster."

"Is there no permanent cure?"

"Sometimes, if you have a well-matched donor, we can do a hematopoietic stem cell transplantation." Sababa said. "But you're getting way ahead of me." He gave Joan some requisitions and asked her to make another appointment with Mercy.

"Thanks, Doctor Sababa." She passed Praj coming in as she left. Before the young resident had a chance to present his case, Mercy interrupted over the intercom.

"Dr. Rivera on line 2, Boss." Sababa put the call on speaker.

"What do you need, Nick?" Sababa asked.

"When you finish your clinic is fine, Sab."

"What you got?"

"I have a young woman in the first trimester of her first pregnancy." Rivera said.

"You know I don't do barbershop, bat shit or babies."

"But you do weird."

"The weirder the better." Sababa said.

"This girl came into the office today." Nick continued. "Strangest thing. She's bleeding from her gums. Says it never happened before."

"It never did." Sababa said. "Where is she now?"

"I sent her to the sat lab for some blood tests." Nick said. "Will you see her?"

"No." Sababa said.

"Why not?"

"Find her, Nick." His voice dropped an octave. "Send her to the ER, now. Call one of their docs and insist on a medivac chopper straight to the on-call hematologist at Vancouver General. Do not pass go. Do not fuck this up."

"What's going on, Sab?"

"She has acute myelogenous leukemia. Her white cell count will be in the sky." He said. "And if she doesn't get her cytarabine and daunorubicin induction chemotherapy within hours, she will be too."

"But she's pregnant." Nick protested.

"I don't remember anyone asking God for clemency." Sababa said. "She's going to lose the baby. Don't you dare tell her. Hop to it. You're wasting time." *Click.*

"Nothing like a little death and mayhem to focus the mind." Sababa said.

"Well, that was heartless." Praj wrinkled his forehead. "Why is it always reasonable in Sababaland to take an emotional problem and sidestep it by turning it into a mechanical problem?"

"Because in Sababaland—and the rest of the universe, by the way—when a question presents itself, it calls for an answer." Sababa said. "There is never any applause on this side of the desk."

"You're such a cynic."

"Cynicism is the art of seeing things as they are instead of as they ought to be." Sababa said. "Now, what you got?"

"Perry Romberg." Praj began. "23-year-old advertising executive for a company called Too Faced Cosmetics. Referred by Tictac Tarmac for a Bell's Palsy of the left side of his face."

"And?"

"He has a Bell's palsy." Praj said. "Except that it's been going on for a month, it's painful, and getting worse."

"So, it's not a Bell's palsy." Sababa said.

"I think it is." Praj insisted. "Lower motor neuron paralysis of the seventh cranial nerve."

"There are many things other than Sir Charles Bell that can cause that." Sababa said. "The symptoms and timing are all wrong. Let's go see." In the resident's room, Praj introduced his mentor.

"This is Doctor Sababa, Perry." The young man said. "He's also neuroatypical."

The patient pulled his hand away from his face. The left half was hardly there.

"So, not Bell's." Sababa said. "When did this begin, Mr. Romberg?"

"About a month ago." Mumbled the right side of him.

"Nope." Sababa said. "I'd bet on a year or more."

"It's only a month."

"How can you be two-faced when you're not even one-faced?" Sababa asked. "Judging by the hypopigmented linear scar where your left forehead used to be, I'd say a year."

"But…"

"We call it a 'coup de sabre' because it resembles the scar of a wound made by a sword." He said. "Sometimes seen in frontal linear scleroderma, but that's not what you've got."

"What have I got?"

"Severe loss of subcutaneous tissue and muscle of the left side of your face, with no apparent involvement of the facial bones. Your mouth and nose have now deviated to the faceless side." Sababa said. "The left eyeball has fallen back into its socket. The drooping eyelid, constricted pupil, red conjunctiva, and reduced sweating are known as Horner's syndrome. Your two irises are now different colours." Sababa tapped what was once his left sideburn. Perry winced in pain. Muscles on the opposite side of his face began to convulse and spasm uncontrollably and spread through his entire right side. The paroxysm disappeared in less than a minute.

"And trigeminal neuralgia. *Tic douloureux.*" Sababa said. "And Jacksonian seizures. Open your mouth."

"I can't." Perry muttered.

"No, you can't." Sababa said. "But I can tell from the little you can do that the left half of your tongue and upper lip is gone. You need a dentist but you're afraid to go. You must live on milkshakes. And you haven't worked for a while, have you." Perry's right eye filled with tears.

"A year." He murmured. "Please help me."

"That's always what we try to do." Sababa said. "First things first; second things never. Dr. Bharmal here will order a blood test for circulating antinuclear antibodies and an MRI of your brain."

"What is it?" He asked.

"It's a rare condition called progressive hemifacial atrophy."

"Can you get my face back?"

"If there is any suggestion of an autoimmune mechanism, we will discuss some more immediate treatment options at your next visit." Sababa said. "Otherwise, it usually goes into remission by itself, although it may take some time."

"Praj, send a referral to Pretty Boy Troy, our local plastic surgeon." Sababa continued. "Perry may also be a candidate for autologous fat transfer or fat grafting, transverse rectus abdominis myocutaneous TRAM or latissimus dorsi muscle or pedicled temporal fascia flaps, cartilage or bone graft, orthognathic surgery, or bone distraction to restore a more normal contour to the face. Send a letter to Dr. Tarmac. The last one we write should go something like this: Did you hear about the guy whose whole left face was missing? He's all right now." Perry forced half a smile.

"And tell Mercy we'll see him in two weeks." Sababa said. "Meet me in the emergency department when you're done."

"Done?"

"Oh right. I forgot." Sababa said. "You're a resident. You're never done."

'Crowds of people lined up inside and out
Just one reason, to rock the house
But in the daytime the streets were clear
You couldn't find a good freak anywhere, 'cause
The freaks come out at night.'
Escape, *The Freaks Come Out at Night*

Outside the automatic frosted glass sliding doors of the Harbour City Regional ER, Praj passed a nurse, her gaze averted, her cigarette smoke streaming a silver sacrifice to the lunar gods above. *It's a marvelous night for a moon dance.*

Inside the *whoosh* of the gates to eternity, beat-up chairs filled with beat-up people. During his training, Praj had discovered two important things about an emergency department: (1) the plexiglass fortress surrounding the reception desk was a terrarium designed to keep the reptiles out, and (2) all the lunatics came out during a full moon, refugees from daytime, sailing in on the painful light of the satellite, basking in the fluorescent illumination of a medical staff at the end of their shifts, and their caring. And this was a harvest moon in an Indian summer. There would be no hiding from the zombie lunacy.

Dr. Gung Ho motioned Praj to stay where he was until he finished speaking to a patient. He read the notice above the consultant's desk while he waited.

Harbour City Regional ER- Weekend Call Schedule

Anesthesiology: Dr. Banjo Paterson is covering anesthesia, except for pain clinic patients who should be referred to their extramural associate Pablo, who will provide narcotic refills for the weekend.

Family Medicine: Dr. Nicholas Rivera is covering all patients for the entire service so he can take next week off for the annual Harbour City Search and Rescue Conference. Please remember that he usually has only one patient in the hospital at a time, but this weekend will have 45. When contacting Dr. Rivera, remember to call his cell phone. After his profane tirade, call back on his pager. Or vice versa. You won't be right the first time. Ever. You can discuss his subsequent complaint with administration on Monday. When Dr. Rivera comes to the emergency department for the admission, have coffee ready, with large amounts of sugar and cream. Also, have the AMA forms available; those he sees tend to sign themselves out of the hospital in anger.

Internal Medicine: Dr. Hacker will be taking call for general internal medicine. Anyone admitted to internal medicine with abdominal pain will require surgical consultation; anyone with diabetes or chest pain or shortness of breath will require transfer. If the patient has any complex abnormality, please know the appropriate metabolic pathways in order to answer obscure questions about why you didn't order enough laboratory studies in the first place.

OB/Gyn: Dr. Olaf Octagon is on call for OB/Gyn. He will be covering patients for Dr. Janice Adkins-Barker and Dr. Margaret Star-Smith. Dr. Moira Harris is on sabbatical until after her elective insertion of a hyphen.

Surgery: Dr. Benway is on for general surgery. Please remember that he does not operate on children or insurance-negative patients. He also considers trauma an enormous inconvenience. If you have gall bladder patients, patients with appendicitis, or patients with acute diverticulitis, you may contact him after the CT scan has been read and the patient is sedated and prepped. Never forget Dr. Benway's axiom. *If it isn't on the CT scan, it doesn't exist.* Dr. Benway is covering for Dr. Falstaff, who will be intoxicated this weekend, but not Dr. Martino, who doesn't trust him. Anything that is only marginally surgical should be admitted to family medicine, and those practitioners may consult him after a lengthy game of telephone tag.

These specialties don't have anyone available:

Dentistry: At no time in the past or future; not ever.

Dermatology: You must be joking.

ENT: Dr. Theodor Billroth is not on call except for his own patients with post-operative tonsil bleeding. Dr. Billroth does not do mandible fractures, facial fractures, blow-out fractures, or facial abscesses. For real airway or vascular ENT emergencies, remember that he lives 20 minutes away. Don't forget Dr. Billroth's axiom. *If it isn't an airway or vascular emergency, you don't need me. If it is, I'll arrive too late to help.*

Neurology: Dr. Oliver Lax is not on call for neurology, as he is our only neurologist and lives on an offshore island. Please perform a detailed neurologic examination before even thinking about calling him, that is obtain any and all possible imaging studies. It is helpful if you can remember some neuroanatomy. Don't forget Dr. Lax's axiom. *If there's blood on the brain, the patient needs a neurosurgeon; if there isn't, then the patient needs to be admitted to internal medicine.*

Pathology: Dr. Juan Leyblanca is occasionally available to physicians whose mother tongue is Castilian Spanish.

Psychiatry: Dr. Robert La Capuche is not on call for psychiatry, especially for those patients he feels our facility is ill-equipped to handle: i.e. the suicidal, the frankly psychotic, the drug or alcohol addicted, the bipolar, the violent/angry, the adolescent, the elderly demented, and the profoundly depressed. Feel free to contact Dr. La Capuche during normal banker's hours for consultation on mild unhappiness, social awkwardness, and fear of open spaces.

"Sababa in the house." Announced the emergency nurse who had just finished her moonlight cigarette. Sab found Gung Ho and Praj perusing a chart.

"¿Qué esta pasando?" He asked.

"Richard Feynman." Gung began. "62-year-old Lake Cowichan secondary school physics teacher with a three-month history of painless masses over his right shoulder and left elbow. Two months ago, he had some bleeding gums after a dental procedure. He's been feeling tired, his appetite is off, and he's lost 5 pounds in the last month. His family doc sent him for some blood tests which showed a low red blood cell and platelet count. His vision is blurry. His wife found another mass lesion on his soft palate."

"Why did he come in tonight?" Sababa asked.

"Nosebleed." Gung said.

"Exam?"

"I told you." He said. "And a right retinal hemorrhage."

"Lab?" Sababa asked.

"All three blood cell lines are down now." Gung turned the patient's pages. "Coagulation profile is abnormal with prolonged prothrombin time and activated partial thromboplastin time. Serum viscosity and LDH are high. Total protein is up but his albumin is down."

"So, some abnormal protein is making up the difference." Praj offered.

"And we know which one, don't we?" Sababa said.

"We do?" Gung looked puzzled.

"Let's go see him." Sababa said. Inside the curtain of cubicle 3, Gung introduced Praj and the professor. Feynmann pointed to his right shoulder.

"You know what this is, Doctor?" He asked.

"Uh-huh." Sababa said.

"What?"

"It's a rare kind of indolent lymphoma." Sababa knew he had Richard's attention. "Named after the man that discovered two patients with it in 1944."

"Who was?"

"Jan G. Waldenström." Sababa said. "You have Waldenström's macroglobulinemia. It's also called lymphoplasmacytic lymphoma, a malignancy affecting two types of B cells, lymphoplasmacytoid cells and plasma cells which are secreting too much serum monoclonal immunoglobulin M. It may have been smoldering for quite some time."

"What happens now?" Richard asked.

"Now, we admit you to hospital to measure your IgM and Kappa light chain levels and some other blood and urine tests, a bone marrow aspiration, biopsy, and soft tissue biopsy, a CT scan of your chest, abdomen, and pelvis, and a search for somatic mutations at locus 6p21.3 on chromosome 6." Sababa said. "And then we'll send you to Vancouver for plasmapheresis to treat your hyperviscosity, and more definitive therapy for the lymphoma."

"Like what?" Richard asked.

"Depends on several factors." He said. "Usually some combination of chemotherapy and biologicals. If you're lucky enough to be in the 90% of patients that have MYD88 L265P mutation-induced activation of Bruton's tyrosine kinase, you'll get ibrutinib, with a 95% success rate at two years."

"Doesn't sound lucky to me." Richard said. "You know anyone else with this problem?"

"French president Georges Pompidou." Sababa said. "And the Shah of Iran."

"Didn't his trip to the US for treatment in 1979 lead to the Iran hostage crisis?"

"Yes." Sababa said. "It was a deal with the devil."

"There ain't no devil." Richard said. "That's God when he's drunk. And I have no intention of meeting him."

"I'll be sure to pass that along." Sababa said. "I dance with him in the pale moonlight. Dr. Bharmal here will see to all these arrangements and I'll check in on you tomorrow." He turned to Praj.

"Meet me over in the overflow ER ward next door when you're done." He said. "Dr. Capitaine admitted Mr. Snapper there late this afternoon."

An hour later, Praj found the stocky savant inside Red's climate-controlled cubicle.

"What have we discovered?" He asked.

"That's what I've been asking the professor here, Dr. Bharmal." The tavern owner sat up and paid attention. He had licked his dinner plate clean. Red's wife held his hand.

"Dramatic response to the solumedrol." Sababa said. "His EEG showed generalized slow waves suggestive of encephalopathy or encephalitis. Cerebrospinal fluid was sterile with a heavy infiltration of eosinophils. Lung function testing disclosed moderate restrictive disease. Echo was remarkable for clots in both ventricles and a global decrease in pump function. Bone marrow revealed hyper-cellularity with eosinophil predominance and no atypical forms."

"So, what is this?" Mrs. Snapper asked.

"With a blood eosinophilia of ≥ 1500/microliter, no other apparent infectious, allergic, autoimmune or malignant causes, and symptoms and signs of eosinophil-mediated organ dysfunction, it's clear Red's eosinophilic meningoencephalitis and biventricular thrombi are due to a condition called hypereosinophilic syndrome." Sababa said.

"From what?" Red asked.

"From what, Praj." Sababa deflected.

"There are six clinical variants of HES." Said the young resident. "A myeloid form, a lymphocytic form, an overlap form, an associated form, a familial form, and…"

"And?" Red asked.

"An idiopathic form." Praj said. "Which is what is going on here."

"What's idiopathic?"

"It means we don't know the cause." Sababa said.

"So how are we any further ahead?" Asked Mrs. Snapper.

"Empiricism." Sababa said. "We know what works anyway."

"So, what now?" Red asked.

"We'll add in some anticoagulation, a measure of hydroxyurea or interferon-α plus or minus the monoclonal antibodies mepolizumab or imatanib mesylate as steroid-sparing agents, and presto change-o, we have a remission."

"And if that fails?" Mrs. Snapper was in the game.

"We still have allogeneic stem cell transplantation." He said.

"When can I take him home to Honeymoon Bay?" She asked.

"Tomorrow morning." Sababa said. "Bright and early. Right Praj?"

"Worms, wheezes and weird diseases." Praj said. "Right you are." And then nothing. Sababa glanced over at his protégé, who had fallen asleep in his chair. *Clunk.*

The young resident awoke to find his monkey wrench on the floor beside him.

"You've had an eventful day, Mowgli." Sababa said. "Why don't you and your mascot take the rest of the night off? I'll handle the bog animals until morning. You can call me with the first contestant."

"Thanks, Sab." Praj said. "Appreciate it." He bolted like Quasimodo through the rafters of Notre Dame, before anyone could change their minds.

It was several hours later, after an exacting evening, that Sababa thought of making his own escape for a few hours of well-deserved shuteye before Groundhog Day began all over again. Dr. Cliff Carlton blocked his exit. "Your dance card has been punched."

"It is my medical advice that you do not leave against medical advice." Cliffy said. "One more, Sab. You need to see her."

"What you got?"

"Laurie Cabot." Cliffy began. "38-year-old Cowichan wool spinner diagnosed with chronic lymphocytic leukemia 4 years ago, treated only with watchful waiting, presents tonight with a week-long history of hard collar bone swelling associated with feverishness, weight loss and night-sweats." Sababa's right eyebrow migrated north.

"B-symptoms." He said. "Rest of exam?"

"Big lymph nodes everywhere." Cliff said. "Enlarged liver. Scar where her spleen used to be."

"Lab results?"

"Real high lactic dehydrogenase." He said. "Smudge cells have disappeared. Chest x-ray was unremarkable."

"I'll go see her." Cliffy thanked the portly professor and left him to see a new patient of his own.

The young woman in the hospital bed behind curtain 7 was as beautiful as she was frail.

"I'm sorry." Sababa said. "I must have the wrong cubicle."

"No." She said. "Everyone thinks I'm supposed to be much older."

"It's unusual to see CLL at your age." Sababa said. "Did anyone find a reason?" Laurie shook her head. Sababa examined her chest wall and lymph nodes.

"Did you ever work in northern Ontario?"

"I planted trees on crown land during my summers as a teenager." Laurie said.

"Did they spray anything from the air when you did that?"

"All the time." Laurie said. "They called it 'brushkiller.' I used to hold up a red, helium-filled balloon on fishing line while low-flying Stearman biplanes sprayed it all around us. And on us. It was supposed to kill what they said were 'weed trees'—birch and maple and poplar and shrubs, although it sometimes killed the black spruce seedlings we were planting as well."

"They didn't only spray the forests." Sababa said. "Ontario Hydro sprayed every power line in Ontario. The highway ministry sprayed the road shoulders. All with no regard for creeks and streams, nor residents and wildlife, running it all off into the lakes. I got drenched one day while picking blueberries in the bush near my hometown."

"They told us that the tough spruce pulp fibres went to produce the Sunday edition of the New York Times."

"All the news that fit to print."

"Something like that." Laurie said.

"Except it wasn't."

"What do you mean?"

"Did they ever tell you what that brushkiller compound was?" He asked.

"I don't think so."

"It was an equal mixture of 2,4-D and 2,4,5-T phenoxy herbicide."

"I don't understand." Laurie looked puzzled.

"It has a more notorious name." Sababa said. "The most widely used chemical in the Vietnam War. The US military, in Operation Ranch Hand from 1962 and 1971, sprayed 20,000,000 gallons of the stuff, a volume of over 30 Olympic-sized swimming pools, in a concentration 13 times the recommended application rate for US domestic use, on 31,000 square kilometres and four million people of Vietnam, eastern Laos, and parts of Cambodia. This 'rainbow herbicide' defoliated twenty percent of South Vietnam alone, destroying 20,000 square kilometres of upland and mangrove forests, twenty percent of the woodlands and 10 million hectares of agricultural land. It caused widespread famine and starvation, a poisoned food chain, animal extinctions, and major illnesses including leukemia, lymphoma, various kinds of cancer and other diseases, and congenital deformities like cleft palate, spina bifida, mental disabilities, hernias, and extra digits in more than three million people. Exposed American veterans had more than twice the rate of aggressive prostate cancer, among other things." *It became necessary to destroy the town to save it.*

"Do you think it caused my CLL?" Laurie asked.

"I do."

"What was the more notorious name?" She asked.

"Agent Orange." Sababa said. "It contained the fat-soluble iso-octyl ester, 2,3,7,8-tetrachlorodibenzo-p-dioxin. In the body, this TCDD binds to the aryl hydrocarbon receptor transcription factor. The resultant protein product moves into the nucleus, where it sabotages gene expression."

"They sprayed me with Agent Orange?"

"More like a Clockwork Orange." Sababa said. "It was just a matter of time."

"What?"

"Until this happened." He said.

"What's this?' She asked.

"Your CLL developed into something worse, Laurie." Sababa shook his head. "Your chronic leukemia has transformed into a fast-growing diffuse large B cell lymphoma. It's called Richter Syndrome."

"Not good?"

"Not good." He said.

"No treatment?"

"We have therapies." Sababa said. "Intensive chemotherapy, radiotherapy, monoclonal antibodies, even stem cell transplantation."

"But they don't work?"

"Not as well as we want."

"How long?

"Median survival of 5–8 months."

"Well, at least I won't die an ugly old hag." Laurie said. And then she beamed a smile Sababa would never forget.

"What now?"

"I'll admit you to hospital, do a fine needle aspiration biopsy of your chest abnormality, and consult our local cancer specialist, Dr. Henry Chibueze." After the biopsy, Sababa shook and then held her hand.

"See you tomorrow." Outside her cubicle, the professor put in a page to the staff oncologist as he sat down to dictate his consultation. A few minutes later, Regina tapped him on the shoulder.

"Dr. Chibueze on line 1 for you, Sab."

"Do you know what time it is?" The voice on the other end of the line was vexed. Sababa selected a tune from his music library on a secret drive hidden deep inside the hospital computer network. *Gonna stimulate some action... We gonna get some satisfaction...*

"After midnight." He said.

"You have an oncology emergency?"

"Hell no, Henry. I just like the sound of your Nigerian accent." Sababa said. "Why do they put nails in coffins?"

"I have no idea."

"To stop the oncologist from giving another round of chemo."

"I assume you had another reason for waking me?" Henry asked.

"Laurie Cabot." He said. "Exquisite 38-year-old woman with Richter's transformation of her CLL."

"Impossible." Henry said.

"Agent Orange. She's here." Sababa said. "And she knows. So, get on with it, but don't promise anything you can't deliver."

"What do you mean?"

"You know how to pick out an oncologist at a funeral?" Sababa asked. "He's the one doing chest compressions. Don't promise her anything you can't deliver."

"Nice beard. The flannel's a good touch. Very authentic.
 What do they call these guys, lumbersexuals?"
"Men. They're called men."
Tiffany Reisz

Dr. Praj Bharmal woke the professor at dawn.
"I have the first contestant, Sab." He said. "You need to come. Now."
"On my way." Sababa, still half asleep, jumped into his clothes and grabbed his keys.
"Pale moonlight." Jane mumbled at a banshee roar careening down their long driveway and into the doppler-distorted distance. Less than six minutes later, the time it takes a brain to die, the closed-circuit camera behind the on-call internal medicine parking bay caught Sababa's dimpled and dented white Honda lurching to a stop in the slot. The driver bounced through the automatic frosted glass sliding doors of the Harbour City Regional ER. *Whoosh.*
"Acute Room, Sab." Michaela shouted. The stocky savant made a sharp left into a resuscitation in progress. A young bearded man covered in sawdust was tilted head down on a gurney. Monitor leads sprouted from his chest inside of an open plaid shirt. Two intravenous lines ran wide open saline into his arms. The rest of him was the colour of a Shady Mile Halloween pumpkin. The screen showed a blood pressure too low and a heart rate too fast. Trace Pangloss barked orders that Dina and Regina ran to complete. Praj stood beside the bedside.
"Tell me." Sababa said.
"Alder Way." Praj began. "24-year-old logger from Honeymoon Bay brought in a few minutes ago unconscious and in shock."
"What kind?"
"What do you mean?" Praj asked.
"Cardiogenic, obstructive, or redistributive?" Sababa asked.
"Redistributive."
"Septic, anaphylactic, endocrine and toxic, or neurogenic?"
"We don't know yet." Trace said. "His jugular venous pressure is low, ECG is normal except for his heart rate, and we've given him volume,

70

epinephrine, and steroids, none of which has done anything to bring up his blood pressure. I was about to start the inotropes."

"Homme orange." Sababa said. *Orange man.* He traced a fingertip across the man's abdomen. A flaring wheal swelled like a cobra behind the scratchmark.

"Dina, give him 25 mg of dimenhydrinate IV." He said. "Regina, give him 150 mg of ranitidine through the IV in his other arm." A minute after receiving the drugs, Alder Way's blood pressure began to rise. When his systolic came up above 70 mmHg, he awoke to the carnage around him.

"What's going on?" He asked.

"We should ask you the same question." Trace hung another litre of saline.

"I tumbled out of a tree." Alder said. "Don't worry. I hugged it first."

"Is there a difference between a faller and a free faller?" Sababa asked.

"I don't usually do it for free." He said.

"How do you feel now?" Praj asked.

"I'm a lumberjack and I'm OK." Alder went to sit up and fell back down. "I am OK, right?"

"You are now." Sababa said. "How many times has this happened?"

"Three episodes in the last month." Alder volunteered. "No one saw them and I recovered quick. Lucky I wasn't working when they happened."

"Lucky." Sababa pulled an infamous hand-scribed Black Book of Remedies from his Columbian leather briefcase. "When sudden deforestation and depopulation occur together, that's how you know a lumberjack has crossed paths with his family tree."

"What do you mean?"

"Your immune system contains mast cells, little blue defenders against bacteria and parasites. They also play a role in wound healing and the growth of blood vessels." Sababa said. "We've never found anyone with too few or no mast cells, so it appears that we may not be able to survive without them."

"You saying I have too few mast cells, Doc?"

"Negatory." Sababa said. "You have too many."

"Wha...?"

"It's a condition we call systemic mastocytosis." Sababa said. "You have too many mast cells, but they're defective. Every so often they degranulate in synchrony, releasing a ton of histamine and other chemical alarms into your bloodstream, like what happens in an allergic reaction, but without the immune trigger. They've invaded your skin, decreased your bone density, given you peptic ulcers and malabsorption, can affect other organ function, and will discharge in unison again when they've refilled their granules."

"You need to fix this thing." Alder said. "Make it go away."

"We'll admit you to the ICU to begin our investigations."

"Can't you fix it without all this fluffy stuff?"

"If you had four hours to chop down a tree, you'd spend the first two hours sharpening the axe." Sababa said. "We need more data so we can decide on the right treatment."

"What do you need?' Alder asked.

"Three things to make the diagnosis." Sababa said. "We'll do a bone marrow and skin biopsy, serum tryptase, and a KIT(D816V) PCR to look for a mutation of the gene coding for the c-kit receptor, mast cell morphology, and mast cell phenotyping for CD2 and/or CD25."

"That's five things."

"We only need three." Sababa said. "Dr. Bharmal and I will see you later in the unit." After giving report to Angie in the ICU, Regina wheeled Alder down a procession of yellow rectangles receding down a passageway to a far-off vanishing point. She hummed a tune to the Death Star. *Follow, follow, follow, follow... Follow the yellow brick road.*

Regina rolled Alder into a small vestibule, furnished with several retro vintage chairs, a coffee table on which sat a vase of withering gladiolas, and a wire rack of support group pamphlets. It could have been a cave if there had been more light. But all the light was straight ahead of him, soft and translucent, behind the frosted automatic door with a hand sanitizer dispenser and a red buzzer button on a brushed metal speaker protruding from its frame. A sign hung overhead. *ICU—Tranquility Base.* Regina pushed on the button. *Whoosh.*

"Bed 6, Regina." Came from a wizened elderly Chinese ward clerk with Coke bottle wire-rimmed glasses and an Empress Consort's demeanor on a raised central platform. He read her nametag as he went by. *Betty Boop.*

"Hello, Alder." The receiving critical care nurse said. "I'm Angie. I'll be looking after you today. You're covered in sawdust."

"You mean man glitter."

"Whatever."

"If you woke up naked in the woods bent over a log, would you tell anyone?" Alder asked.

"Uh, no, probably not."

"Wanna go camping?" Angie ignored him to enter his data on her mobile computer console.

"You having trouble logging in?" He asked. She finished his history and began to examine him.

"Beard rule #7." Alder said. "If you touch my beard, I will touch your butt." He looked across his cubicle to a pastel painting of Cathedral Grove old-growth forest. Pink may have been predominant, but orange was the happiest colour.

"Wow." He said. "I'd sure like to get in there with a chainsaw." Drs. Sababa and Bharmal invaded his space.

"Exquisite painting." Sababa. said. "Calming, but with a hint of nurturing. Offsets the stench of suffering and death."
"Hey, Doc." Alder said. "Did you hear the one about this puny guy applies for a job as a lumberjack?"
"Can't say I have." Sababa said.

"Sorry." Says the head lumberjack, eyeing the man up and down, "You're too small."
"Give me a chance to show you what I can do." The guy pleads. "You won't regret it."
"Okay." Says the boss. "See that giant oak over there? Let's see if you can chop it down." Half an hour later, the mighty oak is felled, amazing the boss.
"Where'd you learn to cut trees like that?" he asks.
"The Sahara Forest."
"You mean the Sahara Desert?"
"Oh sure." He said. "That's what they call it now."

'Look deeply into nature, and then you will understand everything better.'
Albert Einstein

The casual reader can be forgiven for having an affinity with the woodcutter. A simple man doing an honest day's work harvesting the resources and taming the harshness of the wilderness can engender feelings of consonance in the otherwise unenlightened.
Sababa had formed no such bond with these men, although he understood they were but tools in the hands of more avaricious forces— a meme for the most selfish gene in the Anthropocene.
In every rare opportunity, he would climb to the ridges above his lake to be soothed and healed, to have his senses put in order. Autumn won him best in its mute appeal to sympathy for the decay it delivered. On the upper reaches of the mountain, Sababa stood in awe of magnificent trees over a thousand years old, rainforest descendants of a primeval that had driven the glaciers into retreat thirteen millennia earlier.
He found more wisdom in his woods than in his books. The trees and stones haunted Sababa with the idea that by reading their silent riddles, he might learn some secret vital to his own life, a lesson no other master could teach.

Rooted in the earth, touching the sky, the ancient forest calmed his heart. He felt the flow of life and his place in the universe, and the cedar sensitivity to changes of time and light. *Their boughs flop heavy and sometimes float, then they are fairy as ferns and then they droop, heavy as heartaches.*

But a fool sees not the same tree that a wise man sees. These massive organisms providing shelter and food and warmth and protection to all other living things would even give shade to those wielding chainsaws to cut them down. The ones which moved Sababa to exaltation were, in other eyes, only green obstacles in their way. Some saw Nature as all ridicule and deformity, and some scarce saw Nature at all.

In less than twenty more years, any unprotected heritage tree will be logged, and we will never be able to get them back. The timber companies regard their clear cut devastation as normal, second-growth a distraction, and 'sustainability' a speed bump to profit. They redesign their silvicultural plantations to shorten the life of the cyclical timber harvest. They alter the dynamic biodiversity of the rainforest without a clue how their actions will affect the ecology. To maximize the collection of wood fiber today, they gamble with the existence of the forests of tomorrow.

The greatest threat to the planet is the belief someone else will take care of it until it doesn't happen. *When the trees are gone the sky will fall and we and the salmon will be no more.*

'The woods are lovely, dark and deep. But I have promises to keep, and miles to go before I sleep.'

Robert Frost

Autumn isn't so much orange, as russet and tangerine shades of old gold, flushing the outside edges of our senses and browning the margins of our days.

Adelle Davis was her own people person personal trainer until the end of her days, which came sooner than she ever thought possible. Despite the diet and exercise and determination and Google-searched natural remedies and zodiac sign and the positive nature she threw at her multiple myeloma, her pernicious purple plasma cells paid no attention and ran her over with fatal pneumococcal pneumonia before she could reconsider Sababa's recommendation for more conventional therapy.

Bert Sézary's biopsies confirmed the mycosis fungoides that Sababa had suspected. His deflated dermatologist, Dr. Commodus Sitsofsky, picked up the ball he dropped, and treated the park ranger with a combination of topical and systemic therapies, to the benefit of their mutual continuation of gainful employment. Bert has a 66% likelihood of surviving another ten years and is back in Gordon Bay on Lake Cowichan, handing out fines to errant mushroom pickers like Doctor Sababa (except Doctor Sababa).

The solitary lymph node in Morrie Bund's neck did indeed turn out to contain an angioimmunoblastic T-cell lymphoma. The logging truck driver initially responded well to conventional treatment but when he declined consolidation chemotherapy and autologous stem cell transplantation, he shook Doctor Sababa's hand for the last time.

Denis Parsons agreed to Sababa's antiretroviral cocktail and Chibueze's regimen of several cycles of chemotherapy, including the multiple lumbar punctures necessary to deliver it into the fluid around his brain. When his fifty-fifty chance became a hundred percent cure, Denis reduced Doctor Sababa's IT network maintenance cost to zero.

Chilly Marrow was started on hydroxyurea. He continued to have his chest drained and blood transfused every three weeks until it was too difficult. He and Bernadine Soulier renewed their vows under a canopy on the final green of the March Meadows Golf Course three days before he floated up to the clubhouse in the sky.

Red Snapper went home from Harbour City Regional with his wife, the day after he met the professor. His meningitis, heart clots, other organ dysfunction and diagnosis of idiopathic hypereosinophilic syndrome responded to Sababa's blast of solumedrol and anticoagulants and subsequent steroid-sparing agents. Abnormal numbers of pink cells melted into normal numbers of white cells and presto change-o, Red had his remission. He is still babysitting Bossman's hungover loggers in the snake room of the Cutthroat Tavern.

Dmitri Romanowsky's eosinophilic pneumonia and pleural effusion were gone forever inside of eight months. The only pink in his life now is the colour of the cider he delivers to Mercy and Sababa at Manzanita Medical.

Joan Mitchell's genetic testing confirmed Sababa's diagnosis of cyclic neutropenia. She had no further infections with G-CSF and antibiotics at the top of her roller coaster but still wants to be well rid of the problem. She is booked for a stem cell transplant. *There'll be new dreams, maybe better dreams and plenty... Before the last revolving year is through... And the seasons they go round and round...*

The pregnant young woman with the bleeding gums was medevacked from the Harbour City Regional helipad straight to the on-call hematologist at Vancouver General. She died of sepsis during induction chemotherapy for acute myelogenous leukemia. She took the baby with her, in exchange for an endless trail of tears. After reviewing the vivid colours on her initial blood smears, pathologist Juan Leyblanca called Sababa with a panicked profusion of profanity before learning that Dr. Rivera had already transferred the patient out of their jurisdiction.

With the assistance of Doctor Sababa's immunosuppressive therapy and Pretty Boy Troy's plastic prowess, Perry Romberg can once again speak out of both sides of his mouth.

Richard Feynman's Waldenstrom's macroglobulinemia was positive for a somatic mutation in MYD88. His ibrutinib therapy had kept him alive and teaching physics to his grateful students at Lake Cowichan high, a result far more favorable than that experienced by the former Shah of Iran.

Doctor Sababa was at her bedside when Laurie Cabot died from Richter's transformation of her chronic lymphocytic leukemia. Dr. Chibueze didn't promise her anything he couldn't deliver because he couldn't deliver anything at all. No one from the Government of Ontario sent condolences for their recurrent drenching her with Agent Orange, during Laurie's teenage years as a tree planter. She knitted Sababa a Cowichan sweater with a thunderbird motif. He would have plenty of parallel reasons to think of her while wearing it in the savage winter following her departure.

And what of the case of the orange faller? Alder Way had a bone marrow which, together with his high serum tryptase and a positive PCR for a KIT(D816V) mutation, confirmed Sababa's diagnosis of systemic mastocytosis. He had no further episodes of loss of consciousness and his systemic manifestations of the disease all disappeared with a simple cocktail of both kinds of antihistamines, leukotriene antagonists, ketotifen, and calcium-vitamin D. For now. Alder knows there is no cure. But not only his orange but his blues have gone. After Angie touched his beard once too often and Alder took her camping, they became what is known in Honeymoon Bay as an item. Months after they married, Sababa asked Angie what the attraction was.

"He's a lumberjack." She said. "And he's OK."

15. The Case of the Tumescent Tattoos

'Wealth falls on some men as a copper down a drain.'
Seneca the Younger

Eduardo Cazar was no ordinary thief. He was a specialist. When Eduardo drove his Cadillac into his day job as a gas station attendant in Cassidy, no one ever bothered to ask the obvious question. The residents of Cassidy were like that. They were respectful of one another's privacy and stuck to themselves.

Before electricity flipped the switch, the pre-modern world used copper hardened in alloys with other metals. In Doctor Sababa's home province of Ontario, native Ojibway invested the metal with magic and guarded their heirloom stashes of copper fishhooks, needles, and knives with superstitious zeal. Their deity Missibizi lived on a canoe-shaped island in Lake Superior, fifteen miles long and made of solid copper. Missibizi liked to paddle across the waves from his helm on the island's hilly crest, its surf-splashed flanks littered with softball-sized copper nuggets. If a passing fisherman took one, Missibizi struck him dead.

While the Ojibway's story was one of selfishness, the Vancouver Island native history of copper was founded on generosity. After their wars and servitude ended in 1849, the Salish produced large numbers of two-foot-long ornamental shields of beaten copper for their aristocrats. Each sheet was worth as much as a former slave and given as a gift at potlatches.

Modern man cannot survive without copper. Today, an average home is interwoven with 439 pounds of copper wiring and plumbing, with another hundred pounds embedded in household appliances like water heaters, air conditioners, and refrigerators. The average car is strung with more than 600,000 feet of the stuff. In the US alone, 130 million cellphones are retired every year, containing 2,100 metric tons of copper—enough to build twenty-six new copper-sheathed Statues of Liberty. Craft beers and liquors are brewed in shiny copper stills. Fishermen fling Copper John flies with copper-wire abdomens in running waters everywhere. The shiny raw colour attracts trout—just one form in which the metal slays unsuspecting fish.

Eduardo Cazar was a copper thief for the same reason Willy Sutton robbed banks. When Willy was asked why he engaged in such notorious activity, he gave the world Sutton's Law. *Because that's where the money is.* Copper is ubiquitous and useful—corrosion resistant, strong, durable, and endlessly recyclable. Melted down, the metal can be reconstructed into any number of configurations. Copper is a commodity that not only retains its value against the dollar but continually appreciates because of rapid developing industrialization in China and India and rebounding oil prices. Copper theft is lucrative. The US Department of Energy estimates that $1 billion worth of infrastructure damage occurs every year because of it.

Eduardo Cazar's specialty would leave Harbour City streets in the dark for an entire week until BC Hydro could reconnect the disrupted services. On one occasion, he stripped the copper wiring from 23 lamp standards at four locations in one night. Eduardo cut the wiring during the day and returned in the shadows with a large spool on the back of his pickup truck. In another robbery in the south of the city near the airport in Cassidy, he pulled over two kilometres of copper wire from 16 manholes and then stole the manhole covers. He made a profit of over $25,000 in that one night alone. BC Hydro lost $1 million to metal theft every year, and most of that went to Eduardo.

The other question that the residents of Cassidy never got to ask the gas station attendant was his motivation for such a criminal enterprise. For Eduardo was no ordinary thief. He was a methamphetamine addict, and methamphetamine was an expensive hobby, with local unscrupulous scrap metal buyers happy to act as knowing accomplices.

On the night in question, Eduardo broke into what remained of the historic Cassidy Inn.

Built in 1914 as a miner's bunkhouse for surveyors and engineers employed by coal baron Robert Dunsmuir, in later years it had become a biker bar. In between, a colorful proprietor named Napoleon Manca operated the building first as a small store and recreation centre and then, in 1925, after receiving a beer parlour license, as his new Cassidy Hotel. Napoleon bought a unique old player piano. Assembled in Brussels in 1890 by a popular Italian piano maker, the seven-foot-long 1500-pound instrument travelled by ship, train and finally dogsled to its first wealthy owner in Dawson City in 1898, during the height of the Klondike gold rush. It was adorned with a lovely painting of a buxom woman, typical of period pictures that used to hang above saloon bars. To operate the piano, one would put a copper into the coin slot, choose one of ten tunes, and then crank its large handle for the music to begin.

The music stopped for Napoleon Manca when he had to sell the hotel to Mr. Hodge in 1947, for Mr. Hodge in 1953 when he had to sell the hotel to Mr. Osborne, for Mr. Osborne in 1983 when he had to sell the hotel to Mr. Kelly, and for Mr. Kelly in 1990, when he had to sell the hotel to Mr. Charlton, who cultivated a milieu of music, moonshine, and motorcycles.

On any given day, hundreds of chrome choppers from the local Hell's Angels chapter and beyond gathered their gleaming bodies in front of the Cassidy Inn, in a dazzling shimmer of molten reflections that blinded passing motorists. The trajectory of the tavern hit its apogee as a set location for the famous Alaskan loggers' bar scene in the Superman movie *Man of Steel*, where Clark Kent worked as an employee when a patron spilled a beer over his head.

The Cassidy pub spilled downhill from there. New provincial smoking bylaws coupled with harsh drinking and driving legislation led to its closing. The old premises sat neglected for the next few years. Within the boarded-up doors and windows, squatters sought shelter and committed acts of vandalism. Because of safety concerns, the regional district issued a demolition order, which was where Eduardo Cazar re-entered the story.

On the night after the building was condemned, Eduardo brought his tools to the taproom termination, to harvest the thick copper wires that had powered its hundred-year existence. *Can you dance with the devil in the pale moonlight?*

But Eduardo Cazar didn't feel so good, afflicted as he was by the same kind of severe headache and double vision that had landed him in the hospital that many years earlier. Maybe that's why he didn't smell the propane that thieves had released into the air by stripping other copper lines earlier that day. Maybe that's why, in his methamphetamine haze, he didn't realize that the pub's connecting electrical main was still hot, when he drew his hacksaw across the live busbar wires.

Sometimes the goalposts are landmines. All they found in the ashes were his heel bones.

'Drunk on the wind in my mouth,
Wringing the handlebar for speed,
Wild to be wreckage forever.'
James Dickey, *Cherrylog Road*

Ten years before Eduardo Cazar was consumed by his copper conflagration, another young man in Seattle prepared to make his way to the scene of the future crime. Maxie Road was a full-patch member of the Washington Nomads, the state chapter of the infamous Hell's Angels outlaw motorcycle gang. He had been recruited from the ranks of the Sons of Hell breeding ground, up the ladder rungs of 'hang-around' to 'associate' to 'prospect', when he had to visit each charter club in Washington state and introduce himself to every voting hog-rider for their approval. Every potential candidate must own a valid driver's license, a motorcycle over 750 ccs, and have the right combination of personal qualities. Maxie's badass reputation preceded his canvassing campaign. The other full patches already knew that he had once stapled a rival Bandido member's member to a bar, set it on fire, then handed the man a knife.

"You decide." Maxie had said. His formal induction to the club at the 2-Bit Saloon 'church meeting' in Ballard was a unanimous slam dunk. Everyone enjoyed the live music and oil wrestling. In a nation of frightened dullards, there was a sorry shortage of outlaws, and those few who make the grade were always welcome.

Maxie was resplendent in his black leather vest, complete with the fourpiece insignia of his tribe—the 'Death's Head' logo, red and white 'Hells Angels' top rocker, 'Washington' bottom rocker, and the rectangular 'MC' patch below the wing of the Death's Head. There were other patches. The numbers 8 and 1 stood for the respective positions in the alphabet of H and A. The diamond-shaped 'One Percenter' patch was a response to the American Motorcyclist Association comment on the Altamont festival stabbing of 18-year-old Meredith Hunter by a Hells Angel acting as stage security for the free Rolling Stones concert, to the effect that 99% of motorcyclists were law-abiding citizens and the last 1% were outlaws. Maxie also had a title patch which read 'Sergeant at Arms,' and an 'AFFA' patch which meant 'Angels Forever; Forever Angels.' But it was the last two badges which distinguished him from lesser members of his tribe. Here was a strange and terrible saga. The 'Dequiallo' patch signified that the wearer had fought law enforcement on arrest, and the two Nazi-style SS lightning bolts below the words 'Filthy Few' was only awarded to those who had committed or were prepared to murder on behalf of the club. There was a beautiful consistency about Maxie; he was a porcupine among men, with his quills always flared.

The symbols of power and mystique didn't end at his epidermis. Maxie Road's adornment continued below the skin surface. His chest, back, and arms swirled with black and blue body art, fresh from the probing needles of 'Cash' Arnone, a Puyallup tattoo artist. His surname arched over his belly in gothic ink. 'Hell 666 Bound' stretched over his lower back, below the subdermal ink of another Death's Head insignia. His arms and legs and the rest of him danced with the devil in the broad daylight. *H.A... HAMC... Red & White... Route 81... One Percenter... When we do right, nobody remembers. When we do wrong, nobody forgets... The Wild One... Sons of Anarchy... The Wild Angels... Hard as They Come... Sons of Hell...*

Except that Maxie's tattoos weren't his anymore. Something evil had spawned beneath them, pushing them painful and swollen and bulging and inflamed, above the normal surface of his hide. *H.A.... HAMC... Red & White... Route 81... One Percenter... When we do right, nobody remembers. When we do wrong, nobody forgets... The Wild One... Sons of Anarchy... The Wild Angels... Hard as They Come... Sons of Hell...*

There were other things wrong. The light hurt his eyes and his focus fluctuated in and out of bitter blurriness. He was more and more short of breath. Maxie knew he needed to do something, but he wasn't sure what that was. He didn't have medical insurance and couldn't afford to pay what it would cost to get this shit fixed in Washington state. Until he read the article in the Seattle Examiner, he didn't have any options at all.

"The Hells Angels in British Columbia are some of the richest Hells Angels in the world." Said RCMP Inspector Gary Shinkaruk, supervisor of the Outlaw Motorcycle Gang Unit. "The Hells Angels in Washington aren't viewed as that high in the pecking order. They're nothing more than a group of guys who get together to eat an occasional steak and ride motorcycles."

Which is how Maxie Road decided to meet up with his mates on Vancouver Island. He was sure when they saw his patches, and his tattoos, they would help him find some local clinical expertise. And besides, he reasoned, medical care in BC was free. What better road trip could there ever be? If you wait, all that happens is that you get older. Or maybe not. Young riders pick a destination and go. Old riders pick a direction and go. Maxie would go north.

The best alarm clock in the world is sunshine on chrome. On one glorious autumn morning, Maxie Road donned his leather and wheeled his bike out backwards from 'Smilin' Rick' Fabel's garage, to find fifteen Nomad comrades-in-arms assembled in hog formation to escort him to the berth of the Blackball Ferry, headed for Vancouver Island from Seattle.

Smilin' Rick started his engine, and so did 'Frisco' Pete, 'Sweet William' Fritsch, Chocolate George, Sonny 'Buzzard' Barger, Shagrat the Vagrant, Leonard 'Funny Sunny' Sellig, Terry the Tramp, 'Mother Miles' Magoo, Filthy Phil, Charger Charley the Child Molester, Zorro, Lenny 'The Pimp' Janowitz, and Crazy Cross, hard-edged and tense for action. They had the sound of fury in their bones.

All his life, Maxie's heart had sought a thing he could not name. Today it was beside and under him. Beside him were a band of brothers on the only two-wheeled machines on the planet that embodied freedom, independence, rebellion, strength, and masculinity.

Under him was a 1999 Harley Davidson FXR2, one of only 900 special limited-edition CVO bikes with a rubber link and tri-mounted custom 1,340 cc air-cooled Evolution Evo 45-degree Big V-twin aluminum engine manufactured to displace a single, four-lobed, gear-driven camshaft located above the crankshaft axis. The shape of the rocker boxes had nicknamed it the Blockhead, following in the tradition of other ancestral Harley motors—Flatheads and Panheads and Knuckleheads and Shovelheads. Maxie's bike had a Badlander seat, a unique wiring harness, dual fire ignition system, vacuum-operated fuel valve, nine-plate clutch and five-hole derby cover, 'Profile' X shocks, 21-inch spoked front wheel, chromium slotted rear wheel, and just about every other piece of chrome in the catalog. Two messages had been hand-painted on Maxie's rear views. *Warning: objects seen in mirror are disappearing rapidly... Keep thy eye on the tach, thine ears on the engine, least thy whirlybits seek communion with the sun.* Maxie sat tall and pressed the starter. The plug firing sequence of the 45° design of the engine fired the first cylinder, the second rear cylinder 315° later then, after a 405° gap, the first cylinder fired again. *Potato- potato- potato- potato- potato- potato- potato- potato- potato- potato- potato...*

The throaty choppy growling exhaust of sixteen other Touring and Softail and Dyna Harleys roared into a deafening din of desperado derision. Four wheels move the body. Two wheels move the soul. Sixteen souls moved as one organism onto and up the I-5, throttles wide-open way beyond the speed limits, knees skimming black asphalt as they took over the curves. The twisties, not the superslabs, separated the riders from the squids. Two-lane blacktop wasn't a highway—it was an attitude. And the ride was a ritual.

Maxie's FXR2 was also equipped with an integrated blue-tooth-enabled 1000-watt Boss Audio MCBK470B weatherproof 2-channel amp sound system. The thumb control could direct the output to his headset or the handlebar-mounted 3-inch chrome speakers. Today, he chose the speakers and cranked them to 140 decibels.

Get your motor runnin'... Head out on the highway... Lookin' for adventure... And whatever comes our way...

Only a biker knows why a dog sticks his head out of a car window, and how catching a hornet in your vest at seventy miles per hour can double your vocabulary.

I like smoke and lightning... Heavy metal thunder... Racin' with the wind... And the feelin' that I'm under...

Long hair in the wind, beards, and bandanas flapping, earrings and chain whips and swastikas and stripped-down choppers flashed their chrome past the nervous traffic giving way to let the formation pass like a burst of dirty thunder.

Yeah Darlin' go make it happen... Take the world in a love embrace... Fire all of your guns at once... And explode into space...

The highway was jammed with people who drove as if their sole purpose behind the wheel was to avenge every wrong done them by man, beast or fate. The only thing that kept them in line was their fear of death and jail and lawsuits. And that was why they moved over for the Angels. The rules of the road were different for road hogs. Life was too short for traffic. They never traded the thrills of living for the security of existence.

Like a true nature's child... We were born, born to be wild... We can climb so high... I never wanna die...
Born to be wild... Born to be wild...

They left him at the mouth of the Blackball Ferry, with man-hugs and salutes and snarls of feigned indifference to his fate, one they knew they would all share someday. *As you were, I was. As I am, you will be.*

Maxie rolled his hog onto the boat. *Potato- potato- potato- potato- potato- potato- potato- potato- potato- potato- potato...* His speakers spoke Dylan.

Take me on a trip upon your magic swirling ship... My senses have been stripped... My hand can't feel to grip... I'm ready to go anywhere I'm ready for to fade... Into my own parade... It's not aimed at anyone... It's just escaping on the run...

By the end of the voyage, Maxie was convinced that the coffee concoction he had consumed on board was the same 50-weight black lubricant he later found under his Blockhead V-twin aluminum engine. Bikes don't usually leak oil, although it might mark their territory.

On the other side of the Strait of Juan de Fuca, Maxie passed through Canadian Customs with no real questions asked. He pulled into a PetroCanada station to add some oil and fill up with gas. Sometimes it took a whole tankful of fuel before he could think straight.

On the Island Highway an hour north of Victoria in the late Indian summer afternoon, Maxie found the first part of what he was looking for. Hundreds of chrome choppers from the local Hell's Angels chapter and beyond gathered their gleaming bodies in front of the Cassidy Pub, in such a dazzling shimmer of molten reflections that he was blinded by the light.

He backed his bike into the only remaining available spot and took a seat inside where he could see it. It didn't take long. Twelve full-patch bikers closed a circle around him.

"You Maxie?" Asked the biggest beard. The Nomad nodded.

"Mouldy Marvin." He threw down a pint of Dark Matter draft in front of him. "This is Maurice 'Frenchy' Boucher, Fat Freddy, Puff, Dirty Ed, Animal, Tiny, Chuck the Duck, Hambone, Little Jesus, Jonathan 'Thunder' Yates, and the Gimp. Smilin' Rick said you were coming."

"Did he say why?" Maxie asked. The Angels stared at his red raised tattoos.

"You missed a great party last night." Mouldy said. "One guy even died."

"Yeah, he told us." Hambone volunteered. "Although we didn't believe it until we could see it."

"You know anyone who can fix this?" Maxie asked.

"Guy named Sababa." Offered Chuck the Duck. "Knows his shit."

"How do I get to see him?" Maxie asked.

"We protect him. Up at the lake." Tiny said. "He owes us but he doesn't know it."

"Why is that?"

"We protect him."

"From what?'

"Himself." Said Little Jesus. "He looks after us too."

Sometimes it takes a whole tankful of fuel before you can think straight. Maxie was well into his Dark Matter and the new camaraderie when the sunshine came off the chrome caravan outside the Cassidy Pub.

"Time to go." Maxie announced.

"Where to?" Mouldy asked. "You can stay with us if you like." Sometimes the fastest way to get there is to stop for the night.

"I want to be closer to this guy so I can get to see him tomorrow." The Gimp had told Maxie about a campground at the lake near their clubhouse.

"Doc lives up there too." He said. Maxie wished them well.

"Sleep with one arm through the spokes and keep your pants on." Animal and Maxie high-fived as the Nomad pulled away. *Potato- potato- potato- potato- potato- potato- potato- potato- potato- potato- potato...*

"Man of Steel." Mouldy said. They watched his Harley headlight fly north on the Island Highway. His speakers spoke Arlo Guthrie. *'Cause I'd rather ride on my motorcycle... And I don't want to die... I just want to ride on my motorcy...cle...*

Maxie never hesitated to ride past the last streetlight at the edge of civilization. A dark cloud of forest floated above the mist at the roadside. He would rather be riding his motorcycle thinking about God than sitting in church thinking about his motorcycle. Maxie didn't know how close he would come to fusing with both in the blackness. That's why they call it the dead of night. Maxie wanted to leave this world the same way he came into it—screaming and covered in blood. He would almost get his wish. The trees pinned him against a metal sky so dark his tattoos burned. Night licked and sealed his wounded edges.

When Maxie put the lever into fourth, there was no sound except wind. He tightened it all the way over and reached through the handlebars to raise the headlight beam. The needle leaned down on a hundred, and his wind-burned eyeballs strained to see down the centerline, trying to provide some room for his reflexes.

But with the throttle screwed on, there was only the barest margin and no room at all for mistakes. It had to be done right. That's when the strange prickle started when he had stretched his luck so far that fear became exhilaration and vibrated along his arms. He could barely see at a hundred; the tears blew back so fast they vaporized before they got to his ears. The only sounds were wind and a dull roar floating back from the mufflers. He watched the white line and tried to lean with it, howling through a turn to the right, then to the left, and down the long hill towards Harbour City, letting off now, watching for cops, but only until the next dark stretch and another few seconds on the edge. The edge—there was no honest way to explain it because the only people who knew where it was were the ones who had gone over. The others—the living—were those who pushed their control as far as they felt they could handle it, and then pulled back, or slowed down, or did whatever they had to when it came time to choose between Now and Later. But the edge was still Out there. Or maybe it was In.

One flick of his handlebar thumb control switched the Boss audio output to his headset, and another to a local radio station.

This is BC Bud, sitting in for your usual Indian country evening host, Silas Seaweed, CNDN Coast Salish radio, 101.3 FM on your Home and Native Band...

Midnight bugs tasted best. Most motorcycle problems are caused by the nut that connects the handlebars to the saddle. Life may begin at thirty, but it doesn't get real interesting until about a hundred and fifty. Faster, faster, faster, until the thrill of speed overcomes the fear of death. Two hundred, no hands. Damn, that'd be cool... right up to the part where you die.

Silas hit a snag with his ol' lady, that bear in the beauty parlour... the ol' lady asked him what he was doin' with that biker chick... he told her he was helping her with a mechanical problem... but she never said she had trouble with her Harley. She said she blew an Injun... his ol 'lady looked at him with one eye bigger than the other before she beat his ass... if you point with your lips, you might be an NDN... and Silas had pointed his lips one time too many...

Never ride faster than your guardian angel can fly. When you look down the road, it seems to never end, but you better believe it does, and Maxie was on this road for the rest of his life.

Day and night cannot dwell together... the rain falls on the just and the unjust... no deluge can dampen your purpose... you know you are alive...

The only good view of a thunderstorm is in your rearview mirror but if you don't ride in the rain, you don't ride. Maxie saw the rain coming but he didn't see the deer.

A danger foreseen is half-avoided... our fast food has antlers... if you ever shot a deer inside your house... you might be an NDN...

There are those who have crashed and there is those that will crash.

To touch the earth is to have harmony with nature... life is not separate from death... it only looks that way...

The difference between survival and wipe-out in a physical crisis is nearly always a matter of conditioned reflexes. Life is not a journey whose purpose is to arrive at your gravesite in one well-preserved piece but to skid across the line broadside, used up, worn out, leaking oil, and screaming 'Ohhhhh Shiiiiit!' It's the moment when your plan parts ways with reality. Fire all of your guns at once... and explode into space...

There is no death, only a change of worlds...

'I've got you under my skin
I've got you deep in the heart of me
So deep in my heart, you're really a part of me
I've got you under my skin...
  Cole Porter, *I've Got You Under My Skin*

The day before Maxie Road came off his bike, ten years before Eduardo Cazar was consumed by his copper conflagration, Dr. Praj Bharmal paged his preceptor from the Harbour City Regional emergency department. The response on his call display came from the Death Star. "What?" Sababa asked.

"Dr. Ho wants us to see a patient with a weird rash."

"I'm kind of busy right now." Sababa said. "Can I ignore you some other time?"

"OK." Praj sat down at the consultant's desk. "What do you want me to do?"

"Give me half an hour." Sababa said. Ten minutes later, A mess of black curls bounced into the ER to find Praj and Gung Ho pouring over the patient's record.

"I thought you said half an hour." Praj handed him the chart.

"Sometimes your patients get better." Sababa said. "You may have no idea why, but unless you provide a reason they won't pay you. What you got?"

"Christina Pfeifer in Bed 3." Gung said. "28-year-old artist with a three-week history of fever, joint pains, and an unusual rash."

"Unusual how?" Sababa asked.

"Subcutaneous nodules, some of which have healed with depression of the overlying skin. It looks like something attacked the subdermal fatty layers of her tissues." Gung added. "Mostly lower legs but left arm as well."

"I think she has Weber–Christian disease." Praj said. "Relapsing Febrile Nodular Nonsuppurative Panniculitis."

"Do tell." Sababa said. "She been here before?"

"She says no." Gung said.

"When you want to know the truth about someone that someone is the last person you should ask. Did you check for an old chart?" Sababa's question met a baffle of blank stares and silence. "Cheri Sundae, does bed 3 have an old chart?" The ward clerk's fingers ran across her keyboard.

"Yes, Sab." Cheri said.

"You think you can fetch it for us?"

"What do I get?" Cheri asked.

"Box of Purdy's chocolates." Sababa said. "From Dr. Ho here." Praj smiled.

"And Dr. Bharmal." Praj's smile died on his face.

"What kind of artist is she?" Sababa's question met the second baffle of blank stares and silence.

"Let's go see her." Sababa pulled the curtain back from bed 3, to find a young woman with the exact rash his two colleagues had described.

"This is the Doctor Sababa I told you about, Christina." Praj made the introduction.

"Is he as smart as you said he was?"

"He can do both." Praj said. "Wise and otherwise." Sababa raised an eyebrow.

"What kind of artist are you, Christina?"

"I'm a painter." She said.

"Watercolour, latex, oil, or otherwise?" Sababa inspected her skin.

"I use oils." She said.

"Where?" Sababa asked.

"What?"

"No, where?"

"On my canvasses, of course." She said. "Where else would I use them?"

"Indeed, that is the question." Sababa said. "Are you right or left-handed, Christina?"

"Right-handed."

"Funny thing about rashes." He said. "They're usually always symmetrical. Unless."

"Unless what?"

"Unless they're not."

"I'm afraid I don't understand." She said. Cheri handed a chart through the bed 3 curtain. It was two inches thick. Sababa turned to the problem list summary of admissions.

"You told Drs. Ho and Bharmal that you had never been in hospital before." He said.

"It was a long time ago."

"Yes, it appears so." Sababa turned the pages. "But you've had several admissions, and there appears to be a recurring theme."

"Which is?" She asked.

"Most of these encounters were some form of self-harm or mutilation." He said. "Dr. Bharmal here thinks you have a form of panniculitis, a recurrent granulomatous inflammation of subcutaneous fatty tissue, and I agree with him."

"So, what's the problem?" Christina asked.

"He thinks you have something called Weber–Christian disease." Sababa said. "I think you have PseudoWeber–Christian disease."

"What's the difference?"

"Pseudo comes from the Greek." He said. "It means false, not genuine, spurious or sham, supposed or purporting to be but not so, resembling or imitating the real thing. And your Weber–Christian disease comes from your injecting your paint under your skin."

"What?" Christina was furious. "How dare you. I demand to see another doctor."

"And you will." Sababa said. "You've already seen three today, and I'll bet this one will agree with me when I tell you it is possible to inject paint under the skin of your left upper extremity if you're right-handed but near impossible to inject your dominant arm. This is also known as factitious disorder imposed on self, or Munchausen syndrome."

"Who's the other doctor?" Christina demanded.

"Cheri Sundae, can you page Dr. Robert La Capuche for me, please?"

"On it, Sab." Cheri raised her handpiece in the air, less than a minute later.

"Dr. La Capuche on line 3."

"Hey, Bob." Sababa said. "You know the two differences between a psychiatrist and a psych patient?"

"Oh, please." La Capuche moaned. "Make it go away."

"The psychiatrist has the keys." Sababa chortled. "And the patient will eventually get better and go home." The stocky savant relayed his information about Christina.

"Send her down to our unit." La Capuche said. "I know her well. Munchhausen syndrome. Get the other two docs to sign the commission forms."

"This is a world in which the nuts gather the squirrels." Sababa said.

When he told Christina of their decision about her disposition, she was less than appreciative.

"You'll feel right at home there." He said. "They have an arts and crafts room, and the paint is free."

"I'll make sure to complain about my treatment here." She fumed.

"You'll have to wait until your discharge, Christina." Sababa said. "Last time I checked, there was no suggestion box in the Psych Ward." Cheri raised her handpiece in the air, once again.

"Dr. Muldoon on line 2 for you, Sab." The portly professor picked up.

"Hey, Piggy." He began. "What is the orthopedic term for the heart?"

"Ancef pump?" The orthopod groaned.

"There is no orthopedic term for the heart." Sababa said. "What do you want?"

"I need you to see a patient here in the cast clinic."

"On my way." *Click.*

'The tender surgeon makes the wound gangrene.'
Italian Proverb

Sababa and his apprentice made their way down the hallway to the orthopedic outpatients. The cast clinic technician, Michael Eaglefeather slipped a ziplock of smoked salmon into the professor's Colombian leather bag. There was communion. Sababa turned to the knuckledragger.

"What you got, Piggy?" He asked.

"Lili Boulanger." Began the bonesetter. "17-year-old high school student with this necrotic ulcer of her left ankle for 3 months now. Seen by most of your cronies. Our plastics guy, Pretty Boy Troy, grafted it and made it worse."

"Pathergy." Sababa said.

"What's that?" Piggy asked.

"Worsening in response to minor trauma or surgical debridement."

She's in the next room with her parents." Piggy made introductions.

"This is Doctor Sababa, the specialist I told you about. Distraction is what you think he's doing when he's doing something else."

"You'd be the fourth one." Mr. Boulanger said.

"This is my resident, Dr. Bharmal." Sababa said. "May we have a look at your left ankle, Lili?" The young woman pulled up her pant leg to show them the predicament.

"Is it painful?" Praj asked.

"Exquisitely." She said.

"Well?" Piggy asked.

"The ankle bone is connected to the gutbone." Sababa said.

"There is no gutbone."

"That, my dear bonehead, would be a bone of contention."

"What do you mean?"

"This is not any old necrotic ulcer."

"What is it?" They all asked in unison.

"We call it pyoderma gangrenosum." Sababa said. "Horrible name. It's neither an infection nor gangrene. How long have you had diarrhea, Lili?"

"She doesn't have diarrhea." Her mother said.

"About three months or so." Lili admitted. "I didn't think much of it at first."

"What has that got to do with her ankle ulcer?" Demanded her father.

"Everything." Sababa said.

"What causes it?" Mrs. Boulanger asked.

"Immune-mediated neutrophil dysfunction."

"No, I mean what's brought it on."

"Many conditions are associated with pyoderma." Sababa said. "Various forms of arthritis, hematological diseases, autoinflammatory disorders like PAPA syndrome, and one other category."

"What's PAPA syndrome?" Asked Lili's papa.

"She doesn't have acne so it's not that."

"What's the one other category?" Asked his wife.

"The one that's causing this." Sababa said. "Inflammatory bowel disease. Crohn's to be precise."

"Why do you say that, Doctor Sababa?" Lili asked.

"Your clothes are loose so I assume you've lost weight. Your palm creases and conjunctivae are pale from some form of anemia. The white part of your right eye is inflamed, a condition we call episcleritis. And then there is the tobacco tinge on the two fingers of your dominant hand."

"Meaning what?" Lili asked.

"Found twice as often in smokers." Sababa said. "Ergo, Crohn's disease."

Lili's parents looked at Piggy Muldoon.

"Distraction is what you think he's doing when he's doing something else." He said.

"What now?" Mr. Boulanger asked.

"Now, we get Dr. Bharmal here to take a comprehensive history and perform a complete physical exam. He'll look up the histology results from the skin graft biopsy that we hope Pretty Boy Troy sent to pathology." Sababa said. "He will organize some more blood tests, imaging, a colonoscopy with our favorite surgeon Dr. Jules Martino and a referral to our faceless oculist guru, Dr. T.J. Eckleburg. Just don't ask him where he gets his music collection."

"Why not?"

"Lili, Dr. Bharmal will explain the rationale for and send you home with a prescription of 5-aminosalicylic acid and a tapering course of prednisone. He'll dictate a consultation letter to Dr. Muldoon here, with a copy to go to your family doctor. And he'll make an appointment with Mercy for us to see you again in a week at Manzanita Medical."

"Mercy?"

"She's my MOA."

"Moa?"

"Medical office assistant." Sababa said. "Also a large extinct flightless bird formerly found in New Zealand, but less likely to be of any more immediate service." His pager made enough noise for Sababa to answer it.

"Praj, you finish up here and meet me at one in the clinic. I'll see the new consult on the fifth floor."

'He who cheats the earth will be cheated by the earth.'
Chinese Proverb

The delight Samara Morgan felt at seeing the large blur bounce of the fifth-floor stairwell was written on her face. Sababa's Colombian leather briefcase barrel rolled over the nursing station and landed next to her. The fleeting image of her Valentino Garavani silk scarf flashing crimson disappeared when the professor imagined her without her pantsuit. He grabbed a chart off the rack at the nursing station and sat down to pour through it. Samara pulled her hundred-dollar clipboard against her ample chest.

"Have you forgotten all my rules about consultant behaviour?" She made a clicking sound with her tongue. "I always encourage visiting physicians to find a place other than the nursing station to write their reports." Samara pointed to a distant room.

"I'm not visiting, I'm working." Sababa said. "Last time I checked, your new job description was Care Coordinator. I guess it means you're not the head of anything now. What can you tell me about Roscoe Holcomb here?"

"64-year-old man referred down from Campbell River to Dr. Hyde for multiple lung masses." She said. "He's been here a week without anything much happening. Who asked you to see him?"

"Same doc in Campbell River who referred him a week ago." After Sababa had pulled up the patient's imaging studies on a nursing station monitor, he grabbed his Columbian leather bag and headed down the hallway.

"Mr. Holcomb?" The man who nodded looked older than his chronological age. "I'm Doctor Sababa. Dr. Dunsmuir has asked me for a second opinion."

"I've been here a week and haven't had the first one yet." Roscoe said.

"I guess that's why I'm here." Sababa said. "What are your concerns?"

"I've been coughing what's left of my lungs out for over a month now." He said. "I'm getting more and more short of breath, my hands hurt, and my joints are so stiff every morning, I can barely get out of bed. I feel so awful, I even quit smoking, even though everyone knows that smokers live faster. Dr. Hyde said I might have TB, but I haven't seen him for five days."

"Those in a hurry show only that the thing they are about is too big for them." Sababa said. "What kind of work did you do?"

"I was a security guard for the timber mill in town." Roscoe said.

"Did you ever work in the Quinsam anthracite coal mine up there?"

"For about ten years." He said. "But that was thirty years ago. I still remember the cold dirty air. Every day, the suffocating darkness swallowed me so far into those black tunnels, I thought I'd vanish into the dust. My eyes stung and my lungs burned, my muscles ached, and when I left that foul hell hole at the end of my shifts, I didn't recognize myself. I wouldn't taste anything but coal for weeks. So, I quit." Sababa presented Roscoe with questions no one else had asked, and then did a thorough physical examination.

"The joints of your hands are swollen and tender." He said. "You have a positive rheumatoid factor as well as some other antibodies in your serum."

"I have rheumatoid arthritis?"

"At least." Sababa said.

"Is that the cause of my breathing problem?" Roscoe asked.

"Rheumatoid arthritis is associated with various forms of lung disease, but yours is a special case."

"What do you mean?" Roscoe asked.

"Your chest x-ray shows round nodules at the lung periphery, some of which have formed cavities, which is likely why Dr. Hyde mentioned the possibility of TB."

"I don't have TB?"

"No." Sababa said. "You have something called rheumatoid pneumoconiosis, or Caplan's Syndrome, named after Dr. Anthony Caplan, the Welsh physician who first described it in 1953. It consists of rheumatoid nodules and lung fibrosis in coal miners as well as those exposed to other mining dust, like silica and asbestos."

"But I haven't been down a coal mine for thirty years." Roscoe protested.

"No, you haven't." Sababa said. "But Mother Nature doesn't care. She has full recollection of your previous existence, something we refer to as occupational anamnesis."

"What now?" Roscoe asked.

"Now I arrange for you to have a CT-guided thoracic punch biopsy of one of your lung nodules, a set of lung function tests, and a Mantoux to make sure you don't have TB." He said. "I'll start you on a tapering course of corticosteroids and Dr. Dunsmuir can switch them out to a DMARD for your rheumatoid arthritis. You should be able to go home tomorrow."

"Thanks, Doc." He said. "Thought I was a goner."

"Death smiles at us all, Roscoe." Sababa turned as he left. "All any man can do is smile back."

'Comparatively, tattooing is not the hideous custom which it is called.
It is not barbarous merely because the printing is skin-deep and unalterable.'
Henry David Thoreau, *Walden*

"It's congranulation week, Boss." Mercy never looked up from her typing.

"Surely goodness and Mercy shall follow me all the days of my life." Sababa handed Praj the chart off the top of the pile. "You take the first patient while I finish some paperwork." The young resident called out into the waiting room.

"Lisa Monroe?" A thin dark young woman with transdermal metal and subdermal ink, and hair all colours of the rainbow, rose from a chair in the furthest corner and followed him down the hallway.

In his sanctum sanctorum, Sababa waited for Mercy to bring him the first of two mugs of coffee he would enjoy that afternoon. No milk, it was black coffee, pure but strong, that fortified against the powers of darkness which filled the world. Sababa knew that the powers of his mind expanded in direct proportion to the strength volume product of java he consumed, a pure area-under-the-curve quantitation. No work was possible without it. Indeed, there were some problems only black magic could fix. He drank to all the people who remained unharmed because he had a French press and a sense of humour; coffee to help him change the things he could... and wine to help him accept the things he couldn't. Thus fortified, Sababa dictated his way through a mountain of ECGs, Holter monitors, trans-telephonic event recorders, and ambulatory and doppler BP results. He moved on to the pile of patient results Mercy had collated for his perusal. *High calcium based on elk-alkali syndrome... Stool received in boiling water—unsuitable for microscopy or culture. Please resubmit with clinical data... Stress Test: ST segments dipped below one meter at four and a half minutes. Ischemia would head the list of ideological possibilities... Persantine Mibi: small areas of infection in the mid-portion of the anterior wall... Presenting Complaint: Vomited Thursday night after eating 'bad chicken' and diarrhea...*

Next was a stack of solicitations from alternative universes: naturopathy (*I only wish to get referrals from patients who have now become well...*), government-sponsored Therapeutics Initiative panels (*The generic is cheaper but for real savings, go for the placebo...*), addiction practitioners (*Contract in place not to use cocaine but will inevitably use heroin while an inpatient... Need cash for alcohol research...*), and Big Pharma (*Depressed? Overworked? Job Suck? Family Problems? Money Worries? Well Here is a pill for you. Fukitol 1000 g...*).

Sababa sent an email to Jane with the results of his own coronary CTA and Shiva's stool findings. *Good news. Your husband has normal coronary arteries. Bad news: Your dog has worms.*

He looked up to find Praj hovering in his doorway.

"Lisa Monroe." He began even without prompting. "A referral from Dr. Poldy Bloom. 30-year old motorcycle club member with a two-month history of headache, intermittent high fevers, weakness, joint pains, oral ulcers, a red rash of her face and upper chest, hemorrhagic crusting on her lips and firm, tender enlarged lymph nodes in the back of her neck. I think she has lupus."

"It's never lupus." Sababa said. "Let's go see."

The first thing Sababa saw was Lisa's tattoo. *I am good but I'm not an angel. I do sin but I am not the devil. I am just a small girl in a big world.*

"This is Doctor Sababa, Lisa." Praj made the introduction. "He's from the Old Testament."

"Myth to legend to history." Sababa said. "In imaginary time." The young woman permitted the professor to repeat Praj's examination.

"Lupus?" She asked.

"It's never lupus." Sababa turned to Praj.

"Lab?"

"Anemia, low platelets, and a mild elevation of her white blood cell count." Praj said. "Mantoux, Widal, hepatitis B surface antigen, hepatitis C, HIV, VDRL, rheumatoid factor, and chest X-ray were normal. Blood and urine cultures were negative."

"How about the antinuclear and anti-double-stranded DNA antibodies for lupus?" Sababa asked.

"Negative." Praj said. "But she could have seronegative lupus."

"She could have a T-cell non-Hodgkins lymphoma, but she doesn't."

"So what is it?" Lisa asked. "My boyfriend says I have AIDS."

"You don't have AIDS. Some have called this histiocytic necrotizing lymphadenitis or phagocytic necrotizing lymphadenitis or subacute necrotizing lymphadenitis or necrotizing lymphadenitis." Sababa said.

"But most of the rest of us know it as Kikuchi-Fujimoto disease, after the two Japanese physicians that first described it in 1972."

"How do you know for sure?" She asked. Sababa pressed the intercom button.

"Yes, Boss."

"Mercy, see if you can raise Ted Billroth for me, will you?" He said. "Please and thank you."

"On it." She said. It didn't take long.

"What can I do for you?" Asked the ENT surgeon.

"I need an excisional lymph node biopsy, Ted."

"Tomorrow at 10:30 a.m. in my office." He said. "What are you looking for?"

"Kikuchi-Fujimoto disease."

"Whatever the hell that is." Billroth said. "Why can't you ever send me something normal?"

"If it was normal, I wouldn't need to send it to you." Sababa answered. "I'll get Mercy to put in a referral." *Click.*

"What then?" Lisa asked.

"Then we treat you with low-dose oral prednisone for ten days, after which you will get better." He wrote out a prescription.

"Will it come back?"

"In three percent of cases." Sababa said. "So not usually."

"What causes it?"

"We have theories we don't completely understand." He said. "But we don't know. Tell Mercy I'll see you again in three weeks." When Lisa had gone, Sababa reminded Praj about a referral request he had received from Dr. Capitaine in the hospital emergency department. And then read his body language.

"What's the matter, Mowgli?"

"Did you ever have any doubts about your progress as a physician?" Praj asked.

"We should talk about the stages you will pass through." Sababa said. "Friend of mine, Doug Farrago, came up with several sequences. Here's the first, if you like. *I want to help people... I want to make it through this hell... I want to make it through this hell without killing someone... I may have killed someone... I want someone to help me...*

"And where did you end up with that?" Praj asked.

"Back at the beginning." Sababa said. *I want to help people...* "But I'd never admit it."

"Why not?"

"It's the kind of admission that would have disqualified you during any medical school interview." He said. "The interviewer would have told you to go away and become a priest."

"So why is that?"

"Dunno." Sababa said. "Guess they prefer selfish megalomaniacs. If you can fake sincerity, you can fake anything. Sometimes I feel like an incurable anachronism, trying to do good anyway in a world that despises truth-tellers. But at the end of every day, there is only one important question that demands an answer." *Can you dance with the devil in the pale moonlight?*

'Great God! hast Thou given men Thine own image
that it should be thus cruelly defaced by the hands of their brethren!'
Walter Scott, *Ivanhoe*

Behind the automatic sliding frosted glass doors of the wide emergency entrance, Sababa passed a procession of paramedics loitering beside a line of full gurneys. They awaited Dina's green light to enter, as she prioritized and multitasked the multitude. Dirty street blood contaminated the floor of the gateway to the gods. Fresh streams of tears made sad phone calls on the hallway phones.
"Please rate your pain from zero to ten." She asked one candidate. "Zero being no pain, ten being me force-feeding you live bullet ants and tearing off your arms or being on fire."
"Twelve." Said the too calm contender.
"You called 911 figuring we would see you faster." She said. "Follow the black line to the wonderful world of triage."
"Looks like the circus is in town." Sababa said in passing.
"Some asshole who couldn't spell coincidence used the Q word." *Quiet.*
Sababa had sent Praj ahead to see Dr. Capitaine's patient. Everybody was happy to see each other.
"How are you, Myles?" Sababa asked.
"Living the dream."
"Dream as if you'll live forever." Sababa said. "Live as if you'll die today."
"James Dean." Myles noted.
"The same." Said the stocky savant. "What you got?"
"Eduardo Cazar." Praj began. "28-year-old BC Hydro lineman with a week-long history of right-sided headache. Saw his family doctor four days ago who diagnosed him with sinusitis and sent him home on antibiotics."
"And?"
"The pain got worse." Myles said. "Two days ago, he came in here with double vision and a droopy eyelid on the right. Trace thought he had a cluster headache and sent him home with some pain medication."

96

"Today he visited an optometrist who referred him to an ophthalmologist, our faceless oculist guru, Dr. T.J. Eckleburg." Praj said. "T.J. organized an urgent MRI scan. And now he's here."

"Because no matter where you go... there you are." Sababa said. "Exam?"

"Right eye almost completely closed." Praj said. "Adduction of the right eye past midline 25% of normal, and upward gaze 70% of normal. The rest of his neurological exam was normal."

"And the orbital MRI?" Sababa asked. Myles brought up the images on the consultant desk monitor.

"Hmmmm." Sababa mused. "Focal asymmetric enhancement along the lateral wall of the right cavernous sinus posterior to the orbital apex where the right oculomotor nerve should be."

"We did a lumbar puncture to rule out an infection." Praj said.

"And?"

"No infection." He said. "Although some results are still pending— Lyme, herpes simplex, aspergillus, coccidioides, West Nile, syphilis, cryptococcus, histoplasma and blastomyces."

"So what you got?" Sababa asked.

"Painful ophthalmoplegia. Some kind of sterile inflammation behind the right eye." Praj said. "Involving the cavernous sinus and superior orbital fissure. Perhaps a migraine or a craniopharyngioma or a meningioma."

"You think so?" Sababa asked.

"Perhaps." Praj admitted. "I have no idea. Should we go see him?"

"Excellent idea." Sababa said. Behind curtain 6, Myles presented the professor.

"This is Doctor Sababa, Eduardo." He said. "He believes there's nothing in this universe that can't be explained."

"Nothing?"

"Eventually." Sababa said.

"Can you explain what's wrong with me?" Eduardo asked. "My right eye feels like it's going to blow out of my head."

"You have a rare condition called Tolosa-Hunt syndrome." Sababa said. "Named after the two men who first described it in 1954. It's what we refer to as a granulomatous inflammatory condition."

"What causes it?"

"We don't know." Sababa said. "But we can treat it. You should be home in four days."

"How's that?"

"Dr. Bharmal here will admit you to hospital, order additional investigations including referral to our local neurologist, Dr. Oliver Lax, and start you on a three-day course of intravenous methylprednisolone."

"Does it ever come back?"

"You bet." Sababa said. "About 40% of the time. Sometimes years after the first episode."

"Sweet." Eduardo said. "Maybe I should think about a change of career."

"Maybe." Sababa said. "Double vision and climbing power poles are less than compatible situations. But it may not ever happen again."

"I'll take my chances on the ground." Eduardo observed. Sababa shook the man's hand and took his resident aside.

"I have a special general medical staff meeting in about an hour." He said. "Once you finish up here, you're more than welcome to attend, if you're interested. Our new health region managementship has decided to incorporate midwifery into Harbour City Regional's already fragile scientific professional community. The obstetricians are apoplectic. We should go and lend some moral support."

"I'll be there." Praj said. "I would also like to hear more about Farrago's progressive stages of physician evolution."

"Here's the second." Sababa said *"I want to make money... I want to spend money... I want to save money... Where the hell is my money... I need to make money..."*

"And where did you end up with that?" Praj asked.

"I was always somewhere else." Sababa said. *If I do it for the love of solving the problem, the money follows..."*

"That's it?"

"Do not sleep under a roof. Carry no money or food. Go alone to places frightening to the common brand of men."

"Who said that?"

"Miyamoto Musashi."

"Who's he?"

"A 17th-century masterless samurai, philosopher, strategist, and writer considered the Kensei sword-saint of Japan." Sababa said. "Renowned for his unique double-bladed fighting and undefeated record in 61 duels. He wrote *The Book of Five Rings*."

"And was he right about money?"

"Not completely." Sababa said.

"Why not?" Praj asked.

"Because although money can't buy happiness, it can buy good wine."

'The labor we delight in physics pain.'
William Shakespeare, *Macbeth*

There was, as Sababa had foretold, a special general medical staff meeting that evening. It's specific purpose, as the stocky savant had also learned, was for the latest health region managementship to legitimize the medieval craft of midwifery, i.e. the practice of assisting women in childbirth, as a new professional cadre with equal rights and privileges and earning power within the body politic of designated specialists.

The hospital switchboard operator's Big Voice broadcast the assembly overhead, and a hundred accredited physicians congregated into the too-small basement room booked for the occasion. It wasn't the fault of the new version of the health region managementship that doctors were always relegated to the dungeon of the facility. Ever since Sababa and his colleagues had chased the old hospital administration out of their first-floor lair and away to external offices in downtown Harbour City, they had schemed to administer those responsible into the ground. When Sababa and his colleagues chased the next health region administrative incarnation completely out of the city and down to Victoria, the survivors exacted their revenge by dropping the doctor's lounge into a sterile windowless room in the hospital basement and ensured that all their meetings and hopes would forever remain equally subterranean.

The Chief of Staff, the most prepotent master of control, a diminutive general practitioner named Dr. Petronilla de Meath, a Napoleanna bone apart, a harpy hag of a harridan henpecking harassment, made several attempts to call the meeting to order before the noisy hubbub settled into a chaotic commotion.

"Who's the chairperson?" Praj asked.

"Our Chief of Staff." Sababa said. "She's a doctor."

"Oh? Which kind?"

"Witch."

"Which which?"

"Which what?"

"Which doctor?"

"Right." Sababa said.

"Order! Order, please." Petronilla shouted. There came a semblance of lesser disarray among reluctant mutterings. "It is my distinct pleasure to welcome Foster Inclusion, the chief executive officer of our new regional health authority, Island Health." Instead of applause, a faint voice began to sing at the back of the crowded room. *Down the way where the nights are gay and the sun shines daily on the mountain top...*

Petronilla glared. A tanned muscular older man with a full crop of wavy white hair above a wide grin full of perfect white teeth took the podium, behind who sat several management minions from the Underworld.

"Thank you for that glowing introduction, Petronilla." Foster said. "The purpose of our meeting tonight is to welcome to the medical staff a professional cohort of local experts who have long been the victim of discrimination from their more certificated colleagues."

"Objection!" Cried Dr. Olaf Octagon. "Our obstetrical department members have never shown any intolerance towards the more proficient practitioners of midwifery in Harbour City. We have simply advocated

99

for rigorous performance standards and accreditation so we are not called at the eleventh hour to some disaster that could have been anticipated if the midwife had possessed a higher level of proficiency."

"Sit down, Dr. Octagon!" Petronilla insisted. "Mr. Inclusion is here to announce a new era of equal participation and payment in the improved obstetrical milieu we have evolved into. This will happen regardless of whether or not you and your colleagues oppose it."

"Thank you, Petronilla." Foster smiled a smarmy smile. "The moon is not shamed by the barking of dogs. This is all about client satisfaction. Our executive committees have worked long and hard to loosen the grip of elitist professional guilds. Progress demands we move to welcome our alternative colleagues into and under a bigger tent."

"You'll just have a bigger circus." Olaf said. Foster Inclusion went on until he didn't. Sababa had tuned him to the same level of intelligibility his dog heard from him. Blah...blah...blah... blah... blah...

When he finally called for questions, Petronilla saw a hand rise at the back of the throng. She acknowledged the owner's desire to speak before she identified the source.

"Yes, Doctor Sababa." She sighed. "I'm sure this will be relevant."

"And precise." He said. "Do you know the apocryphal story of Mao Tse-tung and Chou En-lai and Deng Xiaoping?"

"I'm sure I don't." She said.

"I'm sure you don't either." Sababa said. "But here we go. Mao had called his two colleagues together to discuss a theoretical issue of concern. 'Do either of you know how to get a cat to bite down on a hot pepper?' He asked."

"Is this pertinent, Doctor Sababa?" Petronilla's neck hairs stood on end.

"Pertinent, your high and mightiness." He said. "Chou En-lai answered first. 'Of course, Mao.' He said. 'Well I would hold the cat's body down under a towel with one hand.' Chou said. 'And push the hot pepper into its mouth with the other, and the cat will bite down on the pepper.' 'But that would be coercion, Chou, and we would never want to give the impression of being willing to use force.'"

"Doctor Sababa!" Petronilla wasn't quite sure what she was railing at but she believed it was for a good cause.

"Bear with me, your excellency." Sababa continued. "'What about you, Deng?' Mao asked. 'I would roll the hot pepper inside a sweet fish filet, present it to the cat, and the cat will bite down on the pepper.' 'But that would be subterfuge, Deng.' Mao said. 'We can never be accused of using deceit to further our aims.'"

"Sababa!" Petronilla was at her wit's end.

"Wait for it, your majesty." He said. "'We're sorry, Mao.' They said. 'We don't know then. What is the best way to get a cat to bite down on a hot pepper?' 'Neither of you was even close to the right answer.' Mao said.

'The trick is to only jam the hot pepper halfway up the cat's ass. The cat will bite down on the pepper.'"

"And what does that have to do with our situation here, Doctor Sababa?" She asked. The resultant cheers and whistles from the medical audience answered the question.

"May I ask a further question?" Sababa asked.

"If it's brief."

"So, if olive oil is made from olives, what is baby oil made from?"

"Sit down, Doctor Sababa." Petronilla said. Praj looked like he had seen a rare white spirit bear.

"What's the next series in Farrago's progressive stages of physician evolution?" He whispered.

"The third." Sababa said. "*I don't know anything... There is too much to know... I will never know all of this... I don't need to know all of this... I only need to know a little... I don't care if I know anything...*"

"And where did you end up with that?" Praj asked.

"I made peace with it." Sababa said. *If I have perfected what I need to know to do in an emergency, I will still have time to look up what I need for any other circumstances...*"

"And now I am no longer young enough to know everything." He grinned a ghoulish grin. "Even though I still remember when I did."

Morning had broken. That's how the light got in.

Sababa and Praj arrived on the bridge of the Death Star in time to watch a cavalcade of mortals and machines wheeling in a new entrant in the game of life.

Harbour City Regional's Head of Anesthesia, Dr. Banjo Paterson, led the cortège, managing the patient's airway and playing the ventilator he pushed like Napoleon Manca's piano. The suction tubing and circuit leaks screamed like a whirlpool at sea.

A nurse from post-anesthetic recovery and another from the ICU flanked the stretcher, steering IV poles and CADD pumps and cardiac and hemodynamic monitors, dinging and buzzing and beeping and alarming in syncopated hair-raising dissonant chords. The caravan was accompanied by loud voices, footfalls, cartwheel squeaks, and cell phone cacophony.

The tail of the transport train was brought up by Dr. Piggy Muldoon, the orthopedic surgeon who had done most of the grunt work, and Dr. Commodus Sitsofsky, the staff dermatologist. It could have been a funeral procession if there had been less electrical power in play.

"It's rare you see a consultation from ortho and derm on the same patient, on the same day." Sababa said.

"This is a special one, Sab." The orthopod said. "I've asked Commodus to see him because of these." Piggy pointed to the patient's tattoos. They were an angry red and raised bas-relief induration embossed above the rest of his skin.

"It's a wonder you can even see them, given the extent of his road rash." Sababa said.

"Look at this one, for example." *TCB*. Sitsofsky traced the outline. *TCB*. "I wonder what that means." Sababa studied others as the convoy changed lines and tubing and resettled onto their landing strip in cubicle 5.

"It means 'taking care of business.' He said. "You have more than your average pigment puncture patient here, gentlemen. This guy is a full-patch Hells Angel. From south of the border, by the looks of his other decorations. How did he get here?"

"Hit a deer with his Harley." Piggy said. "North of the Cassidy Inn, the pub where they filmed 'Man of Steel.' Must have thought he was one as well." Everyone stared at all the stainless external fixation rods and plates and screws that Piggy had tinker toyed his limbs with.

"Looks like he is." Sababa said. "We need to debrief you mongrels while Charmeine saves his life. Call it Sababa's Hierarchy of Needs." Praj and the professor stepped onto the bridge and into the consultant's corner, where Sababa selected a tune from his music library on a secret drive hidden deep inside the hospital computer network.

'Nothing to do, nowhere to go,
I wanna be sedated.'
The Ramones, *I Wanna Be Sedated*

"You first, Banjo." He said. "Who is this guy?"

"Maxie Road." The anesthetist began. "34-year-old biker from Seattle. Came off his Harley just after midnight. Collided with a big stag. The buck stops here, so to speak."

"When did you first see him?"

"I was in the ER when they brought him into Resusc." Banjo said. "The boys were enthusiastic in their religious revival." Sababa had Maxie's imaging on the monitor screen.

"Looks like it." Sababa said. "The correct depth of compression in adult CPR is less than the depth they reached when they broke those ribs."

"They didn't break all of them." Piggy had pulled up a chair from Maxie's cubicle. "In addition to his raging second-degree road rash, he sustained three stable mid-thoracic vertebral fractures, a broken right femur and shinbone and forearm, and a closed head injury. He was lucky he didn't crack his skull or smash his pelvis. To succeed in life, you need a backbone and a funny bone and a wishbone. Steve MacQueen here broke two of them."

"What anesthetics did you use, Banjo?" Sababa asked.

"Nothing but the best, Sab." He said. "None of that local crap, only the imported stuff."

"Which ones?"

"5 mg of STFU-in-a-Bottle Succinylcholine, an infusion of Laughter-is-Not-the-Best-Medicine Propafol, and another of Kick-Me-Again-Asshole Rocuronium."

"Charlie Mayo used to say that the choice of an anesthetic was more often determined by the idiosyncrasy of the operator than the necessity of the case." Sababa said.

"Who's he?"

"Guy from a small town in Minnesota." Sababa said. "They named a clinic after him."

"Whatever." Banjo said. "Look, you may want to lower his oxygen until he turns blue, and then crank it back up enough so he doesn't."

"You're kidding, right?"

"Hell no." The gasman said. "Purple is not a good colour."

"These are my toys, Banjo." Sababa said. "And you can't play with them anymore."

"Hey, I saved this guy."

"Ah yes, the ABCD of anesthesia-led resuscitation." Sababa mused. "Arrive... Blame... Criticise... Depart."

"Know why Hells Angels wear leather?" Banjo asked.

"No." Sababa said.

"Because chiffon wrinkles. See ya." Banjo turned to leave. "Good luck." Sababa turned to the orthopod.

"What did you do, Piggy?"

"You can see for yourself." The orthopod said. "The motorcycle pinned him, fracturing his right femur and tib-fib and crushing those thoracic vertebrae. He put out his right forearm to break the fall and took out his wrist and humerus and ulna. I used the motorcycle rule."

"Which is?"

"Always replace the cheapest parts first." Piggy said. "We've all got stardust in our bones. This guy has some of his bones in the stardust. Listen, I gotta go too, but I've already written my instructions." He handed Sababa Maxie's chart. The professor turned to the order sheet. There was only one entry signed by the orthopedic surgeon. *MWUE.*

"What's that?"

"Mobilise with unrelenting enthusiam." He said. "Know the difference between a Harley and a Hoover?"

"Is that all you guys do in the OR?" Sababa asked.

"The location of the dirtbag." He said. "See you later."

"OK, Piggy." Sababa said. "We'll take it from here."

"What, I don't get a song?"

"But of course." Sababa clicked on the M drive menu as Piggy made for the frosted doors.

> 'On the day I was born the nurses all gathered 'round
> And they gazed in wide wonder at the joy they had found
> The head nurse spoke up and she said 'leave this one alone.'
> She could tell right away that I was bad to the bone.
> George Thorogood, *Bad to the Bone*

Dr. Commodus Sitsofsky was the only other subspecialist left at Tranquility Base, still at the bedside, examining Maxie's road rash and raised tattoos.

In completing her admission, Charmeine had achieved the ultimate ICU nurse trifecta perfecta: (1) her patient was intubated, (2) his 'titrated to comfort' sedation was titrated to her comfort, and (3) He was in restraints, hogtied like Maxie's Harley and the deer. Some things were worth the paperwork. She was about to deal with the unsavory olfactory element of motorcycle disasters—that distinct bouquet of sweat and blood and dirt and gravel with a hint of urine and Dark Matter. Praj and his mentor caught up with Commodus and his magnifying glass. Sababa had pulled his ophthalmoscope from its sanctuary inside the Columbian leather briefcase and peered into Maxie's eyeballs like he was looking for gold nuggets.

"I've never seen anything like this before." Dr. Skin Laser said. "These indelible designs are old and yet the tattoo pigment has acted as a nidus for some kind of granuloma formation. Perhaps he has some sort of systemic disease." Sababa unwrapped his Littman Master Cardiology black and brass stethoscope from around his neck.

"Well, at least we know where to start to find out." Sababa listened to Maxie's chest.

"Where?" Praj asked.

"What's the largest organ in the body?"

"The skin." Praj said.

"We need to get a piece." Sababa said. "Sutton's law skin deep."

"You sound like you already know what's causing this." Sitsofsky said.

"I do." Sababa said. "We don't have much of a history to go on and his physical exam is what it is. But he has eye findings consistent with uveitis, audible dry velcro crackles in both of his lungs, parotid and liver enlargement, enthesitis of his Achilles tendons and a bilateral Jaccoud's sign of his hands." Sababa pulled Maxie's fingers on an angle to his knuckles. "Hemogram shows low lymphocytes and increased monocytes. His serum calcium and liver enzymes are elevated. ECG shows bifascicular block. There is pulmonary fibrosis on his chest x-ray."

"What is it, Sab?" Commodus insisted.

"First described in 1877 by another dermatologist, Jonathan Hutchinson." Sababa said. "It caused French Revolution leader Maximilien Robespierre severe impairment during his time as head of the Reign of Terror. Its name derives from the Greek and means 'a condition that resembles crude flesh.'"

"Sarcoidosis?" Praj was more tentative. "You think he has sarcoid?"

"But of course." Sitsofsky exclaimed. "It's involving his tattoos!" Tattooed people were flawed, a sign of some feeling of inferiority, trying to establish some macho identification for themselves. How convenient when you could see what was wrong with them right away when they wore their sicknesses on their skin.

"We need to prove it." Sababa said. "Before we can treat him."

"I'll biopsy him right now." The dermatologist asked Charmeine for a tray.

"And you, my young protégé, will order the rest of his investigations." Sababa said to Praj. "Serum angiotensin-converting enzyme and immunoglobulins, thyroid function tests, prolactin, and 1,25-dihydroxy vitamin D, and urine calcium, CT abdomen and high-resolution CT chest, and referrals to Ed Hyde and our faceless oculist guru, T.J. Eckleburg. Just don't ask him where he gets his music collection."

"What is that all about, Sab?" Praj asked. "I heard you tell Lili Boulanger the same thing."

"T.J. is a brilliant ophthalmologist but he has one serious failing." Sababa said. "Every day on his lunch break, he goes down to A&B Sound."

"So?"

"Every day he steals six CDs from the classical section of the store."

"Wow." Praj said. "Why don't they arrest him?"

"Bad for business." Sababa said. "T.J.'s kleptomania was first discovered by Iris, his medical office assistant. She spoke to the owner of the music store, and came to a mutually agreeable arrangement, without T.J. even knowing."

"What was the arrangement?" Praj asked.

"Every day after lunch, the music store staff calculate the value of what T.J. stole that day and bill his office. Iris takes it out of petty cash and no one is any the wiser."

"How long has this been going on?" Commodus asked.

"About ten years."

"Wow." Praj said.

"Yeah, wow." Sababa said. "You should see T.J.'s classical music collection."

"What's the next series in Farrago's progressive stages of physician evolution?" Praj asked, once Dr. Skin Laser had finished his biopsy.

"The fourth." Sababa said. *I want to be needed... I love my white jacket... I love the power of the pager... I hate this fucking pager... I don't want to wear a stupid jacket... I want to be left alone...*

"And where did you end up with that?" Praj asked.

"I embraced the captivity." Sababa said. *If I choose to love my servitude, I can expand my horizons in any direction I want.* "Why waste your talent playing with one little predictable organ for the rest of your days? I'd rather spend my life leaping from heart to lungs to pancreas to any other biological body structure that could go wrong at any time. There's nothing wrong with knowing one thing and knowing it well, like there's nothing wrong with being a third-chair oboe in the back of the orchestra. But it's a lot more fun being the conductor. Here's the thing, I love the playing field. Why subspecialize when you can have it all?"

'A fall into a ditch makes you wiser.'
Chinese Proverb

"I wouldn't pull that foley catheter out if you ever want to cough with confidence again." Charmeine said.

"Where am I?" Maxie asked.

"You know, I've been asking myself that same question since I got here this morning." A stocky new attendant with a fancy stethoscope stood beside his bed. "I finally figured out we're somewhere between the end of the line and the middle of nowhere. Now, sometimes you can find yourself in the middle of nowhere and sometimes in the middle of nowhere you can find yourself."

"Where exactly would that be?" Maxie asked. The attendant pointed to heaven.

"It didn't look that far on the map." He said. "If the countryside gets boring, I usually stop, get off my bike, and go sit in the ditch long enough to appreciate what was here before the asphalt came."

"You appear to have perfected that one."

"This is a strange resort, man. I mean, the wheelchair service is great, but that suite I rented, there was another person in it. And for some reason the housekeeper gave me an enema."

106

"Yeah, she's new here." He stared at Maxie's rash. *Road pizza.*

"Who are you?

"This is Doctor Sababa, Maxie." Charmeine. said.

"You're the guy I came to see."

"Congratulations, Maxie. You made it." Sababa said. "But you left a hell of a mess getting here."

"I'm a Hells angel. I always leave a hell of a mess."

"Not like this." Sababa adjusted the ceiling mirror so his patient could see. "He who would make a beast of himself gets rid of the pain of being a man."

"Holy shit." He said.

"I bet that stung." Sababa reassured. "You should have seen the deer."

"At the Cassidy Pub, they called me the Man of Steel."

"You are now." Sababa pointed to Piggy's porcupine of external fixation rods. *There was a beautiful consistency about Maxie; he was a porcupine among men, with his quills always flared.*

"I came off on a steep leaning curve."

"You came off a steep learning curve." Sababa said. "You know what we call motorcycles around here?"

"No. What?"

"Donor-cycles."

"Donor-cycles." Maxie rolled it around in his mouth. "I like that."

"You would." It's not that the portly professor wasn't sympathetic. He did identify with these two-wheeled outlaws and their need for space, their love of binges and their hatred of authority. It's not that he didn't respect those who had seen the dark side of motorcycling and lived. It was just that he hadn't met many. In a more unfortunate turn of phrase, Sababa could be said to have more skin in the game.

"Who's the chick?" Maxie stared at Charmeine.

"She's a Heavens Angel." Sababa said. "Treat her well or I'll give her permission to hurt you. You ever had any problems with drugs?"

"I've never had problems with drugs." Maxie said. "I've had problems with the police."

"Any other medical problems?" Sababa asked. "High cholesterol?"

"I ride way too fast to worry about cholesterol." Maxie said. "The reason I was heading your way was to ask you about my tattoos."

"What about them?"

"They look like this."

"What are they for?" Charmeine asked.

"For?" Maxie said. "They're for my tribe and my social beliefs and the violence with which I will protect them. They're markers of bravery and maturity and cultural acceptance. They keep track of time. They're my right of passage. They're a diary of blood and ink and pain on the outside, to ease the pain on the inside. They're a doomed assertion of mastery of my fate, or at least a defiance of one I can't control. They remake me as something new. That's what they're for."

Sababa had observed three generations of tattoos droop flaccid like moth-eaten upholstery over shriveled biceps and saggy backsides. Most of Maxie's tattoos looked like they were done by a sadistic child on a rainy afternoon. His arms were so inked, they looked like a pair of pajamas. He had a tattoo on the back of his right hand. *I might be wrong.* But it looked like this now. *I might be wrong.* And across his chest. *Try harder. I'm not fucking dead.* He wore his heart on his skin on the skin over his heart. *Try harder. I'm not fucking dead.*

"That will become inaccurate at some point." Sababa pointed out. "Technically, all tattoos are temporary, even permanent ones." And yet, the stocky savant didn't realise that he would live long enough to have tattoos as well—small radiation reminders of what ghastliness the gods had condemned him with.

"You have a rare granulomatous disease, Maxie."

"What the hell is that?"

"It's a condition called sarcoidosis."

"Narco who?"

"Sarcoidosis." Sababa said. "Nobody knows what causes it, nobody knows how long you're going to have it, but with your lungs and eyes and other organs affected, as soon as we make sure it's nothing else, we'll need to treat it."

"With what?"

"Steroids, for starters."

"Great." Maxie said. "Man of Steel."

"Not anabolic steroids." Sababa corrected. "Corticosteroids."

"I need to get out of here as soon as I can."

"We need to discharge you as soon as is reasonable." Sababa said. "But when a doctor and not a motorcycle cop tells you to slow down, you've hit more than a deer, you've hit middle age. Tell me, what is it you plan to do with your one wild and precious life?"

"Dunno." He said. "Look at the sun. Ride, eat, sleep... repeat. I'm a product of the culture that now claims to be shocked at my existence, bound to go to heaven because I've already served my time in hell. You know the local chapter protects you, don't you?"

"So I've heard." Sababa said.

"They say they're protecting you from yourself."

"I have had more trouble with myself than with any other man I've ever met."

"That should be worth some faster way out of this mess, shouldn't it?"

"You made the mess, Maxie." Sababa said. "I'm just cleaning up after you."

"You know I can't pay you, Doc."

"You can pay me by listening to how I plan on getting you on your feet again." Sababa said. "And in here, it's my way or the highway."

"You know which one I'll take." He said. "The minute I can stand." Sababa saw Praj on the bridge of the Death Star, anxious to communicate something.

"Excuse me, Maxie." He said. "I have other responsibilities to attend to."

"See you later, Doc." Maxie shut his eyes. "Keep the paint up, and the rubber down."

Outside the cubicle, Praj was frantic. He handed Sababa a list of twelve names. They were the new consults so far, and it was only eight o'clock.

"We're out of control." He said. "We'll never get on top of this."

"Another day in the Land of the Giants." Sababa said. "We'll be fine."

"Any more of those Farrago's progressive stages of physician evolution?" Praj asked.

"Last one." Sababa said. "*This patient has some interesting problems... This patient has some real disease... This patient needs to be hugged... This patient has a lot of nothing... This patient has Shitty Life Syndrome... This patient needs to leave; I need to be hugged and loved...*"

"And where did you end up with that?" Praj asked.

"Back at the beginning." Sababa said. "Selfless. Doing good anyway."

'We don't come here for our health.
We can think of other ways of enjoying ourselves.'
Prince Philip, on Canada

The casual reader understands Maxie Road's desperation to reach the land of milk and honey for medical treatment. This Hells Angel outlaw had driven up from a republic in which the only essential inalienable rights enshrined in its constitution were those of life, liberty, and the pursuit of happiness. Life did not yet include the right to be saved from a treatable death.

There are legitimate criticisms of the US medical establishment. Even Walter Cronkite said that the American health care system was neither healthy, caring, nor a system. The US spends more on health care than any other country in the world, more than twice as much per capita as other wealthy developed countries—and for that money, its citizens can expect lives three years shorter. Forty countries who spend less have longer life expectancies.

Wealthy Americans with no pre-existing conditions can afford high-quality medicine, while the structural social violence imposed by urban poverty and racism relegate the less fortunate to hoping for and negotiating with whatever safety net might exist in their area. The highest burden of disease correlates with the least access to care. The result is a fragmented patchwork of procedure-oriented symptom suppression services that are enmeshed in a voluminous trail of paper payments, with little relevance to actual medical need. One-quarter of Medicare beneficiaries have five or more chronic conditions, see an annual average of 13 physicians, and fill 50 prescriptions per year.

The main reason for the inertial inequity is simple. The US is the sickest of the rich nations because it does not have a single-payer public medical insurance scheme. The higher the buildings, the lower the morals.

There have been inadequate attempts to fix this. Bill Clinton's effort to reform healthcare turned out to be the second most disgusting thing he did in the oval office. He and his wife created an opening for the worst-of-all-worlds option, the so-called HMO, combining the maximum capitalist gouging with the maximum socialistic bureaucracy. Barack Obama's was less than a junior varsity endeavour.

Because the system administrators in both countries behave irrationally in the name of reason, we get distracted by the vaudevillian aspects of the healthcare debate. Doctor Sababa, accustomed as he was to not getting paid for the treatments he rendered to his American cousins, was always amused when these bureaucrats used health and justice in the same sentence.

If you tell Canadians that you want to interview them for a critical piece on the Canadian healthcare system, they'll put on their best trophy-wife smile for the camera and list its many accolades. But catch them on a day with their guard down in need of actual medical care and the truth spills out.

The cornerstones of the Canada Health Act are the five conditions of universality, accessibility, comprehensiveness, portability, and public administration. Only one of these exists in any significant manner, and all demand their supplicants give their lives for the existential illusion.

There is no universality. In a country as vast as Canada, the geographical imperative guarantees that, no matter how much money is thrown at telemedicine, not all citizens will be able to avail themselves of the wonders of the latest medical technology.

There is no equal accessibility. Access to a waiting list is not access to medical care. And there is not even equal access to the waiting lists that patients with serious diseases die on, because of the usual human foibles that prioritize the pecking order. What does exist is *denial by delay*, real and intentional withholding of medical care because of service rationing in the name of cost containment. The only person who suffers on a waiting list is the patient, and they have no power. The provincial governments, the regional health authorities, and the hospital CEO's save money by making patients wait too long, and there is no incentive in the unions that run the show to improve its performance.

There is no comprehensiveness. Governments can decide not to fund certain expensive medications or more mundane but essential programs while, at the same time, pour millions into gender assignment clinics, illicit drug injection sites, or boondoggle EMR computerization schemes. Physicians find themselves in the conflict-of-interest role of disguised decision-makers and gatekeepers. They negotiate as adversaries, first with government and then with one another about their relative worth, while the 'conqueror' observes and continues to rule. They are forced into providing the quality care that consumers regard as their birthright without having any say about the coercion itself. Given the unpromising nature of the egalitarian ultimatum, they might as well consider all their patients equally dead, for only that can eradicate any differences in fairness. The reductio ad absurdum of cost containment, as Doctor Sababa was always keen to point out, is a seventeen-cent bullet at the frosted front door.

Not only has the concept of comprehensiveness been perverted by the need for cost-containment, the ideological compulsion to ensure the illusion of equality had brought denial of a patient's right to use his resources to access medical care available in other jurisdictions. In an otherwise democratic Canada, it is considered immoral, unethical and illegal for a person to be able to spend their own money on their health care, or on that of a loved one. Indeed, this ideology has reached a level of politically correct arrogance. *I think we have to be very careful about empowering the consumer because they will make choices that are not in their own health interest.* Even prisoners have more rights than the sick. The Supreme Court of Canada has given incarcerated felons the 'right' to vote, but its non-jailed citizens have no such reciprocity in the freedom to bypass the public system when it fails to provide reasonable access to their medical needs.

In 1995, Thea Vakil, BC Government spokesperson and Associate Deputy Minister of Health, was asked about patients on waiting lists seeking care in the United States. She minced no words. *If we could stop them at the border, we would.* What the anti-privatization proponents choose to ignore is that there are other countries in the world beside the US and other ways of delivering health care—some better than Canada's.

There is no equal portability. In a country that considers the term 'two-tier' as seditious as it does, Quebec doesn't pay physicians the same for the treatment their citizens receive in other provinces.

What there is, in no small amount, is the fifth element of the Canada Health Act—public administration. The exponential growth in the sheer number of bureaucrats earning six-figure incomes and golden parachutes in the national health care debacle is astounding. Despite the brilliant manner in which national and provincial governments have increased the number of tax collectors and decreased the number of doctors, the rising cost of health care is unsustainable. The pressure to reduce costs is aimed only at the treatment of real diseases. There is no pressure to reduce the cost of treating fictitious ones. On the contrary, there is pressure to define and pay for ever more types of bizarre alternative disorders and snowflake pseudo-illness. The Ministry of Health will soon be the only Ministry that Canadian taxpayers can afford, and they still won't be able to afford the Ministry of Health.

Costs have exploded as choices have narrowed, in a deluded nation-state unwilling to or incapable of recognizing the difference between *cost* and *cost-effectiveness*. No one is measuring clinical outcomes. The essential problem with Canadian health care is that the government has shielded it from any consumer control or innovation.

Both the American and Canadian health care systems are ineffective and unfair in their own ways, and cruel in the same way. Maxie's country needs to provide insurable services; Sababa's needs to provided service assurances. Nothing that has value, real value, has no cost. Not freedom, not food, not shelter, and not health care.

This is why most medical stories end, not with crash carts and sirens and electric shocks to the chest, but with an empty room, crisp white sheets, and silence.

'... a wondrous work in one volume; but whose mysteries not even himself could read, though his own live heart beat against them... destined in the end to moulder away with the living parchment whereon they were inscribed, and so be unsolved to the last.'

Herman Melville, *Moby-Dick, or, the Whale*

The core principle in the Book of Earth is that you must be able to adapt your strategy to timing with your skill. *As if it were a straight road mapped out on the ground.*

A man cannot be killed in a modern manner without copper. The historic Cassidy Inn didn't die of earth, it died of fire, although it was Eduardo Cazar's act of sawing through the ground that killed them both. Crews from the Cranberry, North Oyster, Cedar and Ladysmith fire departments responded with water but were defeated by wind.

Christina Pfeifer's earth tones looked better on canvas than under her skin. She transmuted her paintings from portraits to landscapes during her confinement in the psychiatric ward of Harbour City Regional.

Dr. Juan Leyblanca reported Pretty Boy Troy's surgical specimen from Lili Boulanger's ankle as pyoderma gangrenosum. Lili's parents presented Doctor Sababa with a fine bottle of Burgundy when her Crohn's disease went into remission.

The owners of Quinsam coal mine near Campbell River closed their operation in response to a decline in coal prices and market demand. Three weeks after his last cigarette, Roscoe Holcomb's CT-guided thoracic punch biopsy of one of his lung lumps revealed that it was rheumatoid nodule surrounded by a palisade of macrophages, typical of Caplan's syndrome. Sababa's steroids and disease-modifying agents landed him on more solid ground.

Foster Inclusion was a man of his words. Despite Sababa's apocryphal parable of the cat and the hot pepper, midwifery joined Dr. Olaf Octagon and the other obstetricians of Harbour City Regional as full partners in the care of their pregnant patients, although it was still only the more certificated colleagues that were called to the more frequent potentially preventable predicaments.

And Maxie Road? As the Washington Nomad recovered, he got to know people he would never have associated with as a Hells Angel. Which was how, during his prolonged convalescence on the Canadian taxpayer's dime, he peered over the shoulder of the man in the thousand-dollar suit, typing his PIN into a hallway ATM. Malcolm Canmore was the Chief Hospital Administrator of Harbour City Regional, the CHA, the CEO, the COO, the COG, the CAD, the CON, the CUR, the grand omnipotent stomper of supermen. But Maxie was the Man of Steel and was so grateful for his treatment at Harbour City Regional, he insisted on giving Malcolm a big long man hug while lifting his crocodile hide wallet, his platinum pen and pencil set, and silver cufflinks.

Maxie Road also got to know one person he would have associated with as a Hells Angel. Lisa Monroe, cured of her Kikuchi-Fujimoto Disease with the same steroid therapy that Sababa had used to treat her new boyfriend, threw her right leg over the seat of Maxie's new Harley Davidson ElectraGlide Road King, purchased with the profits from the multitude of Harbour City ATMs Maxie had visited on the day of his departure. Her silver earrings looked a lot like Malcolm Canmore's cufflinks.

The closed-circuit camera behind the on-call physician parking bay caught their faces as they pulled up to say goodbye to Sababa, opening the driver side door of his dimpled and dented Honda Civic.

"I don't know where you came from." Sababa said. "But I have a fair idea of where you're going."

"I'll call you from my cell." Maxie smiled. *Potato-* *potato-* *potato-* *potato-* *potato-* *potato-* *potato-* *potato-* *potato-* *potato-* *potato...* The professor knew that he would never get paid for looking after the biker. Maxie had told him as much. *You know I can't pay you, Doc.*

But he never expected the courier who delivered the big package from Seattle. Inside was a black leather vest, complete with the fourpiece insignia of the tribe, a title patch which read 'Medic,' and one other embroidered badge. *When we do right, nobody remembers. When we do wrong, nobody forgets...*

The poetry of the earth is never dead.

16. The Case of the Congo Stain

'Coincidences are God's way of remaining anonymous.'
Albert Einstein

The Old Man from Ontario had taken a taxi from Harbour City Regional to his Mercedes camper. It was no small comfort to see that there had been no damage to his vehicle in the week it had sat unattended in the parking lot of Harbour City Mall. He tipped the cab driver, relieved to be finally out of the hospital and back on the road.

The Old Man was accustomed to the finer things in life. He ate the best food, drank the best wine, and mixed with the best people. His extended medical coverage had afforded him a measure of insulation from more intimate contact with the great unwashed, but even in a private room, he knew his blood tests and bowel movements would have shared space with less illustrious inmates.

The Old Man pressed on the ignition of his Mercedes camper and the van roared into life. He wheeled big arcs through the vast mall parking lot before timing his exit onto the Island Highway south towards Victoria. If he was lucky, he would be sipping a glass of First Growth Bordeaux on the terrace of his new waterfront condo in less than two-hours-time.

But the Old Man, although fortunate in other ventures, would not be so lucky in this one.

He had become religious, since the near-death experience that prompted his hospital admission. While he had to acknowledge the skill and ability of the Harbour City Regional internist that attended him, he attributed his rebirth as a Christian as the pivotal event responsible for his survival and resultant recovery. And he vowed to dedicate the rest of his life to Jesus.

Jesus, for his part, would not have been a heavy bettor on the longevity of his new acolyte.

The Old Man never thought about the karma bus, delayed because of high demand, but it was coming. His first encounter with providence was in the form of a local traffic officer, a certain Veronica Marsden, whom Doctor Sababa had warned him about.

The RCMP Ford Interceptor only flashed its firelight finery for three seconds to convince the Old Man to pull over.

"Licence and registration." She was everything Sababa had said she was, and more. The Old Man handed over his documentation.

"Do you know how fast you were drivng?" Veronica said.

"One hundred kilometres an hour." He said.

"Ten kilometres over the speed limit."

"I'm allowed ten kilometres over the speed limit." He said.

"Maybe in Ontario." She said. "But this is British Columbia. And we have rules." Veronica wrote him a ticket, the value of which approached his high level of appreciation. In British Columbia, it appeared, the law was expediency with long black hair. Veronica pushed the ticket onto the Old Man's chest at the same time he memorised her badge number, in case she got lost.

Back on the Island Highway in the south-bound traffic, the Old Man tuned his radio to a local FM station.

Si'em' nu Ts'lhhwulmuhw... Good Morning Harbour City... This is CNDN Coast Salish radio, 101.3 FM on your Home and Native Band. I'm your host, BC Bud...

He counted his blessings to be still alive after his recent brush with death.

Man's law changes with his understanding of man. Only the laws of the spirit remain always the same...

The Old Man looked up at a sign on the overpass for an exit for the BC Ferries terminal to the mainland. His eyes tried to refocus on the road ahead, but in their periphery came a glimpse of something they couldn't quite get the rest of his mind around.

Religion is for people who are afraid of going to hell. Spirituality is for those who have already been there...

Beside the sign on the overpass, he could make out the faint profile of a boy gazing down at the vehicles passing under him. The young man appeared to be balancing a large boulder on the top of the open parapet. *And no rock if there were rock.* The Old Man watched in disbelief as the shadowy figure on the bridge, with a single Herculean heave, dislodged the massive monster from its precarious perch.

God gives us each a song... Sharing and giving are the ways of God... First, we had the land and they had the Bibles, now we have the Bibles and they have the land...

There is a Greek maxim that contends that when you see a rock coming, it's supposed to hurt less. Unfortunately for the ancient van driver, this rock hadn't heard the good news. It was, like the Christian messiah the Old Man had found to be his rock of ages. not a stumbling block but a stepping stone to the great beyond.

Wisdom comes only when you stop looking for it and start living the life the Creator intended for you.

116

Fifty pounds of granite smashed through the windshield, crushing the Old Man's skull and face and jaw and teeth and chest and pelvis and legs. A thousand broken shards of glass split the sunlight into a prismatic rainbow.

Cherish youth but trust old age... Old age is not as honorable as death, but most people want it...

The Old Man went to meet his maker; the young man went to meet his mates at the Harbour City Mall McDonalds. Everyone has a rock bottom.

'Attention all shoppers
It's cancellation day
Yes the big adios
Is just a few hours away.'
Steely Dan, *The Last Mall*

We are shaped not only by our current geography but by our ancestral one as well. One week earlier, Aulds Offramp drove what he knew as the old farm road that once led to a woodland stream, except that now it was a four-lane highway to a strip mall. Aulds was eighty years old, the same age as the farm road and woodland could have also been, except that they were now gone and he was still here.

Aulds had been coming to Vancouver Island every autumn for the last fifteen years since his retirement, when his wife was still alive. This year, he decided to make a permanent move. The thought of lying in a gravesite through the winters in Ontario gave him goosebumps. Far better to wait out eternity in a more moderate climate.

His choice of landing strip had more shopping centres per capita than any other municipality in Canada, and Aulds was heading to the biggest arcade complex of them all, a space station in the rainforest, a surrogate civilization. Somewhere along the way, Harbour City had become a gigantic galleria with an island attached.

It cut into the grey sky like an unholy temple, casting a long shadow on the earth. Harbour City Mall sat on the landscape like some rotting carcass flayed by a hoard of zombie vultures. Retail complexes everywhere cursed us with the tyranny of sameness because the instant connectivity sweeping the earth annihilated all differences. *There's a brand new shopping center, seven stories high... There's bound to be a sale or two; something we can buy...*

Aulds manoeuvred his Mercedes camper through several acres of smooth black tarmac before coming to a halt inside one of a thousand shiny painted rectangles. With how fast Harbour City had outgrown itself in recent years, the suburban shopping plaza was the only surviving place he was sure to find a space to park without colliding with a meter or a fine. Vancouver Islanders retained their frontier spirit for the only frontier that remained in the vast open space between their SUVs and the welcome greeters at the front doors.

Strip malls were the shopping hardware of the twentieth century, in much the same way that Amazon would become the virtual shopping software of the twenty-first—desire, ideology and expenditure floating through the cyberspaced out clouds of ultra-capitalism. In the engine that was Harbour City, they were the final exhaust of all its industry.

The mall was about money. Here, Aulds Offramp could swing a credit card like a scythe through meadows of golden merchandise, in a plastic shrink-wrapped world set off from real life. Credito, ergo sum. *I shop, therefore I am.*

The mall was more than a means to a material end, it was a cult of consumption. The act of shopping was an act of faith and worship. Even Pete Renoir, the Harbour City Salvation Army command commander, had to acknowledge his Christian charity's enslavement to the credo of free-market largesse it depended on. *If money is the route of all evil, then why do they ask for it in church.* More Mecca than Madonna, the mall was a sterile religious place of great pilgrimage for those bereft of the gifts of impulse control and analytical scrutiny. It imposed the same duties of submission on every shopper that the Five Pillars of Islam expected of every Muslim—the *shahada* profession of faith and *salat* ritual observance performed in a prescribed form, the *sawm* abstinence from sexual intercourse, and food and drink (except in the food court), *zakat* almsgiving, and the *umrah*, rather than the *hajj*, because the journey to the mall could be performed at any time of the year. Throngs of adherents swirled around the *Kaaba* sacred square building in the centre of the holiest site and towards which they faced when praying for the deliverance of their earnest hopes and wishes.

Like the desert terrain that spawned the only other true faith, the mall was barren and bereft of greenery. In one of the great ironies of our age, the lack of reverence for the natural world became a dystopian descent into ecocide. There was no weather in the mall. Inside, the walls were stripped of clocks and windows. Without the sun, you couldn't know the time of day or night. The interior was always the same temperature illuminated with the same light, and the air scented with the same chemical perfume, no matter the season. The imperatives of the market governed every life, escalating the danger of destroying the sentient

118

commonwealth of the birds and bees on which we depend for life on planet earth. It was the final footnote for a species that so loved beauty they destroyed what they sought seeking it.

The Harbour City Mall had an architecture that Harbour City Regional Hospital would have killed for. The polished floor shone like the surface of a lake at sunrise. Malcolm Canmore's medical administrative assistant, Paris Hilton, lost her way in walkway tributaries flowing with soporific shoppers and faraway mindless muzak melodies, not a sharp angle anywhere. She took the elevator to the escalator, rode it down and started again, or rode the little carousel in the centre, round and round, and round and round.

The only interruptions were the change in fashions or squeaky carts with wonky wheels or aisle accident announcements. *Attention all shoppers.* In a world of chaos, it was order. In a world of pollution and desecration, it was clean bubble-wrapped perfection. It was where you came to learn about loneliness. *The mall is an oasis that's full of plastic trees... The air is cool, the perfumes sweet, the products aim to please.*

The shops held their mouths open like temptresses, radiating heat and light and a sorbet rainbow of merchandise—bright and tempting candy stores of sensory overload: eye candy, gadget candy, ego candy. All reverberated with the same piped music; only overtures for purchases were permitted inside. Visceral messages and images designed to seduce consumers were wherever their eyes might fall. Everything you wanted and nothing you needed. *We're buying CDs, and we're buying lingerie... We'll put it on a charge account we're never gonna pay.*

If God loved the common people, a trip to Harbour City Mall could convince you that He made far too many of them. In fifteen minutes, you would pass more people than your ancestors saw during their entire lifetimes. Aulds Offramp paused at a bin of pastel baby socks and underwear in the concourse between Thyme Adamant's Releaf cannabis boutique and Hans Klupt's Pipefitter tobacco smoke shop. On the other side of the hallway, Ben Castleman, the owner of Liquidation World bumped into Dr. Zaias' wife, Julia, shopping for a special Halloween costume.

The malls, the advent of which had promised to split the rich from the poor, did just that, then fell into their own gaping chasm of the poor without enough money to shop there and the rich who chose not to rub shoulders with them.

Consumers moved about as if free, but you could see their chains. They were on the billboards of the mall, smiling back at them with perfect teeth. They wanted to be those billboard people so much they handed their children over to daycare as babies. They worked in cubical farms for ten hours a day while dreaming of that one week in the sun and racking up their credit card expenses. Shoppers considered each other as obstacles, both to walk around and wait behind for their turn to reach the tills—teenage girls with glitter eyeshadow and slippery lip gloss, silent wives with sour partners, wobbly women with shopping bags in both arms, waddling women with coffees to go, and widowed grandmothers, overdressed, overweight, and over here. Over there was a man who wore his years on his shoulders, mumbling in German. Herr Doktor Wernher Merkwürdigliebe was a retired German cardiologist. He stood at the escalator, dark hand gripping the rail, frowning, years cutting deep, unable to step on, but his left hand made an embarrassing salute he couldn't control. *Mums with strollers and overweight kids... Sunshades and caps to protect their lids...*

The crowds were clothed in children's tears and plastic shrouds. Every free market slave labour item in the mall had an environmental cost to produce, and no one asked if the expense was worth it. Our addictions were frivolous. How much crap does a child's brain need to develop? Nothing in these boutiques of small and sophisticated mall passions for fall fashions was essential to our survival, our work, or our play. William Mathiseon Macleod, a diving instructor at Sunset Scuba, shopped for something at London Drugs to help him breathe easier. Next door, Polly Poses, a cashier at the Real Canadian Superstore checked out the groceries of Mustafa Erdoğan, the Turkish döner kebap stall owner in an adjacent wing of the mall, and then the trolley of an elderly man from Ontario, who had trouble with pushing his purchases because of the pain in his wrists and tendons. *Shopping for a pair of shoes, shopping for a hat... We're buying some of this, and we're buying some of that.*

Aulds Offramp wheeled his supermarket cart through the food court on his way back to his van. Paris Hilton now sat in the shiny new McDonalds where the bookstore used to be, eating nothing, drinking in the energy of a hundred teenage clones and drones, smiling and nodding at every young face... an alien people clutching their gods. They ordered deluxe triple bacon burgers assembled from the meat of thousands of caged mammals, with fries. Torn plastic pouches, twice the cost of their contents, still contained most of the condiments that littered the abandoned trays. Napkins, packed too tight to be dispensed, were torn out of their sockets.

Aulds found the last washroom near the shopping centre exit, to relieve himself one last time before the long drive south. The usual yellow spray stream he expected to see empty from his eighty-year-old bladder instead splattered the inside of the urinal with a red shower of blood. His legs wobbled under him.

After a day at the mall, stepping back into the lives of grasses and insects and breezes and whatever else was still left of the world, gallons of fresh air poured over Aulds Offramp. But all the oxygen in the world outside the mall in the fall couldn't stop the chaos that detonated in his chest. His heart pounded like a jackhammer looking for a way out of its ribcage, choking off Auld's breath and then his consciousness. One of the welcome greeters started CPR, while another ran off to get the portable defibrillator. *Roll your cart back up the aisle... Kiss the checkout girls goodbye.*

'There is a way of breathing
that is a shame and a suffocation
And there is another way of expiring
a love-breath that lets you open infinitely.'
Rumi

The morning before Aulds Offramp's chest exploded and a week before he hit rock bottom, Dr. Praj Bharmal paged his guru from the ER.

"Yes, Mowgli." Sababa said. "What have you discovered in the human zoo?"

"Patient of Dr. Hyde's."

"Where's Ed?"

"Day off." Praj said.

"So?"

"Dr. Pangloss wants us to see him."

"Hmmmm." Mused the stocky savant. "Trace is usually indecisive, well informed, and compulsive. He doesn't know what he wants, but he knows how to get it, and he knows that he wants it now. Peculiar."

"What do you want?" Praj asked.

"Earlier this morning, I wanted an espresso dopio dopio. Now, I'm drinking an espresso doppio doppio." He said. "Follow your dreams. Coming now." A few minutes later, Praj watched the portly professor prance in through the automatic sliding frosted glass doors. With one effortless arm swing, his Columbian leather briefcase flew a complete barrel roll before coming to rest beside the monitor at the consultant's station. Dr. Trace Pangloss, writing out his referral to Sababa at the same desk, jumped out of his skin.

"Jesus Fucking Christ, Sababa!" He stuttered. "Is that necessary?"

"You called?"

"William Mathiseon Macleod." Trace threw a chest x-ray up on the consultant's view box. "28-year-old Sunset Scuba diving instructor who presented with what I thought was a spontaneous collapsed left lung."

"It's completely black on that side." Praj observed. "No lung at all."

"Not that you can see." Trace said. "Although a pneumothorax can look like that."

"You didn't put in a chest tube?" Sababa asked.

"No, I didn't." The ER doc said.

"Do we get some history and physical findings or are you just going to guess your way through this darkness?"

"He had some recurrent lung infections during puberty but I couldn't find any old imaging." Trace said. "Exam demonstrated decreased to absent breath sounds with hyperresonance to percussion over the entire left upper chest."

"What did Ed Hyde see him for?" Sababa asked.

"Dr. Hyde thought he had something called Swyer–James syndrome." Trace said. "I have no idea what that even is."

"It's a rare result of postinfectious obliterative bronchiolitis." Sababa pulled the hand-scribed Black Book of Remedies from his Columbian leather briefcase and flipped to a page in the middle. "The involved lung grows smaller than the opposite lung, resulting in overdistention of the airspaces together with a decreased blood supply, which gives an x-ray blackout appearance to the side affected. We think it's caused by a type 21 adenovirus."

"Dr. Hyde did a V/Q scan which showed neither perfusion nor ventilation." Trace said. "So that must be what he has."

"Nope." Sababa pulled up more recent imaging on the consultant's monitor. "Mr. Macleod had another study two days ago. Do you remember before the internet, when people thought that stupidity was caused by the lack of access to information?" Trace and Praj nodded.

"Yeah, it wasn't that." Sababa said. "Let's go see him." Trace presented the professor and his protégé to the diving instructor.

"William, this is Doctor Sababa." Trace said. "He handles all the mean curveballs."

"Well, I hope you can help me, Doctor Sababa." Said the diving instructor. "I can't even hold the long notes on my saxophone anymore. Any work I might get has been suspended until I can get my breath back. And I'm cold all the time." He wore a jacket over a flannel shirt. "Dr. Hyde says I have this weird syndrome."

"I don't think so." Sababa said.

"Huh?" William frowned. "Why not?"

"Because your CT scan showed many large air-filled cysts in your left lung, as well as poor blood flow through your left pulmonary artery."

"From what?"

"You were born with cystic malformations where the normal budding of your left primitive tracheobronchial tree should have been." Sababa said. "The air pressure tension inside these big bubbles blocks off the blood supply to that lung."

"Can you fix it?" He asked.

"No." Sababa said. "But I know someone who can." He looked over to the ER ward clerk behind the polycarbonate shield.

"Cheri Sundae." Sababa said. "Can you patch me through to the chest cracker on call in Victoria and get me an ambulance please?"

"On it." She said. Which was how William Mathiseon Macleod entered the process of getting his breath back.

"Another one for you, Sab." Dr. Nicholas Rivera was in an obvious hurry to get to his office."

"What you got?" Sababa turned to face the man.

"Thyme Adamant." The family doctor began. "32-year-old owner of the Releaf cannabis boutique at Harbour City Mall. This is the third time she presents with a spontaneous right lung collapse in less than a year. Dr. Buddy Benway was good enough to put in a chest tube but Thyme says she's not going home until we figure out why this keeps happening. Buddy told her that this is the usual spontaneous pneumothorax we see sometimes, but she's not buying it."

"Where's Buddy?"

"Off golfing at one of the projectile parks this morning." Nick said. "She's been talking with the nurses. Asked for you by name."

"OK." Sababa said. "We'll see her." Nick introduced Praj and the professor.

"Thyme, this is Doctor Sababa." He said. "He tries to stay pointed, like a thorn, so at his side there will always be roses."

"Ooh." Thyme gurgled. Rivera excused himself and skulked off to his clinic.

"Why do you think this is happening, Thyme?" Sababa asked.

"I don't know." She said. "Every few months my lung collapses and they have to put in a chest tube until it reinflates."

"Does it happen in relation to anything you can think of?"

"Like what?"

"Like less than 72 hours after your period begins?" Sababa saw the startled look form on Thyme's face.

"How did you know that?"

"It is my business to know what other people don't know." He said. "That, the blood in your chest tube and that the collapse always occurs on the same side."

"Couldn't that have been Dr. Benway's technique?" Praj asked.

"I would never say anything bad about another doctor." Sababa said. "Buddy may be a useless golfer but he knows how to put in a chest tube. How heavy are your periods, Thyme?"

"Heavy." She said. "And painful. That's how I got into cannabis therapy. How is this related?"

"You have a condition called endometriosis." Sababa said. "Uterine tissue has attached itself to the lining of your lung, forming chocolate-like cysts which menstruate in your chest. The blood and air cause your lung to collapse."

"But how does it get there?" Thyme asked. "And how does the air get in?"

"No one knows about the air." Sababa said. "But we think that endometrial material may enter through defects in your diaphragm or up through your pelvic veins. You have a gynecologist"

"No." She said. "I used to, but he died. Nice man. Warm hands."

"Not anymore." Sababa said.

"Can you do anything?" Thyme asked.

"Dr. Bharmal here can do anything." Sababa said. "He'll order a blood test called CEA-125, arrange for you to have a video-assisted thoracoscopy in Victoria at the beginning of your next period when a chest surgeon may be able to remove the womb tissue in the lining of your right lung, and write a consultation report to Dr. Rivera, your family physician."

"What will you do?" She asked.

"I'll get a gynecologist to see you while you're still in hospital." Sababa handed Praj a piece of paper with three names on it. *Mustafa Erdoğan... Paris Hilton... Wernher Merkwürdigliebe...*

"Call me after you see the first one." Sababa said. "He's on the third floor. The other two are on the fifth floor. We'll both go to see them together."

"We're going to do all this before lunch?" Praj asked.

"Peter Pan." Sababa said.

"Peter Pan?"

"Once you're grown up you can't come back." He said. "Page me when you've finished seeing Mustafa." Sababa left Praj to page the gynecologist on call. It was Olaf Octagon.

"Hey, Dr. Sections and Resections." Sababa said. "Where do you hide a 100-dollar bill from a gynecologist?"

"Why did I pick up this call?"

"What the hell is a 100-dollar bill?" Sababa said. "How's your little hot pepper problem coming along?"

"You were there, so you should know." Olaf said. "Do you have a reason for existing this morning?"

"Need you to see and follow a patient." He said. "She requires some kind of hormone therapy—extended cycle combined oral contraception, Lupron Depot, whatever you guys do for a living."

"Why is that?" Olaf asked.

"She has endometriosis."

"So?

"It's in her lungs."

"Oh." He said.

An hour later, after two more referrals, on his way out of Harbour City Emergency, Sababa found Dr. Zaias' wife, sitting and laughing with a group of nurses on their break. Julia was wearing a gorilla suit from the neck down. The head of the beast sat on the bench beside her.

"What's happening here, Julia?" He asked.

"It's Halloween, Sab."

"The day of domesticated horror." He said. "And?"

"I rented a gorilla suit from the mall."

"OK."

"Dr. Carlton put in a referral to Ernie Hacker as a joke." She said. "Left a referral for hirsutism."

"And?"

"Ernie didn't get it." Julia said. "He came into my cubicle, took one look, wrote out a prescription, and left. Said he had a tee-off time with Buddy Benway." She handed Sababa the prescription. *Triton Creme 15%.*

"Hmmmm." Sababa mused. "Eflornithine HCl."

"What is it?" Dina asked.

"It's a drug first used to treat African sleeping sickness." Sababa said. "The second stage of the disease caused by a West African organism, *Trypanosoma brucei gambiense*, found in the same region of the Congo as your gorilla. The drug was later reformulated by Gillette to inhibit hair growth. Suicide inhibitor of ornithine decarboxylase."

Michaela handed Sababa the referral sheet that The Big Easy had scrawled on. *Dx X-linked congenital terminal hypertrichosis. Dr. Ernie Hacker*

"What the hell is that?" Regina asked.

"X-linked congenital terminal hypertrichosis." Sababa said. "Ambras Syndrome, named after the Austrian castle near Innsbruck, where portraits of the first known family with the disease were found. They were all descendants of Petrus Gonsalvus of the Canary Islands, the 'man of the woods' documented by Altrovandus in 1642. It's caused by genetic changes on chromosome 17 resulting in the addition or removal of millions of nucleotides. Extremely rare, it's also called 'werewolf syndrome.' Those affected sometimes end up as circus acts—Fedor Jeftichew *Jo-Jo the Dog-faced Man*, Stephan Bibrowski *Lionel the Lion-faced Man*, Jesús Aceves *Wolfman*, Annie Jones *The Bearded Woman* and Alice Elizabeth Doherty *The Minnesota Woolly Girl*."

"And Ernie Hacker thought I was one of these people?" Julia asked.

"He would have got the diagnosis right." Sababa said. "If it had been the right diagnosis."

"He's given me a follow-up appointment." She said.

"You should go." Sababa's pager hummed a tune in his pocket. It was Praj, calling from the first floor.

"Let me know how it works out."

> 'Death is the black camel that kneels before every door.'
>> Turkish proverb

"Günaydın, Mustafa." *Good morning.*

"Günaydın, Doktor." *Good morning.*

"N'aber?" *How are you.*

"Nefes almakta zorlanıyorum." *I'm having trouble breathing.*

"Türkiye nerelisin?" *Where are you from in Turkey.*

"Lıyım Tuzköy." *Tuzköy.*

"Kapadokya'da?" *In Cappadocia.*

"Evet." *Yes.*

"Goreme gittim." *I've been to Goreme.*

"I speak English." Mustafa said.

"I know."

On his way to see Mustafa, Sababa had met Marquis Shu Ying, entering the emergency department as the stocky savant was leaving.

"How's the yin-yang duality today, Shu?" He asked.

"Leading you to the oneness of the Tao." He said. Sababa felt his eyes roll back.

"I have a consult on floor 3." He said. "Any thoughts?"

"The Five Elements live even on the surgical ward of Harbour City Regional." Shu smiled. Chinese metaphysics weighed in heavy.

"This patient you're going to see there—according to the theory, his viscera is lung, his colour is white, his environmental factor dryness, his five senses smell, his taste spicy..."

"Come on, Shu." His colleague continued.

"His direction is west, his emotional activity grief, and his sound..."

"Is?"

"Crying." Shu said.

A few minutes later, Sababa had entered the sterile surgical setting of the third floor. No flowers or scents, or other forms of natural beauty were allowed entry to aid in the healing process. In their efforts not to offend or inspire, the bureaucrats had succeeded in sinking the spirit. The walls were just cream, the floor just gray.

"Morning, Sariel." He said. "Where's my boy?"

"He's in room 304 with Mr. Erdoğan." The head nurse pointed down the hallway.

Praj was surprised to hear Sababa greet his patient in Turkish. He wasn't surprised when the professor refocused his attention on him.

"What you got?"

"Mustafa Erdoğan." Praj said. "55-year-old döner kebap shopowner in Harbour City Mall. Two-month history of fatigue, weight loss, chest wall pain, shortness of breath, cough, wheeze, hoarseness, and blood in his sputum. Admitted yesterday with a right-sided hydropneumothorax. Dr. Falstaff put in the chest tube and the referral."

126

"Exam?" Sababa corroborated Praj's physical findings.

"Imaging?" The two physicians excused themselves to bring Mustafa's radiology into view on a hallway monitor.

"Chest x-ray before Dr. Falstaff's reinflation act showed collapse of his right lung, fluid, and thickening of the lining."

"We have on our hands an ailing gentleman—sick man of Europe." Sababa said. "Did John send the fluid for histology?"

"The chart says he did." Praj and Sababa walked back down to the nursing station where the stocky savant dialed up the big brain in the basement.

"¿What do ju want, Cabrón?" It was Juan Leyblanca.

"John Falstaff sent you some pleural fluid yesterday from a patient named Mustafa Erdoğan."

"JesuCristo." Juan let loose a string of Patagonian profanity. "Thees ees not Taco Bell. Ju need to wait jor turn."

"I know you've seen it." Sababa said. "What was in it?"

"¿What do ju theenk?"

"The patient is from Tuzköy in Cappadocia." Sababa said. "For the first fifteen years of his life, he inhaled a fibrous silicate zeolite mineral called erionite which the locals carved their houses out of. He presents with a collapsed lung, a thickened pleural lining, and looks like death eating a cracker. I think he has the same disease that killed Steve McQueen and Warren Zevon and Malcolm McLaren of the Sex Pistols."

"Maleegnant mesotheeleeoma." Juan said.

"Epithelioid subtype?"

"Stateesteecally, ju would be correct." Juan said. "But he has the sarcomatoid form."

"Not good."

"Not good." Juan said. I call ju." *Click.*

Back in Mustafa's room, the patient had been waiting patiently.

"Neden nefes darlığı çekiyorum?" *Why am I short of breath.*

"How much do you want to know, Mustafa?"

"Bilmemek değil, öğrenmemek ayıptır." *There is no shame in not knowing something; the shame is in not being willing to learn.* Sababa laid out the problem for him.

"You're saying that I got this cancer forty years ago?" Mustafa asked.

"No." Sababa said. "You inhaled the cause forty years ago."

"Can you treat it?"

"We have radiation, chemotherapy, and surgery, Mustafa." Sababa said. "Your breathing function is not good enough for the kind of more aggressive slashing we do in certain selected patients, but we can keep your right lung reinflated by placing some talc between the lung and the lining."

"Talc?"

"It's strange, because we know that exposure to talc can also cause this type of cancer."

"How long have I got?" Mustafa asked.

"Always difficult to be sure." Sababa said. "The paleontologist Stephen Jay Gould lived for twenty years after they discovered his mesothelioma and died from a completely unrelated cancer. After his diagnosis, he wrote *The Median Isn't the Message*, insisting that statistics like median survival are useful abstractions, not destiny."

"But I will have a different destiny from your Mr. Gould." Mustafa said.

"Typical survival despite surgery is between 12 and 21 months." Sababa said. "But you have some worse prognostic factors. Çıkmayan candan umit kesilmez." *Hope springs eternal.*

"İlk nefes ölümün başlangıcıdır. İt ürür, kervan yürür." *The first breath is the beginning of death. The dogs bark, but the caravan passes on.* "You will speak to my wife?"

"I will speak to your wife."

Malcolm: How does your patient, doctor?
Sababa: Not so sick, my lord, as she is troubled
    with thick-coming fancies that keep her from rest.
William Shakespeare, *Macbeth* Act 5 Scene 3
(with apologies to the Bard)

Doctor Sababa respected Praj for his intellect, although he never would have admitted it. On their way to see the other ward referrals, the young resident shared his excitement over a recent clinical article. Sababa told him the results were invalid.

"But this paper demonstrates..." Praj complained.

"I never met a study I couldn't refute." Sababa said. They dropped a floor into the hospital basement, on a detour to resolve the opinion difference. In the sterile subterranean windowless room of the doctor's lounge were a few staff photographs and paintings on bone-white walls, a bank of printers that spat out corrugated patient lists, shelves of medical texts and clinical journals, and bulletin boards which advertised lectures and concerts and rental properties and second-hand sales and the latest creative pursuits of professional spouses. There were odours of ozone and cleaning fluids and old Code Brew coffee and pastry butter. Praj and Sababa hovered in front of a framed formula.

Bennett's Classification for Reading Medical Articles

Medical Student: Reads entire article but does not understand what any of it means

Intern: Uses journal as a pillow during nights on call

Resident: Would like to read entire article but eats dinner instead

Chief Resident: Skips articles entirely and reads the classifieds

Junior Attending: Reads and analyzes entire article in order to pimp medical students

Senior Attending: Reads abstract and quotes the literature liberally

Research Attending: Reads entire article, reanalyzes statistics, and looks up all references usually in lieu of sex

Chief of Service: Reads references to see if he was cited anywhere

Private Attending: Doesn't buy journals in the first place but keeps an eye out for articles that make it into Time or Newsweek

Emeritus Attending: Reads entire article but doesn't understand what any of it means

"A man cannot understand the art he studies if he only looks for the result without taking the time to delve into the reasoning of the study." Sababa said.

An older family physician, Dr. Charles Russell, approached the two men. "Sababa, I'd like to speak to you about the blood products you ordered on one of my patients." He said. "I'm wondering if there are any other options."

"How about death?" Sababa said. "Death is still an option." The professor explained the interaction with Praj.

"Dr. Russell here is some kind of holy man minus the holiness." Sababa said. "He belongs to a specific cult which rejects scientific thought. Rational arguments don't work on religious nutbars. Otherwise, there would be no religious nutbars. Dr. Russell once asked me to become a Jehovah's Witness. I told him I hadn't seen the accident."

"You don't believe in God?" Charles asked.

"I did." Sababa said. "Then one day I had hair in places I'd never had places before."

"I know you want to believe, Sababa."

"I also want to wake up and find myself in a forest of trollop trees and harlot hedges and floozie flowers but that road runs right past the Kingdom Hall. If you talk to God you're religious. If God talks to you, you're psychotic. Now if you'll excuse us, Charlie, my disciple and I have real live patients to see on the fifth floor."

Samara Morgan met their arrival with mixed enthusiasms.

"You need to get these two swivel heads off my ward." She said. "I need the beds."

"Good to see you too, Samara." Sababa said. "Whose bed would you like first?" Samara pulled a chart from the rack.

"Paris Hilton, here." She said. "Malcolm Canmore's former squeeze. She was his administrative assistant, although she did her best work on his desk, rather than beside it. He's down there waiting for you." Praj looked at Sababa who looked back at Praj.

"Do we get a story?" Sababa asked.

"Who am I, Margaret Atwood?" Samara fumed. "53-year-old admitted by Dr. Cliffy Carlton and reviewed by our neuroleptic, Dr. Oliver Lax. He said she has Alzheimer's. I say she's nuts."

"Why do you say that?" Praj asked.

"Because she's hitting on everything in pants except me." Samara said. "One day she's eloping with Tom Cruise, the next she's having children with George Clooney."

"Like a reverse DeClarembault syndrome." Sababa said.

"What?"

"DeClarembault syndrome." Sababa said. "It's a delusional disorder in which a woman believes that a man of higher social status is in love with her. Paris Hilton's love story is the other way around."

"It's not a delusion." Samara said. "She says she knows these relationships are in her head and not real."

"So if they're not delusions and she has Alzheimer's, these must be confabulations." Praj said. "Imaginary experiences fabricated to compensate for her loss of memory."

"It's not that either." Samara became impatient. "The psychometric testing Lax order showed that her memory is normal."

"Then she doesn't have Alzheimer's." Sababa said. "Whatever she has is causing her to have 'fantastic thinking.'"

"Well, I would appreciate it if her and her fantastic thinking can find another place to live." Samara said. "I'm starting to take some major heat from the bed Nazis."

"Let's go see her, Praj." Sababa and his apprentice headed down the hallway. They found Malcolm sitting by Paris' bedside. His welcome was Macbethian. *Canst thou not minister to a mind diseased, pluck from the memory a rooted sorrow, raze out the written troubles of the brain, and with some sweet oblivious antidote cleanse the stuffed bosom of that perilous stuff which weighs upon her heart.*

"You can help me." He said. "I asked for you."

"We'll try our best." Sababa said. "What did Oliver Lax say?"

"He said she has Alzheimer's." Malcolm said.

"Tell us how she came to be like this."

"She was fine until about five years ago." He said. "And then her personality and behavior changed. Dr. La Capuche treated her for depression but that didn't do a thing. She became more and more disengaged, developed false beliefs, and started to daydream about having relationships with celebrities. Her motivation disappeared and she began to neglect her housework and then her hygiene. She became impulsive, repetitive, and inappropriate in her comments and gestures, and she developed an appetite for sweets. She wouldn't step on cracks in the sidewalk. She picked at her fingers, pinched her lips, ground her teeth together, rubbed her right knee or right cheek, and swayed back and forth when standing."

"Apathy, disinhibition, loss of social graces, and compulsive behavior." Sababa said.

"All that." Malcolm said. Sababa looked at Paris, smiling and staring into space. She didn't look up, even when he called her name. His exam told him more.

Praj showed him the results of her Mini-Mental Status Examination. She had a perfect score. But her neurobehavioral assessment and MRI were abnormal. "Pronounced bifrontal atrophy." Praj said. "Especially of the medial frontal and anterior temporal lobes."

"Yep." Sababa said. "I'll bet that, if we did a single-photon emission CT, we'd see poor perfusion of her ventromedial frontal lobes causing impaired subjective feelings of reality and her role of self within that reality, her dorsolateral frontal lobes compromising her ability to separate altered feelings of reality from her intact understanding of reality, her right orbitofrontal cortex producing fouled up self-monitoring and inhibition, and her ventral and dorsomedial frontal lobes triggering her fantastic thinking."

"Right." Praj said.

Back in Paris' room, Malcolm had questions.

"Can you can do anything for her Alzheimer's?" He asked.

"She doesn't have Alzheimer's, Malcolm." Sababa said.

"But..."

"Which came first, her personality change or her memory loss?"

"Her personality change."

"It's the other way around in Alzheimer's." Sababa said.

"Then what is this?"

"It's bvFTD." Sababa said. "Behavioral variant frontotemporal dementia. When I trained, we used to call it Pick's disease, named after Arnold Pick, a professor of psychiatry from Charles University in Prague, who first described it in 1892."

"What causes it?" Malcolm asked.

"We don't know exactly." Sababa said. "But there is an excess of a protein called β-amyloid in neural cells, causing inflammation and cell destruction by the immune system. To be sure we would have to do a brain biopsy."

"But you're sure already."

"Sure."

"Anything you can do for her?"

"We can put her on a low dose of quetiapine for her behaviour." Sababa said. "But she will continue to deteriorate. I'm sorry." *A tear fell into the glass he raised to his dear. He drank the wine and then he drank the tear.*

"Me too." Malcolm said. "Who else had this condition?"

"Ralph Klein, the former premier of Alberta."

"He had fantastic thinking?"

"He did." Sababa said.

"Like our young Prime Minister."

"Nope." Sababa said. "He's a camp counsellor, nightclub bouncer, and snowboard flouncer. And a deluded liar."

'The Jumping Frenchmen of Maine
Were often considered insane:
Whatever you'd say
They would leap to obey,
Those excitable Frenchmen of Maine.'
    E.C. Bentley, *The Jumping Frenchmen of Maine*

Samara's frame filled the one around the door.

"Your other referral said he knows you." She said.

"He does?" Sababa asked.

"Yeah, poor bastard." Samara clutched her hundred-dollar clipboard. "60-year-old retired German cardiologist admitted by Dr. Gung Ho last night with a 3-week history of cognitive and memory deterioration, behavioral changes, incoordination, visual hallucinations, and involuntary movements. The found him saluting the bottom of an escalator at Harbour City Mall. I guess it's only reasonable that the bed Nazis would want to get rid of a real one. If you want to see Dr. Strangelove before he goes off for his MRI, you'd better get on it."

"Coming now." Sababa shook Malcolm's hand and promised to speak to him later.

Praj fetched a new chart from the nursing station. Together they went to see the retired cardiologist.

"Herr Doktor Wernher Merkwürdigliebe?" Sababa asked.

"Jawohl, mein kollege." The man had snow-white hair and wore silver wire-framed glasses. At the same time his left hand rose in an involuntary but provocative salute, his right hand struggled to bring it down from above his head.

"Whoa." Praj said. "You don't see that every day." Dr. Merkwürdigliebe's left hand began unbuttoning his shirt while at the same time his right hand followed in rebuttoning it.

"There appears to be a functional disentanglement thought and action between right and left, an intermanual conflict." Sababa placed a chair in front of the cardiologist and asked him to pull it forward with his right hand. Merkwürdigliebe's left hand pushed it away.

"Hmmmm." Sababa said. "Agonistic dyspraxia." He handed Wernher a book on the bedside table. The patient began to turn over the pages with his right hand while his left hand tried to close the cover.

"Diagonistic dyspraxia." Sababa observed. "He may be German but if his brain was a block of cheese, it would be Swiss Emmenthal."

"Meaning what?" Praj asked. Merkwürdigliebe put an apricot into his mouth with his right hand but before he could swallow it, his left hand pulled it out and tossed it away.

"Meaning that Herr Doktor Merkwürdigliebe here has *le signe de la main étrangère*, the Fisher Group I collosal variant of Alien Hand syndrome." When Wernher's phone rang, his left hand wrestled his right in a fight to answer it. "From a transmissible spongiform encephalopathy forming tiny holes in the brain where whole areas of nerve cells have died."

"What kind?" Praj asked.

"Sporadic Creutzfeldt–Jakob disease, although there are other forms." Sababa said. "Caused by a spontaneous mutation of a gene for a prion protein which causes a misfolding of the dominant alpha-helical regions into beta-pleated sheets, a change in conformation which disables the ability of the protein to undergo digestion. The misfolding of the prion-protein propagates itself in an exponential cascade of a self-sustaining accelerated positive feedback loop. The toxic protein aggregates form dense plaque fibers, killing off brain cells in massive numbers."

"Prions?"

"Abnormal protein molecules that form amyloid." Sababa said. "There are familial forms and acquired forms from contaminated electrodes and brain products, infected corneas and meningeal tissue and pituitary hormones, and the blood-born new variant from affected cattle we know as BSE, or Mad Cow disease—there are even people in Kentucky who acquired it from eating squirrel brains."

"It's not OK to feed bog animals to each other or eat brain material?" Praj asked.

"No, it's not." Sababa said. "Mother Nature will punish us for engaging in unrestrained venereal addictions, interfacing with other species, turning herbivores into cannibals, or screwing with the blood-brain barrier. One form of vengeance consists of these prion or slow-virus diseases—kuru in humans, scrapie in sheep, and chronic wasting disease in deer."

"There are other prion disorders?" Praj asked.

"The Fore of Papua New Guinea engaged in endocannibalistic funeral practices, in which relatives consumed the bodies of the deceased to return their 'life force' to the village." Sababa said. "Corpses of family members were often buried for days then exhumed once infested with maggots, at which point the loved one would be dismembered and served with the maggots as a side dish. Because the women and children consumed the less desirable body parts, including the brain where the prion particles concentrated, they were nine times more likely to contract what they call kuru 'laughing sickness,' after the classic muscle tremors that came with it. The incubation period was 20 to 50 years. Australian patrol officers thought it was psychosomatic, caused by the trauma of colonization and perpetuated by beliefs in sorcery and witchcraft."

"And Scrapie?" Praj asked.

"Another transmissible spongiform encephalopathy that affects sheep and goats." Sababa said. "It's characterized by compulsive scraping off fleece on rocks or trees or fences, lip-smacking, altered gaits, and convulsive collapse. Misfolded prions that first appear in lymph nodes and the Peyer's patches of the small intestine invade the brain through the spinal cord by creeping up the autonomic nervous system." He put his index finger to his lips.

"Watch." He whispered. Together he and Praj tiptoed back into Wernher's room undetected. Sababa clapped his hands together. Herr Doktor Merkwürdigliebe jumped out of his skin.

"Startle reflex." Sababa said. "Well-recognized sign in Creutzfeldt–Jakob disease. But there are other startle conditions such as the truncal hypertonia of genetic hyperekplexia, and some which represent simple benign culturally-specific behavioral peculiarities."

"Like what?" Praj asked.

"Like the verbal or behavioral imitation, compulsive obedience or negativism of Imu among the Ainu women of Japan, the screaming, cursing, dancing, uncontrollable laughter, and trance-like mimicry of Latah in Malay middle-aged women, the Mali-mali or Silo in Filipinos, the Bat-schi among Thais, Miryachit in Siberia, and then there is my favorite Hyperstartle-Plus syndrome."

"Which is?"

"The Jumping Frenchmen of Maine." Sababa said. "In 1878, George Miller Beard described the plight of French-Canadian lumberjacks in the Moosehead Lake region of Maine who, when startled, would jump and yell, and obey any sudden command, even if it meant striking a loved one. In the observations of fifty cases, Beard noted that the men were 'suggestible' and that they 'could not help repeating the word or sounds that came from the person that ordered them any more than they could help striking, dropping, throwing, jumping, or starting.'"

"And Herr Doktor here?" Praj was startled by the vacant look in the old cardiologist's eyes.

"Wernher's EEG showed the characteristic triphasic periodic sharp waves of rapidly progressive Creutzfeldt–Jakob." Sababa said. "He already has fulminant dementia, myoclonic jerks, and extrapyramidal and cerebellar dysfunction. Ninety percent of those afflicted are dead within a year of diagnosis, most within four months."

"Do we ever do a brain biopsy to be sure?" Praj asked.

"It's a dangerous procedure for obvious reasons." Sababa said. "Only if the clinical suspicion is not sufficiently high or low. Mein kollege will die of a one in a million disease, and not even know it."

They watched him put on his reading glasses with his right hand. And remove them with his left.

'All empires are created of blood and fire.'
Pablo Escobar

"It's protein deposition and bad lungs week." She said.

"Pity is between Mercy and sorry." Sababa smiled, pulling the first chart off the stack and handing it off to Praj.

"Hans Klupt." He called. An elderly man rose from a chair in the waiting room and followed the young doctor down the hallway to the resident's area. Sababa took the second chart.

"Pete Renoir." A thin shadow of a man accompanied Sababa into his office and took one of the two seats opposite the desk. The professor poured through the details of his referral documentation from Dr. Poldy Bloom. *72-year-old Salvation Army command commander followed by Dr. Ed Hyde for a five-year history of idiopathic pulmonary fibrosis. Has requested a second opinion. I thought of you...*

"How can I help?" Sababa looked up from the chart. His patient was pink and puffing.

"I want to talk to you about Jesus."

"Oh, no." Sababa said. "What's he done now?"

"You're an atheist?"

"Only during holy days." Sababa raised an eyebrow. "The rest of the time it doesn't matter."

"Myself, I've been with the Church my entire adult life." Renoir said.

"It may well be your only marketable skill." Sababa said. "Why would you want a second opinion if you believe in magic?"

"Faith is not a disease."

"No." Sababa agreed. "But it is communicable and kills a lot of people."

135

"I asked to see you because to find out why, after all my prayer and medical care, I'm no better." Pete said. "God's not supposed to work in trial and error."

"His mistakes are well-documented." Sababa said. "If he'd done everything right the first time, there'd have been one plague and zero great floods."

"He may have planned this for me." Pete said.

"I have observed that even those who claim that everything is predestined still look both ways before they cross the street." Sababa said. "What did Dr. Hyde tell you?"

"He said I have a disease of progressive scarring in my lungs and nobody knows what causes it."

"But I know." Sababa said.

"What do you mean?"

"What's the motto of the Salvation Army?"

"Blood and Fire." Said the command commander. "It describes the blood of Jesus shed on the cross to save all people and the fire of the Holy Spirit which purifies believers."

"I gave instructions to Dr. Bloom for you to have some blood of Jesus tests before I saw you."

"And?"

"And I got the fire of the Holy Spirit which purifies believers." He said. "The results show a positive rheumatoid factor and anti-CCP and antinuclear antibodies, and a high ESR and C-reactive protein."

"What does that mean?" Pete asked.

"You don't have idiopathic pulmonary fibrosis, you have pseudoidiopathic pulmonary fibrosis." Sababa said. "You have rheumatoid arthritis—rheumatoid lung sine arthritis, to be more precise."

"But I don't have any problems with my joints." He protested.

"You will."

"After the five years I'd had this condition?"

"Even then."

"Is there treatment?"

"You bet." Sababa said. "I'm going to add azathioprine and prednisone to the N-acetyl-l-cysteine that Dr. Hyde put you on. It would have helped, even if you had what he said you had."

"How do you know that?"

"It is my business to know what other people don't know." He said. "I know because the triple-therapy arm of the PANTHER-IPF trial was terminated early."

"You would be most welcome to join the Salvation Army, Doctor Sababa." Renoir offered.

"I'm afraid my vices are incompatible with your organization, Pete." Sababa said. "For me, the Salvation Army is like Franklin Roosevelt's

New Deal—it began by promising to save humanity and ended by running flop-houses and disturbing the peace. Although you do save me money on laundry. When the shirts I donate are washed and put on hangers, my wife can buy them back the next morning for half the cost of me having them dry cleaned. What a friend we have in Jesus." Pete and Sababa laughed together.

"Tell Mercy to make a return appointment in three weeks." He saw Praj trying to get his attention from the hallway. Pete and Praj changed positions.

"And?" Sababa asked.

"Hans Klupt." Praj said. "77-year-old Harbour City Mall smoke shop owner referred by Dr. James Ruben Andrews for worsening arthritis. He first presented with fever, diarrhea, and painful ankles and left knee after receiving a fluoroquinolone antibiotic for patchy pneumonia at the base of his right lung. They pulled off some fluid from the knee and found aseptic synovitis. Stool testing for Clostridium difficile was positive for toxin. They assumed his joint involvement was reactive arthritis from the organism."

"So?"

"So despite a course of oral vancomycin and prednisone his ankle pain didn't improve, his fingertips looked more and more like doorknobs, and he had a bone scan which demonstrated digital clubbing and the 'tramline' appearance of tubular bone periostosis."

"What you got?"

"I'm sorry."

"Praj, I can't teach you if you're going to be this repentant all the time." The professor said. "Sababa's Three Rules of Medical Analysis: (1) What you got you got, (2) What you don't got, you don't got, and (3) Context is everything. Now, what you got?"

"You mean the hypertrophic osteoarthropathy? HOA?"

"Also known as osteoarthropathia hypertrophicans or Pierre Marie-Banberger syndrome, after Austrian internist Eugen von Bamberger and French neurologist Pierre Marie." Sababa said. "The triad of digital clubbing, long bone periosteal reaction and painful limb tenderness, especially in the lower extremities, sometimes with synovial non-inflammatory effusions of large joints. What are the causes?"

"HOA can represent the rare hereditary disease of pachydermoperiostosis or acquired sarcoidosis and chronic infections, polyarteritis nodosa, familial Mediterranean fever, Takayasu's arteritis, and rheumatoid and psoriatic and reactive arthritis. More often, it's a secondary distant effect or paraneoplastic disorder related to certain cancers."

"Which ones?" Sababa asked.

"Ovarian, adrenal or lung malignancies." Praj said. "Usually lung."

"And what does Mr. Klupt do for a living?"

"He owns the Pipefitter Smoke Shop."

"And does he smoke?"

"No, but he did." Praj said. "Seventy pack-years."

"Any other history of note?" Sababa asked. Praj shook his head.

"Let's go see him." The two clinicians entered the resident's room to find a pale elderly man stripped to the waist.

"Dr. Bharmal here has told me of your problems, Hans." Sababa said. The smoke shop owner looked at his hands.

"They told me it was from the colitis." He said.

"It wasn't." Sababa said. He turned to Praj.

"Exam?"

"As you see." Praj held the man's hands out flat. "And he has fine crackles at the base of his right lung. Could be scarring from his previous pneumonia." Sababa had placed a chest x-ray up on the view box.

"It's not." He said. "This film was taken two days ago."

"It looks like he still has his pneumonia." Praj said.

"What?" Hans blurted.

"It was never pneumonia."

"What?" Hans and Praj blurted.

"Hans, this is an unusual kind of lung cancer." Sababa said. "We call it lepidic pattern adenocarcinoma because it grows along the surface of intact airspace walls without invasion. Even with just a sublobar resection, we see survival rates of a hundred percent."

"What happens now?" He asked.

"We need to confirm exactly what this is." Sababa said. "Dr. Bharmal here will get our local respirologist, Dr. Hyde, to arrange a bronchoscopic biopsy and write a letter to Dr. James Ruben Andrews. Your bone pain will respond to simple over-the-counter COX-2 inhibitors." Sababa handed him a prescription. "Tell Mercy I'll see you after your biopsy results become available."

"We'll see this last office referral together." Sababa told Praj after Hans had left. The stocky savant called into the waiting room as Praj grabbed the chart.

"Ben Castleman." In his inner sanctum, Sababa and Praj read the referral letter from Dr. Tictac Tarmac.

40-year-old Liquidation World owner with a 2-year history of cough, fatigue and mild shortness of breath with no associated fever. He was diagnosed with pneumonia and treated unsuccessfully with antibiotics. I told him you would find out what this is and fix it. Don't make me look bad.

"Is your cough productive, Mr. Castleman?"

"I'm a businessman." Ben said. "Of course it's productive." Praj asked to examine the man's chest.

"There's nothing here, Sab." Praj said. "His lungs sound normal."

"Absent air movement in occupied distal airspaces." Sababa said. "Don't worry, there's more. His lab results show increased hematocrit, gammaglobulins, lactic dehydrogenase, and carcinoembryonic antigen." Praj threw a chest x-ray up on Sababa's viewbox."

"Bilateral symmetric airspace densities affecting the lower lung zones, in a pattern of a batwing or butterfly distribution." He said.

"Differential diagnosis?" Sababa asked.

"Broad." Said the young resident. "Chronic opportunistic infections like mycobacteria or nocardia or fungi, malignancy, rheumatoid nodules, sarcoidosis, pneumoconiosis." Sababa found other results in Ben's referral.

"High resolution CT scan of his chest showed diffuse reticulonodular opacities and ground-glass densities in a continuous pattern with a thickened interstitial pattern of polygonal structures.

"Polygonal structures?"

"Hmmmm." Sababa mused. "Crazy paving?"

"Meaning what?" Ben asked.

"Meaning that you have rare lung disorder characterized by diffuse abnormal accumulation of formless lipoproteinaceous material within your airspaces impairing your pulmonary gas exchange and lung expansion." Sababa said. "The condition leads to difficulty breathing and a predisposition to infections."

"You got a name?" Ben asked.

"Pulmonary alveolar proteinosis." Sababa said. "PAP."

"What causes it?"

"There are several kinds." The professor opened his hand-scribed little Black Book of Remedies. "Yours is an autoimmune problem, the most common kind. Your B cells produce anti-GM-CSF autoantibodies to granulocyte-macrophage colony-stimulating factor, a critical stimulus to the development of airspace macrophages."

"Macrophages?"

"White blood cells that eat bugs and scavenge wreckage at sites of infection. They also clear surfactant, the liquid your lungs produce to reduce surface tension" Sababa said. "In their destruction, they fail to develop and function, leading to impaired phagocytosis and disturbed surfactant production. PAS-staining phospholipid and apoprotein derivatives pile up in your airspaces without causing any inflammation. It's like drowning on dry land in your own juices."

"Liquidation World." Ben said. "So, I'm a dead man?"

"Hell no." Sababa said. "Dr. Bharmal here will set up an appointment with our special local pulmonologist, Dr. Ed Hyde."

"What can he do?"

"Get us a diagnosis and treat you at the same time." Sababa said. "You'll have a bronchoscopy in which Dr. Hyde will take a biopsy and perform what's called a bronchoalveolar lavage. That will serve two purposes—the washings will contain diagnostic information that our pathologist can analyse, and the whole lung lavage will flush away the accumulated material. You may go a long time before you need another."

"Nothing else?"

"We do have GM-CSF injections, and lung transplantation for refractory cases, although I hope you won't need them."

"Well thanks, Doctor Sababa." Ben said. "I think."

"You know, the first series of 27 patients with pulmonary alveolar proteinosis was reported in the June 7, 1958 edition of the New England Journal of Medicine by Sam Rosen and two other doctors." Sababa said. "One of them was a physician named Averill Leibow who had a beautiful way of introducing new medical students to his discipline of pathology."

"What was that, Sab?" Praj asked.

"In the Beginning there was chaos..."

'The practice of medicine is not a state activity, and doctors who are over-identified with the state, or with the language of the state, have sold out. There are times when medicine has to be subversive. Doctors who cannot act, think and speak subversively can be dangerous.'

Dr. William Osler

On the eve of the monthly Medical Advisory Committee meeting, that strange, solemn, sacrificial, satanic, shamanic ritual of collision (or collusion, depending on the machinations of the participants) between the medical staff and the health authority bureaucrats, Sababa would get as close to the dark matter of the universe as he ever dared.

The conclave was held in the Boardroom, that same Oracle of Oversight, that identical morgue of ambition, in which Dr. Zaias chaired his Department of Medicine meetings. The only differences were that the light green-yellow padded walls were fuzzier from the static electricity, the white stippled acoustic tile ceiling worked harder to absorb the screams of the defeated, and the Mayline chairs fabric seats running the length of the long teak conference table held fatter asses and more of them. The particulate debris lurking under the table became even more agitated.

At the far end of the room, new graffiti marred the melamine whiteboard on an easel:

A cowboy named Bud was overseeing his herd in a mountainous pasture on Vancouver Island when suddenly a brand-new BMW advanced out of a dust cloud towards him.

The driver, a young man in a Brioni suit, Gucci shoes, RayBan sunglasses, and YSL tie, leans out the window and asks the cowboy, "If I tell you exactly how many cows and calves you have in your herd, will you give me a calf?"

Bud looks at the man, obviously a yuppie, then looks at his peaceful grazing herd and calmly answers, "Sure. Why not?"

The yuppie parks his car whips out his Macbook Pro, connects it to his iPhone satellite modem, and surfs to a NASA page on the Internet, where he calls up a GPS satellite to get an exact fix on his location which he then feeds to another NASA satellite that scans the area in an ultra-high-resolution photo.

The young man then opens the image in Adobe Photoshop and exports it to an image processing facility in Hamburg, Germany. Within seconds, he receives an email on his iPhone that the image has been processed and the data stored. He accesses an MS-SQL database through an Excel app spreadsheet and, after a few minutes, receives a response.

Finally, he prints out a full-color, 150-page report on his miniaturized HP LaserJet printer and turns to the cowboy and says, "You have exactly 1,586 cows and calves."

"That's right." Bud said. "Well, I guess you can take one of my calves."

He watches the young man select one of the animals and looks on amused as the young man stuffs it into the trunk of his car.

Then Bud says to the young man, "Hey, if I can tell you exactly what your business is, will you give me back my calf?"

The young man thinks about it for a second and then says, "Okay, why not?"

"You're a Ministry of Health apparatchik for the NDP government," says Bud.

"Wow! That's right," says the yuppie. "How did you guess that?"

"No guessing required." answered the cowboy. "You showed up here even though nobody called you. You want to get paid for an answer I already knew, to a question I never asked. You tried to show me how much smarter than me you are. And you don't know a thing about cows: this is a herd of sheep. Now give me back my dog.'

"What is this, some joke?" Asked Malcolm Canmore.

"Joke." Sababa said.

The committee was made up of medical staff departmental representatives—Jules Martino from Surgery, Juan Leyblanca from Pathology, Mako Brisk from Radiology, Trace Pangloss from Emergency, Banjo Paterson from Anesthesia, and Eleazar Sababa from Internal Medicine; and courtiers from the Palace of Administration, and all their urbane appurtenances—Malcolm Canmore, the Chief Hospital Administrator of the silk ties, linen handkerchiefs, and manicured fingernails, minus his silver cuff-links and platinum pens, Foster Inclusion, the new CEO of Island Health, Big Nurse Mildred Ratschet, the Grand Galactic Governess of Nightingales, sporting her string of cultured natural pearls, and a gaggle of other suits and pantsuits. They would collaborate to achieve the magnetic goals that drew their obscene destinies together, always ready and willing to judge and bludgeon the independent outsider.

But the committee chairperson, the most prepotent master of control, was a diminutive general practitioner named Dr. Petronilla de Meath, a Napoleanna bone apart, a harpy hag of a harridan henpecking harassment.

Petronilla picked up a handset from the multifunction business-class conference digital phone console and dialled zero.

"Lana, can you announce the beginning of the Medical Advisory Committee meeting?" The hospital switchboard operator's Big Voice broadcast the assembly overhead.

Petronilla called the council to order and requested approval of the previous meeting's minutes. A cacophony of grunts echoed around the table.

"I've tabled the old business." She said. "So we can hear a progress report from Foster Inclusion, the new CEO of the brand new expanded Health Authority.

"A modest man, who has much to be modest about." Sababa muttered.

"Foster has brought three associates up from Victoria." She said.

"One to read, one to write, and a third to keep an eye on the two intellectuals."

"Doctor Sababa!" Petronilla shouted. "Manners."

"Manners can replace intellect by providing a set of memorized responses to any situation in life." He said. "All the perfumes of Arabia will not sweeten this little hand."

"Foster, please proceed." She said. Inclusion rose to the occasion.

"Thank you for that excellent introduction, Petronilla." He said. "Let me begin by thanking you for your patience during the reconstitution of our new Regional Board, and efforts expended necessary to refine our Vision and Mission Statements." One of Foster's ill-suited accomplices adjusted a far wall bank of controls and switches and potentiometers dimming the photons and heat focused by the bored-out pot lights and railway yard grooves of track lighting. "First slide please..."

"The name of our new authority is Island Health." The slide had two words, as did Sababa. *Down the way where the nights are gay and the sun shines daily on the mountain top...*

Petronilla glowered in the dark. "Next slide..." A rainbow flag of many colours flew a caption. *Love is Healthy.* "Next slide..."

"We know that experience comes from bad judgment and we're at our best when we don't know what we're doing. To the five cornerstones of Canada Health Act, universality, accessibility, comprehensiveness, portability, and public administration, we have added two more. Next slide..."

TQM = Total Quality Management

"The previous health authority, VIHA, had already adopted the two disciplines of infrastructure change—the continuous value innovation of organizational and cultural development and the continuous value enablement of information technology development." Foster said. "TQM is the last of the five disciplines of change methodology, preceded by the four we have already perfected: strategic visioning, enterprise redesign, value stream reinvention, and procedure redesign. TQM consists of organization-wide efforts to install and make permanent a climate in which our organization continuously improves its ability to deliver high-quality services to our clients."

"There is nothing so useless as doing efficiently that which should not be done at all." Sababa's comment died from a lack of oxygen.

"TQM is not just a quality control program. Oh no. TQM is focused on everyone's satisfaction." Foster said. "TQM is an unyielding, continuing, improving effort by everyone in our organization to understand, meet, and exceed the expectations of our customers. Simply put, TQM is a management approach to long-term success through client satisfaction."

"Things which matter most must never be at the mercy of things which matter least." Sababa was once more ignored.

"Island Health has embraced the six disciplines of enterprise development: pick an important problem, get the facts, analyze the facts, find the underlying truth, plan a method of improvement based on the underlying truth, test it to verify that it works, standardize the new method, and then cycle around again to get a positive result."

"In the arena in which I work, a positive result is not a good thing." Sababa said. "Even W. Edwards Deming, your guru of Quality management, once declared that 'the most important things we need to manage can't be measured.' Idealism always increases in direct proportion to one's distance from the problem."

"I do understand completely, Doctor Sababa, why you are considered an unreasonable man." Foster could have spat bullets if he hadn't been so disarmed.

"The reasonable man adapts himself to the world; the unreasonable one persists to adapt the world to himself. Therefore, Foster, all progress depends on the unreasonable man." Sababa continued. "The more you hardwire total quality management, the more you hurt breakthrough innovation. The mindset that is needed, the capabilities that are needed, the metrics that are needed, the whole culture that is needed for discontinuous innovation, are all different. What's your second gift to humanity?" Foster called for the next slide.

Definition
Personalised, co-ordinated, and enabling, Client-directed Healthcare treats clients with dignity, compassion, and respect.

"First it was radical reform, then incremental change, now—finally—we're ready for client-directed healthcare—taking into account service users' needs, preferences and strengths, and providing an opportunity to make informed decisions about their care and treatment, in partnership with their health and social care practitioners. As a starting point, we have just published our... Next slide..."

Island Health Declaration
Client-directed Healthcare sets out to describe what client-directed Healthcare should look like.

"We're asking clients and stakeholders who want to see a real change towards client-directed care to sign up and pledge their actions and make their declarations to support their family and friends and community. Next slide..."

Objective
To help facilitate the provision of a seamless service to clients through a multidisciplinary team approach to client-directed treatment.

"We encourage clients to think about what client-directed care means to them, talk to others about it, and practice being client-directed in their interactions with clinicians and stakeholders. Clinicians will need to change from asking "What's the matter with you?" to "What matters to you today?" This will enable clients to co-produce their care and help a different conversation happen with different results for all concerned. Last slide..."

Client-directed Care in Action
1. Client-owned care and support page plans will be taken with them wherever they engage the system to support consultations.
2. Clinicians will write their letters with the client in the room.
3. Care Coordinators will help clients navigate around the system.

"There is evidence that client-directed care improves clinical outcomes, quality of life and reduces cost; but more importantly it can help people living with long term conditions thrive rather than just survive. We want to make this way of working together with patients become the norm. Any questions?"
"You plan on making vulnerable and traumatised and unenlightened patients responsible for their clinical outcomes?" Sababa asked.
"Our most unhappy customers are our greatest source of learning."
"Our most unhappy customers are dead, or dying needlessly because, instead of front-end loading the expertise that might save them, you're dismantling it in the name of administrative progress." Sababa said.

"Every new bigger iteration of the oxymoronic 'health authority,' weakened by cowardice, decadence, mediocrity, and spiritual exhaustion, confirms the close relationship between corruption of language, corruption of thought, and corruption of action. But 'tis strange: And oftentimes, to win us to our harm, the Instruments of Darkness tell us truths, win us with honest trifles, to betray's in deepest consequence... So well thy words become thee as thy wounds..."

"Macbeth?" Malcolm asked.

"It's just so right." Sababa said. "When the hurlyburly's done, when the battle's lost and won... there is nothing serious in mortality."

"I don't know what you're objecting to, Sababa." Foster said. "You and your fellow clinicians will still have a major input."

"This is not my first rodeo, Foster." He said. "I know how the bureaucracy works in Obfuckistan. Listen... Agree... Sidestep... Ignore..." There was a smell of sulphur.

"Never own a horse you can't ride." Sababa said. "Now give me back my dog."

Sababa entered the Harbour City Regional emergency department on a wind-blown dark cloud. He didn't even acknowledge Praj and Gung Ho waiting for him at the consultant's desk before he pulled up Rage Against the Machine from his music library on a secret drive hidden deep inside the hospital computer network. Eventually, he turned to reengage his transmission.

"What you got?" He asked.

"Polly Poses." Praj said. "24-year-old Real Canadian Superstore checkout cashier at Harbour City Mall who presents tonight with low blood pressure, high heart rate, abdominal pain and black, tarry stools.

"Sounds surgical." Sababa said. "What are we doing here?"

"That's just it, Sab." Gung said. "I expected to find peritonism—guarding, rebound, that sort of thing, but her abdomen is soft and nontender and unremarkable. No air-fluid levels on a flat plate x-ray even."

"You're transfusing her with matched whole blood." Sababa said.

"Six units." Gung said. "Her initial hemoglobin was in her boots. I called the surgeon on call tonight, Buddy Benway, but he won't see anyone who hasn't had a CT scan. *If it isn't on the CT scan, it doesn't exist.*

The porter, returning from radiology, wheeled a gurney back into an assigned cubicle. She was wearing rags and feathers from salvation army counters.

"Let's go see her." The professor said. Gung made introductions.

"Polly, this is Doctor Sababa, the consultant that Dr. Bharmal and I told you about. Gung said. "He squeezes the universe into a ball to roll towards some overwhelming question."

"My favorite TS Eliot poem." Polly said. "*The Love Song of J. Alfred Prufrock.* What's the question?"

"The most important question is 'What's the question?'" Sababa turned to Praj. "And what is the most important thing?"

"What we do with the most important question?" Praj ventured.

"The most important thing is to keep the most important thing the most important thing." Sababa said. "So what's the question?"

"What's causing me to bleed inside?" Polly offered.

"You bet." Sababa said. "Rest of her exam?"

"Normal." Gung said. Sababa put on a pair of surgical gloves.

"Open wide, Polly." He said. "Shine the light, gentlemen." Gung and Praj pointed their penlights onto flat dark freckle-like macules on Polly's eyelids, lower lip, gums, hard palate and the inside of both cheeks.

"Oh." Said both Illuminati.

"Stare." Sababa said. "It's the way you educate your eye and more. Stare, pry, listen, eavesdrop. Perceive that which cannot be seen with the eye. Die knowing something. Anyone else in your family with these freckles, Polly?"

"Dunno." She said. "I was adopted. What are they?"

"They're pigmented patches we see in a hereditary disorder called Peutz–Jeghers syndrome." He said. "Caused by a mutation in the STK11/LKB1 gene on chromosome 19. They come with hamartomatous polyps in the gut."

"Hamartom..."

"Kind of like tumours of malformed teeth." Sababa said.

"I have teeth in my bowel?"

Sometimes these hamartomas can cause intussusceptions, the telescoping of one loop of the intestine within another." Sababa left the cubicle with Gung and Praj to pull up Polly's CT scan on the consultant monitor. This produced many sounds of concordance.

"Cheri Sundae." Sababa asked. "Please raise Buddy Benway for me."

"On it, Sab." Cheri held her handset in the air less than five minutes later.

"Dr. Benway, line 1."

"You know how you smack something to get it to work. Sometimes I have to do that with people." Sababa said. "Can you dance with the devil in the pale moonlight?"

"She was supposed to have a CT scan." Buddy protested.

"She had it." Sababa said. "It shows multiple ileo-ileal small bowel intussusceptions. She has Peutz-Jeghers syndrome with a Rockall score of 3 with an 11.2% risk of rebleeding and a Blatchford score of 14, indicating a high likelihood of the need for further intervention, so you not only get to perform an emergency laparotomy, but she'll also need an upper GI endoscopy, the kind you like because it pays well."

"I'll be in." Buddy said. "Does she know about the other stuff?"

"Not yet." Sababa said. "I'll tell her now." *Click.*

Praj and Gung and the professor returned to the bedside.

"There's one other thing you need to know about Peutz-Jeghers, Polly." Sababa said.

"What's that?"

"It comes with fifteen times the normal risk of developing cancer." He said. "Not only gastrointestinal adenocarcinoma but also extra-gastrointestinal malignancies in the breast, lungs, liver, pancreas, uterus, and ovary. You'll need close monitoring with frequent endoscopy and imaging."

As he finished his dictation, Sababa caught a glimpse of two shapely legs in fishnet stockings sashay past the consultant's desk. Nice shanks. He looked up into the mascara of Dr. Sid Shalimar.

"Happy Halloween, Sab." His colleague grinned and threw a handful of candy.

"I wish I could believe that you only cross-dress like that one night a year Sid." The professor sighed.

"How do you hide a hundred-dollar bill from an internist, Sab?" Sid asked.

"Dunno."

"Put it under a dressing." Sid said. "Or, in my case, a cross-dressing." Mutual groaning ensued. The hundred dollars Dr. Shalimar produced bought Mambo's pizza for the ER nurses.

Later that night, Sababa picked Jane up from the concert she had attended at the Harbour City Theatre. He drove up Jingle Pot road onto Westwood Lake when the vault of heaven was breached by a torrential downpour followed by a sound and light show bursting from the RCMP Ford Interceptor that exploded out of a small side road.

Sababa floored his dimpled and dented white Honda Civic.

"What are you doing?" Jane asked.

"FIDO." He said.

"FIDO?" She asked.

"FIDO." He said. "Fuck It Drive On."

"You need to stop, Sab." Jane said. "I think it's that Marsden creature." The professor pulled over onto the road shoulder.

A study in kevlar exited her vehicle and approached his driver-side door. As he rolled down his window, Veronica Marsden shone a full-beam flashlight into his eyes.

"Licence and registration." Sababa rifled through his glove compartment looking for coupons that he might redeem for his freedom.

"I notice your eyes are bloodshot." Veronica said. "Have you been drinking?"

"I noticed your eyes are glazed over." Sababa said. "Have you been eating donuts?"

"Do you know why I pulled you over?" Veronica asked.

"Loneliness?"

"Your registration sticker is out of date." She said. "Where's your new one?"

"It's right here on the dashboard."

"What's it doing there?" She asked. "Why haven't you placed it on your back licence plate."

"I was waiting for a sunny day." Sababa thought the pause lasted far too long.

"Sonny." She said. "It's a sunny day."

'Here the ways of men divide:
   if you wish to strive for peace of soul and happiness, then believe;
   if you wish to be a disciple of truth then inquire.'
                               Friedrich Nietzche

On a crisp autumn morning in Harbour City, Praj and Myles Capitaine paged Sababa earlier than usual. They watched the Columbian leather briefcase fly a loop the loop before soft landing beside the ER consultant's computer.

"How are you, Myles?"

"Living the dream."

"Big dreams. Good music. Expensive taste."

"That would be the man in cubicle 3." Myles said. "You need to see him."

"Why?"

"Aulds Offramp." Myles said. "80-year-old retired civil servant from Ontario brought in last night in atrial fibrillation."

"And?"

"We shocked him."

"And?"

"He went back into sinus rhythm."

"And?"

"It's way too slow." He handed Sababa an ECG.

"Hmmmm." Sababa mused. "Also extraordinary low voltage as well as a left bundle branch block. You didn't give him digoxin."

"How do you know?" Myles asked.

"Cause he'd be dead."

"Why is that?"

"For the same reason his heart rate and conduction are slow and his voltage is low and he's eighty-years old." Sababa said. "Why didn't you call the internist on call last night?"

"Because he seemed stable enough." Myles said. "And we love you more."

"It takes a tough man to make a tender chicken." Sababa said. "Let's go see him." Praj introduced his mentor.

"Mr. Offramp, this is Doctor Sababa." He said. "He's our village explainer."

"So explain." Aulds said. "Why am I so tired, so short of breath and dizzy? Why do I pee blood and why do my legs swell? Why can't I sleep and, when I do, why does the numbness in my hands wake me up?"

Sababa took Auld's hands and flexed them together at the wrists. Aulds winced in pain.

"Positive Phalen's manoeuvre." Sababa said. "Carpal tunnel syndrome. Further confirmation."

"Of what?" Aulds asked.

"Stick out your tongue."

Aulds stuck out his tongue.

"Just as I suspected." Sababa said. "Normal."

"And if it wasn't?"

"If it was enlarged I would have thought you might have systemic amyloidosis but it's not, so you don't."

"So what have I got?" Aulds asked.

"We used to call it senile systemic amyloidosis but it's now known as wild-type transthyretin amyloid, or ATTRwt. It's a chronic progressive condition linked to abnormal deposition of misshapen normal protein, which cannot be degraded and eliminated by cell metabolism. The amyloid protein accumulates in the heart and tendons and bladder of elderly people."

"But I've always taken such good care of my health." Aulds protested.

"Getting older is no problem. You just have to live long enough. Remember the twenty extra years you added to your life through clean healthy living?" Sababa asked. "Well, these are them."

"Are you sure I have this weird condition?" Aulds asked. Everyone watched his ECG monitor take a six-second pause, except Aulds, who went unconscious until he wasn't.

"Sure." Sababa said. "Tell you what we're going to do. I'm going to put in a temporary pacemaker until one of our surgeons can give you a real one. Dr. Bharmal here will order an NT pro-BNP and troponin and immunoglobulin electrophoresis and echocardiogram. He'll get 'Doc' Martin, our in-house urologist to cystoscope you and our plastic surgeon, Dr. Christian 'Pretty boy' Troy, to do a carpal tunnel release and send the surgical samples for the same Congo Red staining that 'Doc' Martin will send your bladder biopsy for, and we'll have our diagnosis."

"If you find it, can you treat it?" Aulds asked.

"We can treat your diastolic heart failure and electric conduction problem." Sababa said. "You may be a candidate for diflunisal."

"How long have I got?"

"Median survival is six years from symptom onset." Sababa said. "2.7 years from diagnosis."

"I have less than 3 years from now?" Aulds asked.

"You may anyway. But you also may have been diagnosed early." Sababa said. "We try to do that around here."

"Is there no cure?" He asked.

"Liver transplantation." Sababa said. "Good luck with that one at your age."

"Old people shouldn't be born." Aulds reached across the railing of his bed for a New Testament.

"You believe that book has all the answers?" Sababa asked.

"To morality." Aulds said. "Maybe not science."

"The book is irreconcilable with science." The professor raised an eyebrow. "How many young witches did it burn to death because of psilocybin mushrooms, how many epileptics did it torture because they were possessed, how many did the Inquisition kill by for not converting to your definition of morality?"

"I'm not the hypocrite here." Aulds said. "You act like you don't care but here you are, saving lives..."

"Solving puzzles." Sababa said. "Saving lives is collateral damage."

"I just find it hard to believe that Jesus let all this happen to me."

"I wouldn't pin it on Christ." Sababa said. "He has enough nails in him."

"He died for your sins."

"Maybe somebody's, but not mine."

"Where's the fun in that? A finite un-mysterious universe."

"It's not about fun." Sababa said. "It's about truth. I must have missed rehearsal because I appear to be on the 'truth is good' side. Isn't that your part?"

"My faith is my truth." Aulds said.

"You are entitled to your own opinion." Sababa said. "You are not entitled to your own truth. And the one truth that affects everyone is that as soon as one part of your life starts looking up, another falls to pieces."

"Don't you believe in miracles, Doctor Sababa?"

"I believe that for every drop of rain that falls, a flower grows."

"Jesus will provide me a sign."

"You mean like his silhouette on your chicken sandwich?" Sababa dug deep into his music library on a secret drive hidden deep inside the hospital computer network. "Religion is not the opiate of the masses, Aulds. Religion is the placebo of the masses. Oh no, I've said too much..." R.E.M. filled the awkward spaces. *That's me in the corner, That's me in the spotlight, Losing my religion...*

"Now, if we have exhausted all the epiphanies, you might pray that Jesus will guide my Hindu associate Dr. Bharmal here in putting in your pacemaker." Praj did a Hindu head bobble, just for fun.

'So Occam's razor—Occam says you should choose the explanation that is most simple and straightforward—leads me more to believe in God than in the multiverse, which seems quite a stretch of the imagination.'
Richard Dawkins

The casual reader could be forgiven for thinking that Sababa was cavalier about youth and retirement and old age and life and death, and the roles that faith and truth played in the progression.

Aulds Offramp thought he would live forever, although the question that went begging was 'for what?' But, even with Jesus, our bodies would always break down and there was never any nobility in it. You could live with dignity but you couldn't die with it. It was always ugly.

Sababa couldn't conceive of retirement from his calling. He had planned to live his life in the saddle, do his work, then take his hat. *I trust that age doth not wither nor custom stale my infinite variety.*

Ahead of him, as with his patients, inevitable decline lay in ambush—hardening arteries, weakening heart and kidneys, thinning bones, and failing immunity and memory. Evolution had evolved an inevitability of systemic deterioration, resulting in a health authority prepared to invest in our repair only as much as their formula calculated we were still worth. Life is hard. A near-death experience, it eventually kills. Life is pleasant. Death is peaceful. It's the transition that's troublesome. In between, our devious minds will do anything to make it more interesting.

Death is more universal than life; everyone dies but not everyone lives. It takes no bribes and pays all debts. Sababa was as squeamish about death as anyone else. When someone close to him died, he moved seats. Some solace came from the writings of his masterless samurai, Miyamoto Musashi. *Do not be intent on possessing valuables or a fief in old age... Fixation is the way to death. Fluidity is the way to life... While on the Way, do not begrudge death... the Way of the warrior is resolute acceptance of death.*

Despite his ridicule, Sababa was not without certain kinds of faith. He chose to believe that the white light his patients claimed they saw were chemical reactions that took place when their brains shut down, but there was no conclusive science. Like the patients who clung to their superstitions and religions, Sababa chose the outcome he found more comforting—to believe that this wasn't simply a test. And that no statement should be believed because it was made by an authority.

For Sababa, existence was not a choice between truth and beauty, it was a choice for truth and beauty, for there was some of each in the other, as in Marquis Shu Ying's forces of *yin-yang* duality. Man... woman... birth... death... infinity. Even in his own demise, he would find some way of pouring a bag of popcorn kernels down his feeding tube to make the cremation more interesting. *From my rotting body, flowers shall grow and I am in them and that is eternity.*

'Management is doing things right; leadership is doing the right things.'
Peter Drucker

The human mind treats a novel idea the way the body treats a strange protein; it rejects it.

With brand new shiny pills and pacemaker, Aulds Offramp's mind rejected the novel idea of a massive boulder arriving from a direction he himself intended to go someday. The rock, as we now know, rejected his rejection, and no one knows in which direction he went next.

The chest cracker in Victoria performed a posterolateral thoracotomy on William Mathiseon Macleod, the young Sunset Scuba diving instructor. A brand new LUL segmentectomy restored enough blood flow to Bill's left lung to permit his eventual return to the underwater

152

world he so loved. Sababa got free diving lessons for his dream trip to Micronesia.

Her CEA returned high, but the combination of the same chest crackers's video-assisted thoracoscopic removal of the chocolate cysts menstruating in her chest and a brand new oral contraceptive prescription from Dr. Olaf Octagon fixed Thyme Adamant's endometriosis and saved her from requiring any more chest tubes. She is still the owner of the Releaf cannabis boutique at Harbour City Mall and has completely forgotten her ordeal, although she did remember to send Doctor Sababa a novel hemp hat with his name on the front.

Dr Zaias' wife, Julia, didn't attend her scheduled follow-up appointment with Dr. Ernie Hacker for her hairy experience, although she did mail him a novel 'after' selfie photo, completely cured of whatever that problem was.

Malcolm Canmore's paramour and former medical administrative assistant, Paris Hilton, died of her Pick's disease not long after Sababa saw her in consultation for her novel fantastic thinking. The young prime minister is still a deluded liar. Herr Doktor Wernher Merkwürdigliebe was also dead within two months of Sababa's diagnosis of Creutzfelt-Jackob Disease. He punctuated his last moments with Nazi salutes and exotic echolalia... *mein kollege... mein kollege... mein kollege...*

The black camel knelt before Mustafa Erdoğan's door not much later. His viscera was lung, his colour was white, his environmental factor dryness, his five senses smell, his taste spicy, his direction was west, his emotional activity grief, and his sound was crying. Sababa spoke to his wife.

Command commander Pete Renoir's rheumatoid lung disease responded well to Sababa's cocktail of medications. With his new blood and fire, he can be found every Christmas ringing his bell and filling his Salvation Army kettle outside the Harbour City Mall. Hans Klupt is back at his Pipefitter Smoke Shop, surgically cured of his lepidic lung cancer. His COX-2 inhibitor therapy did wonders for his bone and joint pains. He received a windfall payout by joining a novel class-action suit against the manufacturer.

Ben Castleman's lung biopsy proved he had pulmonary alveolar proteinosis. Ed Hyde's bronchoalveolar lavage worked well enough for long enough for Ben to liquidate his Liquidation World shop in the mall. Sababa has sent in a new form for a special release of injectable granulocyte-macrophage colony-stimulating factor.

Buddy Benway performed a laparotomy on Polly Poses, the young Real Canadian Superstore cashier with Peutz-Jeghers syndrome. He reduced multiple small bowel intussusceptions without the need for surgical resection and removed her polyps by enterostomy. In addition to following Doctor Sababa's new monitoring protocol for the development of malignancy, Polly was able to find her real family, most of whom had freckles where the rest of their faces should have been.

Sababa rejected Foster Inclusion's Total Quality Management and Client-Directed Healthcare for the strange proteins they were. Foster emailed the professor an article on time management. Sababa sent Foster a Dali print with a melting clock. *Come what come may, time and the hour run through the roughest day.*

Dr. Sid Shalimar and Dr. Eleazar Sababa celebrated their birthdays together at the Nori Restaurant with pine mushrooms that the portly professor had collected off the mountain. And Veronica Marsden would let them finish, her RCMP Ford Interceptor waiting in the silent shadows, radar gun set to stun.

17. The Case from the Crack of Doom

'Don't forget this fact, You can't get it back, cocaine
She don't lie, She don't lie, She don't lie, cocaine'
J. J. Cale, *Cocaine*

Popcorn Sutton drove the second last car off the Queen of Alberni B.C.
Ferry that had just docked in Departure Bay from the lower mainland.
The guy in the last vehicle beside him was beside himself—riled, ranting,
raving, raging, ratshit ropeable beside himself.

Popcorn didn't understand why the deckhands had held him up for so
long after the rest of the cars in his lane were allowed to leave, but he
could appreciate why the man was furious about it. No one likes to spend
a second longer in any ferry lineup than providence deems necessary.

What Popcorn didn't know was that the last driver didn't own the last
vehicle, nor was he renting, leasing, or borrowing it from who it belonged
to. The last driver had carjacked the BMW roadster in West Vancouver
and thought he had succeeded in making his escape to the Island. It was
a shame about the broken bones and bullet wounds he left behind, but
such were the hazards of clinging to something you loved. And the owner
of the BMW the last driver took it from loved it a lot.

Popcorn thought the last driver might have been a bodybuilder. He
looked too much like a condom full of walnuts. His manner suggested
more than a casual involvement with anabolic steroid use. 'What does it
profit a man to gain muscle and suffer the loss of his brain?' Popcorn
wondered.

He also wondered what all the RCMP Ford Interceptor police cruisers
were doing, assembled as they were at the mouth of the offramp onto
Stewart Avenue, and the final common pathway to everywhere on the
island. In his rearview mirror, Popcorn could see the last man's vehicle
blocked by two of the cruisers. One young female officer, in particular,
seemed far too enthusiastic in the way her Smith and Wesson pistol flew
out of its holster as she took aim behind her driver-side door. The last
driver screamed at his entrapment, pulled out a weapon of his own, and
shrieked at Constable Veronica Marsden's threatening pose. But the last
driver was about to learn the difference between shooting your mouth off
and someone else doing it for you. In his mirror, Popcorn saw the flashes
from her firearm before he heard the discharges. The last driver foamed
in the same stroboscopic incandescent flashing colours of the cruiser
lights surrounding his last breath. It was the hail of lead that he had
foreseen with Sababa.

A reporter from the Harbour City Star later asked Popcorn about the takedown.

"I counted sixteen shots." He said, although witnesses always get that wrong. "Then it was all quiet, really, really quiet." The same reporter interviewed Officer Marsden about the impact that the shooting may have had on the ferry employees and other witnesses.

"Their long-term needs are being taken care of." She said.

'She was a Phantom of delight
When first she gleamed upon my sight;
A lovely Apparition sent
To be a moment's ornament.'
William Wordsworth, *She Was a Phantom of Delight*

A month before the last driver lost his speech, and a few blocks away, pathologist Juan Leyblanca awoke in his Nob Hill fourth-floor penthouse condo to find a woman on the lawn below his bedroom window with a garden hose up her dress.

The original Nob Hill was an exclusive conclave in San Francisco, named after the Central Pacific Railroad's Big Four nabob tycoons, or 'nobs'—Leland Stanford, Mark Hopkins, Collis P. Huntington, and Charles Crocker, who built their granite palaces there. The mansions were all destroyed in the earthquake firestorm of 1906, but the Hill recreated itself as the home of upper-class families and affluent young urban professionals with landscaped parks of fountains and playgrounds. The downtown Nob Hill of Harbour City had no such illustrious provenance, although one could contrive appropriate double entendres from the surrounding San Francisco neighbourhoods of *Tenderloin* and *Market* and *Union*.

The prostitute douching herself on Dr. Leyblanca's front lawn was not a singular phenomenon. The Harbour City Regional pathologist would often hear the water flow within his walls at all hours of the night. Juan was not naive enough to think that he could put a stop to the illicit activity, and all the attendant problems of drug abuse and profiteering and violence and disease that followed.

In his native Argentina, prostitution was a schizoid compromise between Catholicism and copulation. More than a service industry, mopping up the overflow of male demand (which always exceeded female supply), prostitution was an old testament to the amoral power struggle of sex, which even the Catholic bishops and priests had never been able to stop. Prostitutes and their patrons marauded in the forest of archaic night.

156

Men were confused. They were conflicted. They wanted a woman who was their intellectual equal, but they were afraid of those women. They wanted a woman they could dominate, but then they hated her for her weakness. It was an ambivalence that went back to the relationship with their mother—source of his life, centre of his universe, object of both his fear and his love. Every man wanted a woman to appeal to his better side, his nobler instincts and his higher nature, and another to help him forget them. Every man slept with his wife, whose lips kissed his children, or with *putas*, whose lips kissed other parts of him, money making up the difference in beauty or desire. And the big difference between sex for money and sex for free is that sex for money costs a lot less. The men were not paying for sex. They were paying to act out a fantasy or for companionship or to be seen with a well-dressed young woman or for someone to listen to them. And for the wives, the difference between marriage and prostitution was that in marriage they only had to make a deal with one man.

Whores were deliberate bloody sacrifices on the altar of monogamy. That was why Jesus hung out with them. They took the money from under the lamp instead of in Versace. The Church condemned the sin but the community accepted the sinners, even condoned by that angelic doctor, St Thomas Aquinas. *Prostitution in the towns is like the cesspool in the palace: take away the cesspool and the palace will become an unclean and evil-smelling place.* The Church was a body, and the body was a business, and it all amounted to the same thing.

Juan recognized the similarity between prostitution and war. In war, as in prostitution, amateurs were often better than professionals. Juan knew of the similarity between prostitution and politics. Politics and prostitution were the only jobs where inexperience was considered a virtue. They bore a striking resemblance to each other in many other ways, although prostitution was the only career in which the maximum income was paid to the newest apprentice.

Juan understood that the prostitutes were victims. In the Anglo-Saxon countries he had trained and settled in, the prostitutes looked to him as if they purveyed, along with sin, the attendant pains of hell. They attracted a wide species of preying criminals. Every call girl was obliged not only to sell her genitals but her human dignity as well. Sex killed. And love was just a long succession of empty bottles and used condoms and syringes.

Juan understood the patrons who used up the prostitutes. They only thought about one thing, is it was big enough and where could they put it. That's why they called it a joystick.

The only way for Nob Hill prostitutes to purge their penetrations was with water, and the only accessible water came from the faucet connected to Dr. Leyblanca's garden hose. And the most persistently profuse user of Juan's water was a streetwise student of economics.

Every harlot was once a virgin. Honey Drive hadn't selected her current occupation as a first choice. She simply hated poverty more than she hated sin, and the career path Honey had chosen sure beat the hell out of waitressing. In every honest nocturnal transaction, she presented her bill upfront.

But Honey wasn't just your average hooker, oh no. Honey was a crack whore. She wasn't addicted to cocaine; she just liked the way it smelled. Honey loved cocaine from the first time she tried it but, as with all of her other loves, the feeling didn't last. Chemistry can be a good and bad thing. Chemistry is good when you make love with it. Chemistry is bad when you make crack with it. Cocaine was terrific if you wanted to stay awake for three weeks with unconscious naked people you didn't know. It was bad for everything else.

There were three things Honey had learned about cocaine: (1) there was no such thing as enough, (2) it would never be as good as the first time, and (3) your brain will settle into a puddle around your sinuses. When it snows in your nose, you catch cold in your brain.

Cocaine came without a happy ending. You either died, you went to jail, or else you ran out. In fact, the main purpose of buying cocaine was to run out of it. When Honey ran out, she was empty inside.

And now she had new problems of fatigue and shortness of breath, bruising, and blood in her urine that even a garden hose couldn't wash away.

Everyone who doesn't live in a prostitute's bed on a diet of cocaine snow is an ascetic these days. Juan Leyblanca was such a desert saint. He poured his morning coffee from a French press, sat with his morning paper, and turned on his radio.

This land is my land this land ain't your land... a big shout out to you recent immigrants... This is CNDN Coast Salish radio, 101.3 FM on your Home and Native Band. I'm your host, BC Bud...

Juan turned to the Harbour City Star's crime page and obituaries, which often gave him a good idea about how his week would go.

Happy Columbus Day to our American cousins... Party like it's 1491 BC... Before Columbus...

There were the usual eulogies to the ancient Ontarians and Albertans and prairie rats who had managed to live longer by retiring to the island and leaving their surviving family members to fend for themselves back east.

It started with a lack of cohesive border security... In the great Columbian exchange, you brought us smallpox and scarlet fever and we gave you syphilis...

158

He read the list of recent arrests for burglaries and assaults and drug dealing and other petty crimes. There was a series of unexplained carjackings on the mainland with the vehicles ending up on this island.

Call me cynical, but I'm so over multiculturalism... but we're getting it all back in the casinos and bingo halls... one house at a time...

Real estate prices had continued to climb.

Life is not a fairy tale. If you lose your moccasin at midnight, you're drunk... Many have fallen with the bottle in their hand...

There were reports of cases of local blindness. Someone was making moonshine with the methanol still attached.

For all you whitebacks out there looking for BC Bud's smoke signals... show me your papers...

The Tilray marijuana facility was going literal gangbusters out at Duke Point, driving down the price of less legal local weed.

I had a deer hoof for a roach clip... My circle was so small, I used to pass the joint to my other hand, and hit it again...

Cries of distress from below his harbour view interrupted Juan's morning musings. The washer woman doubled over in pain. Her last sigh fell to the ground.

Remember kids... Smoke salmon, not drugs...

The pathologist did something he never had to do with any of his other patients. He dialled 911.

Those that lie down with dogs, get up with fleas...

There is a little crack in everything, that's how the light gets in.

> 'Tis the strumpet's plague
> To beguile many, and be beguil'd by one.'
> William Shakespeare, *Othello*

The morning before Honey Drive collapsed under Dr. Leyblanca's window, and a month and a morning before the last driver lost his speech, Dr. Praj Bharmal paged his guru from the Harbour City Regional ICU.

"Why are there so early?" Sababa asked.

"Dr. Harry Martin asked me to admit one of his patients."

"What for?"

"He said it was a dermatological emergency."

"Doc Martin is a dick doctor." Sababa said. "And a pisshead. The only kind of skin he deals with are foreskins."

"This guy is sick, Sab." Praj said.

"On my way in." He said. "Give me twenty." Fifteen minutes later, Praj had to duck a Columbian leather briefcase flying aerobatics over the bridge of the Death Star, before it came to rest beside the consultant's computer.

"OK, Mowgli." Came the voice behind. "What you got?"

"38-year-old souteneur who saw Dr. Harry Martin a week ago."

"Souteneur?" Sababa asked. "You mean like 'pimp?'"

"My word is kinder." Praj said.

"Holding things in can give you cancer." Sababa said. "Let's call him a pimp."

"He also deals in illicit substances."

"Let your spine reach your brain." Sababa encouraged. "He's a pimp and a drug dealer. Why is he taking up space in my critical care unit?"

"I'll show you." Praj went over to cubicle 4 and pulled back the curtain and watched as both of his mentor's eyebrows rose in acknowledgement of the young resident's rectitude in admitting the patient.

Mary tended to a young man in serious distress. Most of his skin and mucus membrane surface area was raw and blistered and peeling.

"Looks like a refugee from a sunlamp." Sababa noted.

"Who the fuck are you?" The man garbled.

"If they fight you, they're still alive." Said the professor.

"This is Doctor Sababa, Joe." Mary said. "He's the specialist I told you about."

"I thought that was Doc Martin."

"He was the last doctor." She said. "Doctor Sababa is the one after that."

"What happened here, Praj?" Sababa asked.

"Joshua 'Joe' Jackson." Praj said. "Saw Doc Martin for erectile dysfunction three days ago."

"I once tried to Google impotence, but nothing came up." Sababa said. "And?"

160

"Gave him a prescription for sildenifil."

"Abracadabra, I'm up like Viagra." Sababa said. "Little young for that, aren't you, Joe? You use your own cocaine?"

"Hell, no. It provokes the desire, but it takes away the performance." He said. "I only take Viagra when I'm with more than one woman."

"It's a Disneyland device. You wait an hour for a two-minute ride." Sababa said. "Like putting a new flagpole on a condemned building. People who think there's no good way to die have never heard the phrase 'drug-fueled-sex heart attack.'"

"Sex is one of the most beautiful, natural, wholesome things that money can buy." Joe said.

"You specialize in prostitutes?"

"Just the sight of one of my girls touches some ascetic, hidden corner of my soul."

"It turns out that your penis is not the largest organ in your body, Joe." Sababa said. "Your skin is." He encouraged Praj to tell him more.

"One day after he took 100 mg of Viagra, he spiked a fever and developed a sore throat and cough and fatigue and burning eyes. He saw a Doc-in-the-Box at one of the walk-in clinics who prescribed a course of antibiotics but, even before he took the first pill, his skin reddened and bubbled and came off in layers, and painful ulcers formed on his lips and in his mouth and genital and anal regions. The prescribed antibiotic wasn't a sulfonamide or one known to cause this kind of reaction. He stopped eating because of the agony. Came into the ER late last night with severe dehydration. Asked to see Doc Martin."

"And?"

"Turns out that the urologist was in house up on floor 6 dealing with a lower urinary obstruction of some kind." Praj continued. "He came down to see Joshua there and then called me to admit him."

"This makes no sense." Sababa said. "Where were the ER docs and the on-call internist in this fustercluck? Why didn't Harry consult our local dermatologist, Commodus Sitsofsky? And why wasn't this guy shipped down to a burn unit where he belongs?"

"Dunno." Praj said. "All I know is that he has a bad SCAR that I've been trying my best to look after."

"Scar?" Joe gurgled."

"Severe cutaneous adverse reaction." Sababa said. "There are five kinds—Stevens–Johnson syndrome, toxic epidermal necrolysis (TEN), Stevens–Johnson/toxic epidermal necrolysis overlap syndrome, acute generalized exanthematous pustulosis, and DRESS syndrome."

"I bet I have the dress reaction." Joe said.

"It would be the most fitting revenge." Sababa said. "Drug reaction with eosinophilia and systemic symptoms. But I don't think that's what's going on here. Anything else to help us, Praj?"

The young resident slid a gloved index finger across a small area of Joe's torso. Everyone watched the souteneur's skin slide off behind it.

"Nikolsky's sign." Sababa said. "Tobacco kills tens of thousands of people a year from lung cancer and there's no telling how many lives have been ruined through drinking. But to my knowledge, Mr. Jackson, no one has ever died of a blow job. You could be the first."

"From what?" Joe muddled.

"Dehydration, sepsis, pneumonia, multiple organ failure. Take your pick." Sababa said. "You have toxic epidermal necrolysis."

"Sab, his SCORTEN scale is three." Praj said.

"Man, you guys are so medical I can only understand every third word." Joe said. "What does that mean?"

"It means you have more than a 35 percent chance of dying from this." Sababa said.

"It's that serious?" Joe jumbled.

"That serious." Sababa said. "Dr. Bharmal has done an excellent job so far by giving you adequate pain medication, antihistamines, antibiotics, intravenous immunoglobulins, and fluid replacement, topical corticosteroids, nasogastric tube feeds, and consulting an ophthalmologist, but you'd be better off in the burn unit in Victoria. Which is exactly who I'm going to contact now to arrange transfer." But before Sababa could make his call, Betty Boop held up her handset.

"Doc Martin on line 1, Sab." She said.

"It's a good thing you didn't prescribe any prune juice with that Viagra, Harry, or your procurer wouldn't have known if he was coming or going."

"My procurer?" The urologist stammered.

"The only reason for you to have shown so much interest in Joshua Jackson was if there was some quid procurer quo going on." He said.

"That's an insult." Harry protested.

"I'm not insulting you." Sababa said. "I'm describing you."

"How did you know?"

"I like being a detective, I like the work." He said. "Why else could he come to a stream team specialist without a referral to get samples of a drug he could have received a prescription for in in any general practitioner's office?" There was a lull on the line.

"You won't mention this to anyone." Harry said.

"Physician-patient confidentiality protects me from annoying conversations."

"Thanks, Sab." Harry said. "You ever hear the one about the Harbour City woman 'of a certain age' who visited her physician to ask for his help in reviving her husband's sex drive?"

"Can't say I have." Sababa said.

"'What about trying Viagra?" The doctor asked.

"Oh, no, doctor, I couldn't do that." She said. "He won't even take an aspirin."

"Not a problem." The doctor said. "Drop it into his coffee. He won't even taste it. Give it a try and call me in a week to let me know how things went."

It wasn't a week later, that she called the doctor, who inquired about her progress.

"Oh, doctor." The poor dear exclaimed. "It was horrid. Terrible."

"Oh." The doctor said. "What happened?"

"Well, I did like you said and slipped it into his coffee." She said "The effect was almost immediate. He jumped himself straight up, with a twinkle in his eye, and with his pants bulging something fierce. With one swoop of his arm he sent the cups and tablecloth flying, ripped my clothes to tatters and then, he took me right then and there, making wild, mad passionate love to me on the tabletop. It was a nightmare."

"Why so terrible?" The doctor asked. "Was the sex not good?"

"No, no, Doctor. The sex was fine, the best I've had in 25 years. But I'll never be able to show my face in Tim Hortons ever again.'"

Betty Boop held up her handset.

"Two more in emerg for you, Sab." She said.

"Tell them we're on our way." The professor grinned at his young associate.

"How are you possibly in a good mood?" Praj asked.

'A junky runs on junk time. When his junk is cut off, the clock runs down and stops. All he can do is hang on and wait for non-junk time to start.'

William Burroughs, *Junkie*

Dr. Gung Ho was overjoyed to see Sababa and his apprentice.

"You need to help me sort this guy." He said.

"Which guy?" Sababa asked.

"That one." Gung pointed to the disheveled intubated middle-aged man the respiratory technician was bagging in a corner of the acute room.

"William Burroughs." Gung said. "47-year-old with a 20-year history of substance abuse, recently resorted to 'skin popping' after 'using up' all his veins, including that dorsal one that used to drain the venous blood from what's left of his penis. I had to put in a central line and an endotracheal tube. He's been here twice in the last two days."

"What for?" Praj asked.

"First time he came in complaining of blurred vision and trouble swallowing. Cliffy gave him 0.4 mg of 'wake-the-fuck-up' and told him his party was over. He came back yesterday with double vision, droopy eyelids, and slurred speech. Exam showed an abscess of his right thigh, which I drained, numerous uninfected skin lesions at other subcutaneous and intradermal injection sites, and multiple cranial nerve palsies and some limb weakness, for which I referred him to our neurologist, Dr. Oliver Lax."

"Diagnose. Adios." Sababa said.

"Yep." Gung said. "Said he'd had a brainstem stroke even though nothing showed on his brain CT. Ollie doesn't admit his patients, so Sweet William here waited in limbo until one of the GP hospitalists could take over his care."

"And?"

"He never made it."

"The patient?" Praj asked.

"No, the hospitalist." Gung said. "Early this morning Burroughs developed generalized weakness. A few minutes ago, he had a respiratory arrest. And here we are."

"Let's go see him." Sababa suggested. The respiratory technician hooked William up to a ventilator while the three physicians conferred at the bedside.

"What's the drug?" Praj asked.

"Not coke." Sababa said. "Note the absence of central pallor surrounded by hemorrhage of his injection sites, a pattern characteristic of the vasoconstrictive properties of cocaine."

"It can't be a narcotic." Gung said. "We've given him umpteen doses of intranasal and parenteral naloxone this time with no improvement."

"But it did have some effect the first time." He said. "Junk is the ideal product, the ultimate merchandise. No sales talk necessary. The client will crawl through a sewer and beg to buy." Sababa went through William's cranial nerve exam and went on to examine his extremities. He pulled his antique Queen Square reflex hammer from its resting place in his Columbian leather briefcase and tapped the addict's tendons. There was no reaction.

"It's not a stroke." Sababa said. "He has symmetric flaccid paralysis, not an asymmetric spastic process."

"I didn't think so." Gung said. "Must be Guillain–Barré syndrome."

"It's not Guillain–Barré syndrome." Sababa said.

"But he has complete paralysis of all his limbs and cranial nerves." Gung protested.

"Guillain–Barré causes an ascending paralysis." Sababa said. "Mr. Burroughs here has a descending paralysis."

"From what?" Praj asked. "From narcotics? It doesn't make sense."

"When you cannot be deceived by men you will have realized the wisdom of strategy." He said. "When you have attained the way of strategy there will be nothing that you cannot understand. You will see the way in everything."

"What's the way?" Gung asked.

"The way of strategy is the way of nature." Sababa said. "If you are to practice the way of strategy, nothing must escape your eyes."

"OK, Sab." Gung said. "Enough Miyamoto Musashi mumbo jumbo. What's escaping our eyes?"

"What could William Burroughs have been skin-popping that could have caused his symmetric descending flaccid paralysis?"

"Dunno." Praj and Gung said together.

"Contaminated Black Tar heroin from Mexico 'cut' with shoe polish, wood pulp, coffee grounds, and dirt." Sababa said. "Dissolved in a weak acid like lemon juice mixed with saliva and heated to boiling."

"Contaminated with what?" Gung asked.

"Something that thrives in the heated anaerobic conditions that would destroy every other bacterium in the neighbourhood." He said. "Something that can cause this kind of neurological presentation."

"A neurotoxin." Praj had a eureka moment. "From the germinating spores of Clostridium botulinum."

"Head of the class." Sababa said. "Wound botulism." He looked over at William Burroughs who couldn't hear either of the two Sababas in his visual universe.

"What can you do for him?" Gung asked.

"Praj here will order serum for botulinum toxin in a standard mouse bioassay and neutralization antibodies, send wound tissue samples for Clostridium botulinum culture, write Sweet William's Death Star and ventilator setting orders, give him a dose of trivalent equine botulinum antitoxin and a 10-day course of benzylpenicillin 1.8 g qds plus metronidazole 500 mg tds, and get 'Pretty Boy' Troy to debride his skin lesions."

"You need a plastic surgeon to do that?" Gung asked.

"Not at all." Sababa said. "But I know how much it will make his day complete."

"Anything else?" Praj asked.

"Yeah, get Ollie Lax to come back and do some nerve conduction studies." The professor handed him three names on a piece of paper. "And then we have to see these other inmates. The first is on the first-floor telemetry unit. Call me when you're done with her. We'll see the last two together." *Fiera Carpenter... Popcorn Sutton... Bettino Ricasoli...* The young resident flew at it.

"Little tough on Praj, aren't you, Sab?" Gung asked.

"Some of our little birds don't learn to fly until they lose all their feathers." He said.

"Hey, I sent that guy home." Cliffy Carlton peered over at Gung's ventilated patient. "His chief complaint two days ago was that he needed Dilaudid and a turkey sandwich and a cab voucher home."

"We'll need to talk about that, Cliffy." Sababa said. "He's got wound botulism."

"You can't fix stupid but you can intubate and sedate it." Cliffy put an arm on Sababa's shoulder.

"What else do you want?"

"I need you to see the Rasta man in bed 4." He said. "Impeccable Williams, 61-year-old quality control technician at Tilray Cannabis brought in barely conscious by EMS, found by his landlord after a 3-week history of nausea, malaise, and frequent bouts of vomiting thought due to hepatitis A. Family history of a dead brother who had sickle cell trait and travel history of a trip back to Jamaica two months ago for one of their groundation meetings."

"Nyabinghi issemblies."

"What?"

"That's what their communal meetings are called now." Sababa said. "Nyabinghi issemblies."

"Whatever." Cliffy continued. "Anyway, he comes in confused and dehydrated with jaundice and sky-high liver tests. Viral and autoimmune hepatitis serology ordered by his family doc last week was negative, as was toxicology screen for drugs of abuse and acetaminophen today. He's anemic with some sickling noted on his peripheral smear, and has impaired coagulation. I gave him a bolus of D50W for his low blood sugar."

"So, what you got?" Sababa asked.

"I got some pothead with fulminant liver failure speaking dreadtalk I can't understand." Cliffy grinned. "And I got you, Babe."

"Let's go see him." Behind the curtain that divided bed 4 from the rest of the known universe, was a thin middle-aged black man with a long salt 'n pepper beard and a medusa of coarse dreadlocks barely contained by a crocheted round rastacap the colours of Africa.

"Impeccable, this is the specialist I told you about." Cliffy said. "He's an infinite web of golden threads."

"Ahoy bredren, wa gwaan?" Sababa asked. Cliffy didn't even think of inquiring.

"Bwai, ya done know seh mi deya gwaan easy." Impeccable said. "Jah bless bretta. One love."

"Fiyah bun kaaz dis Ball head Bumba clot taament me."

"What's he say?" The ER doc asked.

"I don't think he likes you, Cliffy." Sababa leaned over the rails.

"Wapen, Impeccable?" He asked.

"Ah, mi nuh have nutten fi complain bout." Impeccable said. "Mi life irie."

166

"Hold up your hands." Impeccable lifted his arms into the air and his hands try to flap away from his wrists.

"Asterixis." Sababa said.

"Hepatic encephalopathy." Cliffy added.

"Do you use any drugs, Impeccable?" Sababa asked

"Ah, I only smoke 'oly 'erb." He said. "In spliff or in chalice. 'Erb is the healin' of a nashun, alco'ol is the destrucshun. But I 'aven't even dun dat the last tree weeks caaz I sick sick."

"What's your favorite food, Impeccable?" Sababa asked.

"Man a rasta man, mi only nyam ital food." He said. "I like mi ackee and saltfish too much much."

"Too bad you can't get it on the island."

"Ah, I make it at mi 'ome."

"When was the last time you ate ackee and saltfish?"

"Tree weeks ago." He said. "Solomon sent me a new package of oven-dried ackee fram Jamaica."

"Solomon?" Sababa asked.

"Solomon Williams." Impeccable said. "Mi bretta in Kingstun."

"Did you get sick just after eating the new ackee." Impeccable's yellow eyes grew wide.

"Six iwas after eatin' the saltfish I get belly pain." He said. "And den I cyaan stop vomitin' until now."

"Genesis 1:29." Sababa said. *And God said, Behold, I have given you every herb bearing seed, which is upon the face of all the earth, and every tree, in the which is the fruit of a tree yielding seed.* "Excuse us for a few minutes, Impeccable." Sababa and his referring emergency physician left the patient cubicle to confer well out of hearing range.

"What's going on here, Sab?" Cliffy asked.

"Funny thing about the fruit of the ackee tree." Sababa said. "It's safe and delicious when ripe."

"But?"

"But if you eat its unripe arils or seeds or husks, you'll get JVS."

"JVS?"

"Jamaican vomiting sickness." Sababa pulled his own Book of Revelations from his Columbian leather briefcase. "The immature fruit still contains up to ten thousand times more hypoglycin A, a toxin which, when metabolized to methylenecyclopropylacetic acid, inhibits fatty acid oxidation and depletes a cofactor necessary for making glucose. Once liver glycogen stores are gone, the body cannot synthesize glucose, resulting in severe persistent low blood sugar."

"Is it usually this serious?" Cliffy asked.

"No, although it can be fatal all by itself." Sababa said. "But Impeccable has sickling on his peripheral smear so he must also have sickle cell trait. The hepatotoxic effect of the unripe ackee fruit he ate synergized with sickling-induced ischemic injury, causing massive liver failure."

167

"So he needs a new liver?"

"He needs a new liver."

"What can you do?"

"Get him one." Sababa turned to catch the emergency ward clerk's attention. "Cheri Sundae, please patch me through to Ziggy Stardust in Vancouver."

"On it." She said. Two ER nurses recognized the call request and migrated towards Impeccable's cubicle.

"Regina, please give Mr. Williams here vitamin K 10 mg, erythropoietin 2000 IU, and hang 2 bags of cryoprecipitate." Sababa said. "Michaela, please piggyback a bag of D10W at 50ml/hour onto his IV, and tack on octreotide by my protocol to reduce his pancreatic insulin secretion."

"Ziggy Stardust on line 3, Sab." Cheri Sundae held up her handset.

"How come you only call me when you're after something." Ziggy asked. "What do you want?"

"I need a liver, Zig." Sababa said.

"What for this time?" Dr. Stardust was the best liver guy in the big city.

"Unripe ackee fruit and sickle cell trait." Sababa told him the Rasta man's story. "Everyday buckit a go a well, wan day he battam drap out." Ziggy said. "Send him ova by choppa. You overstand de odds." *Click.*

"Call in the Big Bird, Cheri." He hung up his handset and watched the ward clerk pick hers up again.

Sababa and Cliffy went back into Impeccable's cubicle.

"Ah, what do I and I do now, Iya Sababa?" He asked. Sababa took the time to explain the lack of options and his one chance at survival.

"Jah Jah protect mi fram mi enemy dem."

"Ziggy Stardust." Sababa said. "'e's a 'epatologist. Look fi 'im."

"Mi, I mo' need a rastalogist." He said. Sababa grinned.

"Nah skin yer teet bai!" Impeccable said. "Give thanks. Praise Jah. I apprecilove you livication and dat you is truely 'epin' mi. I and I is evalivin', evafaithful, evasure. Ras Tafari. I-men."

"Yes I, a so it go still." Sababa said. "Not 'n na gwaan, but we a keep di faith, nuh true?"

"Ah, yeh man, orange yellow but yuh nah know if it sweet jus-now." Impeccable said. "Lickle more, seen? Jah Jah bless."

"Lickle more." Sababa said. "Me a go."

Ten minutes later, a racket of rotors rocked the Harbour City Regional emergency dependent. *Dubdubdubdub whumpawhumpa whupwhup wuppawuppa whopwhop batabata tocotoco flacflac chakkchackk chakachak akk-chk thiththith ssssssssss...*

Five minutes after that, two blue air ambulance jumpsuits followed their noses to a holy herb smell wafting out of cubicle 4. Dey din overstand der greetin'.

Cool alyuh.

'I smoke two joints in time of peace
And two in time of war
I smoke two joints before I smoke two joints
And then I smoke two more.'
Sublime, *Smoke Two Joints*

'We are all primary numbers divisible only by ourselves.'
Jean Guitton

An hour later, Doctor Sababa rolled through the frosted doors of the Harbour City Regional first floor telemetry unit.

"Morning, Serafina." He said. "Where's my boy?"

"Bed 3, Doc." She said. "He's quite a serious young man." Sababa called into the curtain."

"Coming now." Praj emerged with a chart and motioned Sababa to join him out of hearing range of the patient.

"Tough one, Sab."

"Not for you, Mowgli." He said. "What you got?"

"Fiera Carpenter." Praj said. "19-year-old professional model. Patient of Dr. de Meath."

"Petronilla referred me a patient?"

"She's on holiday." Praj said. "It was her locum."

"You had me worried there." Sababa said. "For a moment, I felt a shift in the polarity of the planet."

"Nope." Praj said. "All still the same. Anyway, this girl came in yesterday with metabolic madness."

"That's not a diagnosis."

"I know, but her acid-base balance is weird."

"We do weird." Sababa said. "Try me."

"Her potassium was low when she hit the door." He said. "I mean like 1.9 mEq/L."

"Cardiac arrest and pontine stroke range."

"Hence the need for telemetric monitoring."

"Why didn't she have the on-call internist involved yesterday?"

"She came in late and when the locum tried to get Ed Hyde to see her, he said he needed his sleep." Praj said. Sababa raised an eyebrow.

"What's her potassium this morning?"

"Well, that's the weird part." Praj said. "She's been getting oral supplements and slow IV boluses and high concentration infusions of potassium all night long but her serum level hasn't budged."

"That's a prolonged QT interval." Sababa pointed to the saccades on Fiera's ECG monitor. "What else?"

"In the last six months, she was admitted seven times with the same pattern of low potassium and low chloride and metabolic alkalosis." Praj said. "Buddy Benway scoped her both ends looking for any cause of GI potassium loss. Last week, she saw a nephrologist in Victoria who diagnosed her with Bartter's syndrome."

"How did he come up with that diamond?"

"He said that with her normal blood pressure, high aldosterone level, and metabolic alkalosis, her chronic low potassium and chloride must be due to losses through her kidneys, ergo Bartter's."

"What's her urine chloride content?"

"Low."

"Well, that shoots the Bartter's theory out of the water." Sababa said. "She's not losing chloride in her urine. She's losing it from her gut. Her chronic low potassium comes from a state of systemic chloride depletion induced by renal-independent factors. Reduced circulating volume activates her renin-angiotensin-aldosterone axis. The high renin adds to the effect of her high aldosterone which acts on the distal renal tubule which further exacerbates the low potassium and metabolic alkalosis, in a self-perpetuating vicious cycle. And round and round we go. She doesn't have Bartter's syndrome. She has Pseudo-Bartter's syndrome."

"But how does she lose potassium and chloride and volume from her gut?" Praj asked.

"That, Mowgli, is the most important question." Sababa said. "Let's go see her."

Inside the curtain of bed 3, the young resident introduced his mentor.

"Fiera, this is Doctor Sababa." Praj said. "He's in the business of light."

"I'm light." She said.

"How light?" Sababa asked.

"This light." Fiera held out a slender arm like an artist showing off an original creation. Dull and dry brittle hair and pale yellowish bruised skin stretched thin over her skull. In between the eye shadow and lipstick, her cheekbones looked as if they had been dug out with a spade. She ran her hands down her body like she was waving it good-bye. Where was it supposed to go? Every rib protruded, trying to escape its cage. Razor-sharp hips rose on both sides of her abdominal concavity. Her knees would never meet without force. She made small persistent movements of her fingers and toes. Her feet were orange.

"Beautiful, aren't I?"

"Her body mass index is 16.15 kg/m^2, Sab." Praj said. "Pretty low."

"But still pretty." Fiera said.

"You're a model?"

"Why, yes."

"When was your last period."

"Oh, I'm so lucky." She said. "I don't have time for periods." Sababa examined the remains of her breakfast tray. Fiera had cut her omelette into four pieces, cut each of those four pieces into four more pieces, and had eaten the smallest one of those. The ketchup smear on her plate was untouched. Ketchup was sugar, and sugar was fat, and fat was unthinkable.

"How was the omelette?" Sababa asked.

"What do you mean?" Fiera asked.

"How did it taste?"

"Like shame." She said.

"How many calories did what you ate have?"

"Not quite a hundred." Fiera was a cruel cartoon of skin and bone, a garish caricature of the dozen other waiflike, angular models smiling up from the dozen glossy magazine captioned covers on her tray table. *Thinspiration... fitspiration...* "I'm such a glutton."

"The young always have the same problem." Sababa said. "How to rebel and conform at the same time. They have now solved this by defying their parents and copying one another." He asked if he could examine her.

"I'm cold." Fiera clutched her gown around what was left of her. Her breath smelled like juicy-fruit gum and death. Sababa noted the enlargement of her parotid glands, thin ragged scars on both wrists, and Russel's sign, knuckle calluses on the dorsal aspect of her dominant hand from the repeated introduction of the hand into her mouth to induce vomiting.

"Say 'Ahhh,' He said.

"Ahhh." She said.

"Hmmmm." Sababa mused. "Faint longitudinal scarring of the soft palate."

"What does that mean?" Fiera asked. Sababa unwrapped his Littman Master Cardiology black and brass stethoscope from around his neck and listened to her heart.

"Mitral valve prolapse." He said.

"What about my palate?" She said.

"It's scarred." Sababa said. "Because you push your fingers down your throat to vomit."

"I do not!" Fiera objected.

"Sure you do." The stocky savant continued. "For the same reason you starve yourself and take laxatives."

"I do not!" She insisted. "You have no right! You have no proof!"

"But I do." Sababa said. "Dr. Benway didn't find the cause of your low potassium in your gut but I did. The pathologist, Dr. Leyblanca, reported that your colonic membrane was hyperpigmented with melanin. The only way to get a suntan in your cecum is to use too much cathartic. The only way for you to get a serum potassium that persistently low without losing chloride in your urine is with surreptitious self-induced cyclic vomiting and laxative abuse."

"I have Bartter's syndrome." Fiera said. "The nephrologist in Victoria told me."

"You have Pseudo-Bartter's syndrome." Sababa said. "From your eating disorder. You have serotonin pathway dysfunction. You have a fear of food, sitophobia. You have depression, anxiety, abnormal interoceptive awareness, metacognition, and alexithymia, the astounding illusion that you can escape the flesh, and, by association, the realm of emotions. And you have a compulsion to destroy yourself."

"You think I have an eating disorder?"

"Anorexia nervosa, purging type." He said. "When your mother told you could be anything, you heard something else. *You have to be everything.* Eating disorders are like a gun assembled by genetics, loaded by cultural ideals, and triggered by unbearable distress. Girls developed eating disorders when society established a standard of beauty that couldn't be achieved by being healthy. We turned skeletons into goddesses and looked to them to teach us how not to need. When unnatural thinness became attractive, girls did unnatural things to be thin. That's the secret, isn't it, Fiera? To be thin. Thin is good, thin is strong; thin is safe. You can always find each other, you girls with secrets. And the thinner you get the meaner you become. Until your organs fail."

"What now?" Fiera broke down into uncontrollable sobbing.

"In here, if you see someone crying, it's not because of their haircut." Sababa said. "Now, we fix your metabolic madness with potassium-sparing aldosterone-antagonist medication and as much potassium as we can get into you via every route we can for as long as you need it. Now, we increase your caloric intake slowly so as not to cause refeeding syndrome and drop your phosphate and potassium into your boots."

"And then I can go home?"

"Not quite." Sababa said. "Anorexia nervosa patients have the highest death rate of all mental illnesses, with a suicide risk 56 times higher than in the general population. I'll send you to our provincial Eating Disorders Unit team for nutritional rehabilitation and cognitive behavioral therapy." No one said anything until they did.

"I hope it works this time."

"Me too." Sababa sent Praj to the fifth floor to get on top of the second ward patient's problems. As he sat down to write out his consultation at the nursing station, he selected a tune from his music library on a drive hidden deep inside the hospital computer network, and yet another secret. *We've only just begun...*

'You moonshine revellers, and shades of night,
You orphan heirs of fixed destiny...'
William Shakespeare, *The Merry Wives of Windsor*

Dr. Praj Bharmal paged the professor an hour later, two hours after Impeccable Williams took his first and last helicopter ride.

Sababa moved vertical and horizontal in a similar pattern of lift and propulsion, landing on floor 5 in a near collision with the Medical Nursing Director. Edith Mortley was wearing her string of natural pearls, uncultured.

"Why are you here?" Sababa asked. "Where's Samara Morgan?"

"Samara is away on a professional development day."

"She'll need more time." Sababa said. "Why can't we have Sophia back? She's the best head nurse you almost never had."

"Well, for one, she's back in the Philippines." Edith said. "And two, it's complicated."

"Call me when you sort it out and find her." Sababa watched Praj coming down the ward hallway towards them.

"If your phone doesn't ring, it's me." Edith watched Dr. Bharmal return down the hallway to the nursing station. "Your resident seems like a nice young man. Try not to ruin that too much."

"Life is good, Edith." He said. "You should get one." He turned to his apprentice.

"Popcorn Sutton." Praj said. "46-year-old patient of Dr. Nicholas Rivera. Won't tell me what he does for a living."

"Interesting." Sababa said. "I assume you have more history."

"Dr. Rivera admitted him last night for an exacerbation of gout." Praj said. "He also complains of headaches, fatigue, insomnia, memory problems, visual blurring, nausea, abdominal pain, constipation, muscle aches and pains, and tingling in his hands and feet, going on for the last three months."

"Exam?"

"Hostile. Called me a Paki, which is just so wrong, because I'm a Sikh. My family came from Punjab a hundred years ago." Praj said. "His skin is pale and grey, his blood pressure is high, his nerve conduction hearing reduced, and he has cataracts, decayed dentition, slurred speech, and a foot drop on the right, opposite to the left big toe affected by his gout."

"Lab?"

"Microcytic anemic with hypochromasia and basophilic stippling." He said. "His kidney function is poor. I suspect he might have Fanconi syndrome."

"Let's go see." Sababa said. His protégé presented the portly professor to Popcorn.

"This is Doctor Sababa, Mr. Sutton." Praj said. "The pulse of life dances against his shore."

"Yeah, well he can dance with the devil for all I care." Popcorn said.

"And in the pale moonlight." Sababa added. "You have a drinking problem, Mr. Sutton?"

"What?" He said. "There's something wrong with my hearing."

"Do you have a drinking problem?"

"I don't have a drinking problem." He said. "Except when I can't get a drink."

"What's your poison?"

"I make my own." He said. "But lately it tastes like a rusted tin can."

"Mind if I examine you?"

"Why not?" Popcorn said. "Doesn't hurt to check up on young Mahatma here." Both physicians ignored the insult.

"I can't see so well." He said. Sababa tested his visual fields.

"Hmmmm." He said. "Bilateral central defects. Possible toxic optic neuritis. Show me your teeth." Popcorn pulled back his gums. Sababa pointed to a blue line along the man's gum margin with a bluish-black edging to the teeth.

"Well, howdy." He said. "Burton line." Praj felt bad for missing it.

"Let me ask you again, Popcorn." Sababa said. "What's your poison? And is it also what you do to make money?" Sutton was crestfallen.

"How'd you know that?"

"It is my business to know what other people don't know." He said. "You make moonshine."

"A third of worldwide alcohol consumption is moonshine." Popcorn was agitated. "When I sell liquor, it's bootlegging. When the provincial government sells it, it's a business. When my customers serve it on a silver tray in Hammond Bay, it's hospitality."

"I've met some of your customers." Sababa said. "They had methanol poisoning."

"It's a tricky thing to get the shine just right." Popcorn protested. "I test every batch to make sure it's safe."

"How do you do that?"

"Flame test." He said. "Pour some in a spoon and set it on fire. Most times it burns with a blue flame. Means it's safe. A yellow flame means it's not."

"Methanol burns invisible." Sababa said. "You must have missed that class. Ever get a reddish flame?"

"All the time." Popcorn said. "Never gave it no never mind."

"What burns red and makes you dead, Praj?" Sababa asked. The young resident looked puzzled.

"Dunno."

"Think about Popcorn's symptoms and signs and lab results." Sababa said. "What was first mined in Anatolia 8500 years ago? What did the

Greek botanist Nicander describe as the cause of colic and paralysis in the 2nd century BC and the Greek physician Dioscorides blame for the mind 'giving way' three hundred years later? What caused the fall of the Roman empire, leached from its *fistulæ* water supply pipes in a concentration a hundred times more than in local spring waters, boiled down into *defrutum*, *carenum*, and *sapa* fruit musts in contaminated cookware to preserve their cuisine and cosmetics, and added as an acetate sugar to sweeten the wine which caused their saturnine gout? What white carbonate in yellow and white oil pigments killed off the painters Caravaggio, Francisco Goya, and Vincent Van Gogh? What caused Beethoven's hearing loss and death? What wine adulterated with *litharge* caused the colic and death of hundreds of monks in the 17th century, what rum distilled in the 'worm' wreaked havoc among slaves and sailors in the colonial West Indies, and what cider made in presses lined with the stuff poisoned Devonshire residents in the 18th century? And what, after adjusting for confounding factors, causes higher violent crime rates through history and around the world?"

"I'll most likely die in a hail of lead." Popcorn said.

"Exactly." Sababa agreed. "Lead burns red and makes you dead. Your saturnine gout and all your other symptoms are from lead poisoning."

"Where would it come from?" Praj asked.

"From the old solder in the repurposed parts he used to make his still." Sababa said. "But I agree, there could other sources as well. Do you take any other remedies, Popcorn?" The bootlegger opened his bedside table and pulled out a small packet of orange powder.

"Only Azarcon." He said. "From my Mexican naturopath."

"Also known as alarcon, coral, luiga, maria luisa, or rueda." Sababa said. "Contains about 95% lead. Natural, like uranium and arsenic."

"What can you do about it?" Popcorn asked.

"First, you get a new line of work, or at least learn how to distill moonshine." Sababa said. "Second, my brilliant young resident here, who you will quick smart develop a healthy respect for, will order your blood lead and erythrocyte protoporphyrin levels, and start you on iron, calcium, and zinc. He'll arrange initial daily infusions of dimercaprol followed by EDTA four hours later, chelating agents that should eventually get rid of the lead, although we may have to repeat it at intervals, as it comes out of your bones."

"Why do I need two drugs?"

"The first one prevents the second one from redistributing the lead into your central nervous system."

"What kind of life will I have?" Popcorn asked.

"We are here and it is now." Sababa said. "Further than that, all human knowledge is moonshine."

Praj and Sababa left Popcorn Sutton to see the last ward patient further down the fifth-floor hallway. They met Dr. Poldy Bloom coming out of his room.

"What can you tell us, Poldy?" Sababa asked.

"Bettino Ricasoli." The family physician said. "57-year-old owner of the Gold n' Fleece pawn shop downtown."

"The one with the inspirational signs?" Sababa asked. *Please remove ski mask and unload before entering... Surly staff. Poor selection. High prices. Terrible quality... Shoplifters will be beaten to death...*

"That one." Poldy said.

"I think I saw him in consultation and follow-up at Manzanita Medical about ten years ago." Sababa remembered.

"I think I sent him."

"As I recall, at his first visit he brought me a gift of a bottle of homemade wine." Sababa said. "It was terrible. Jane poured it down the sink."

"He's the guy."

"On his second visit, he brought me two bottles." Sababa said. "When he asked me how I liked it, I made the mistake of lying."

"And then?"

"On his fourth follow-up appointment, he dragged in two cases of flagons." Sababa continued. "I finally had to tell him how bad it was."

"Was he offended?"

"He told me that none of his family or friends would go near it, so that's why he gave it to me."

"That was Bettino." Poldy said.

"Was?"

"Different man now."

"How so?" Sababa asked.

"Since his wife died a year ago, Bettino has become progressively depressed and aggressive with loss of ability to perform particular purposive actions and loss of control of his body movements. He came in yesterday with a seizure."

"What else?"

"His exam demonstrated impaired short-term memory and garbled speech with intact cranial nerves and long tracts. His bloodwork showed an elevated white blood cell count and AST."

"He needs an MRI." Praj said.

"He had one." Poldy said. "Although I haven't seen it yet."

"Let's go look." Sababa said.

The three men pulled up Bettino's imaging studies on a nursing station monitor.

"Hmmmm." Sababa said. "MRI shows abnormal high diffusion-weighted imaging and T2 signal in the splenium of the corpus callosum with sparing of dorsal and ventral layer and no mass effect or edema."

"What does that mean?" Praj asked.

"That means Bettino has Marchiafava–Bignami disease."

"What's that?" Poldy stared harder at the images on the monitor, looking for an answer.

"It's a progressive neurological disease characterized by corpus callosum demyelination and necrosis and atrophy." Sababa said. "First described in 1903 by the Italian pathologists Amico Bignami and Ettore Marchiafava in an Italian Chianti drinker."

"Why did Bettino get it?"

"When his wife died, he started drinking more of his own bad wine and developed thiamine deficiency because she no longer prepared his meals." Sababa said. "It's wiped out the middle part of his brain that connects the two hemispheres."

"What can we do?" Poldy asked.

"We'll start him on high-dose intravenous thiamine 500 mg three times a day for 5 days as well as oral vitamin B complex." Sababa said. "He'll need to pour all the rest of his wine down the drain. Let's go see him."

Inside the patient's room, the pawnshop owner recognized Sababa.

"Hey Doc." He said. "You wanna some of my wine?"

"All of it, Bettino." Sababa said. "I want all of it."

'I have absolutely no pleasure in the stimulants in which I sometimes so madly indulge. It has not been in the pursuit of pleasure that I have periled life and reputation and reason. It has been the desperate attempt to escape from torturing memories, from a sense of insupportable loneliness and a dread of some strange impending doom.'

Edgar Allan Poe

"It's drug abuse and poison week, Boss." Praj and the professor had arrived at Manzanita Medical a few minutes before their afternoon clinic was due to begin.

"Mercy triumphs over judgement." Sababa picked up the first chart on the pile and handed it to his apprentice. Praj called into the assembled multitude.

"Marshall Applewhite." A thin elderly man struggled out of his corner chair and followed the young resident down the hall to an examining room. He wore a black shirt and sweatpants, brand new black-and-white Nike Windrunner athletic shoes, and an armband. *Heaven's Gate Away Team*. Sababa picked up the next one.

"Ben Johnson." The young man looked like a condom full of walnuts. He expanded into the waiting room air like a balloon animal and lurched behind Sababa into his office. No one said anything until the Sage of the

Salish Sea had finished reading the referral letter from his family physician.

Dear Doctor Sababa,

Please see this 25-year-old bodybuilder admitted last year with an acute superior sagittal sinus thrombosis, an associated cortical based acute infarct in the right parietal lobe, and focal seizure secondary to a 2-year history of anabolic androgenic steroid use (cycled with an estrogen modulator to prevent breast enlargement and luteinizing hormone stimulants to prevent testicular atrophy). He made a full recovery since his discontinuation of performance enhancement drugs.

Ben presented again three days ago with bilateral thigh and calf pain after increasing the intensity and duration of his cross-trainer workouts. I gave him a course of diclofenac but his muscle pain has, if anything, worsened. Sent him for some bloodwork at the same time I placed this referral.

Thank Mercy for fitting him in.

Kind Regards.   Dr. James Ruben Andrews

"How can I help?" Asked the Sage of the Salish Sea.

"All my muscles are cramped up." Ben said. "I can barely walk."

"What medications do you take?"

"Just the anti-inflammatory that Dr. Andrews prescribed." Ben was surly.

"If you tell the truth, you don't have to remember anything." Sababa said, and then he didn't say more.

"What makes you think I'm taking something else?" Ben demanded.

"Oh, I don't know. Let me see. Your creatine phosphokinase this morning is 22,226 IU/litre, about a hundred times more than what it should be." Sababa read the lab results. "And your urine is loaded with myoglobin, which has clogged up your kidneys so much they're barely functioning. How's that?"

"OK. I do take creatine powder." Ben admitted. "I guess you need a good bedside manner with doctors or you get nowhere."

"Mendax interminabilis."

"What's that?" Ben asked.

"Latin." Sababa said. "It means 'interminable liar.'"

"You're calling me a liar?"

"I tried. You didn't. I'm done. Have fun."

"OK." Ben rubbed his sore muscles. "OK. I've been injecting WinstrolTM and PrimabolanTM. What doesn't kill you makes you strong."

"Stanazolol and metenolon." Sababa said. "Sometimes what doesn't kill you makes you stroke. Or have you forgotten?"

"OK." Ben said. "So, what's wrong with me?"

"You mean other than your room temperature IQ?" Sababa channelled his inner demons. "What shall it profit a man to gain muscle and suffer the loss of his brain? It's called anabolic steroid-induced rhabdomyolysis,

178

Ben. Your muscles are melting, and your kidneys are playing goalie. We'll need to act fast or you get to meet Dr. Hemodialysis." He pressed his intercom button.

"Mercy, get me an ambulance and one of the ER docs please."

"On it, Sab." She said.

"Now what?" Ben asked.

"Now you get to take a seat in the waiting room until your ambulance arrives, while I write out your hospital admission orders and dictate your consultation."

"You're admitting me to hospital for my sore muscles?"

"No, I'm admitting you to hospital for your failing kidneys." Sababa said. "At the least, you'll need an orthopedic consult to rule out a compartment syndrome, a muscle biopsy, MRI of your legs, EMG, IV fluids, urinary alkalinization, an osmotic diuretic, and a course of methylprednisolone."

'What's that?"

"Strangely enough, it's a steroid." Sababa said. "Another kind."

"I have wheels." Ben pointed out the window to a Mercedes convertible in the parking lot.

"The universe doesn't care." Sababa pointed to his office door. Back in the waiting room, Ben approached the red-headed medical office assistant with the cat-eyed frame glasses and fast feline typing fingers.

"Who pissed in his Cheerios?" Mercy never looked up from her transcription.

"Must have been a fruit loop." She pointed to the photo above her counter, a bowl of multicoloured cereal with a diagonal red line through it.

A few minutes before Praj was ready to present his first patient, Mercy patched an outside call into Sababa's sanctum sanctorum.

"In-Site program director on line 2, Sab." She could hear the intercom groan.

"Courtesy phone."

"Good afternoon, Doctor Sababa. This is Lucretia Miller, Island Health's In-Site program director for the Harbour City downtown core." A voice said. "I assume you read the letter from our regional Medical Health Officer, Dr. Spud Hasselbeck about bringing your clinic into our downtown needle exchange program."

"You mean the guy with no patient rapport, stunted interpersonal skills, and incredible hostility to informed views he doesn't agree with, qualities consistent with most fifth column physician government bureaucrats who have gone over to the dark side?"

"But you did get his letter?" Lucretia asked.

"I got it and at first I threw it away, but then I decided that wasn't a grand enough gesture, so I made it into an origami of the HIV virus and set it on fire."

"That's not in the least bit amusing, Doctor Sababa." Lucretia said. "That letter was a formal notice that we expect the central location of your practice to support our needle exchange program. Dr. Hasselbeck and I are in the business of harm reduction."

"You mean like the business of procuring young children for the pedophiles in our community so they don't have to source their own?" He said. "Patients whose moods are affected by the thoughtlessness, ugliness, and impoverishment of their surroundings are in no state of mind to join as partners in their treatment, Lucretia. When you watched *Alien*, which side did you root for?"

"We have hard data to support our program funding." She said.

"You have data that proves you convert a single addict into a drug-free petting zoo paragon of virtue?" Sababa asked. "Do you have cost-benefit data that justifies the extraordinary price of this white elephant at the expense of important medical priorities that more productive members of our society might benefit from? You have data that supports your commandeering of my little erudite solo practice for the blanket provision of safe spaces and free illicit drug paraphernalia? If a stone falls on an egg, it is bad for the egg; if an egg falls onto a stone, it is still bad for the egg."

"We have data that proves we save lives." She said. "Is it better to stick needles in the living or scalpels in the dead?"

"Sometimes the best drug is karma." Sababa said. "No problem is insoluble given a big enough plastic bag."

"Your principles are old fashioned and obsolete, Doctor Sababa." Lucretia said. "And completely divorced from humanity."

"Me and humanity, we got married too young." He said. "But if you disapprove of my principles, I have others."

"I take it that you will not provide syringes and needles for our clients?" Lucretia said.

"If they're diabetics and using them for insulin, you betcha." *Click.* He looked up to find Praj trying not to laugh.

"How many Island Health bureaucrats does it take to change a light bulb?" Sababa asked. Praj shrugged.

"One, carefully following recommendations by a core panel of regional, municipal, and provincial government representatives, local community activists, First Nations, industry and environmental spokespersons." He said. "What you got?"

"Marshall Applewhite." Praj began. "Referral from Dr. Dasco Boet."

"Dasco Boet doesn't send referrals." Sababa said. "Dasco Boet receives referrals. There isn't anything I do that Dasco can't handle himself."

"Nonetheless, he sent Mr. Applewhite."

"Alright." Sababa said. "Continue."

"67-year-old California retiree with a history of Whipple surgery for pancreatic adenocarcinoma two months ago. Follow-up imaging revealed metastatic disease to his liver and lungs. He declined chemotherapy and went to see an alternative holistic medicine doctor instead." Praj watched one of Sababa's eyebrows migrate in a northerly direction.

"If it looks like a duck, it's a quack." He said.

"He prescribed what he called vitamin B17 tablets, 500 mg a day which Marshall took for a month."

"Apricot kernel extract." Sababa said. "Also known as amygdalin. It ain't no vitamin."

"In a subsequent appointment, the holistic guy tripled the dose. Approximately 45 minutes after taking the first 1500 mg, Mr. Appelwhite developed an altered mental status, along with sweating, rapid heart rate, vomiting, dizziness, and crampy abdominal pain. A friend called an ambulance. In Harbour City emergency, Marshall was confused and making incomprehensible sounds. His initial pulse oximetry at 3 liters/minute nasal cannula demonstrated an O2 saturation of 67%. He dumped his blood pressure but that responded to a litre bolus of saline. His bloodwork returned showing a high-anion-gap metabolic acidosis with a sky-high lactate of 14.2 mmol/L. That's when they asked Dr. Boet to see him."

"What did Dasco do?"

"He gave Mr. Appelwhite five grams of hydroxocobalamin." Praj said.

"Why?"

"Dr. Boet found blue lines in his nailbeds and a cherry red colour in his cheeks and extracted the story of the apricot kernel extract." Praj said. "With everything else, he made a diagnosis of acute on chronic cyanide poisoning. The hydroxocobalamin worked and his clinical condition improved overnight in the ICU. He was discharged home the next day with instructions to stop the amygdalin and follow up with his oncologist."

"I still don't know why Dasco wanted us to see him." Sababa said. "He nailed the diagnosis. What did he write on the 'reason for consultation' line?

"Hand on bladder."

"That's code." Sababa said.

"For what?"

"For snowflake." Sababa cracked a grin. "Dasco has trouble problem solving for idiots. I assume that Mr. Appelwhite still consumes the natural born killer his quack prescribed."

"At a lower dose, yes."

"Let's go see him." Down the Manzanita Medical hallway, the young resident made the introduction."

"Marshall, this is Doctor Sababa." Praj said. "He's a singular person who fell out of infinity."

"I heard a great joke about Jonestown the other day." Sababa said. "I don't remember the build-up, but the punchline was killer."

"Didn't it contain cyanide?" Marshall asked.

"Funny you should remember." Sababa said. "That's what your 'vitamin' was hydrolyzed to by beta-glucuronidase in your small intestine. Every 500 mg pill contains 30 mg of cyanide, 40 times more potent than if we gave you cyanide intravenously. The amount you took the other day was 1.8 times higher than the minimum lethal dose."

"But my naturopath..."

"Gave you amygdalin, a poisonous cyanogenic glycoside first isolated by French chemists in 1830, first used as a treatment for cancer in Russia in 1845, and then in the United States, in the 1920s. A simpler semisynthetic version called laetrile was patented in 1961, but it's the same poison. Do you remember the actor Steve McQueen who died during surgery at Oasis of Hope Hospital in Tijuana? The laetrile that his de-licensed orthodontist quack, William D. Kelley, gave him for his mesothelioma was subsequently tested in expensive scientific studies and found useless.

However, there is one thing that cyanide is good for—killing people. The Prussians used what was called prussic acid even before the Nazis manufactured 56 tonnes of hydrogen cyanide Zyklon B pellets to murder millions at Auschwitz, Majdanek, and Mauthausen-Gusen concentration camps, and to kill themselves and their Aryan children at the end of the war. In 1954, the Enigma decoder Alan Turing used an apple injected with cyanide solution to commit suicide after being convicted of having a homosexual relationship and forced to undergo hormonal castration. From mining accidents to mass murder, cyanide has been the grand cru of carnage through history. And now you're paying with your life to play the same game."

"I'm going to die anyway." Marshall said.

"We're all going to die." Sababa said. "You might prefer to do that without suffocating your mitochondrial cytochrome c oxidase and committing revolutionary suicide and enriching the parasites who prey on my palliative patients."

"OK, I guess you're right, Doctor Sababa. I'll stop the B17." Marshall said. "Why did Dr. Boet refer me to see you?"

"Not sure, myself, Marshall. Dasco is an alchemist." Sababa said. "That hydroxocobalamin he gave you converted your false vitamin B17 to real vitamin B12 and saved your life for now."

"Maybe he was just showing off some magic."

"More and less than that." Sababa said. "Most magic consists of knowing one extra fact. Dasco knows more than anyone else outside this room."

182

'If I had money
I'll tell you what I'd do
I'd go downtown
And buy a Mercury or two.'
Alan Jackson, *Mercury Blues*

Praj and Sababa pulled two more charts from the afternoon clinic pile. "Raoul Bensaude." The young resident took the next patient. "Louis Alcott." The professor called the one after that. A middle-aged man followed Sababa into his office. There was a brief silence as the internist read the referral letter from Dr. Tictac Tarmac.

43-year-old plumber recently discharged from hospital for bilateral pneumonia. Radiologist reported immunosuppression or aspiration. Respirologist said it was an atypical organism. You tell me.

"How can I help you, Mr. Alcott?" Sababa asked.

"Dunno." He said. "I'm not even sure why I'm here."

"Dr. Tarmac thinks we're missing something." Sababa pulled up the man's imaging on his desk computer. "You have any idea what that might be?"

"No idea." Louis said. "All I know is that I got pneumonia and now it's gone."

"You're a plumber?"

"Uh-huh."

"Wife and kids?"

"One wife, two kids." Louis said. "Boy and a girl."

"Ever been in hospital before?"

"No."

"Says here you were seen in emergency three months ago by our psychiatrist, Dr. La Capuche, for gambling addiction and suicidal thoughts."

"Oh, yeah." Louis said. "I forgot about that."

"How's your financial situation?"

"Not so hot." His voice cracked. "I'm about to lose my house."

"So, I'm thinking Louis, that your profound nausea and vomiting and abdominal pain and enlarged lymph nodes and gum inflammation and generalized rash and anemia and elevated white blood cell count and liver tests and negative cultures don't support the diagnosis of infectious pneumonia."

"I had a high fever and a bad cough." Louis protested. "They said the rash was from one of the antibiotics and I saw the patches of pneumonia on the chest x-ray."

"Did you see these dense globules in the region of the stomach and hepatic flexure of the colon on the chest x-ray?" Sababa pointed to his screen.

"No."

"Neither did the shadow puppet who reported it." Sababa. said. "So, I'm thinking Louis, what heavy metal a plumber with a gambling addiction and financial strife and suicidal thoughts would have easy access to, such that he could heat up and inhale, in the hope that his family could collect some money he bet would be there for when they needed it?" Sababa said. "I'm thinking about what could account for your clinical presentation. I'm thinking the Roman god of eloquence, skill, trading, and thieving, herald and messenger of the gods, Louis. I'm thinking mercury. You inhaled a lot of mercury vapour."

Louis's face crumpled and he cried.

"A pound." He said. "I heated a pound of elemental mercury with a propane torch under the stove hood in my kitchen and sucked in the fumes. I didn't want to kill myself, I just wanted to cause enough damage to get a letter from Dr. Tarmac saying that I had a shortened life expectancy so that I could collapse my locked-in RRSPs. And I nearly made it." Tears ran down his cheeks.

"You haven't made it yet, Louis." Sababa handed him a lab requisition.

"What's this?"

"It's a request for a 24-hour urine sample for mercury." Sababa said. "Tell Mercy to make a return appointment to see me two weeks after you hand it in."

"Will I be alright?" Louis asked.

"You'll likely need a course of chelation therapy to get rid of the mercury in your system." Sababa said. "But if your family loves you and you love them, and you get some proper counselling, you should be alright. I'll write Dr. Tarmac and tell him all about it."

Louis thanked Sababa and left his office to see Mercy. He heard the faint sound of music behind the closed office door. *I'm gonna buy me a Mercury and cruise it up and down the road...*

Mercy's intercom broke into Sababa's interlude.

"College of Physicians and Surgeons on line 1 for you, Sab." She heard a groan from the other side.

"Good afternoon." He said.

"Doctor Sababa, this is Dr. Ballast at the College."

"Oh joy."

"Are you aware of the letter you wrote to Dr. Sludge, the chairperson of the provincial Therapeutics Task Force?" She asked.

"How could I not be?" Sababa said. "I wrote it, didn't I?'

"Are you aware that, in that letter, you referred to Dr. Sludge as a prostitute?"

"Bureaucracy masquerading as scholarship is to knowledge what prostitution is to love." Sababa said. "Are you aware that love uses the same neurotransmitters as addiction and this prostitute is addicted to meddling. He overruled my prescription of a specific H2 inhibitor and substituted a cheaper one without asking my permission."

"What's wrong with that?" Dr. Ballast asked. "That's his job. He's a medical consultant, not a prostitute."

"In silk and in scarlet walks many a harlot. Becoming this kind of medical consultant is like prostitution. First, you do it for love, then you do it for others, and finally, you do it for money. The drug he substituted is potentially hepatotoxic and my patient already has liver dysfunction. The indication for what I prescribed is off label, ancillary treatment for her systemic mastocytosis. Cost-effectiveness is not just about cost."

"You are directed by the College to write a formal letter of apology to Dr. Sludge for referring to him as a prostitute."

"I'm sorry I hurt Dr. Sludge's feelings when I called him a prostitute. I thought he already knew. Also, he has syphilis." Sababa said. "The fight against syphilis demands a fight against prostitution, against prejudices, old habits, against previous conceptions, general views among them not least the false prudery of certain circles."

"Who said that?" Dr. Ballast asked.

"Adolf Hitler." Sababa said. "And me. What will the College do if I don't write this snivel letter?" There came a pause.

"Well, uh... er, that is." She stammered. "I suppose there's nothing we can do officially. It's not the kind of thing we hand down punitive measures for. But in circumstances such as this, we generally try to use moralsuasion to resolve any sense of personal injury."

"Your righteousness has a stench of sincerity. Tell you what I'm going to do." Sababa said. "Nothing. How does nothing work out for you?" *Click.* He looked up to find Praj trying not to laugh.

"What was that about?" Asked the young resident.

"Some prostitute working for the provincial Therapeutics Bumbledom." Sababa said. "I hurt his feelings. We let the darkness in so we can see the stars. And do what good we can. What you got?"

"Raoul Bensaude." Praj said. "51-year-old Croatian insurance broker referred by Dr. Christian Troy, the plastic surgeon."

"What does 'Pretty Boy' want?" Sababa asked.

"He wants a diagnosis."

"How odd." Sababa said. "Most plastics patients usually come with one. What's the story?"

"Mr. Bensaude has a two-year history of bilateral progressive painless swellings in his upper arms and face and neck. There is no other history."

"Exam?"

"As I mentioned." Praj said. "Bilateral subcutaneous swelling of the submandibular, cervical, nuchal, upper back region and upper arms, movable, non-tender. The masses feel doughy and vary in size up to 10 centimetres. Labwork all normal. CT scan showed extensive fatty accumulation in the cervical and upper thoracic region. Dr. Troy performed a biopsy."

"What did it show?" Sababa asked.

"Normal fat tissue."

"So what is it?"

"Some guy with a lot of big benign fatty tumours involving his upper body." Praj said. "I have no idea."

"Let's go see him." Sababa seemed to wander off-topic as they walked together down the hallway.

"There's an imposing statue the archeologists found in the Abruzzi region of Italy." He said. "It has a unique somatic aspect characterized by big hips and wide shoulders. Dates from the sixth century B.C. It's called the Warrior of Capestrano." Praj opened the door.

"And here he is."

"Permit me to introduce Doctor Sababa, Mr. Bensaude." Praj said "You may weary of his perspicacity."

"What are you guys talking about?" Raoul asked. "Why did Dr. Troy send me here?"

"Dr. Troy wants to know why you're built like Popeye." Sababa said. "Why you have hamster cheeks and a horse collar and buffalo humps and a pseudoathletic appearance."

"So why do I?" He asked.

"Mr. Bensaude's appearance is also depicted in ancient Egyptian carvings of the Queen of Punt." Sababa said. "This is a spot diagnosis. You either know it or you don't. How much alcohol do you drink, Raoul?"

"I like my slivovitz." He said.

"How much plum brandy?" Sababa asked.

"A bottle a day."

"Sometimes two?"

"Sometimes two." Raoul admitted. "What is this thing?"

"You have a hereditary condition that has several names—benign symmetric lipomatosis, multiple symmetric lipomatosis, lipomatosis simplex indolens, and symmetric adenolipomatosis. It was first described by Sir Benjamin Brodie in 1846. In 1888, the German surgeon Otto Wilhelm Madelung reported the first series of 33 middle-aged men of Mediterranean origin with lipomas associated with alcoholism. To date, there have been only 200 patients with Madelung's disease reported in the literature."

"Will it hurt me?" Raoul asked.

"It's a cosmetic disfigurement, although these lipomas can affect breathing." Sababa said. "The embryological brown fat deposits are metabolically innocent, the result of a defect in the catalytic unit of adenyl cyclase leading to the abnormal synthesis of intracellular cyclic adenosine monophosphate. It may be due to an A8344G mutation of mitochondrial DNA in the fat tissue, peripheral nerve, muscle, and central nervous system. Alcohol acts as a cofactor by reducing the number of β-adrenergic receptors, thus hindering the lipolytic effect of norepinephrine; it hampers β-oxidation leading to decreased lipolysis and promotion of lipogenesis. Insulin and glucose metabolism are normal. Lipid profile shows increased HDL and low LDL."

"I didn't get any of that." Raoul said.

"Me neither." Praj agreed.

"What's the treatment?" Raoul asked.

"Diet doesn't make any difference although abstinence from alcohol prevents disease progression in the size of the fat masses." Sababa said. "Surgery works. Lipectomy or liposuction or phosphatidylcholine injection lipolysis are the treatments of choice. I'll write Dr. Troy and tell him."

"Thank you Doctor Sababa." Raoul said. "You like slivovitz? I make my own. I bring you some."

"Alas, I was forced to give it up after it tried to murder me one night in Dubrovnik." Sababa said.

"It make you sick as dog?" Raoul asked.

"As a thousand and one Dalmatians."

'And night shines as day, for your darkness is as light.'
Psalm 139:12

Praj and Sababa were on call for Internal Medicine that evening. Their first referral waited for them behind the frosted sliding doors of the Harbour City Regional emergency department as soon as they had finished their afternoon clinic at Manzanita Medical.

"How are you, Myles?" Sababa asked.

"Living the dream."

"I do not know whether I was then a man dreaming I was a butterfly, or whether I am now a butterfly dreaming I am a man."

"Well, this butterfly can't see where she's going." Dr. Capitaine said.

"What do you mean?" Praj asked.

"Carrie Underwood." Myles said. "38-year-old Weight Watchers meeting room leader sent over from our faceless oculist guru T.J. Eckleberg's office. Said even though she can't see you, you should see her."

"Why?"

"He said she has retinal hemorrhages." Myles said.

"From what?"

"Her blood pressure when she rolled in here was up in scientific notation." He said. "But it's not your classic hypertensive emergency.

She's the one on the nitroprusside drip in bed 9. Nothing that a little cyanide won't fix."

"Let's go see her... since she can't see us." Sababa had Myles introduce them.

"Carrie, this is Doctor Sababa and his resident, Dr. Bharmal." Myles said. "They're two of our shiny happy experts."

"Well, I hope they can fix my vision." She said. "That eye doctor wasn't much help. Wait a minute. Doctor Sababa? You're looking after a good friend of mine."

"Who's that?" The professor asked.

"Fiera Carpenter." She said. *You can always find each other, you girls with secrets.*

"If the camera adds ten pounds, do you actually exist?" Sababa asked. "Trying to lose weight, Carrie?"

"Always." She said. "It's what I do for a living."

"Dr. Capitaine here said you don't take any medication."

"No chemicals." Carrie said. "But I have started taking a natural fat burner."

"The medical profession is irritated by lay knowledge." Sababa said. "And what, pray tell, might that be called?"

"Ma Huang." Carrie said. "It's an herb used for centuries by practitioners of Chinese medicine. It was first mentioned 3,000 years ago in the *Shen Nong Ben Cao Jing*, The Divine Farmer's Materia Medica."

"Ah yes, *Ephedra sinica.*" Sababa said. "But the Chinese never used it as a dietary supplement for purposes of weight reduction and energy enhancement, Carrie. It was a weak formulated remedy for asthma, coughs, congestion, and other lung problems. When ma huang was introduced to the West, we supersized it to concentrate its active alkaloid compounds, ephedrine, and pseudoephedrine. You may have heard of them. They're the prodrugs used to make methamphetamine."

"Speed?" Carrie asked.

"Banned in the States." Sababa said. "Ever since the heatstroke deaths of Minnesota Vikings offensive lineman Korey Stringer and Baltimore Orioles pitcher Steve Bechler. It is not a performance-enhancing drug."

"But ephedra is natural." Carrie protested.

"So are its adverse effects." Sababa said. "Like the high blood pressure and stroke that just knocked off the blood supply to the back of your eyeballs."

"Will I get my vision back?" She asked.

"My general approach is that you mustn't generalize." Sababa said. "But most likely. We'll admit you to Tranquility Base until your pressure comes down and we can take you off your infusion. You've already figured out the other important lesson here. Every moral has a story."

Sababa's pager detonated in his pocket. It was Dr. Olaf Octagon, calling from the second-floor obstetrical unit. At the same time, Dr. Trace

Pangloss mimed that he had another referral. Sababa held up an ISIS index finger and picked up his page.

"I'll send my magician's apprentice to reconnoitre." He turned to Praj.

"Mowgli, Dr. Weed Puller has some improvised explosive device about to detonate on floor 2." He said. "Be a good chap and call me when you've defused it." Praj melted through the frosted glass doors.

"What you got, Trace?" Sababa asked.

"Michael Bulles." He said. "23-year-old stock clerk at Bed Bath & Beyond brought in by the RCMP a half hour ago."

"You're consulting me when you haven't even worked him up?"

"He's already more than worked up." Trace pointed to a naked young man singing and making faces and twitching. "The guy strapped into bed 6 in four-point restraints. No one can get near him."

"Why did the police bring him in?"

"Arrested as a public nuisance. Took six big cops to restrain him." Trace said. "He was hallucinating, aggressive and violent, and paranoid. When he used his teeth to tear up the back seat of the patrol car, they brought him here. He thinks he's ten feet tall and bulletproof."

"Did you get to examine him?"

"Not much." Trace said. "His pupils are dilated wide, his heart rate and blood pressure are sky-high, and he has a lot of involuntary muscle movement."

"Hmmmm. Excited toxic delirium." Sababa mused. "MDPV."

"Huh?"

"Methylenedioxypyrovalerone." Sababa said. "It's a bad synthetic cathinone."

"Well, that helps a lot."

"You know about the leaves and stem bundles of the native East African mountain flowering shrub that the Horn of Africa uses as a stimulant? Sababa asked.

"You mean khat?"

"Khat. *Catha edulis*." Sababa said. "They have to chew it fresh because the active amphetamine-like ingredient, cathinone, is not stable and breaks down fast. They have to chew it continuously because there isn't much active drug concentrated in the greenery. For a dealer, it's the perfect commodity—addictive, short shelf and half-life, and controllable supply-side economics. Whole countries are dependent on it. Committed aircraft fly in twenty tons a day from Kenya to Somalia. The Yemeni government has proposed relocating large populations to the Red Sea coast, because of water shortages produced by its cultivation. The World Health Organization classifies it as a drug of abuse 'capable of producing mild to moderate psychological dependence' but manic hyperactivity is a far better description of its effects."

"What does this lunatic have to do with your herbal essence chewing gum story?"

"Mr. Bulles here has ingested or injected or smoked or snorted a designer drug, a more addictive synthetic cathinone, khat on steroids."

"You have a name?" Trace asked.

"PABS." Sababa said.

"PABS?"

"Psychoactive bath salts."

"This guy is the Incredible Hulk because of Epsom salts?"

"No." Sababa said. "These psychotic crystalline granules are marketed as true bath salts to throw off the regulators. Even the packaging is deceptive." *Not for human consumption.*

"It's not a mild sedative?"

"No way." Sababa said. "Worst drug imaginable. Pure evil. "PCP on crack, a synergistic combination of methamphetamine's paranoia and aggressiveness, LSD's hallucinations, and PCP's extreme paranoia resulting in unpredictable behavior. There were a couple of grisly crimes in Florida that got our attention. In the first, video footage captured by surveillance cameras on the Miami Herald building recorded an 18-minute horrific zombie-like attack in which a naked bath salts addict ate the face off a homeless man he had dragged into an alleyway. When police officers arrived on the scene and told him to stop, the man growled and continued chewing. They shot him with more bullets than they needed. In another incident in Panama City, an intoxicated woman tried to behead her 71-year-old mother."

"How can you be sure that's what he's got?" Trace asked.

"Gas chromatography-mass spectrometry can detect MDPV in urine, but I'm sure that Dr. Leyblanca would have his own stroke if I were to order it." Sababa said. "No, tonight the diagnosis is a clinical one—I can smell it in his hair. Bath salts reek of the nasty and unkempt fear and impending doom and darkness they were supposed to cleanse."

"How do we treat him?"

"I'd prefer to manage him in the ER overnight. We don't want a serial killer in the Death Star unless there is some reason for us to admit him tomorrow morning when he's transmogrified back into Bruce Banner." Sababa said. "Spear him with two milligrams of Vitamin H. That should allow us to get in some intravenous Ringer's, labetalol to block his alpha and beta-adrenergic tsunami, and get some baseline blood work, ECG, and chest x-ray. Leave a string of garlic, a silver bullet, and a hammer and a wooden stake at the bedside."

"Anything else?"

"If we don't get him through a proper detox, it will destroy his life. It will destroy his family. It will destroy everything." Sababa said. "Now, if you'll excuse me, I have to attend to a more immaculate conception on the second floor."

"Cleanliness is next to godliness." Trace grinned.

"Bed Bath & Beyond."

190

The protective sisters of mercy responsible for the labour and delivery of the next generation of humanity were quick to challenge the bouncing blur that came off the second-floor stairwell. But they backed away from the Columbian leather projectile like it was Thor's hammer. The briefcase landed beside Dr. Bharmal as a Zen koan.

"I wish you wouldn't do that." He said.

"What am I, a genie?" Sababa said. "What's your second wish."

"I wish I'd gone to law school."

"What?"

"I wish I'd gone to law school."

"What?"

"Law school."

"Talk into my bullet hole. Tell me I'm fine." Sababa said. "Praj, you are on the verge of becoming a medical superspecialist, standing on the shoulders of giants, dedicating your pathetic short existence to solving nature's most challenging mysteries, and you're talking about becoming a bottom feeder?"

"I like internal medicine." Praj said. "But I also like law."

"I like coitus and cognac but I don't want to end up a fucking tosspot." Sababa was incandescent. "Internal medicine is a calling. It's a métier. It's the last proper priesthood of masterless samurai."

"They're turning you into civil servants, Sab." Praj said. "They're replacing what used to be knights-errant with a standing army of rule-bound vassals."

"We need to talk about this." Sababa said. "But not right now. Tell me why we're on the weed puller floor."

"Paula Broca." Praj said. "27-year-old $P_1G_0A_0$ pharmacist at 12-weeks gestation admitted yesterday for dizziness, anorexia, dehydration, and a weight loss of 14 kg. She had persistent vomiting over the previous two months. Fetal conditions were good except for mild oligohydramnios. Her hemoglobin level was 9.2 g/dl and her sodium and potassium and urea were down. Dr. Octagon treated her for hyperemesis gravidarum with metoclopramide and rehydrated her with saline and 40 mEq/L of KCl."

"And so?"

"Today Mrs. Broca's mental status deteriorated." Praj said. "She lost all perception of time, people, and places, and was unable to articulate her words. That's when Dr. Octagon called us."

"What did you find now?" Sababa asked.

"Oriented in only one of three spheres." Praj said. "Short-term memory is completely shot. Her visual acuity is down in both eyes, 20/100 in the right and 20/400 in the left, possibly at least in part from the small peripapillary retinal hemorrhages and pale optic discs I see on ophthalmoscopy. There is bilateral upbeat nystagmus and extraocular muscle paralysis, with binocular diplopia reported on both extreme lateral gazes. I found symmetrical rigidity in both upper and lower limbs. She is almost too weak to stand because of her dizziness and her gait is ataxic."

"So what you got?"

"Not sure."

"Not sure?" Sababa asked. "You describe a classical triad of paralysis of extraocular movement, gait ataxia, and disturbance of mentation and consciousness combined with memory loss in a pregnant woman with a history of malnutrition from hyperemesis gravidarum, and you're not sure?"

"Uh..."

"I'll give you a hint." Sababa said. "We used to call it dry beriberi until a pathologist whose first name was Carl called it polioencephalitis haemorrhagica superior in 1881. And then we named it after him."

"If she was an alcoholic, I would swear she has Wernicke's encephalopathy." Praj said.

"You don't have to be an alcoholic to be thiamine-depleted." Sababa said. "During pregnancy, the demand for thiamine increases three-fold, and with her vomiting and catabolic state, she hasn't kept up. Let's go see her." Sababa turned to a nurse, flipping through the messages on her phone.

"Excuse me." He said. "I wonder if you could give Mrs. Broca a stat dose of thiamine 50 mg IV now, followed by an IV infusion of thiamine hydrochloride 500 mg over the next 30 minutes."

"I'm down the other end of the hall tonight." She said. "Her nurse is on her break, but she should be back in half an hour or so."

"I'm afraid we don't have much 'or so' left to play with." Sababa said. "Perhaps you could find a way to help us with this."

"I'm not sure we stock that particular drug on the ward."

"Is it possible to find out?"

"I'd have to call pharmacy." She said. "But they go home in twenty minutes."

"Is it possible for you to look, or call them?"

"Is it possible for you to look, or call them?"

"Of course." Sababa said. "So that way, when I dictate my consultation, I'll be sure to get everyone's spelling right to explain why a 12-week primip had her emergency treatment delayed by indolence." The charge nurse squirmed in her seat.

"I'll give pharmacy a call, but I'm only working a half shift."

"I've just written these stat orders in Mrs. Broca's chart so our erudite conversation is now a matter of record." Sababa said. "Dr. Bharmal and I will leave you to see her now. I do hope this all works out for everyone concerned, and even those less concerned." The charge nurse reoccupied herself with the screen of her mobile phone.

Praj introduced Doctor Sababa but Paula Broca was away with the fairies. They reviewed the young resident's neurological findings.

"Her ocular muscle and gaze palsies are due to lesions of the sixth and third nerve nuclei, the nystagmus is from lesions in the regions of the vestibular nuclei in the adjacent tegmentum." They spoke of transketolase and the pentose phosphate pathway and pyruvic and lactic acid accumulation and benfotiamine inhibition of the hexosamine pathway, the advanced glycation end-product formation pathway, and the diacylglycerol-protein kinase C pathway. They spoke of glyceraldehyde-3-phosphate and fructose-6-phosphate, and NF-kappaB activation. And then they didn't speak at all.

'Pharmacy must be out in the fucking jungle gathering the raw materials to make it from scratch." Sababa fumed. "Let's go back to the nursing station." But there was no one there to talk to. The professor called the bridge of the Death Star.

"This is Charmeine." She answered. "How may I help?"

"Charmeine, this is Doctor Sababa." He said. "I wonder if you can get someone to send up a 50 mg IV thiamine bolus and a bag with 500 mg of the stuff to obstetrics ASAP."

"Coming now, Sab." *Click.*

Five minutes later, Mrs. Broca had received her medication, Praj and Sababa were speaking to her husband, who had been visiting his family to bring them into the picture, and Paula's nurse had returned from her break with more questions than answers. But Sababa had the most important one. *Can you dance with the devil in the pale moonlight?*

No, not that one. This one: How was it possible for a lifesaving fifty-cent vitamin to be so difficult to locate in a billion-dollar health care system like Island Health?

When he told Olaf Octagon the story, the obstetrician offered a partial explanation.

"On my ward, if it's not bleeding, it's not an emergency."

'Welcome to the jungle, we've got fun and games
We got everything you want Honey, we know the names
We are the people that can find whatever you may need
If you got the money, Honey we got your disease.'
Guns N' Roses, *Welcome to The Jungle*

"What?"

"Dr. Cliffy Carlton wants us to see a patient in the ER." Praj said.

"What time is it?"

"Sixish." He said.

"Mowgli, there is Irish, Swedish, and Jewish but there is no Sixish."

"Five forty-five."

"Who's the patient?"

"Honey Drive." Praj said. "23-year-old sex worker..."

"Quel charme." Sababa said. "You mean like prostitute?"

"My word is less judgemental." Praj said.

"My word is more judge and less mental." Sababa said. "Let's call her a prostitute."

"Anyway, Dr. Leyblanca sent her in by ambulance."

"Is she dead?"

"No."

"What's a pathologist doing calling an ambulance?"

"Good Samaritan, I guess." Praj said. "She was douching herself outside his window."

"I would have paid good money to see his reaction to that." Sababa said. "What's her problem?"

"She has TTP." Praj said. "Thrombotic thrombocytopenic purpura."

"I know what TTP is, Mowgli." Sababa said. "Why do think she has it?"

"She comes in with four of the classical signs." He said. "Microangiopathic hemolytic anemia, acute kidney failure, low platelet count, and high blood pressure."

"No fever or neurological signs?"

"She complains of headache and feeling tired." Praj said. "No fever."

"On my way in." *Click*. Sababa jumped in his shower, dressed hurriedly, and kissed his sleeping wife's forehead on his way out the door.

"Something serious?" Jane mumbled half awake.

"Only way to find out." Sababa said. "Bed Bath & Beyond." He fired up his dimpled and dented white Honda Civic, and flew down his long driveway on the lake. Six minutes later, he pulled up in the Internal Medicine on-call parking bay outside Harbour City Regional emergency. Cliffy Carlton was the first to meet him behind the automatic sliding frosted glass doors, holding two cups of coffee.

"French press?" He held one out to Sababa.

"Funny." Sababa took the coffee.

"We need to rename these cubicle bed numbers to more useful labels like 'Boozehound' or 'Drug Seeker' or 'Crazy Bitch.'" Cliffy said. "That tells me a hell of a lot more than 'I need help in bed 4.'"

"Where's your referral?" Sababa sipped his coffee.

"Cubicle 5." Cliff said. "In behind the curtain with your resident and Regina, who's trying to restart her IV. No veins. Smells like a civet cat."

"Every harlot was a virgin once." Sababa said.

"I'm afraid her virginity is gone forever, Sab, just like my patience now." Cliffy said. "It's that servo in her knees, wired to words coming out of other peoples' mouths. Whatever she's got has turned her crabs into sabretooth crotch crickets."

"The percentage of honest and competent whores is higher than that of plumbers and much higher than that of lawyers. And enormously higher than that of professors." Sababa suggested. "Let's go see her."

Cliffy and Sababa slid through the curtain opening of cubicle 5. Regina was on her third attempt to find a vein.

"I hate needles." Honey said.

"You have eight facial piercings, nipple rings, and tattoos covering three-quarters of your body." Said the ER nurse. "You don't get to cry when I try to restart your IV. You have any veins left?"

"You sure you know how to start an IV?" Honey asked.

"Honey, I've blown more veins in my life than you've... never mind."

Sababa slid a #14 intercath into a vein in Honey's thumb and hooked it up to her IV infusion bag. He began to pour through the lab results in her chart.

"Slick." Honey said. She scowled at Cliffy. "I can tell you like me. I saw your pants move. God, I hate men."

"Don't women need men for sex?" Cliffy asked.

"Do we need so many?"

"Party girls are fun until they puke on your shoes." He said. "I brought you a coffee." Cliffy held out the cup but she waved it away.

"I hate that stuff." She said. "It tastes like feet."

"How would you know what feet taste like?" He asked.

"I just know."

"Crack is really evil coffee, Honey." Cliffy said. "Your cocaine eyes can't hide your face."

"Imagine trying to live without air." Honey said. "Now imagine something worse. It digs out the happiness that lies within."

"She's right, in a way." Sababa said. "Crack cocaine releases large amounts of dopamine in the user's brain. But it causes them to become addicted the first time they try it."

"It's not habit-forming." Honey laughed. "I should know, I've been using it for months. I can give it up any time, as long as it's next week."

"What else have we got here, Praj?" Sababa noted Honey's diffuse skin bruising. She was bleeding from her gums. "What kinds of TTP are there?"

"About 60% of TTP is an idiopathic autoimmune process." He said. "From autoantibody-mediated inhibition of the enzyme ADAMTS13, a metalloprotease that cleaves large multimers of von Willebrand factor into smaller units. According to the Furlan-Tsai hypothesis, the increase in these circulating multimers results in small platelet clots that shear off and rupture red blood cells. This causes anemia and potentially life-threatening bleeding."

"First described by Dr. Eli Moschcowitz at Beth Israel Hospital in New York in 1925." Sababa said. "Any other kinds?"

"There is a rare, autosomal recessive form of TTP called Upshaw–Schulman syndrome that results from an inherited deficiency of ADAMTS13."

"Anything else?

"There are two related syndromes." Praj said. "Hemolytic-uremic syndrome and atypical hemolytic uremic syndrome."

"I don't mean them." Sababa said. "Think about it. Honey didn't have the usual influenza-like or diarrheal prodromal symptoms before she developed her illness."

"You can't just eliminate a symptom." Praj protested.

"I can if it's not a symptom."

"Well, what is it then?" He asked.

"Not a symptom."

"You mean secondary forms of TTP?" Praj scratched his forehead.

"The other forty percent." Sababa said. "Seen in bone marrow transplants and pregnancy and HIV and with some drugs and medications."

"Drugs?" Honey asked. "That's the only word I understood."

"You don't have the usual form of what Dr. Bharmal and I have been discussing, Honey." Sababa said. "You have something called pseudo-thrombotic thrombocytopenic purpura, from cocaine."

"Are you admitting me to hospital?" She asked.

"Not this one." Sababa said. "Here we'll give you corticosteroids and fresh frozen plasma. We have to be careful not to give you too much fluid because your kidneys aren't working. Which is why I'm sending you to a nephrologist friend in Vancouver, who will treat you with plasmapheresis and dialysis and more kinds of medications."

"Will you transfuse her with blood and platelets?" Cliffy asked.

"No." Sababa said. "That would add fuel to the coagulopathy fire." Sababa and Praj and Cliffy Carlton left to organize Honey's treatment and arrange her transfer. They found Dr. Juan Leyblanca at the consultant's desk.

"You know the difference between an internist, a surgeon, a psychiatrist, and a pathologist?" Sababa asked. The pathologist rolled his Spanish eyes.

"The internist knows everything and does nothing. The surgeon knows nothing and does everything. The psychiatrist knows nothing and does nothing. And the pathologist knows everything and does everything, but too late."

"I've looked at her blood smear." Juan said. "She has TTP."

"She's going to Vancouver for treatment." Sababa said. "You need to do something about that garden hose tap of yours. It's popular."

196

"And it ees now padlocked behind a steel cage." Juan said. "The next one to use it weethout a key will need a cutting torch."

'Hey baby won't you please come quick
This old cocaine's makin' me sick
Cocaine all around my brain.'
Bob Dylan, *Cocaine Blues*

'

We had two bags of grass, seventy-five pellets of mescaline, five sheets of high powered blotter acid, a salt shaker half-full of cocaine, and a whole galaxy of multi-colored uppers, downers, screamers, laughers... and also a quart of tequila, a quart of rum, a case of Budweiser, a pint of raw ether and two dozen amyls. Not that we needed all that for the trip, but once you get locked into a serious drug collection, the tendency is to push it as far as you can.'
Hunter S. Thompson, *Fear and Loathing in Las Vegas*

We can forgive the casual reader for any prejudices about addiction. We can even forgive our casual readers for their addictions. Addiction is everywhere. It has no walls. It bleeds across every socioeconomic class line.

Our most beloved fictional detective had much in common with Honey Drive. *Holmes remained... alternating from week to week between cocaine and ambition... pray what remains for you?' 'For me,' said Sherlock Holmes, 'there still remains the cocaine bottle.'*

The father of psychotherapy, Sigmund Freud, was just as afflicted. *I was making frequent use of cocaine at that time ... I had been the first to recommend the use of cocaine... And if you are forward, you shall see who is the stronger, a gentle little girl who doesn't eat enough, or a big wild man who has cocaine in his body.*

The imaginary internist from Princeton based on Sherlock Holmes, not quite as erudite as the Sage of the Salish Sea, is addicted to oxycontin. *'You stash your drugs in a lupus textbook?'... 'It's never lupus.'*

The road to addiction is sure and swift. It begins with the hope that something 'out there' can instantly fill up the emptiness inside, temptation driven first by the search for pleasure, and then by the avoidance of pain. It turns a lack of impulse control into a compulsion and then an addiction. The difference is not great. Addictions are sought after more as a source of pleasure than guilt while compulsions are experienced more as a source of guilt than pleasure. A rabid dog cannot choose but bite.

The nature of addiction feeds on our attempts to master it. You can get the monkey off your back, but the circus never leaves town. It's the difference between the world as your arena and the world as your prison. If addiction is seen as a moral failing, it will be condemned. If seen as a deficit in knowledge, it will be educated. If viewed as an acceptable aberration, it will be tolerated. If considered illegal, it will be prosecuted. If viewed as an illness, it will be treated.

Some experts would maintain that no drug causes the fundamental ills of society, that the source of our troubles isn't drugs, but stupidity and ignorance and greed and narcissism.

But many of Sababa's contemporary cupcake colleagues would maintain that addiction is indeed a disease. A disease is defined as an incorrectly functioning organ that interrupts or modifies the performance of the vital functions. It comes from *dis-*, a prefix expressing negation, or denoting reversal or absence of an action or state; and *ease*, the absence of difficulty or effort or rigidity or discomfort or worry or problems. If addiction is any kind of disease, it must be a brain disease—a wiring disorder that impairs how we process information about motivation, reward, and punishment. But it is also a personality disease, a motivational disease, a social disease, a cultural disease, and a bunch of other stuff that are not diseases, although it becomes an incubator for all kinds of them.

Addiction is a shifting cultural concept. Addiction replaces people with obsession. It is a symptom, not the cause, of personal and social maladjustment. Addiction is a self-inflicted adaptation. Addiction is an experience that grows out of an individual's subjective response to something that has special meaning for him, from which he seeks safety that nothing else provides. Addiction is not a chemical reaction or a biological entity or you. It is the cage you live in, a form of slavery which commands that a part of us boss the rest of us. Addictions make your most crucial decisions about life. And they're dumber than earthworms. All sin tends to be addictive, and the terminal point of addiction is damnation. The terrible irony is that most addicts are already victims of a vicious world.

So what's it going to be? Prohibition? Criminalization? Hospitalization? Harm reduction? Legalization? When does your civil liberty right to poison yourself whenever you want in whatever manner you choose become a matter for your family or society at large to intervene on your behalf?

Perhaps reality is just a crutch for people who can't handle drugs. In the 1960s, people took acid to make the world weird. Now the world is weird, and people take drugs to make it normal. If God dropped acid, he would likely see these people. Jazz was born out of the whiskey bottle, raised on marijuana, and will expire on cocaine. Drugs have taught an entire generation of American kids the metric system. Addiction does keep the cause of death from being a total surprise. There is an incentive not to do drugs—if you do drugs you'll go to prison, and drugs are expensive in prison.

And what of our stocky savant. What is his addiction? Some would say pinot noir, but Sababa is not dependent on pinot noir, he is merely in love with it, granting that love may be the cruelest addiction.

Every form of addiction is bad, no matter whether the narcotic is alcohol or morphine or idealism. Doctor Sababa is addicted to puzzles. He shows all the classic behaviors— intolerance, competitiveness, conflict, and an inability to stop no matter how devastating the consequences. The critical element is the resolution of the puzzle rather than the restoration of the person. His addiction comes from failing to realize that he is already what he's looking for. Addiction is addiction is addiction. *Rose is a rose is a rose.*

> 'I height Don Quixote, I live on peyote,
> marijuana, morphine and cocaine.
> I never knew sadness but only a madness
> that burns at the heart and the brain.'
> John Whiteside 'Jack' Parsons, *I Height Don Quixote, I Live on Peyote*

Addiction, for the most part, obeys the three laws of thermodynamics: (1) You can't win, (2) You can't break even, and (3) You can't get out of the game.

William Burroughs, Sababa's patient with the wound botulism from skin-popping contaminated Mexican black tar heroin was on a ventilator in the Death Star for six weeks. Because the binding of botulinum toxin at the neuromuscular junction is irreversible, his recovery could only take place through terminal axonal sprouting and reinnervation, which took that long to occur. Oliver Lax confirmed the diagnosis with his neurophysiology studies. There was a steady improvement in his oculobulbar and limb function, and William began to stand with support. However, he still saw two Sababas, the persistence of which likely contributed to his ultimate enrollment as a star pupil in Island Health's methadone program.

Impeccable Williams, the Rastafarian Tilray Cannabis quality control technician with Jamaican vomiting sickness came through Ziggy Stardust's liver transplantation without technical complication and with minimal blood loss without the need for vasopressor support. As disappointed as he was to have eaten his last meal of salt fish and ackee, he finds consolation in catching and eating his salmon which, like the holy herb he still worships, he likes to smoke.

Fiera Carpenter died of her anorexia nervosa a month after Praj and Sababa saw her in consultation. It was Einstein's relativistic equation that defined the relationship of mass to light. It was no one's fault that Fiera had resolved to convert the solidity of the first variable into the ethereal photons of the second.

Carrie Underwood's vision returned completely and she heeded Doctor Sababa's advice about never going near Ma Huang again. It never occurred to here that Mormon Tea, growing in the wild in the Fiery Furnace area of Arches National Park near Moab, Utah, was *Ephedra funerea*, a close relative of what had caused her blindness. She just didn't see the relationship.

Popcorn Sutton's blood lead level of 70 µg/dL got the bootlegger two course of infusions of dimercaprol followed by EDTA chelation, two months apart. But although Popcorn's flame test started to burn blue instead of red, his saturnine gout had formed kidney stones. He never had an opportunity to entertain the painful speculation about whether gout or stone was the worst disease. Sometimes the stone, on passing, kills the patient, without waiting for the gout.

With the aid of thiamine and B-complex infusions, Bettino Ricasoli recovered from his Marchiafava-Bignami disease. He regained his speech and memory and returned to the eclectic transactions of his Gold n' Fleece Pawn Shop. Bettino poured his remaining barrels of homemade wine into the drain behind his establishment, drowning most the Harbour City sewer rats in the process, the agony, and the misfortune.

Two months after he stopped the amygdalin cyanide tablets prescribed by his alternative holistic medicine doctor, Marshall Applewhite went through Heaven's Gate in his sleep. They found him with his arms crossed, dressed but barefoot. Someone on the *Away Team* had flown off with his new Nike Windrunners.

The results of Louis Alcott's 24-hour urine collection for mercury were reported two weeks after his consultation with Doctor Sababa at 2377 nmol/L, fifty times the amount considered toxic. He underwent a 19-day course of oral meso 2, 3-dimercaptosuccinic acid chelation, and a second course four months later to get rid of the rest. With successful counselling for his gambling addiction, he and his family reunited, he got to keep his house, and returned to work as a plumber. When Doctor Sababa called him out one night to fix a leak, Louis refused payment but told the professor what he would have otherwise charged him.

"I don't make that as a medical specialist." Sababa said.

"Neither did I when I was a specialist." Louis grinned.

'Pretty Boy' Troy removed most of Raoul Bensaude's Madelung disease fatty tumours with ultrasound-assisted liposuction. The Croatian insurance broker no longer looks like the Warrior of Capestrano, although he often sneaks the odd swig of slivovitz when his wife isn't watching.

Olaf Octagon's pregnant patient, Paula Broca, recovered from her Wernicke's encephalopathy with the prompt administration of thiamine from the Death Star, except for her memory which took several months to return in full. At Olaf's urging, Sababa gave an inservice to the nurses on the second floor about medical obstetrical emergencies. It was well attended and well received, except for one outlier, a union rep who spent the lecture scrolling her cell phone screen and watching the clock. She left on her break as Sababa reached the part in the story where the patient's life is saved by a cheap vitamin.

Michael Bulles' hallucinations, paranoia, and agitation resolved with an extra dose of haloperidol. His kidney failure and muscle breakdown settled over three days in the ICU with supportive treatment. He confessed to taking three packets of 1500 mg of bath salts throughout the day of his admission. Michael listened hard when Doctor Sababa told him that if he ever did it again, he would eat his face off.

Ben Johnson was admitted to Harbour City Regional for the investigations Doctor Sababa told him about in his office, and management consisting of intravenous hydration, osmotic diuretic and urinary alkalinization, and a course of the other kind of steroid. A month later he died in a hail of lead at the Departure Bay ferry terminal. Constable Marsden thought he looked like a condom full of walnuts, but she liked the car he had been driving.

Honey Drive received plasma exchange and dialysis in Vancouver for her cocaine-induced pseudo-thrombotic thrombocytopenic purpura. A month later, she did it again.

In between the two presentations, in between the top of Nob Hill and the bottom of Honey Drive, pimp and drug dealer Joshua 'Joe' Jackson, recovered from his Viagra-induced skin eruption, pumped the oxygen blast trigger of his cutting torch to blow away the steel cage around Juan Leyblanca's garden hose faucet. *Cleanliness is next to godliness... Bed Bath & Beyond.*

18. The Case of the Sensitive Smurf

'Thou rascal... hold thy bloody hand!
Why dost thou lash that whore? Strip thine own back;
Thou hotly lust'st to use her in that kind
For which thou whipp'st her.'
Shakespeare, *King Lear*

Martina Benno withered and turned brown. Six months before the ordeal, Martina had been a happy Harbour City cosmetician with a good reputation and a loyal clientele.

Jennifer Gonif's afternoon appointment would change the rest of that. An obese, androgynous troll wearing a juvenile pastel hoodie bumbled into Martina's salon fifteen minutes late.

"I'm sorry, Ms. Gonif, but you've missed your consultation."

"I'm not a Ms. yet." He/she said. "I'm still undergoing reassignment therapy. I used to be Jason before I became Jennifer. My LGBTQ2 pronouns are they/them/their."

"It appears you requested our Brazilian-wax services." Martina said. "But we only offer that to our female clients. We don't do Manzilians. Testicles are different from bikini lines."

"But I want to be all shiny and new." They showed her a rainbow flag, tattooed on their left arm. "And I do so want you to wax my balls."

"Again, I'm sorry, Jennifer." Martina said. "But I don't think that would be appropriate."

"You're not the first turban-fucker to refuse me service." Jennifer said. "Pure discrimination against trans-activists. I've won all 15 complaints I lodged with the BC Human Rights Commission against other estheticians who refused me service. One tribunal member wrote that 'waxing can be critical gender-affirming care for transgender women.' Have a look at my Twitter feed. I'm a global internet personality and social justice warrior."

"You may have weaponized your chosen gender but I'm afraid I don't have any interest in identity politics." Martina said. "I'm just a simple beautician who runs a business from her home. I'm asking you to leave."

"Maybe you need some stimulation." Jennifer pulled an X26P device from their handbag. White knuckles fired two taser barbed wires at Martina's chest. The implantation discharged a shaped pulse product of voltage and current that tetanized the cosmetician flat on her face.

Paralyzed with an electrical storm and frozen with fear, Martina could only watch the boot, coming down from their smouldering stare.

'Fruitcakes in the kitchen, fruitcakes on the street
Struttin' naked through the crosswalk, in the middle of the week
Half-baked cookies in the oven, half-baked people on the bus
There's a little bit of fruitcake left in everyone of us.'
Jimmy Buffett, *Fruitcakes*

And God made a baker. Tom Turnabout was a baker, celebrated in Harbour City for good humour and generosity.

His Cascadia Bakery was organic and alive. Every morning Tom rose, like his dough, well before dawn, He put on his soft cotton apron and ran the daily balancing act of time, temperature and ingredients through his mind.

By the time the early morning light slanted through the bakery windows, it was already warm inside. The jingle of the bell on the bakery door rang in the first customers. Ovens and display cases filled so much of the shop that customers had to squeeze in and out and by each other. No one ever made the distance across the checkerboard of black and white tiles, worn and cracked from three decades worth of boots and shoes, before being seduced by the rapture.

A steaming hot front of thick, buttery fumes and sugary vapors lay in ambush inside. Powerful and intoxicating, more delicious than any other aroma in the world, the air inside the Cascadia Bakery was a spiritual experience. The sweet smells of yeast and cinnamon and chocolate and gingerbread and caramel and apples and toasted almonds and coconut and currants and coffee floated in its atmosphere. The air in the Cascadia was so fine you wanted to bottle it and take it home. It was the hypnotic smell of good bread baking, indescribable in its evocation of innocence and delight. When you die, you will enter a room of bright light, and smell this baking around the corner. It was the aroma of kindness to strangers. There was no therapy, no dance, no ascetic discipline, no hour of meditation in any Buddhist temple that could leave you emptier of bad thoughts than this ritual, this ancient alchemy of flour and heat. Tom built it, and they came. *If thou tastest a crust of bread, thou tastest all the stars and all the heavens.*

The dated countertops were well-polished. The barrel in the corner held slim baguettes, each with a crinkled brown paper coat. Inside the cold display cases, pastries gleamed in translucent icing or sparkled with powdered snow. Tom's patrons knew that a party without cake was just a meeting. They fogged up the glass with the breath from their noses.

Every kind of Harbour City resident came to Tom's Cascadia Bakery to buy the inspired tribal pastries that he prepared each morning. Tell me what you eat, and I will tell you who you are.

Diane de Poitiers, the goldsmith, and Émile Zola, the shisha bar employee, came to buy Tom's faithful renditions of French boulanger and patisserie—croissants, macarons, baguettes, beignets, bichons au citron, broyés poitevin, canelés, dacquoises, gâteaux Basque, gibassiers, Kouign-Amanns, madeleines, pain au chocolat, pain aux raisins, pain de Gênes, palmiers, pithiviers, puits d'amour, tartes des Alpes, and tartes tatin.

Thomas Ham, the butcher, and Marsha Mallow, the horticultural therapist, bought English gingerbread men, Bakewell pudding, Coventry Godcakes, Eccles cakes, and flies' graveyards.

Frederica Flückiger, the housesitter, Robert Heinz, the sculptor, and Gina Rinehart, the colloidal silver therapist, came for Tom's versions of German rye bread, black forest cake, marzipan, Aachener Printen, allerheiligenstriezel, cremeschnitte. moorkops, and streusel.

Tristano Martinelli, the waiter, and Martina Benno, the cosmetician, bought Tom's Italian ciabatta, baicoli, biscotti, bruttiboni, cannoli, ciambella, ciarduna, pasticciotto, pizzelle, sfogliatella, and torta Caprese.

Even Jack Tu, the bicycle shop owner, and Westwood Ho, the medical student and composer, patronized the Cascadia Bakery for Tom Turnabout's Chinese almond biscuits and mooncake.

Jabba Desilijic Tiure, the Albanian taxi driver, came for the Danish, and RCMP constable Veronica Marsden, bought cinnamon buns, beaver tails, butter tarts, and Nanaimo bars (but mostly donuts), for her detachment. Tom was the king of croissants, the tsar of sourdough, the prince of pastry, the earl of éclairs, and the baron of baguettes. It was a wonderful loaf.

No one bothered to ask why Tom's stereo always played the blues. Refrains from Baker Shop Boogie, Black Coffee, Brown Sugar, Cakewalk into Town. Custard Pie Blues, I Need a Little Sugar in My Bowl, Mr. Jelly Roll Baker, Spoonful, and Sugar Blues filled in the little remaining space that the smells hadn't occupied.

Tom had been fortunate to breathe the sacred air of his own making. It should have ensured that his work would never turn into just another day at the office. But man cannot live by bread alone and a baker can't live on bread he made yesterday.

Broken sleep and oven-scorched eyebrows, varicose veins, and floury underwear came with the territory. Tom's hands had become swollen, thickened by the constant painful pressure of kneading. The strain and diarrhea and weight loss and fatigue were taking their toll. His rash had become so itchy, he scratched the blisters off his skin, the appearance of which his clientele found so repulsive as to cause them to shun the Cascadia and bring Tom to the point of insolvency. He went from kneading the dough to needing the dough. Of complaints, he had a baker's dozen. One ingredient entered his baking, more concentrated than any extract, more pungent than any spice; an ingredient that everyone would recognise, no one could name, and rose with every new frustration.

Anger is an acid that can do more harm to the vessel in which it is stored than to anything on which it is poured. Tom's wrath was a wind that blew out the lamp of his mind. His itch drove him mad, his work drove him into a trap, his financial difficulty drove him to desperation, and his business insurance policy drove him into criminal intent.

One early morning, instead of playing his blues collection, Tom turned on the radio. And then he turned on his ovens.

Good morning, Blueberries... this is CNDN Coast Salish radio, 101.3 FM on your Home and Native Band... I'm your host, BC Bud... Time for a hearty breakfast of bannock and fried Indian bread...

Tom changed his creations from confections to convections, fueled by gallons of kerosene accelerant. His fury burst out from within, in snarls and bites of crimson rage and wrath. Of the many ways he could retaliate on the world for his misfortune, fire was the most beautiful weapon of them all.

The way of the troublemaker is thorny... A hungry stomach makes a short prayer... Better to live on Indian cakes.

Molten plumes lit up the blackness. Ferocious flames exploded and engulfed, flickered and flared, licked and leaped, spat and swept, and devoured and roared and rampaged into an uncontrollable blazing inferno.

Weaving under the spell it was sparked from, the fire crackled and rumbled into a freight train. Embers leaped and twirled in a fiery dance. Showers and fountains rolled the giant wave in on itself, like a running river roaring through its tributaries, splashing broad strokes of bright yellow and red and orange autumnal colour on the black charcoal canvas behind.

The rainbow is a sign from Him who is in all things... The soul would have no rainbow if the eye had no tears... Universe closed, use rainbow...

The firestorm undulated like some grotesque famished beast, a great hungry serpent winding itself around posts and beams, devouring everything in its way. It belched thick black poisonous clouds of acrid smoke, ascending in darkness and misery. It choked the air and swallowed the sky. There was a sound of sirens but Tom knew that no firefighter would rush into such an inferno. Grey ash floated towards the ground like dirty snowflakes before being blown away, empty on the wind.

Even a small mouse has anger... There is nothing as eloquent as a rattlesnake's tail... It is better to have less thunder in the mouth and more lightning in the hand...

The bakery cracked and wilted under the force of the weightless fire. It smelled of incense and extermination. From across the street, Tom watched his dreams die. Everything he loved was gone in minutes, crumbled on the ground. When one burns one's bridges, what a very nice fire it makes.

When you know who you are... when your mission is clear and you burn with the inner fire of unbreakable will... no cold can touch your heart...

The onlookers had been excited at first, behaving like a crowd on bonfire night. They snapped selfies with their phones and emailed them into the ether. But a shift in the wind direction brought noxious smoke and ash raining down into their hair and eyes.
The heat was oppressive. It burned their lungs, cooking them from the inside. Most fled to their cars, hands and clothing clamped to their mouths. It was chaos as they all tried to leave, honking horns and struggling to see through the grey debris that coated their windshields.
And then Tom Turnabout turned the most amazing shade of blue...

'You will not be punished for your anger, you will be punished by your anger.'
Buddha

'There's no physician
What could he tell me to use
No liquid or pill I'm sure
Ever did or will cure
A woman alone with the blues.'
Peggy Lee, *A Woman Alone with the Blues*

This was also the colour of Sababa's first patient in the ICU the morning before Tom Turnabout torched his treasury and a month before Martina Benno was translocated and transacted and transpierced and transfixed and transformed and transmuted and transubstantiated.
"Why so blue?" Sababa bounced into the Death Star. It was a new day.
"Didn't get much sleep." He said.
"Not you, Mowgli." Sababa said. "Your patient."

"Frederica Flückiger." The young resident opened the curtain of cubicle 6 wider. Mary was suctioning a sapphire. "20-year-old house-sitter admitted by Dr. Ernie Hacker last night. He was on call."

"Where is the Big Easy today?"

"Playing pale projectiles at some local golf club." He said. "Day off."

"Diga me."

"Chronic liver disease from Hep C." Praj continued. "History of portal hypertension and esophageal varices banded by Dr. Falstaff. Refused antiviral therapy and follow-up. Admitted last night with shortness of breath and cyanosis and clubbing."

Sababa and Praj joined Mary in cubicle 6.

"Exam?"

"Enlarged spleen, spider nevi, that's about it."

"You missed her heart and lungs." Sababa said. "Rather important if you're telling me she's not getting enough oxygen."

"That's also what I'm telling you." He said. "Normal. Chest x-ray also normal."

"Some of our predecessors have claimed that man is a rational animal." Sababa had unraveled the Littman Master Cardiology black and brass stethoscope draped over his shoulders and listened to Frederica's chest. "All my life I have been searching for evidence which supports this."

"And?" Mary asked.

"Not a trace anywhere." He said.

"Her oxygen saturation was 85%." Praj said.

"What was it when you stood her up?"

"I didn't stand her up." Praj said.

"Let's stand her up." Sababa said. Frederica's oxygen saturation dropped to 65% on standing."

"What the hell was that?" Praj gnashed his teeth.

"Platypnia." Sababa said.

"What the hell is that?" Sababa turned to the ward clerk, counting down to her next cigarette.

"Betty Boop, can you raise whichever shadow puppet is on for ultrasound today please?"

Less than a minute later, Betty's left hand gesticulated in the air as she held the handset high.

"Dr. Brisk on line one." She said. Sababa picked up line one.

"The blues had a baby and they named it rock 'n roll."

"What?"

"Mako, I need a portable contrast-enhanced transthoracic echo in the Death Star." He said. "Bring your bubbles." *Click.*

"Bubbles?" Mary asked.

"Champagne for your real friends, real pain for your sham friends." Sababa said. "It helps us follow the flow."

A few minutes later, they heard the whoosh of the translucent door, sliding sideways with ease. An ultrasound technician guided a large mobile Zamboni through the unit like he was driving a Ferrari through a bad neighbourhood.

"Bed 6." Betty Boop pointed toward Frederica's cubicle. A few minutes later, Dr. Mako Brisk entered, scowling at Doctor Sababa.

"I'm on call for nuclear medicine today." He said.

"You mean unclear medicine?" Sababa said. "I should have asked for a 99mTc-macroaggregated albumin lung perfusion scan."

"I would have said no." Mako said.

"That's why I ordered this one."

"Whatever." Mako said. "What do I write down as the reason for this unscheduled bedside conference?"

"Why is her oxygen saturation low?"

"Isn't that why they hired you?"

"And that's what I'm about to find out." Sababa said. "This job is a test. Had it been an actual job, I would have received raises, promotions, and other signs of appreciation. Did you bring your bubble-maker?" Mako held up a bag of warmed saline.

The technician had already set up the study windows for Frederica's ultrasound. Sababa and Brisk, and Praj and Mary hovered beside the screen. The radiologist shook the bag of saline, piggybacked it into the patient's central line, and squeezed. As he adjusted his probe, an effervescent stream of shooting stars sparkled across the screen.

"Whoah." Sababa let out a low whistle. "Left-sided circulation.".

"Should be on the right." Mako said. "Pulmonary vascular dilatation."

"Intrapulmonary shunting." Sababa said. "Frederica has hepatopulmonary syndrome."

"What causes it?" Mary asked.

"Nobody knows."

"What's the treatment?" She asked.

"Oxygen." Sababa said. "Or liver transplant. Survival is 70%."

"I have this feeling you're about to make one of those Ziggy Stardust phone calls." Praj said.

"Cry me a liver." Sababa selected a tune from his music library on a secret drive hidden deep inside the hospital computer network.

'When whippoorwills call
And evening is nigh
I hurry to
My blue heaven.'
  Leon Redbone, *My Blue Heaven*

White was the colour of the other referral in the Death Star that morning. "Thomas Ham." Praj said. "Elderly retired butcher back-transferred from his cardiologist in Victoria last night."
Which one?"
"Dr. Wineburger." Praj said.
"Two of my favorite comestibles." Sababa raised an eyebrow. "Why did he send him back? I'm a simple village internist."
"His transfer letter says that you'll figure out what's wrong."
"Flattering." Sababa said. "Do tell."

Dear Doctor Sababa,
Thank you for accepting this 73-year-old patient with recurrent coronary syndrome without associated stenosis, fever, marked inflammatory syndrome, and anemia. His past medical history is noteworthy for two episodes of DVT and pulmonary embolism. This year we treated him for two consecutive acute coronary episodes within a 1-month interval, while on continuous anticoagulation with warfarin.
Both presentations were inferior location heart attacks associated with intraluminal thromboses of his right coronary artery. Both opened with balloon angioplasty. No stents were placed because of his fever of unknown origin. Antiplatelet therapy was added to his anticoagulation, ASA the first time, and ASA with clopidogrel the second. We informed Mr. Ham of the much higher risk of bleeding with triple therapy. His urine is red.
We are sending him to you to find out what the hell is going on here.
Dr. Ricardo Wineburger

"OK, Praj." Sababa said. "What the hell is going on here? What you got?"
"Mr. Ham is anemic, with elevated reticulocyte count and lactate dehydrogenase and bilirubin and C-reactive protein, reduced haptoglobin and negative direct antiglobulin test."
"So?"
"So non-immune hemolytic anemia." Praj said. "All tests for infectious, systemic inflammatory diseases, and vasculitis are negative."
"What's he doing in the Death Star with stable vital signs?" Sababa said. "Why didn't you admit to the telemetry unit on floor one?"
"He developed severe abdominal pain without much in the way of surgical signs late last night." Praj said. "Dr. Buddy Benway said he wouldn't see him without a CT scan. Dr. Statham the radiologist came in to read the one I ordered."
"And?" Praj brought the images up on the consultant desk monitor. "It shows hepatic vein thrombosis and multiple clots affecting his small abdominal vessels."
"In a guy on triple therapy?"
"In a guy on triple therapy." Praj said.

"Let's go see him." Sababa said. "Betty Boop, please find Dr. Leyblanca for me."

"On it." She said. Praj made introductions at Mr. Ham's bedside in cubicle 5.

"Thomas, this is the specialist that Dr. Wineburger sent you back to see. He tries to keep clear and still as water does with the moon."

"Doctor Sababa." Thomas said. "We old roosters must be cautious. Apparently, I've been trying to outwit my arteries."

"Spectacular fail, Mr. Ham." Sababa saw Betty Boop's handset reaching for the stars with two fingers extended. "Please excuse me. I'll be back in a minute." He picked up line 2.

"Hola amigo mio." Sababa said.

"¿What do ju want, Cabrón?" It was Juan.

"I need a flow cytometry test for CD55 and CD59 on white and red blood cells, or a fluorescein-labeled proaerolysin." Sababa said. "Thomas Ham. Bed 5 in the Death Star."

"Ju don't need my permeesion."

"But I get it done faster if I kiss the ring, right."

"Send the blood." Juan said. "I call ju." *Click.*

"So, what's wrong with me?" Thomas asked.

"We need to find out why you continue to have so many unusual and unexplained blood clots on maximum therapy to prevent them." Sababa said. "I think you have a condition called paroxysmal nocturnal hemoglobinuria."

"What's that?"

"It's a rare acquired nonmalignant clonal hematopoietic stem cell disorder." He said. "A somatic mutation of the X-linked phosphatidylinositol glycan class A gene responsible for the expansion of hematopoietic stem cells lacking a functional GPI anchor. The aberration results in a deficiency of complement inhibitory proteins causing complement-mediated hemolysis, and activation of monocytes, granulocytes, and platelets with formation of prothrombotic microparticles. The combination of hemolysis with the liberation of high levels of free hemoglobin leads to nitric oxide scavenging, which results in platelet activation and aggregation."

"I didn't get any of that." Thomas said.

"Me neither." Praj said.

"You have a condition in which platelets and the lining of your blood vessels are stimulated by broken red blood cells, nitric oxide deficiency, and acceleration of the complement pathway."

"Still don't get it." Thomas said. "What causes it?"

"It's complicated." Sababa said. "And we don't know. But we can treat it."

"How?" He asked.

"First, we have to confirm the diagnosis with a test called flow cytometry, which looks for the PHN clone." Sababa said. "You'll need a bone marrow smear. Then, when we have confirmation, we have treatment that should work."

"In the meantime?"

"We have to wait two weeks after your vaccinations against meningococcal and pneumococcal infections. We continue your triple therapy, transfuse you as needed, organize antibiotics to cover you during your treatment, and apply to the Federal Government to release the special humanized monoclonal antibody you need."

"You have to ask Ottawa?" Thomas asked. "Is it that difficult?"

"You have no idea." Sababa excused himself to call the special release program in the nation's capital. He was astounded to speak to a human on his first attempt.

"What is it you want this time, Doctor Sababa?" The voice asked.

"I need you to release eculizumab."

"What?"

"I need you to send me some eculizumab." Sababa thought the coughing on the other end of the line would never stop.

"You do know it costs more than half a million dollars a year, don't you?" Asked the voice. "It's one of the most expensive pharmaceuticals in the world."

"You have all our money." Sababa said. "You can afford it."

"What's the indication?"

"Paroxysmal nocturnal hemoglobinuria." Sababa said. "Eculizumab blocks the terminal complement pathway by binding to C5."

"Whatever." Said the voice. "Just fax me the forms." Sababa faxed him the forms, then gestured to Praj.

"Call the blood bank, Mowgli."

"Why?"

"Nothing fancy." He said. "But Thomas here could use a couple of litres of the house red." Blood will have blood.

Out of the corner of his eye, he saw Betty Boop lift her handset and three fingers in the air. Sababa picked up line three. It was Cherie Sundae.

"Two more in emerg for you, Sab." She said.

Trace Pangloss waited for Sababa and his apprentice on the other side of the automatic frosted sliding doors.

"I have no idea." He said.

"I haven't asked you yet."

"Just trying to stay ahead of the ritual." Trace said. "Émile Zola. 24-year-old male brought in by EMS after falling unconscious at work."

"Where does he work?"

"At the Harewood hookah lounge near the university." Trace watched one of Sababa's eyebrows migrate north.

"What does he do there?"

"I didn't ask."

"Let's go ask." Trace's patient had regained consciousness but held on to his head and his chest. Sababa noticed the waveform changes in the rapid heartbeat running along the patient's cardiac monitor. He mimed the placement of leads on his chest to Dina (and tapped his wristwatch), who repeated the same movements to Cheri Sundae behind her polycarbonate protection, who called for a stat ECG.

"Émile, this is the specialist I told you about." Trace said. "He's cool but he cares."

"I don't feel so good."

"What were you doing when you fainted, Émile?" Sababa asked.

"Lighting the coals in the narghiles." He said. "I was nearly finished."

"What are narghiles?" Trace asked.

"Waterpipes." Praj said. "Charcoal-heated hookahs."

"How many did you light?" Sababa asked.

"Forty."

"How do you light them?"

"I torch a butane lighter next to the charcoals and inhale through the hose to draw the flame across to light them."

"The paramedics said he was out for ten minutes before they got to him." Trace said. "Vital signs were normal except for a fast pulse rate of 105/minute and a respiratory rate of 18/minute. Portable chest x-ray, complete blood count, serum chemistry panel and alcohol, cardiac enzymes, and urine tox screen were all normal."

Sababa took a small device from his Colombian leather briefcase and placed it on one of Émile Zola's fingertips.

"He already has a pulse oximeter on the index finger of the other hand." Trace pointed at the number on the screen. "See, it shows pulse oximetry of 98% on a 15 L O2/min nonrebreather mask. Why does your pulse oximeter read only 35%."

213

"Because it's not a pulse oximeter." Sababa said. "It's a CO-oximeter. By evaluating the light absorption of the specific types of hemoglobin in the capillaries, it measures carboxyhemoglobin, not oxyhemoglobin. Your device can't tell the difference." He mimed the pointing of his radial artery to Dina (and tapped his wristwatch), who repeated the same movements to Cheri Sundae behind her polycarbonate protector, who called for a stat arterial blood gas.

"You're saying he has carbon monoxide poisoning?' Trace asked.

"Traditional charcoal-heated shisha hookahs deliver ten times the carbon monoxide of a standard cigarette." Sababa said. "Émile did forty of them before he lost consciousness. Strange that Indian and Persian physicians in the sixteenth century invented the first water pipe as a less harmful method of tobacco use." The bedside filled up with ECG and respiratory technicians.

"Isn't he supposed to be a bright cherry-red colour?"

"Only if he's a corpse." Sababa said. "Every murdered victim at Treblinka and Sobibor and Belzec died with cherry red cheeks from the Russian tank engines they used to gas them with carbon monoxide. It's a silent killer that gives no warning—you can't see it; you can't smell it; you can't taste it. The meat in your local supermarket is the same colour for the same reason."

"They use Russian tank engines to turn our meat red?"

"I do the metaphors, Trace." Sababa looked at the ECG coming off the machine. "Cheri Sundae, please patch me through to the Oceanside Hyperbaric Unit in Parksville."

"On it." She said. Dina handed Sababa Émile's arterial blood gas results. "Émile's COHgb is 33.8 %." He turned to the respiratory technician. "Switch him over to 100 % oxygen via a high flow, nonrebreather mask." The changeover was quick.

"Carbon monoxide shifts the oxygen-hemoglobin dissociation curve to the left." Sababa said.

"What does that mean?" Émile asked.

"Carbon monoxide has 230 times more affinity than oxygen for the four hemoglobin oxygen binding sites." Sababa said. "Its attachment at any one of them increases the affinity of the three remaining, causing hemoglobin to hang on to oxygen that would otherwise be delivered to the tissues. This prevents the blood from carrying and delivering oxygen."

"Anything else?" He asked.

"Carbon monoxide binds myoglobin sixty times stronger than oxygen can. Its late release can then attach to hemoglobin and delay recovery. Also, binding to cytochrome oxidase interferes with ATP synthesis. Cells switch to anaerobic metabolism, causing lactic acidosis, and cell death. Finally, carbon monoxide releases nitric oxide from endothelial cells and platelets. Oxygen-free radicals cause lipid peroxidation and Grinker myelinopathy, white matter demyelination which results in swelling and necrosis within the brain. Never ride in the back of a pickup truck."

"Sweet." Émile said. "Can you fix it?" Cherie Sundae interrupted the conversation with the solution.

"Oceanside Hyperbaric Unit on line 1, Sab." She said. Sababa picked up line 1.

"You have a referral?" Asked the technician.

"Red skin pigment anomaly of New Guinea." Sababa said.

"Huh?"

"Just kidding." He said. "I have a 24-year-old unintentional non-fire-related carbon monoxide poisoning with ECG changes consistent with cardiac ischemia." There was hardly a pause.

"Send him up." Sababa mimed the movement of rotating siren to Cheri Sundae behind her polycarbonate protector, who called ambulance dispatch.

"Will I be alright?" Émile asked.

"The Roman emperor Julian suffered from carbon monoxide poisoning in Paris in 350 AD." Sababa said. "He lived to write about the experience and you should too. But you may need to change your line of work to something other than a hookah lounge lizard."

"And if I don't?"

"You'll end up dead in the afterdamp." Sababa selected a tune from his music library on a secret drive hidden deep inside the hospital computer network. "Like that canary in the coal mine."

> 'I'll take a quiet life
> A handshake of carbon monoxide
> With no alarms and no surprises...'
> Radiohead, *No Surprises*

Dr. Myles Capitaine made his approach.

"You might be an ER doctor if you stand and wolf your food even in the nicest restaurants." Sababa said. "How are you, Myles?"

"Living the dream."

"In the face of everything, in the face of life, the true dream is being able to dream at all." Sababa mused. "What you got?"

"Jack Tu." He said. "70-year-old bicycle shop owner with a five-year history of polycythemia rubra vera treated with intermittent bloodletting, but he missed his last two phlebotomy appointments. Patient of Dr. Henry Chibueze, who recently stopped his low dose aspirin because he thought it worsened his gout."

"Henry's unique, like everyone else." Sababa said. "You know why medical oncologists know how to perform CPR?"

"Dunno."

"In case they need to pump the chemo." He said. Praj let out a groan.

"Anyway, Mr. Tu has associated problems of diffuse itching and gout."

"OK."

"He presents today with a four-day complaint of headache, fatigue, and severe burning pain in the hands and feet accompanied by swelling and a reddish-blue discoloration of the skin."

"Exam?"

"As described." Myles said. "Also plethoric facies, an enlarged liver and spleen, and gouty nodules."

"Labs?"

"Hemoglobin is up at 190 g/dl with a hematocrit of 70%." He said. "Platelet count up at 680k. Recent tests from Henry's records show low erythropoietin and ESR and raised leukocyte alkaline phosphatase."

"Let's go see him." Sababa said.

Inside the curtain of his cubicle, an elderly oriental gentleman glowed at the extremity of his extremities.

"Mr. Tu, permit me to introduce the professor I told you about and his resident, Dr. Bharmal." Myles said. "Doctor Sababa is usually all in favour of spontaneity, providing it is carefully planned and ruthlessly controlled."

"Can you get rid of this terrible burning pain in my hands and feet?" Jack asked. "And this itch? It's driving me mad."

"We can do that, Jack." Sababa said. "First thing we'll do is give you back your aspirin with another medication to protect your stomach. That will make this secondary erythromelalgia go away."

"Wait a minute, Sab." Praj said. "Didn't we have another case of secondary erythromelalgia earlier in the autumn? Perry Lepistopsis, that specialty food importer back from a buying trip in France."

"Good memory, Praj." Sababa said. "But his secondary erythromelalgia came from eating the paralysis funnel mushroom, *Clitocybe amoenolens*. If Mr. Tu had eaten the Asian funnel cap, *Clitocybe acromelalga*, I might be more persuaded, but his is from his PRV." Cheri Sundae held up her handset and motioned to Praj. He left the ER after taking the call, having informed his mentor that he would page him after he had seen the new consult.

"Anything else you can advise, Doctor Sababa?" Jack asked.

"We'll take a couple of units of blood off this morning." Sababa said. "You'll need to get back on your regular phlebotomy schedule. There are also cytoreductive agents like hydroxyurea, interferon injections, anagrelide for your high platelet count, and the monoclonal inhibitor, ruxolitinib, but I'll remind your oncologist of these options and tell him what we've done. Then you can hit the road."

Back at the consultant's desk, Sababa asked the Big Voice to put in a page for Dr. Chibueze.

"To what do I owe this pleasure, Sab?"

"How many medical oncologists does it take to carry a coffin, Henry?"

"Six?"

"Seven." Sababa said. "Six to carry the coffin, one to hold the chemo."
Oncologists are not known for their sense of humour. There came a brief
silence.
"I saw Jack Tu in the ER." The professor said.
"Whatever for?" Henry asked.
"Erythromelalgia."
"What did you do?"
"I told him to take two aspirins and call you in the morning."

'Brown skin girl, ya skin just like pearls
Your back against the world...'
Beyoncé, *Brown Skin Girl*

"You calling from the Psych Ward?" Sababa knew all the extensions.
"Yeah."
"It was just a matter of time since that law school thing."
"It's not me." Praj protested. "It's a referral from Dr. Robert La
Capuche."
"We don't do crazy." Sababa said. "Did you tell him?"
"He says he doesn't do internal medicine."
"We'll call it a draw, then, shall we?"
"No, Sab." Praj said. "He's got a real case here. She's sick."
"I'll be down." He said. "But she better not be a loon."
Dr. Robert La Capuche waited with Praj to welcome the stocky savant
to his ward.
"How's everything here, Bob?" Sababa asked.
"Pure bedlam." He said. "Nuts."
"Did you hear the one about a guy who walks into a psychiatrist's office."
"Do we need to do this?"

"Hey, Doc." He said. "My brother's crazy. Thinks he's a chicken."
"Why don't you turn him in?" The shrink asked.
"I would." He said. "But I need the eggs."

"I want you to see this patient, Sab." The psychiatrist said.
"OK. Tell us the story, Praj."
"Martina Benno." The resident said. "43-year-old esthetician admitted
four days ago with soft tissue injuries from an assault in her salon. But

she also presented with a six-month history of generalized anxiety disorder characterized by progressive difficulty concentrating, insomnia and fatigue, as well as anorexia, weight loss, mild gastrointestinal distress associated with altered bowel habits, dizziness, sweating, and muscle and joint pains. She attributed her state to worry about the financial status of her family. Her symptoms compromised her occupational and social function. Prior medical history was unremarkable except for burnt-out Hashimoto's thyroiditis, treated with l-thyroxine 100 μg daily. Dr. La Capuche prescribed a benzodiazepine and an antidepressant agent.

"Exam?"

"Dehydration, with a rapid pulse and blood pressure drop on standing, and diffuse brown hyperpigmentation," Praj said. "She's as brown as I am."

"I'll back him up on that." La Capuche volunteered.

"You're a shrink, Bob." Sababa said. "You don't remember how to do a physical exam. Labs?"

"None here of course." Praj continued. "In the ER, she had low sodium, high potassium, borderline low blood sugar, and high levels of antithyroid antibodies. There were too many eosinophils on her blood smear. Some bright light ordered a plasma adrenocorticotropic hormone."

"And?"

"It just came back." Praj said. "Elevated."

"How elevated?" Praj showed him the result. One of Sababa's eyebrows migrated north.

"Let's go see her." He pulled a cylinder from his Colombian leather briefcase. Dr. La Capuche introduced the portly professor.

"Martina, this is Doctor Sababa." Bob said. "He does all our hard cases because he's one himself."

"Pleased to meet you, sir." She said. Sababa handed her the cylinder, the contents of which she devoured with enthusiasm.

"Likewise." He said. "Positive Pringle test."

"Meaning?" Dr. La Capuche asked.

"Salt craving." Praj said. "From salt wasting. I got this one, Sab." The professor bowed.

"Make me proud."

"Schmidt's syndrome." He said. "First described by Schmidt in 1926. Also known as Type II autoimmune polyglandular syndrome—combined occurrence of primary adrenal insufficiency and Hashimoto's thyroiditis. Only 1 out of 100 patients with thyroid disease will develop adrenal insufficiency."

"And who first described this primary adrenal problem?" Sababa asked.

"Thomas Addison, at the University of Edinburgh medical school in 1855." Praj said. "His original six cases were all from tuberculosis, although I forget the name of his paper." *On the Constitutional and Local Effects of Disease of the Suprarenal Capsules.*

"But Martina doesn't have TB." Sababa said. "She has an autoimmune adrenalitis, an antibody reaction against the adrenal enzyme 21-hydroxylase. Order circulating adrenal cortex autoantibodies and an adrenal CT scan. No time for a long ACTH stimulation test. We need to get into real treatment now or else we'll have an adrenal crisis on our hands."

"What does that mean?" Martina asked.

"If your levels of adrenal hormones get too low, we can run into some serious trouble." Sababa caught the attention of the charge nurse.

"Excuse me." He said. "I wonder if it might be possible to give Martina here a litre bolus of IV saline, and then piggyback D5W at 45 ml/hour onto saline at 75 ml/hr." He said. "She needs 100 mg of IV hydrocortisone stat and every eight hours until we can rely on her gut absorption, and please give her the first dose of daily 0.1 mg of fludrocortisone."

"We're not allowed to start IV's or administer those kinds of drugs here." She said.

"I can see how that can be a problem." Sababa said. "You do have a funny farm here, Bob. It's like what Jung said about how the unconscious is revealed through the dream imagery which expresses our innermost fears and desires."

"Jung said that?" La Capuche asked.

"I think it was Jung." Sababa said. "Or maybe Leonard Cohen. Damn it, Bob, I'm an internist." He turned to his resident.

"Praj, before you meet me at Manzanita at one, please transfer Martina to the medical ward, dictate her consultation report, and write her orders." And back to the patient.

"Martina, you'll need lifelong therapy for this condition, the doses of which you'll need to increase during times of stress." He said. "We'll also arrange a MedicAlert bracelet and an injectable form of cortisol to carry with you. You should begin to feel much better in a couple of hours."

"It's the Medical Nursing Director on the line, Sab." Praj interrupted. "She says there are no medical beds."

"I teach you to lie and cheat and steal and as soon as I turn my back, you wait in line?" Sababa took the phone."

"I need this bed, Edith." He said. "This girl is sick."

"You need to call bedline, Doctor Sababa." She said. "They will find her a place in another hospital."

"Unless she gets the right treatment, and soon, you'll be transferring a corpse to the morgue." Sababa said. "Rock the house harder."

"The answer is no."

"OK."

"OK?" Edith was puzzled. "You're not going to even argue with me."

"Hell, no." Sababa said. "Dr. Bharmal and I will simply wheel this patient up to the big automatic frosted sliding doors of our emergency department and admit her there. What goes around comes around."

"You wouldn't dare." Edith said. "On second thought, yes you would."

"I can make you famous." Sababa said. "Evening news. Make sure you're wearing your string of natural pearls, uncultured."

"I'll find a bed."

"I just went to my happy place. Edith." Sababa said. "Find it fast." *Click.*

"And?" Dr. La Capuche asked.

"Like every time." He said. "It ain't over 'til the fat lady sings."

"It's colour my world week, Boss."

"The truth has to do with Mercy." Sababa took the first of two steaming mugs she had placed on the counter and motioned for Praj to take the second.

"Life is like coffee." He handed the first chart of the afternoon clinic to his resident. "The darker it gets, the more it energizes."

"Marsha Mallow." Praj called. A young woman wearing cotton gardening gloves rose from her chair and followed him down the hallway to the resident's room. Sababa picked up the next folder.

"Westwood Ho." Sababa called. A young Asian male jumped up and shook the professor's hand with enthusiasm.

"Westwood." Sababa said. "Still want to be an internist?" The young composer nodded.

"How's your brother, Gung?"

"Since his encounter with that Singapore Sling you ordered for him at Raffle's Long Bar, he only drinks green tea."

"It's not my fault he was born without alcohol dehydrogenase." The professor protested. "What does Dr. James Ruben Andrews think I can help you with today?"

"He referred me for an abnormal hemoglobin A1c." He said.

"You've been a Type I diabetic for ten years already." Sababa said. "The test may be elevated as a reflection of poor glycemic control."

"It's low." Sababa raised an eyebrow.

"How low?"

220

"1.6 percent." Westwood said. "Four times less than it should be if my sugars were normal."

"Hmmmm." Sababa mused. "Interesting. You know how they perform the test, don't you?"

"They grind up red blood cells and count the number of radiolabelled glucose receptors." He said. "This determines how much excess sugar has been in your system in the previous three months, a weighted average of blood glucose levels during the life of these red blood cells."

"Correctamundo, Grasshopper. A measure of the beta-N-1-deoxy fructosyl component reaction produced through a Schiff base and an Amadori rearrangement. separated on cation exchange chromatography." Sababa said. "And what are the determinants of that determination?"

"I don't understand."

"What makes the test unreliable?" Westwood looked puzzled.

"HbA1c is unreliable in many circumstances." Sababa said. "After blood loss, after surgery, blood transfusions, anemia, or high erythrocyte turnover, in chronic renal or liver disease, and after high-dose vitamin C or erythropoietin treatment. Higher-than-expected levels are seen in people with a longer red blood cell lifespan, as with vitamin B12 or folate deficiency."

"But mine is low."

"Right." Sababa said. "Which is seen in people with shortened red blood cell lifespans, as with blood donation, G6PD deficiency, sickle-cell disease, or any other condition causing premature red blood cell death."

"And I have such a condition?"

"You and your brother, Gung, have beta-thalassemia minor." Sababa said. "We used to call it Mediterranean anemia."

"But we're Chinese." Westwood protested.

"You'll have to take that one up with Marco Polo."

"Can you prove that this is the cause of my low result?" Westwood asked.

"We could do a chromium-51 red blood cell survival study, to show that you have a high turnover of red cells." Sababa said. "But it's not necessary. We can measure something else."

"What?"

"The test we use in cats and dogs." He said. "Serum fructosamine—just as accurate and provides a better indication of what your blood sugar has been doing in the last three weeks." Sababa handed him a lab requisition.

"That's it?" Westwood asked.

"Unless or until you have a real problem." Sababa waved his fingers and rose to meet the resident in his doorway.

"This one is interesting." Praj began.

"They're all interesting." Sababa said. "When they're not, you go to law school." The young resident winced in psychic pain.

"Marsha Mallow." He said. "25-year-old horticultural therapist." Sababa rolled his eyes back into his brain. Down the hallway in the resident's examining room. Praj introduced his mentor."

"This is Doctor Sababa, Marsha."

"What does he do?" She asked.

"He's the wizard of ahhs." Praj asked Marsha to extend her arms. "Two-month history of fragile skin and blistering, erosions, and scarring on the back of both her hands." He continued. "Red face of healing erosions and excessive hair growth. There doesn't appear to be any mucosal involvement."

"Labs?"

"Less than I thought." Praj said. "Mild anemia and elevation of her sedimentation rate and ALT. Strange that her plasma and urine porphyrins were both negative but maybe they need to be repeated. However, her skin biopsy showed subepidermal blistering with a mild lymphocytic infiltrate, results consistent with the diagnosis."

"Which is?"

"Classical case of porphyria cutanea tarda."

"Your eyes can deceive you, Mowgli. Don't trust them." Sababa took a small sterile specimen container off a shelf and pointed to the washroom across the hallway.

"Marsha, do you think you could give us a urine sample?" The young woman nodded and left the room. When she returned, the professor asked her to place the container on the desk.

"Turn off the lights, Praj." He pulled a thick flashlight from his Columbian leather briefcase. He clicked on the button at the end. A thick beam of purple light lit up the darkened room like a combat lightsaber.

"In a dark place we find ourselves, and knowledge lights our way."

"What's that?" Marsha asked.

"Wood's lamp." Sababa said.

"What's that?"

"Ultraviolet light source." He said. "Now watch. Your focus determines your reality." Sababa shone the beam first on her face and teeth and then on the urine sample. Nothing happened.

"So what?" Praj asked, turning the room lights back on.

"There was no fluorescence." Sababa said.

"So what?"

"If she had porphyria cutanea tarda, her skin and urine should glow with coral pink radiation."

"And her teeth?"

"Would glow if she had erythropoietic porphyria." He said. "She doesn't have porphyria. But the sun... it burns."

"Huh?"

"What is the distribution of her skin lesions?"

"I don't understand." Praj said.

"They are only present on her face and the back of her hands." He said. "Sun-exposed areas."

"So?"

"What photoactive molecules other than porphyrins can cause vesiculo-erosive skin disease?"

"I imagine there are hundreds of chemical compounds that become phototoxic when exposed to light." Praj said. "Some medicines, but Marsha doesn't take any."

"What does Marsha do?" Sababa asked.

"I'm a horticultural therapist." She said.

"It's a shame that you don't have porphyria, Marsha." Sababa put the Wood's lamp back into his Columbian leather briefcase. "For you would have found yourself in illustrious historic company—King Nebuchadnezzar of Babylon, Mary, Queen of Scots, King George III, 'Maria the Mad' of Portugal, Vincent van Gogh, and Vlad Țepeș of Transylvania, also known as Vlad the Impaler, the literary inspiration for Bram Stoker's Dracula, who may have started the notion that vampires were allergic to sunlight. Many plant products have the ability to cause your skin lesions—bergamot oil and parsley and lime juices and direct contact with giant hogweed."

"I don't take any of those therapies." She said.

"But there is one extract that you do take, isn't there Marsha?" Sababa said. "The one you neglected to mention to Dr. Bharmal. The mother of all molecules found in all green plants, algae, and cyanobacteria."

"I do take chlorophyllin to detoxify." Marsha said. "But only 1200 mg a day."

"The interaction between light and matter is at the basis of life on our planet." Sababa said. "The reaction from which chlorophyll accepts an electron stripped from water is how photosynthetic organisms produce all the oxygen gas in the Earth's atmosphere."

"What does that have to do with my rash?" Marsha asked.

"The big doses of chlorophyll pigment you took were metabolized to pheophorbide-A which, along with the singlet oxygen toxic free radicals produced, were responsible for killing your sun-exposed skin cells. Chlorins are evolutionary relatives of the porphyrins found in hemoglobin. They share a common biosynthetic pathway, including the precursor uroporphyrinogen III. So, you may not have porphyria, but you definitely have chlorophyll-induced pseudoporphyria."

"You think?" Praj was skeptical.

"I find your lack of faith disturbing." Sababa said. "You want to know something else? Both chlorophyll in plants and hemoglobin in animals have the same tetrapyrrole ring structure. The only difference is the metal at the centre. The metal at the centre of the chlorophyll molecule is magnesium; the metal at the centre of the hemoglobin molecule is iron. Plants use the ring to produce oxygen; animals use the ring to deliver it to their tissues. Animals exhale carbon dioxide; plants turn it back into oxygen. One ring to bring them all, and in the darkness bind them. Today's diagnosis has been brought to you by the colours green and red."

"What should I do now?" Marsha asked.

"You can't be a plant and an animal. Pick a side." Sababa said. "Stop taking the extract. Stay out of the sun. Tell Mercy I'll see you in eight months."

"Eight months?"

"It can take that long to resolve." Sababa and Praj escorted her to Manzanita's reception area and said goodbye.

"Let's see this last patient together." The stocky savant took the final folder from Mercy's counter.

"Tristano Martinelli." He called. A middle-aged couple followed the physicians into Sababa's sanctum.

"How can I help?" Sababa asked when everyone was seated. The woman spoke first.

"My husband's English is not so good." She said. "I am his wife, Francesca. Dr. Tarmac and Dr. Sitsofsky make this appuntamento."

"Go on." Sababa encouraged.

"My husband he..." She hesitated. "Diventa un mostro quando facciamo sesso, Dottore. Capisci Italiano?" *He becomes a monster when we have sex, Doctor. You understand Italian.*

"Io non sono quel tipo di dottore, signora." Sababa said. *I'm not that kind of doctor.*

"No, non è così. Diventa un arlecchino." *No, it's not like that. He becomes a harlequin.*

"Come mai?" *How so.*

"Il lato destro del viso e del collo e braccio e petto diventa rosso e sudato, proprio in mezzo al suo corpo." She said. *The right side of his face and neck and arm and chest becomes red and sweaty, right down the middle of his body.*

"E la sua parte sinistra?" Sababa asked. *And his left side.*

"Niente." *Nothing.*

"Deve essere preoccupante." *That must be worrisome.*

"Non ne conosci la metà." Francesca broke into tears. *You don't know the half of it.*

"Oh, ma lo faccio." He said. *Oh, but I do.*

"Daverro, Professor?" *Really, Professor.*

"Veramente." *Really.*

"What is she saying?" Praj couldn't take it anymore.

"She says that half of her husband flushes and perspires during exertion." Sababa said.

"Which half?"

"The right half." Sababa motioned to Tristano to follow his resident. "Praj, I'll leave you to perform a physical exam. Then set Signore Martinelli up on the treadmill for us."

"We're going to do a stress test?" He asked.

"After a fashion."

"Che tipo di lavoro fai, Tristano?" *What kind of work do you do, Tristano.*

"Sono un cameriere, Dottore." Tristano had found his voice. *I'm a waiter.*

"Da quanto tempo hai questo problema?" *How long have you had this problem.*

"Quasi tre mesi ormai." He said. *Almost three months now.*

Sababa returned to interrogate his resident about his examination.

"Niente." Praj said. *Nothing.*

Sababa pressed the button to start the treadmill. Tristano began a slow walk which increased in speed with every increment of the exercise protocol. Five minutes into running on an incline, Sababa punched the button to stop the test. Everyone stared at Tristano. The right side of his face and chest was blood red and drenched with dripping sweat. His left side was not. Right down the middle.

"Classical harlequin sign." Sababa noted. Back in the resident's room, Praj was surprised how much English the Martinellis had learned in such a short time.

"What is wrong with my husband, Dottore?" Francesca asked.

"He has an unusual condition called harlequin syndrome." Sababa said. "Something has gone wrong with what we call the chain of sympathetic nerves that supply the left side of Tristano's face."

"What is the reason?" She asked.

"Most of the time we don't find a cause." Sababa turned to Praj. "Primary, idiopathic, congenital, secondary, organic lesion, or iatrogenic causes." He refocused his attention on the Martinellis.

"We will look for one." He said. "I'll book Tristano for an MRI of his brain and spine, a CT scan of his chest, Holter monitor and tilt table test, and a skin biopsy. But I don't expect to find anything else abnormal."

"And the treatment, Dottore?" Tristano asked.

"No therapy is necessary as long as we're convinced that nothing else is going on, Tristano." Sababa said. "But sometimes, for social or psychological reasons, we can try botulinum toxin, stellate ganglion blocks, or surgical sympathectomy if your symptoms are too much or your ability to function is too little."

"Ne avrà uno, Dottore." Francesca furrowed her forehead. *He'll be having one of those.*

"Sospetto che probabilmente lo farà, Francesca." *I suspect he likely will.*

They both looked over at Tristano, who had fallen asleep and was snoring.

"Ha solo due facce quando è sveglio." She said. *He's only two-faced when he's awake.*

The portly professor handed several requisition forms to Francesca and asked her to make a return appointment with Mercy when Tristano was awake. He and Praj wished them well and retired to Sababa's sanctum.

"Well, that was entertaining."

"A true commedia dell'arte." Sababa said.

"A what?"

"The Italian Late Renaissance template of every theatrical production since. Plotlines of sex, jealousy, love, and old age." He said. "All those things you have to look forward to after your residency."

"Unless I go to law school."

"We're on call tonight." Sababa handed Praj his pager.

'His silver skin laced with his golden blood.'
William Shakespeare, *Macbeth*

Dr. Gung Ho won the prize for the first referral to Internal Medicine that evening. He was waiting for Praj and the professor inside the automatic sliding frosted glass doors of the emergency department, at the end of a long shift and a short tether.

"I saw your brother, Westwood, today." Sababa said.

"How is he?"

"Better than you, by the look of things."

"Hey, I heard they found piranhas in your lake last week." Gung said. "You may have to wear a steel armoured cup on your swims next summer."

"It should keep the tourists away."

"I also heard they found a gigantic yellow boa constrictor up near you at Ammonite falls."

"It's a tough neighbourhood, Gung." Sababa said. "What you got?"

"I need you to see this crazy lady in bed 4." Gung said.

"Why?" Praj asked.

"Gina Rinehart." Gung said. "53-year-old self-described rare earth therapist who presents with a two-month history of extensive blue-gray discoloration of the face, torso, and arms."

"That's it?" Sababa asked.

"That's it."

"And she came here for help?" Praj asked. "Why didn't she go to her family physician?"

"Says she doesn't believe in allopathic medicine."

"But she's happy to take up a bed in a busy emergency ward?" Praj was upset. "We already saw the only two-faced patient in our afternoon Manzanita clinic. I don't think I'm going to like this one."

"Easy, Mowgli." Sababa said. "You don't have to like your patients. You just have to fix them. Let's go see."

Behind the curtain of bed 4, Gung introduced the professor and his protégé to a woman the colour of gunmetal.

"Gina, this is Doctor Sababa." He said. "He's one of the few partisans in an age of ascendant orthodoxy. And this is his resident, Dr. Bharmal."

"What brings you to the ER tonight?" Praj asked.

"I'm changing colour." She said. "It's affecting my referrals."

"You see referrals?"

"I see clients in my rooms at Down to Earth Ecotherapy." Gina said. "I'm a practitioner of the Rasa Śāstra discipline of Ayurvedic medicine."

"What exactly is that?" Praj asked.

"I'm surprised you don't know, Mr. Bharmal." She said. "You're from India, aren't you?"

"Never been there." Praj frowned. "What is it you do?"

"I use a 7000-year-old system of metal therapy to restore my clients to wellness."

"What kind of metal therapy?"

"Many kinds of metals." She said. "I use *parada* and *swarna* and *rajata* and *tamra* and *loha* and *sisaka* and *vanga* and *pittala* and *kamsya*."

"What?" Praj asked.

"Mercury and gold and silver and copper and iron and lead and tin and brass and bronze." Sababa interrupted.

"We use *shodhana* calcination in fires of *puttam* cow dung to purify thin metal sheets, *ayaskriti* to reduce them to micro-fine powdered *bhasma* ash, and then immerse them in *taila* oil, *takra* extract, or *gomutra* cow urine." Gina said.

"But many of these preparations must be toxic." Praj protested.

"Any Western claims of toxicity are due to a failure to follow traditional practices in the production of these preparations." She said. Sababa studied the scattered blue-gray and white patches these sounds had emanated from.

"आप कितना कोलाइडल सिल्वर लेते हैं?" He asked. *Aap kitana kolaidal silvar lete hain.*

"I don't understand."

"I'm sorry." Sababa said. "I thought you spoke Hindi."

"No." She said.

"I asked how much colloidal silver you take?"

"How did you know?" Gina asked.

"It is my business to know what other people don't know." He said. "How much?"

"I'm taking Rajata Bhasma 120 mg a day for my Morgellons disease."

"Morgellons disease?" Praj asked.

"Bugs in my skin." She said. "Parasites. Painful crawling and biting and stinging parasites. Our wounds are often openings into the best and most beautiful part of us. I'm a survivor."

"You're a fruitcake." Praj said. "The only kind of person who can't brag about being a survivor is a corpse. What is this raja... raja..."

"Rajata Bhasma." Sababa said. "It's a combination of 60% metallic silver, 15% ferric oxide, 10 % calcium, silver chloride, and traces of free sulphur, sodium, potassium, and aluminum."

"Besides being able to kill superbugs, it has 51 other health benefits." Gina said.

"Sterling." Sababa took her right hand. "Look at her proximal nail beds, particularly the lunulae of the fingernails." He said.

"Lunulae?" Gina asked.

"The crescent-shaped area of your nailbeds." Sababa broke into song. *By the light...by the light... of the silvery moon...* "Every silver lining has a cloud. What is the differential diagnosis for slate-gray discoloration of the skin, Mowgli?"

"Exposure to other heavy metals, central cyanosis, methemoglobinemia, ochronosis, and Addison's disease." Praj said. "And drug-induced pigmentation from medications—antimalarial therapy, amiodarone, and minocycline."

"Which is why Arceus created the universe with three states of matter and three hundred solid and liquid poisons that could cause this presentation." Sababa beamed. "Head of the class."

"Which one have I got, sir?" Gina asked.

"Oh, you still have argyria, you silver-tongued star of the silver screen." He said. "First described by Ernst Fuchs in 1840."

"Argyria?"

"Bang! Bang! Maxwell's silver hammer came down upon her head." Sababa sang. "Congratulations, Gina. You've poisoned yourself with silver. Who says you can't take it with you?"

"Is there anything you can do about it?" She asked.

"There is no silver bullet." Sababa said. "But we can start with you not ingesting any more of your metallic mumbo-jumbo and staying out of the sun. Dr. Bharmal here will order a serum silver quantitation and take 4-mm punch biopsies from the front of your ear and lateral forehead."

"Will it go away?" She asked.

"Alas, no." Sababa said. "But it isn't causing you any real harm."

"But I can't afford to look like this." Gina protested.

"I know a guy with a picosecond 755-nm alexandrite laser." He said. "I'll see what I can do. You may have to sell the family silver."

Dr. Cliffy Carlton stuck his head through the curtain.

"Got a live one for you, Sab." He said.

"Let me finish up my silver service here." Sababa and Praj and Gung drifted over to the consultant's desk. The professor selected a tune from his music library on a secret drive hidden deep inside the hospital computer network. The William Tell Overture blared across the ER.

"Hi Ho Silver Away." He turned his attention to Cliffy.

"What you got?"

"Jabba Desilijic Tiure." Cliff said. "49-year-old taxi driver. Yellow tub of muscle and suet topped by a shaggy skull."

"Not that you're being judgmental."

"He's the slug in bed 7." Cliffy said. "All yours."

"Don't I at least get a history and physical."

"Sure." He said. "Six months of sloth and gluttony. Great custard-coloured mobile miasmic mass."

"You always were a stickler for detail."

"A little inaccuracy sometimes saves tons of explanation." Cliffy said.

"I'm done, Sab. I need a cigarette and I don't even smoke."

"Praj and I will see him." Sababa said. "If your pager doesn't go off, it'll be me."

"Mr. Tiure?" The professor opened the curtain to a strange orange mountain of flesh.

"Yehehehss." It was more of a juggernaut jug-o-rum basso profondo croak than a greeting. His expressionless face was puffy, and the rest of him was swollen with fluid.

"Jaffa the Hutt." Praj muttered under his breath.

"I understand you're a taxi driver." Sababa wondered how he fit behind the steering wheel of his vehicle.

"Yehehehss."

"Which company?"

"Yehehellow Cahahab."

"Of course." Sababa said. "Silly me. What brings you to the ER tonight?"

"Vehehry weaheaheak ahand cohold ahand slohohw." He said.

"Stick out your tongue." Sababa said. A large rump steak rolled from Tiure's mouth. Sababa then showed Praj how his patient's temperature was below normal and his deep-tendon reflexes were delayed.

"Why is he yellow, Praj?" Sababa asked.

"Could be bilirubin." The resident was hesitant.

"Are his eyes yellow?"

"Uh, no."

"So, it ain't bilirubin." Sababa said. "He's yellow from too much carotene. And you know the three causes of that."

"Too much ingestion, too high lipid levels, or some other secondary disease state."

"Exactly." Sababa said. "Like what?" Praj shook his head.

"This is one of those spot diagnoses that you either know or you don't, Mowgli." Sababa said. "And you need to know this one. Anytime, anywhere." The professor took another blood pressure.

"I don't like this." He said. "He should have high diastolic pressure."

"And?" Praj asked.

"It's low." Which is when Jabba Desilijic Tiure fell asleep and stopped breathing.

What happened next occurred so fast that Praj would remember it as a blur. He rubbed his eyes to find the patient surrounded by medical staff. Tiure's tongue had been too big to allow an endotracheal tube to pass. Sababa had performed an emergency cricothyrotomy through which one respiratory technician ventilated him with an Ambu bag while another set up a ventilator.

"This is myxedema coma, Mowgli." Sababa said. "This is how it can present. I will leave you to order his bloodwork, administer an initial 300 µg IV dose of thyroxine, 200 mg of hydrocortisone, glucose infusion, cautious normal saline volume expansion, and passive warming, to dictate his consultation report and write his Death Star orders and to find out what the precipitating event was. Your job is to turn this toad back into a prince."

"Where are you going?" Praj saw Dr. Ho wave from across the ER.

"To see Gung's next referral." Sababa said. "Join me when you've tucked him in. *Now, don't it always seem to go that you don't know what you've got till it's gone...*"

"Patient in bed 3." Dr. Ho said. "Robert Heinz. 33-year-old sculptor with a one-day history of painless jaundice and anemia."

"If it's painless, the surgeons won't be interested." Sababa said. "Why is he jaundiced? Indirect or direct hyperbilirubinemia?"

"His elevated bilirubin is unconjugated, so indirect." Gung said. "He has raging hemolytic anemia."

"Immune or non-immune hemolytic anemia?"

"His direct Coomb's test is negative, so non-immune." Gung said.

"OK." Sababa said. "So, what you got?"

"I got squat, Sab." Gung said. "The man doesn't take any drugs or toxins, there's no mechanical reason for this, he's not infected with anything, and he doesn't have any evidence of a membrane disorder or microangiopathic features."

"Hmmmm." Sababa said. "What did he have for dinner last night?"

"How the hell should I know?"

"Because you might have asked him." Sababa said. "Let's go see."

Behind the curtain of bed 3, Sababa met Mr. Heinz.

"Robert, this is the specialist I mentioned." Gung said. "All men have limits. They learn what they are and learn not to exceed them. Doctor Sababa ignores his."

"What did you have for dinner last night, Robert?"

"I ate some liver with a nice bottle of Chianti." He said.

"Anything else?"

"Fava beans."

"Bingo." Sababa said. "Where is your family from, Robert?"

"Vancouver Island." He said. "What do you mean?"

"I mean where did your ancestors live in the Mediterranean?" Sababa asked.

"We didn't come from the Mediterranean." Robert said. "My great grandfather was from an Iraqi town called Dokho."

"What was his name?"

"Nahom be Hamo Xanci." He said. "He was an innkeeper."

"He was a Jewish Kurd." Sababa said.

"Jewish Kurd?" Praj asked.

"What a friend we have in Cheesies." Sababa smiled. "Which explains everything."

"What do you mean?" Praj and Robert asked together.

"Half the population of Kurdish Jews have an inborn error of metabolism called hereditary glucose-6-phosphate dehydrogenase deficiency, or G6PDD. It's a disorder that protects against malaria, much like sickle cell anemia does."

"What does have to do with fava beans?" Praj asked.

"Fava beans, or broad beans, contain high levels of vicine, divicine, convicine, and isouramil, all of which create free oxygen radicals. Red blood cell oxygen carriers are sensitive to oxidative stress and are protected by normal levels of G6PD. If there isn't enough enzyme around, the red cells get destroyed."

"You have a name?" Robert asked.

"It's called favism." Sababa saw the pained grimace on his face. "Don't worry. Your ancestors weren't alone. Broad beans scared the ancient Greeks to death, some literally. Pythagorus, himself, was killed by his enemies from Crotonia because he refused to cross a field of fava beans."

"Can you prove this theory of yours?" Robert asked.

"In a couple of weeks, we'll order a Beutler fluorescent spot test." Sababa said. "That will show it."

"Is there anything I can do?"

"Learn to love chickpeas." Sababa watched as Cliffy Carlton made another flyby.

"One more, Sab." He said. "Diane de Poitiers. 36-year-old goldsmith in bed 2, gowned and raped."

"You mean gowned and draped, don't you?"

"Whatever."

"It's a wonder they haven't pulled your license, Cliffy." Sababa said.

"They've been pulling on everything else." Echoed in the hallway down which he disappeared. Sababa opened the curtain on bed 2.

"Hello, Diane." He noticed her hand deformities and made a mental tally of other signs. "I'm Doctor Sababa. Dr. Carlton has asked me to see you."

"Thank you for making a special trip." She said.

"I was already here." He said. "But all my trips are special. What seems to be the problem?"

"I've had rheumatoid arthritis for ten years." She said. "It's taking a toll on my jewellery-making skills. I have trouble with the strength and function I need in my hands to file and solder and saw and forge and cast and polish my material."

"And?"

"Six weeks ago, my rheumatologist gave me a choice of second-line disease-modifying antirheumatic drugs."

"And you chose gold." Sababa said. "Chrysotherapy."

"Of course." She said. "A goldsmith has to remain loyal to her precious metal. You know that wealthy women in the medieval French court consumed gold because they thought it made them look younger. They believed it harnessed the power of the sun, which would be transferred to the consumer."

"The mistress of the 16th-century French king, Henry II, drank solutions of gold chloride and diethyl ether." Sababa said. "She was 20 years older than her royal lover but drop-dead gorgeous."

"What do you mean?" Diane asked.

"It killed her."

"How?"

"We're not completely sure."

"But it could affect me the same way?" She asked.

"Possibly." Sababa said. "Gold salts are toxic to the liver and kidneys."

"My rheumatologist started me on auranofin 6 mg daily." Diane said. "I did well until a week ago when I became tired and unable to sleep. After some diarrhea, my hands and feet and face swelled, I started to gain weight, and I had to get up at night to pee. My urine is foamy."

"Your urine has oval fat bodies and fatty casts and a high amount of protein in it." Sababa said. "Also, your blood pressure and serum creatinine are elevated."

"From the gold?"

"Possibly." Sababa said.

"How do we find out?"

"The first thing we do is to get you to stop taking it." He said. "I'll order some investigations, including a serum anti-PLA2R antibody titre. You'll need a kidney biopsy, Diane."

"Oh."

"You have a condition we call membranous nephropathy.

"Can you treat it?"

"Most definitely." Sababa said. "First, we reduce the salt in your diet and start you on a loop diuretic and an ace inhibitor and a statin. You made need to be on blood thinners. Depending on your biopsy results and some other factors, you may require more aggressive therapy."

"Or I may not?"

"That's what I'm hoping." Sababa said. "About a third of these cases get better by themselves."

"And the other two thirds?"

"One-third will have a chronic condition, and the other third will progress to end-stage kidney failure."

"Oh."

"We'll do our best, Diane." Sababa said. "Have you any other questions?" She shook her head.

"Silence is golden." Sababa excused himself to dictate his consultation report and write orders at the consultant's desk. Praj arrived to musical accompaniment from an old sunshine superman. *They call me mellow yellow (Quite rightly) They call me mellow yellow (Quite rightly) They call me mellow yellow...*

"All done?" Sababa asked.

"Yep."

"You mean for now." Sababa handed Praj his pager and the heavy monkey wrench from under the desk. "Maybe you'd like to play first base tonight before you head off to law school."

"I'll call you if I need you." Praj sighed.

But the karma of the arrangement would be heavier than the monkey wrench. Sababa drove home to catch a few hours of sleep. He may have been speeding. On the last curve to the lake, the night sky erupted in a flaming kaleidoscope of blue and red light. Its reflection in his rearview mirror pulled his dimpled and dented white Honda over onto the road shoulder.

An interior light of an RCMP Ford Interceptor illuminated the occupant, checking Sababa's vehicle details on her mobile data computer. After what seemed like hours, a female officer exited the police car and made her way towards his driver's side window. Sababa knew her profile and movement well. Veronica Marsden's flashlight found its mark in the middle of his face.

"Is there a problem, officer?" He said.

"You were speeding." She said. "Can I see your license please?"

"I'd show you but I don't have one."

"Don't have one?"

"Lost it four years ago." He said. "Drunk driving."

"I see." She said. "Can I see your vehicle registration please."

"I can't do that either."

"Why not?"

"I stole this car."

"Stole it?"

"Yep." Sababa said. "And killed and hacked up the owner."

"You what?"

"His body parts are in plastic bags in the trunk if you want to see them."

Veronica Marsden backed away to her car and called for backup. Within minutes, three police cars blocked off Sababa's Honda. A senior officer approached the car, clasping his half-drawn weapon.

"Sir, could you step out of your vehicle please." He said. Sababa stepped out of his vehicle.

"Is there a problem, Officer?"

"One of our members reported that you stole this car and killed the owner."

"Killed the owner?"

"Please open the trunk of your car." Sababa opened the trunk of his Honda. There was nothing inside.

"Is this your car, Sir?"

"Of course." Sababa said. "Here's my registration."

"One of our members claims that you don't have a driver's license." The senior officer seemed stunned.

Sababa handed his license to the officer, causing even more consternation.

"Thank you, Sir." The senior patrolman handed back Sababa's license and registration. "One of our officers stated that you didn't have a license, that you stole this car, and that you murdered and dismembered the owner." Sababa smiled.

"I suppose she told you I was speeding as well."

'Blueberry Pie, he's from the upper-crust;
Rolling in dough, he's half-baked and bound to bust...'
Bette Midler, *Blueberry Pie*

"You're gonna want to see this, Sab?" It was early, and the Good Doctor was still asleep.

"What time is it?" He asked.

"Just after five." Praj said. "But you're gonna want to see this."

"What is it?"

"You have to see it."

"Where are you?"

"Death Star."

"Give me twenty." Sababa passed through his shower on the way through his clothes and into his dimpled and dented Honda. Inside of six minutes, it flew down his long driveway on two tires and lurched to a stop in the Internal Medicine on-call parking slot outside Harbour City Regional emergency. A bear he hadn't seen in his trajectory had bearly made it out of the way.

The stocky savant bounced through the automatic frosted glass sliding doors of the Harbour City Regional ER, opening and shutting in symphonic saccades. *Whoosh... Whoosh...*

At the end of the dark hallway to the Death Star, Sababa passed under the sacred sign above a soft, translucent radiance straight ahead. *ICU— Tranquility Base.*

Inside, Praj waited on the bridge, cradling his monkey wrench like a newborn.

"Cubicle 5." He said. "You're gonna want to see this."

"So you keep saying." Sababa pulled back the curtain to find Charmeine suctioning the endotracheal tube of her ventilated patient.

"Why so blue?" Sababa asked.

"I'm working a double shift."

"Not you, Charmeine." He said. "I was asking my resident."

"You might think that our patient here could be a Blue Fugate from the hills of Kentucky or one of the Blue Men of Lurgan from Ireland, but he's not."

"Don't fuck with me, Mowgli." Sababa said. "I haven't had my coffee yet."

"Coffee first. Save the world later." Mary handed the professor a large styrofoam cup of black sludge. "Only two kinds of people drink their coffee black, Sab. Cops and serial killers."

"I'm a little of both today, Mary." He sipped and heard the hiss of daybreak extinguished.

"Talk." He said. "Tell me about Little Boy Blue here."

"Tom Turnabout." Praj said. "44-year-old bakery owner brought in an hour ago with blueness."

"Blueness is not a diagnosis." Sababa said. "He didn't get his colour from a blueberry pie."

"I know." Praj said. "History of dermatitis herpetiformis treated with dapsone."

"As had French revolutionary and physician Jean-Paul Marat, which is why his murderer knew to find him in his bathtub." One of Sababa's eyelids migrated north. "He's a baker, and he has celiac disease?"

"It would appear so." Praj continued.

"Be not a baker, if your head be of butter." Sababa checked the ventilator settings.

"His skin condition has been driving away his business as of late resulting in some financial difficulty." Praj said. "Angry man."

"There are two things a person should never be angry at." Sababa said. "What they can help, and what they cannot. And?"

"His bakery burned to the ground tonight." Praj said. "EMR found him collapsed and unconscious at the scene."

"So why is he blue?" Sababa asked.

"This is the cool part." Praj said. "You know about a form of hemoglobin that contains the Fe_3+ ferric form of iron. Unlike the ferrous Fe_2+ tetramers in normal hemoglobin, ferric iron causes impaired affinity for oxygen leading to a reduced ability of the red blood cell to release oxygen to tissues, with the associated oxygen–hemoglobin dissociation curve shifted to the left. This form of hemoglobin is called methemoglobin. When its concentration is elevated in red blood cells, tissue hypoxia can occur from disruptions in NADH methemoglobin reductase, NADPH methemoglobin reductase, and the ascorbic acid and glutathione enzyme systems. His blood is chocolate-brown."

"And?" Sababa perused the baker's chart.

"Tom Turnabout took dapsone for his skin disease." Praj said. "Dapsone is one of the drugs known to cause methemoglobinemia."

"His methemoglobin level is only 8% by co-oximetry." Sababa said. "Not enough to turn him blue."

"Except for the other kind of hemoglobin that made it worse." Praj said.

"Hmmmm." Sababa mused. "Carboxyhemoglobin from the fire, like our shisha bar worker who lit the hookahs."

"Exactly." Praj beamed. "It didn't take much inhaled carbon monoxide to accentuate the adverse effects from his otherwise low level dapsone-induced elevated methemoglobin levels. Plus, the smoke inhalation could have even caused higher levels of methemoglobin without the dapsone effect. Additive or synergistic."

"So, what have you done for him?" Sababa asked.

"Supplemental oxygen and about to start a 1% infusion of methylene blue, 2 mg/kg over five minutes."

"What will that do?" Sababa asked.

"Provide an artificial electron acceptor to allow his NADPH methemoglobin reductase generated via the hexose monophosphate shunt to function at five times their normal levels, and thereby reduce his ferric ions to a ferrous state." Praj said. "OK, Charmeine, let 'er rip. Watch this, Sab."

Sababa watched the blue man turn pink.

"What do you think?" Praj asked

"Amusing parlour trick, Mowgli." Sababa selected a tune from his music library on a secret drive hidden deep inside the hospital computer network. John Coltrane's tenor saxophone drove *Blue Train* through the heavy air of the Death Star. "You need to rethink this law school thing." Betty Boop's handset, ascending into the atmosphere, interrupted his sentiment.

"Dr. Carlton in the ER for you, Sab." She said. "Line 1." Sababa picked up line one.

"What?"
"I need you to see a guy."
"Why?"
"Imports cars from China." Cliffy said. "Thinks he picked up some virus in a Wuhan restaurant. Short of breath and his chest x-ray sucks. Batshit crazy."
"Hmmmm." Sababa mused. "Put him in a negative pressure isolation room and tell everyone to stay away until I get there."
"Is that necessary?"
"Consider him in the same way you contemplate your penis." Sababa said. "The exposure may have already ruined countless numbers of human lives."

'Anger is a fuel. You need fuel to launch a rocket. But if all you have is fuel without any complex internal mechanism directing it, you don't have a rocket. You have a bomb.'

Gil Schwartz

The casual reader may not appreciate the difference in the anger of Tom Turnabout and Doctor Sababa.

One might wonder how a baker could become so filled with wrath. The aromas of his creations, like the sounds of flowing water, indescribable in their evocation of innocence and delight, tasted of all the stars and in the heavens. Tom Turnabout was a poet with pastry as his medium.

But his rash chased away his customers and threatened his livelihood. Tom got the blues. He converted his grief to rage, holding onto it like he was grasping a hot coal. It burnt him and his bakery to the ground. Anger is like taking poison and waiting for another guy to die. In Buddhist thought, anger was one of three poisons, the others being greed and ignorance. Together, they caused delusion and suffering. The delusion was of a particular kind, a belief that he was separate from other living things and the physical earth. Tom kept his own wounds green, like the chlorophyll that produced the carbohydrates he needed to make his poetry. Dr. Bharmal not only ventilated the blue baker's lungs, but he also aerated Tom's ire towards forgiveness through distance and delay.

Anyone who knew Doctor Sababa well had seen him angry. His wrath was as red as hemoglobin and as black as the bile he could summon in any extraordinary circumstance. Despite the speed of his deliberations and actions, the Sage of the Salish Sea was a patient man. If he decided to be patient in a moment of anger, he knew he could escape a hundred days of sorrow. But he always maintained that compassion was seven-tenths passion. Like all passions, anger had degrees, ascending from slight indignation through deepening clouds to outrage, and finally to that fury of the patient man, which was a black and horrible tempest. In its mid-region, where it was neither too little to be motive nor too furious to be ungovernable, it had usefulness. For all feeling was as fuel, and where there was none life had no fire, and then no flame of ascent.

Sababa's anger was always directed towards problems, not people, energy he focused on answers, not excuses. Often, it was a reaction to the violation of his boundaries. The product of his anger and imagination was also poetry. It would be one of the last things within him to grow old.

'Colours are the deeds and sufferings of light.'
Johann Wolfgang von Goethe

Colour was the deep and mysterious dream language of these poets, the place where their brains and the universe met. Colour was a mid-point between pure light and pure darkness, a consequence, never a cause.

And the consequences of each colour in the visible spectrum Sababa attended were all different, for he looked after the whole box of crayons. Frederica Flückiger survived her hepatopulmonary violet cyanosis and Ziggy Stardust's liver transplant only to be run over by a methamphetamine addict in a stolen car.

Tom Turnabout's blues resolved in the ICU but returned in another form when Veronica Marsden arrested him for arson on his discharge from the hospital. After accepting a brief job opportunity in the Harbour City Correctional Centre, Tom was able to borrow enough from his former clients to reopen two gluten-free bakeries, Just Desserts and Torte Reform. His skin and conscience are now clear.

It took Marsha Mallow eight months for her chlorophyll blisters to resolve. The enthusiasm for her calling as a horticultural therapist waned as a function of the number of permanent scars she acquired in her convalescence. It's not easy being green.

Further along the chromatic spectrum, there emerged two successful recoveries in the key of yellow. Jabba Desilijic Tiure awoke from his myxedema coma and his carotene levels returned to normal after several months of thyroid replacement therapy. He can now fit into the driver's seat of his yellow cab. The Beutler test on Robert Heinz confirmed his glucose-6-phosphate dehydrogenase deficiency. He has had no further attacks of favism. The sculptor presented Doctor Sababa with a three-foot carving of a broad bean, now displayed at a rather obscure site in his garden at the lake.

The brains of our ancestors registered red first, the color of blood and fire. The cheeks of Émile Zola never saw that flush, because the Oceanside Hyperbaric Unit fixed his carbon monoxide poisoning. He quit his job as a shisha lighting technician at the Harewood hookah lounge for the more lucrative and safer activity of geoduck diving.

Jack Tu's polycythemia-induced erythromelalgia improved from a schedule of serial phlebotomies, every unit of which Sababa took home to fertilize Jane's roses. When Jack returned to his bicycle shop, he put his entire inventory up for sale, and bought a boat.

Westwood Ho's fructosamine levels provide an accurate measurement of his diabetic control. He applied and was accepted to the UBC residency program in Internal Medicine, despite his brother's attempts to talk him out of it.

Tristano Martinelli, at the insistence of his wife, received several courses of botox for his harlequin syndrome. Even with the improvement, Francesca still insisted that he takes the bottom position during their conjugal activities. Jane and Sababa always get the best table on those rare occasions when they go out to eat at his restaurant.

There are five colours hidden in or missing from the visual spectrum of light—white, black, gold and silver, and brown.

White is the colour of all colours. Thomas Ham's pale white face and paroxysmal nocturnal hemoglobinuria improved with administration of the expensive eculizumab that the bureaucrats in Ottawa released to treat him. Eight months later, Thomas developed refractory anemia with excess blasts. Because of his age and other factors, he was ineligible for a bone marrow transplant and died of septic shock two months later, his family at his side.

Black is the colour of no colours, and the colour of death. And out of the darkness came the hands that reach through nature, moulding men. Sababa lived his life in colour and told his truth in black and white, *dancing with the devil in the pale moonlight.*

Diane de Poitiers' membranous nephropathy resolved completely with the discontinuation of her gold therapy. Her rheumatologist put her on another disease-modifying agent, with even better improvement of her rheumatoid arthritis. In her goldsmithing gratitude, she crafted a special pendant for Jane Sababa.

Gina Rinehart's silver complexion didn't respond completely to alexandrite laser therapy, although her parasites have disappeared, and she finds it easy to choose jewelry that looks good with her skin tone.

Which leaves us with two stories of brown. Martina Benno's Schmidt's syndrome vanished with the right hormonal replacement therapy. Her anxiety state didn't disappear quickly, driven by the PTSD that persisted from Jennifer Gonif's assault in her home salon. But karma waited in the wake of it. The judge in the case gave Martina a large cash settlement from the assailant and waxed the defendant's balls for a long time.

And Dr. Praj Bharmal? The professor found his monkey wrench in the consultant's chair on the bridge of the Death Star, with a note taped to the metal. *Got into law school. Thanks for helping me make the decision. Click the link on the screen.*

Sababa clicked the link on the screen. One of the tunes from his music library, on a secret drive hidden deep inside the hospital computer network, filled the unit with grunge.

> 'What have we done with innocence?
> It disappeared with time, it never made much sense
> Adolescent resident...
> Don't wanna be your monkey wrench...'
> Foo Fighters, *Monkey Wrench*

Epilogue

'Autumn wins you best by this, its mute
Appeal to sympathy for its decay.'
Robert Browning, *Paracelsus*

So, how was your Harbour City homecoming? I hope your return visit was enlightening and even illuminating.

Having now lived through three seasons of *The Casebook*, I would love to bring you one more. As spectacular as spring and summer and autumn were in Sababaland, it is only in winter that one finds closure.

The portly professor's creator has renewed his Faustian pact with the devil that, if he is allowed to survive that much longer, he would write the final stories of the Sage of the Salish Sea.

Wait for them.

Characters

Family
Eleazar Sababa
Jane Sababa
Shiva (deceased)

Administrators
Malcolm Canmore- Site Administrator, Harbour City Regional
Hospital
Foster Inclusion- Chief Executive Officer, Island Health
Dr Petronilla de Meath- Chief of Staff, Harbour City Regional Hospital

Moa
Mercy

Paging Operator
Lana

Internal Medicine
Dr Peter Zaias
Dr Eleazar Sababa
Dr Marquis Shu Ying
Dr Ernie 'The Big Easy' Hacker
Dr Dasco Boet
Dr Wayward Woods
Dr Edward Hyde (Respirology)
Dr Sidney Shalimar
Dr Commodus Sitsofsky (Dermatology)
Dr Henry Chibueze (Oncology)
Dr Oliver Lax (Neurology)

Surgery
Dr Theodor Billroth (ENT)
Dr Buddy Benway (General)
Dr John Falstaff (General)
Dr Jules Martino (General)
Dr Olaf Octagon (OB/GYN)
Dr TJ Eckleburg (Ophthalmology)
Dr Piggy Muldoon (Orthopedics)
Dr Christian 'Pretty Boy' Troy (Plastics)
Dr Harry 'Doc' Martin (Urology)

Anesthesiology
Dr Banjo Paterson

Pathology
Dr Juan Leyblanca

Psychiatry
Dr Robert La Capuche

Radiology
Dr Alan Statham
Dr Mako Brisk

GPs
Dr Tictac Tarmac
Dr Poldy Bloom
Dr Petronilla de Meath
Dr James Ruben Andrews
Dr Nicholas Rivera
Dr Charles Russell (Jehovah's Witness)

ER Physicians
Dr Myles Capitaine
Dr Trace Pangloss
Dr Cliffy Carlton
Dr Gung Ho

Ward Clerks
ICU- Betty Boop
ER- Cheri Sundae

Nursing
Grand Galactic Governess of Nightingales (Big Nurse)- Mildred Ratschet
Director of Medical Nursing- Edith Mortley
Director of Surgical Nursing- Daisy Daws
ER- Dina, Michaela, Regina
ICU- Mary, Charmeine, Angie
Floor 1- Serafina
Floor 3- Sariel
Floor 5- Samara Morgan
Floor 6- Shekina

Internal Medicine Resident
Dr Praj Bharmal

Biomedical Engineer
Murray 'Leatherman' MacGyver

Medical Advisory Committee
Dr Petronilla de Meath
Malcolm Canmore
Dr Jules Martino
Dr Eleazar Sababa
Dr Juan Leyblanca
Dr Trace Pangloss
Dr Mako Brisk
Dr Banjo Paterson

RCMP
Veronica Marsden

Patients

13. The Case of the Universal Veil
Tim Leery- VIU student
Elias Ashmole- VIU Philosophy Professor
Duke Point- Mushroom Compost Worker
Rollrim Brown- Lifeguard
Perry Lepistopsis- Specialty Food and Foie Gras Importer
Smokey Crescent- Fungiculturist
Tippler Spain- Commercial Printer
Stoney Ridge- VIU Mycology Professor
Holly Hill- VIU Coed

14. The Case of the Orange Faller
Alder Way- Faller
Adelle Davis- Personal Trainer
Bert Sézary- Gordon Bay Provincial Park Ranger
Morrie Bund- Logging Truck Driver
Denis Parsons- IT Guru
Chilly Marrow- Golf Course Golf Pro (married to Bernadine Soulier)
Red Snapper- Cutthroat Tavern Manager
Dmitri Romanowsky- Cider Maker
Perry Romberg- Advertising Executive
Joan Mitchell- Folk Singer
Richard Feynman- Cowichan Secondary School Physics Teacher
Laurie Cabot- Cowichan Wool Spinner

15. The Case of the Tumescent Tattoos
Maxey Road- American Hell's Angel
Christina Pfeifer- Painter
Lili Boulanger- Student
Roscoe Holcomb- Retired Coal Miner

Lisa Monroe- Bikie's Girlfriend
Eduardo Cazar- Gas Station Attendent

16. The Case of the Congo Stain
Aulds Offramp- Retired Civil Servant from Ontario
William Mathiseon Macleod- Sunset Diving Instructor
Thyme Adamant- Releaf Cannabis Club Owner
Julia Pastrana- Dr Zaias' Wife
Paris Hilton- Medical Administrative Assistant
Herr Doktor Wernher Merkwürdigliebe- Retired German Cardiologist
Mustafa Erdoğan- Turkish Döner Kebap Shopowner
Pete Renoir- Salvation Army Command Commander
Hans Klupt- Pipefitter Headquarters Smoke Shop Owner
Ben Castleman - Liquidation World Salesman
Polly Poses- Real Canadian Superstore Checkout Girl

17. The Case from the Crack of Doom
Honey Drive- Downtown Hooker
Joshua Jackson- Pimp
William Burroughs- Drug Addict
Impeccable Williams- Tilray Cannabis Quality Control Technician
Fiera Carpenter- Model
Popcorn Sutton- Bootlegger
Bettino Ricasoli- Gold n' Fleece Pawn Shop Owner
Ben Johnson- Body Builder
Marshall Applewhite- Cancer Patient
Louis May Alcott- Plumber
Raoul Bensaude- Croatian Insurance Broker
Paula Broca- Pregnant Pharmacist
Carrie Underwood- Weightwatchers Meeting Room Leader
Michael Bulles- Bed, Bath & Beyond stock clerk

18. The Case of the Sensitive Smurf
Tom Turnabout- Baker
Frederica Flückiger- Housesitter
Thomas Ham- Butcher
Émile Zola- Hookah Bar Employee
Jack Tu- Bicycle Shop Owner
Martina Benno- Massage Therapist
Marsha Mallow- Horticultural Therapist
Westward Ho- Composer/Medical Student (brother of Gung Ho)
Tristano Martinelli- Waiter
Gina Rinehart- Colloidal Silver Therapist
Jabba Desilijic Tiure- Taxi Driver
Robert Heinz- Sculptor
Diane de Poitiers- Goldsmith

The Further Analects of Doctor Sababa

A. The Science

1. Bennett's Classification for Reading Medical Articles

Medical Student: Reads entire article but does not understand what any of it means

Intern: Uses journal as a pillow during nights on call

Resident: Would like to read entire article but eats dinner instead

Chief Resident: Skips articles entirely and reads the classifieds

Junior Attending: Reads and analyzes entire article in order to pimp medical students

Senior Attending: Reads abstract and quotes the literature liberally

Research Attending: Reads entire article, reanalyzes statistics, and looks up all references usually in lieu of sex

Chief of Service: Reads references to see if he was cited anywhere

Private Attending: Doesn't buy journals in the first place but keeps an eye out for articles that make it into Time or Newsweek

Emeritus Attending: Reads entire article but doesn't understand what any of it means

B. The Snowflakes

1. Prachett's Guide to Mushrooms

(1) All fungi are edible.

(2) Some fungi are not edible more than once.

C. The System

1. Instructions for Strategic Filibustering at your Next Hospital Committee Meeting

(1) Ask for more data—This always works. Use phrases like 'level of confidence is low' or 'statistically insignificant' to scare the members into searching for more data. This data is never available.

(2) Ask for whatever data you have to be 'analyzed' in a more effective manner—use phrases like 'confounding variables' or 'background noise' to make the members skeptical.

(3) Ask for more members to be added to the group—everyone knows that more is better, but since everyone hates committees, you'll never get anyone to join.

(4) Ask to have a consultant brought in—somehow this fools even the best of them. You have to first debate if a consultant is needed, and debate what type of consultant to get. Even if you get an answer

on this, you still have to find a way to pay the consultant. There is never money in the budget to pay a consultant.

(5) Ask to have the group broken down into smaller task forces, steering committee or action groups—by the time you define what the goal of the 'microcommittee' is, you will head right into the realization that no one will volunteer to be on it.

(6) Ask to bring the issue to the largest group of the hospital (general staff meeting, etc.)—by the law of averages, some crotchety bastard will hate the issue enough to force it back into the smaller committee again where you filibuster it all over again.

(7) Try bringing up a point and then slowly, but deliberately go tangential—by the time the committee realizes you are on another topic, you make sure that new topic is really controversial. That will piss off your 'hothead' in the group enough to have him speak his mind about the new topic and you are now off to the races. Sit back and enjoy.

(8) Ask to have a consensus on the issue and they try to have the committee define *consensus* and see if they can have a consensus on that definition.

(9) Ask your 'slowspeaker' in the group to give the in-depth opinion and where he does, ask him more questions so he can elaborate on what he just said.

(10) Ask if the issue at hand is really that important when so many other issues are critical (they never are)—try to table this issue and promise to bring it up in the next meeting and then reapply any one of the top nine techniques.

Songs and Poems

Sababa's Playlist (from a secret drive hidden deep inside the hospital computer network)

13. The Case of the Universal Veil
Allman Brothers, *One Way Out*
Allman Brothers, *Blue Sky*
Harry Belafonte, *Jamaica Farewell*
Van Morrison, *Philosopher's Stone*
My Chemical Romance, *Blood*
Basho, *Out mushroom hunting*

14. The Case of the Orange Faller
Monty Python, *Lumberjack Song*
John Mayer, *Your Body is a Wonderland*
Don McLean, *Vincent (Starry, Starry Night)*
Joni Mitchell, *Circle Game*
Escape, *The Freaks Come Out at Night*
Eric Clapton, *After Midnight*
Harold Arlen, *Follow the Yellow Brick Road*
Robert Frost, *Stopping by Woods on a Snowy Evening*

15. The Case of the Tumescent Tattoos
James Dickey, *Cherrylog Road*
Steppenwolf, *Born to Be Wild*
Bob Dylan, *Mr. Tambourine Man*
Arlo Guthrie, *The Motorcycle Song*
The Ramones, *I Wanna Be Sedated*
George Thorogood, *Bad to the Bone*

16. The Case of the Congo Stain
Warren Zevon, *Down in The Mall*
Steely Dan, *The Last Mall*
Jo Walton, *Mall Poem*
Rumi, *There is a way of breathing*
E.C. Bentley, *The Jumping Frenchmen of Maine*
Rage Against the Machine, *Know Your Enemy*
T.S. Eliot, *The Love Song of J. Alfred Prufrock*
R.E.M., *Losing My Religion*

17. The Case from the Crack of Doom
J.J. Cale, *Cocaine*
William Wordsworth, *She Was a Phantom of Delight*
William Burroughs, *Junkie*
Sublime, *Smoke Two Joints*
The Carpenters, *We've Only Just Begun*
Alan Jackson, *Mercury Blues*

Guns N' Roses, *Welcome to The Jungle*
Bob Dylan, *Cocaine Blues*
John Whiteside 'Jack' Parsons, *I Height Don Quixote, I Live on Peyote*

18. The Case of the Sensitive Smurf
Jimmy Buffett, *Fruitcakes*
Willie Nix, *Baker Shop Boogie*
Sarah Vaughan, *Black Coffee*
Rolling Stones, *Brown Sugar*
Taj Mahal, *Cakewalk into Town*
Sonny Terry and Brownie McGhee, *Custard Pie Blues*
Bessie Smith, *I Need a Little Sugar in My Bowl*
Leon Redbone, *Mr. Jelly Roll Baker*
Howlin Wolf, *Spoonful*
Ella Fitzgerald, *Sugar Blues*
Peggy Lee, *A Woman Alone with the Blues*
Leon Redbone, *My Blue Heaven*
Gus Edwards, *By the Light of the Silvery Moon*
Carole King, *Pleasant Valley Sunday*
Radiohead, *No Surprises*
Beyoncé, *Brown Skin Girl*
Crosby, Stills, and Nash, *Helplessly Hoping*
Gioachino Rossini, *William Tell Overture*
Donovan, *Mellow Yellow*
Bette Midler, *Blueberry Pie*
John Coltrane, *Blue Train*
Foo Fighters, *Monkey Wrench*

Other Works by Lawrence Winkler

Westwood Lake Chronicles

Orion's Cartwheels Quadrilogy
Orion's Cartwheel
Between the Cartwheels
Hind Cartwheel
The Final Cartwheel

Stories of the Southern Sea

Wagon Days

Samurai Road

Stout Man

Fire Beyond the Darkness

The Bolthole

Void Vast Infinite

Bandits of Madagascar

The Casebook of Doctor Sababa